The
WOODEN NICKEL

WILLIAM CARPENTER

The

WOODEN
NICKEL

LITTLE, BROWN AND COMPANY

BOSTON NEW YORK LONDON

Library of Congress Cataloging-in-Publication Data

Carpenter, William.
   The wooden nickel / William Carpenter.
       p.   cm.
   ISBN 0-316-13400-7
       1. Lobster fishers — Fiction. 2. Maine — Fiction.
I. Title.
PS3553.A7622 W66 2002
813'.54 — dc21   2001034445

10 9 8 7 6 5 4 3 2 1

Q-FF

DESIGNED BY CATHRYN S. AISON

Printed in the United States of America

This book is dedicated to my tireless muse and critic, Donna Gold. It would not have been possible without the support of many others, especially Elmer Beal, Philip Campbell, Hans Duvefelt, M.D., Ron Gold, Howdy Houghton, Majo Kaleshian, Sylvester Pollet, Dr. Sean Todd, Clinton Trowbridge, my editors Michael Pietsch and Asya Muchnick, and my extraordinary agent, Alison Bond.

His clothes always smelled
of gasoline and fish.

— Leo Connellan,
"By the Blue Sea"

The
WOODEN NICKEL

I

HE'S SOUND ASLEEP, no dreams, nothing, then a
hand touches his forehead and he surfaces slowly, as if they're hauling
his brain off a fifteen-fathom ledge. The voice sounds like a stranger,
though it's the same one that has whispered him awake for twenty
years. "*Lucas.* It's almost quarter of five."

She gets up even before he does, checks out the forecast on the
scanner, arranges his clothes on the bedroom recliner so he can feel
for them in the dark. He can tell the weather from what's laid out for
him. Today it might as well be January, she's got the union suit, two
sweatshirts, wool pants, two pair of socks. "What the hell?" he says.

"Look."

He raises the blind. The red GMC pickup down in the driveway
is covered with snow.

"Jesus H. Christ, Sarah. It's *April.*"

"Quiet, you'll wake the kids. The weather radio says it's changing to rain. And you know, Lucas, it's not just April, it's the fifteenth. Have you mailed the tax forms?"

"Fuck them bastards. I paid them last year."

"You didn't, Lucas. It was the year before. And I wound up doing it."

April 15 may be a black moment for the lawful citizen, but it's Opening Day for the lobstermen of Orphan Point, and the *Wooden Nickel*'s sitting out there in the predawn darkness with forty-eight brand-new wooden traps weighing down the stern. He was up till near midnight loading them on because that son of a bitch Hannaford put him on last for the dock crane. Clyde Hannaford blames everyone in town for his wife problem but for some reason Lucky most of all, though he knows god damn well Lucky's married with two kids and Sarah does not cut him much slack to frig around.

He is tired and pissed, mainly at himself for not putting the pickup in the garage so he has to scrape two inches of wet slush off the windshield, and for taking the big Fisher plow off the hook already and storing it out back. Forty-six years in Orphan Point, you'd think he'd seen enough April blizzards to know better, but this is the year they said global warming was supposed to kick in. Fucking environmentalists, nothing but broken promises. If you have your head up your ass, naturally the world is going to look like shit.

He would have liked to plow Sarah out before going to work. Now he can't. The pickup's got thirty-three-inch Wranglers, it can steam through this fluff without even going into four-wheel drive. But her little blue Lynx with the twelve-inch tires won't be able to claw its way out of the garage. Kyle won't shovel her out either, because she'll let him sleep till ten minutes before his ride like he was still in the second grade. Well fuck her, he thinks, she has dug her own grave with that kid, she'll be lucky if he doesn't end up in Thomaston like Howard Thurston's son that robbed the convenience store, three and a half years and one suspended.

Now she's bent over in the half-light, going through his pockets. "Just making sure you have your medication along. There won't be any drugstores out there."

"And checking for cigarettes."

"We do want to keep you alive, Lucas, even if it's against your will. You know what young Dr. Burnside said, and I'm not going to be along to remind you."

She doesn't find them. Fact is, the Marlboros went aboard already, along with the gear, fuel and bait.

Thick snow blows towards his windshield so it feels like he's stopped dead and the white world is swimming past. He drives the still-unplowed road around the back side of the cove towards Hannaford's wharf. Other pickups are coming from other directions, their lights illuminating the snowflakes like darting schools of shiners as they converge on the waterfront. Lucky of course knows every truck, every driver and passenger, even in the predawn darkness, and he would know them if struck blind, so long as he could hear their individual engines and the wake of their oversize tires through the snow.

Every boat wants to be first out of the harbor on opening day, so they are all heading straight down to the wharf and out to sea, without stopping for coffee and crullers at Doris's. He, Lucky Lunt, was once among the first men out with the most traps, but last season Kyle stopped sterning for him, he had to do all the work out there, and he slowed down. One string of traps and he'd break into a sweat, have to stop, have a cigarette, a beer maybe, rest half an hour before hauling the next string. Then in the fall he shot the moose up in Ambajezus and couldn't get it out of the woods. They found him passed out on top of the christly thing, at first they couldn't tell which one was dead, him or the moose. The paramedics had to use his own four-wheeler to haul him out to a field where the chopper could land. They flew him to the Tarratine hospital and found his arteries choked up like a saltwater engine block. Eleven years since his last checkup. They did the first angioplasty on the spot and sent him home, he was out on the water in a week. They drill right through your crotch up into the coronaries and inflate a long skinny five-thousand-dollar condom which is supposed to push the layers of butter and french fries back against the arterial wall. Sarah served the moose for Thanksgiving dinner, next morning he was back in the heart ward for another try. The second time, when they pulled the balloon out they left a stent to keep the stuff in place, a few inches of stainless steel plumbing that will still shine like starlight when the rest of him's eaten up by worms.

Sarah had a hard time adjusting to a metal part inside her husband, but the way he sees it, the stent brings him that much closer to the hearts of his boat and truck, an honorary member of the mechanical world.

After the operation they poisoned him with vegetables and put him on three or four different-colored pills, which he's long since mixed together in the same brown bottles, one in the pickup, one over the bathroom sink. He takes a handful of them now and then when Sarah reminds him, though they make him seasick in front of the TV. Well fuck that, he'd rather listen to country, though when the stock car races are on he clings to both arms of his chair and watches anyway.

He's also under strict orders to slow it down, not drive straight to his chained-up skiff but pause for a cup of decaf at the Blue Claw, and if Doris is not yet open, spend a moment relaxing in the pickup cab with the heater on listening to High Country 104. Course it will make him the last boat on the water, an honor that used to belong to Alonzo Gross, but now the *Wooden Nickel* will bring up the fucking rear. He used to be right up there with Art Pettingill, who goes to bed at half past seven and rises at three, but now he's supposed to cut his stress level in half and take time "for himself," as Dr. Burnside told him, but who the fuck is himself? There's lobsters, there's the *Wooden Nickel* and there's the sea. That's it.

Doris opens the Blue Claw sharply at five-thirty, but he's already in the parking lot at twenty past. He knows she's in there because her old Plymouth minivan's out back with the faded blue claw on its two front doors. The restaurant windows are fogged already with coffee steam, but the CLOSED sign is still up and she's not going to flip it around till five-thirty even if the coffee is turning to creosote at the bottom of the urn.

There's enough light now to make out the silhouette of the *Wooden Nickel* moored among the Orphan Point fleet, all of them stern down and low in the water under their first-day load of traps. A wheelhouse light snaps on in one of the boats, then another, then red and green running lights that blur through the light snow like it's still Christmas. The first diesel kicks in, maybe Pettingill's but nope, it's a straight-six, probably Dennis Gower in the *Kathleen and Brian,* which he repowered with a Volvo 102 last year but it already sounds like an old man farting himself to death. Big dumb Swedes, twenty-four hours of daylight and still they can't build shit.

The diesel sounds float in over the water and fill his heart with anxiety and competition till he feels the medication kick in and slow it down. How is he going to cut his christly stress level in half if he has to sit here hearing the other boats start up? He takes the pill bottle out of his lunchbox and puts it in the glove compartment instead. Fuck that. He's not going on the water with that stuff.

The DJ is still playing his mellow wee-hours material, it fits right in with the sky clearing and the late stars coming through the clouds. He even lets himself cue up Garth Brooks's "Go Tell It on the Mountain" because of the weather, must still be winter up in the mountains where their studio is. On the western side of the harbor, lined with gloomy vacant summer estates, there's not a sign of life. On the east, though, all along the shore he can make out the lights of fishermen's homes through the colorless snowy haze of dawn. The men are already at work but their wives are cleaning up after the first-shift breakfast and getting ready to rouse and feed the kids. He knows the town so well it's like X-ray vision, he can see through the walls, knows each woman in each kitchen, each kid in bed, the contents of the refrigerator and what station she's tuned to waiting for the sun to come up, country mostly, but some will have the Christian station or the talk show, then they'll all switch over to Rush when he comes on.

It was torture to see Art Pettingill and his boy drive past him in their big crew-cab F-350, not even turning to look at the Blue Claw, straight to the mooring. Art's boy will be straining at the oars, Big Art in the stern, skiff sinking under his whale's body and the twelve-pound lunch pail in his lap, Art putting the sponge to her every ten seconds because she's still full of shotgun holes from when the Split Cove boys gave him a piece of advice. He hears their boat start up, old Caterpillar 320 with dual pipes up through the wheelhouse roof. The *Bonanza. Banana,* it should be called, it's got the hog shape and the yellow hull covering the rust that drips off of all Art's gear. Still, he is a highliner and he brings them in. Thirty-five thousand pounds of lobster last season and his wife won't let him trade the boat. Alma Pettingill's a churchgoing woman and she's got him securely by the nuts.

Art's son is fifteen, sixteen, great big kid, just the right age for a sternman. Another year or two and they want their own boats, then you have to hire a stranger who half the time won't know what the fuck is going on. Sternperson, that's what you're supposed to call them now, though somehow that word makes him think of doing it dog style, he can't say why. Things have changed, there's a lot of female sternmen. Wives, daughters, girlfriends, it does improve the morning if you can get laid down in the cuddy after a few strings, but for Lucky Lunt the purpose of going out on the water is to catch lobsters, and like his old man used to quote out of the Bible, a man's not supposed to mix fish and flesh. The day Ellis Seavey took that Tarratine girl with the bikini top out to show her his trapline, Lucky shouted, "Going after crabs today?" and Ellis didn't speak to him for a month. That whole summer Ellis had one hand under his oilskins, scratching away, till his uncle Lester lent him his tube of Captain Scratch's crotch ointment and they found someplace else to live.

Twenty-five past. He keeps the pickup idling in park, not just because it's cold but he also likes the sound of the rods just turning the crankshaft over in its bath of oil. The pickup's only a 350 but it's a 4-barrel, and its low, rumbly, slow-turning V-8 with just the right hint of exhaust failure sounds enough like his Chevy 454 marine to get his blood moving even before his first sip of the morning regular Sarah won't give him but Doris might.

Just light enough to see Art Pettingill's old Cat diesel farting black soot like a Greyhound bus as the *Bonanza* casts off and smokes out towards Sodom Ledge into the April fog. Art's got a CB tuned to the truck channel because his brother drives for Irving Oil, another radio on VHF 64, which is the Orphan Point fishermen's party line, and a third radio on Christian Country 88.5, all at top volume, though Art can't hear any of them through the Cat's exhaust.

He leans his head back against the reassuring hardwood stock of his .30-06 Remington Standard on its rear-window rack. He used to carry two guns back there, one for Sarah, but after Oscar Reynolds shot his old lady and glassed her into a hull mold, Sarah asked him to lock hers away in the gun cabinet. Each year, as the hair on the back of his head thins, he can feel the oiled walnut stock more clearly against the exposed nerves of his scalp.

The .30-06 hasn't left its rack since the ill-fated Ambajezus hunting trip when he wound up getting butchered along with the moose. He likes the gun there, though, it's a warmer headrest than the plate glass window.

He can see the whole harbor now as the snow subsides and the day brightens over Doris's parking lot. The Blue Claw sits at the head of the harbor just east of the bridge over Orphan Creek. Over on the westward side, where there's water enough to float a vessel at all tides, is the wharf of Clyde Hannaford, buyer and dealer for the Orphan Point lobster fleet. Like it or not, you catch lobsters, you deal with Clyde. Otherwise you might as well eat the fucking things yourself. Clyde has a monopoly, that's how it is and has always been. Over in Split Cove they have a socialist co-op, maybe they pay a cunt hair more than Clyde does, but if you don't like the American way, you might as well move up to Canada and sit back and let the government pay you not to fish.

Beyond Clyde's, passing down Summer Street where the Money shore begins, there's Phelan's boatyard, full of sailboats shrink-wrapped for winter like a field of tent caterpillars. Then comes the row of summer shops — the Quiche Barne, Bloom's Antiques, the Cockatiel Café. Then the Orphan Point Yacht Club, dues alone more than a working man makes in a year. Then a chocolate-colored Episcopal church with a fancy brown-shingled steeple that starts tapering at the ground and terminates in a golden cross. The summer people have that cross gilded every June with fourteen-karat gold leaf, slapped on by some bearded asshole they get up all the way from Philadelphia. After that church Summer Street peters out into a dirt road running behind the row of big spooky summer mansions they used to break into to smoke and jerk off when they were kids.

On the other side of the harbor, there's Main Street, where the year-round fishermen live, there's the Blue Claw, Lurvey's Convenience & Video and Ashmore's Garage. There is also the regular Methodist church with a normal white steeple, so these two churches separated by water both reach for the sky like a couple of guys giving each other the finger. A brown guy and a white guy, if you thought of it that way, which Lucky doesn't. He doesn't give a fuck what a man is, though everyone knows the Asians are taking over the earth. And they can have it. Lucky hasn't set foot in church for fifteen years, except for a handful of funerals when Sarah dressed him up like the corpse and made him go.

If you spend enough time offshore you realize all those steeples are pointing the wrong way. If there was to be a God, which is not likely in this numb universe, He would be down under the surface where the real power is, in the cold invisible currents of the sea.

He focuses his ear on the soft well-tuned drum of the idling V-8. It doesn't waver, it doesn't skip a beat. Now if they had a church with a truck engine up at the altar end, that would mean something and he might sign on. If you're going to worship anything it should be something you can get your hands on and you don't have to argue whether it's there or not. You can trust an engine. When you're over the horizon, past sight of land, maybe it's thick of fog, cold, with the wind rising, nothing around you but freezing black salt water and cold-blooded predators that don't give a fuck, no invisible spirit is going to help you. That can be proved by Dennis Gower's cousin Calvin Willey, a God-abiding Mormon that never touched a drink or smoke, but his RV stove exploded a couple of Julys ago after the Stoneport races and everyone trapped in the back of it was killed. All God-fearing Mormons, every one of them burned to a crisp. Now a V-8 engine is something to believe in, made by honest American working stiffs with their own hands. You won't find a V-8 in a rice-burner. It can be steaming out beyond Shag Ledge at fifteen knots with the stern half sunk beneath a load of traps, hard-driving the hydraulic winch to haul a thirty-fathom trapline, or patiently waiting in neutral as you cull the catch, rebait, dump them in again. Your wife may cheat on you and your friends may forget you ever lived. Your own body starts fucking you over the minute you're born, the heart lurks in your chest like a land mine, the brain goes useless as a fistful of haddock guts. But an internal combustion engine is another matter. Long as you take care of the bastard, when there's nothing else on earth to count on, it will get you home.

He feels all the clothes Sarah put on him, the Grundens oilskin bib trousers and the wool sweater and the long underwear and beneath the clothes, his own skin wrapped around him like a survival suit. Under that layer there's a circulation no different from the heart of a big-block V-8, the Havoline 10-40 gushing from the pump to lube the pistons stroking in and out of their cylinders like a tight-holed fuck, the nervous gossipy valves jumping in their seats, the spinelike crankshaft turning in its bath of oil. His body idling in the front seat, the engine idling under the hood, they're the same fucking thing.

Not that it's true for every vehicle. Take Sarah's Mercury Lynx, which is an aluminum-block four-cylinder piece of shit. When she started insisting on a car of her own, he planned to buy her something American at Harry Pomerleau's Lincoln-Mercury up at the Narwhal Mall in Norumbega. Gas mileage is everything for Sarah, she doesn't want to take any more than she has to from those nice Arab sheiks and their Rolls-Royces and their dozen wives. Harry Pomerleau sold her a four-cylinder Lynx whose engine sounds like an ice-fishing auger but Honest Harry told her the thing would get ten miles on a quart of gas. That's the word that slick son of a bitch used on her, a *quart,* like they were going to put milk in the fucking thing. They had the Lynx three months before Virge Carter told him it was built in Oakville, Ontario. He should have known it from the name, Lynx, must be the national mammal up there in Molsonland. The laws of marriage force him to keep a car in his garage built under a Communist government by slave labor, same as their socialist cooperatives and government-funded fucking Canadian piers so they can give lobsters away while just over the border a free people starve to death.

So he doesn't set foot in his wife's car with its lawnmower engine, and Sarah won't ride in the truck because it smells like fish. *I don't mind it on you, Lucas, but then I don't have to climb inside you, do I?* When they go out together they take both vehicles, even on the thirty-mile run to the Tarratine mall, the navy blue Lynx tailgated by the big red pickup, Lucky behind the wheel looking down at his wife's neck through the Lynx's rear window and thinking, Fuck fuel economy, I'd like to see the EPA rating on us.

After the angioplasties last November, he was supposed to recuperate on an exercise schedule with walks of gradually increasing distance. He skipped the exercise and went right for the boat engine instead. Within a month of the operation he had cleaned the garage and fashioned an engine bed out of railroad ties, which he couldn't lift and he had to pay Kyle a dollar apiece to lug them in. Then he flushed out the water-cooling passages with hydrochloric acid. He ran the acid over and over through the engine block the same way they'd done it with the artery balloons run up past his nuts and guts into his own chest. When he was finished the acid came out the same as it went in, swift-flowing, colorless and clear: no rust, no clots. As soon as they let him drive again he dropped the block back in the

Wooden Nickel, balanced the shaft and flywheel, and at 3000 rpm it ran fifteen degrees cooler. He drove over to the clinic and said, "Check me out."

That exercise program did the job for your husband, that's what young Dr. Burnside told Sarah when they ran into each other in the IGA.

At exactly five-thirty, Doris flips the sign around. OPEN. Just at that moment Clyde Hannaford shows up in his blue three-quarter-ton Dodge Ramcharger with the bright yellow Fisher plow still on the hook. Clyde's never lowered it yet, not wanting to dirty her up with snow.

CL. HANNAFORD DEALER
LOBSTER CLAMS ~~GROUNDFISH~~
ORPHAN POINT

He's got groundfish crossed out because there's none of them left, and what there are the government won't let you have, their goal being to starve the fishermen off the water and turn the Atlantic Ocean into the world's biggest national fucking aquarium, look but don't touch. It's good to have your name on a truck. As long as your name isn't Lunt. The one time Lucky tried it, the weekend wasn't over before it became

LUCAS M. CUNT
LOBSTERS

Scrape it off as he tried, it kept reappearing, even when he painted the whole fucking door it would be there again when he got in from a day's fishing. Lucky Cunt.

Now Clyde is bringing his thirty-year-old child bride Ronette to her job as Doris's counter girl at the Blue Claw. Lucky can't figure why she works there. Clyde Hannaford is not some dumb fisherman in debt for fuel and bait, scraping to meet his boat loan. Clyde owns a wharf and fuel dock that he inherited from his old man, Curtis Hannaford, a first-class prick who diddled the fishermen for about fifty years and now writes postcards from Miami Beach. It's his boy Clyde who buys and sells every lobster that comes into Orphan

Point, and in the winter he now has the urchin trade. With his brother Arvid he runs a lobster takeout in back of the wharf. Come June first they get out a copper kettle big enough to boil four or five New Jersey tourists in and they sell a one-pound shedder with a boat price of three bucks for eighteen ninety-five. Not to mention the daily dock markup that probably nets him ten thousand a month while a man like Lucky, out at sea all day doing the work, can barely scrape up the payments on his gear.

Clyde's truck door opens to the sound of a Patsy Cline tape and Ronette Hannaford bounces down from the high cab in a black winter parka over her little waitress miniskirt, showing some places that don't often see the light of day. She looks like what Paula Jones *should* look like, if they had a real president in there, only Paula Jones is a dog if you study the pictures, while Ronette's got a face that makes her look naked even with an overcoat on. She was a cheerleader at Norumbega High, can't be more than ten or twelve years back, while Clyde Hannaford was two years ahead of Lucky and Sarah at the old red brick high school in Orphan Point. Sarah went out with him too, the years Lucky was a motor-pool mechanic for Uncle Sam, but that was all over when Lucas Lunt came back to town.

Lucky taps the horn, cries out, "Ain't you cold?" through the closed window which she probably can't hear over Clyde's exhaust.

Ronette looks embarrassed and pulls the skirt down, wraps the parka tight around her tits and flashes a mean look, fake mean since Ronette Hannaford does love to be noticed. It's Clyde that is shooting over the mad-dog stare, then he backs up fast with a lot of unnecessary noise, spins his slick nine-fifty by sixteens and heads for the wharf to drink hazelnut decaf and count the profits. Lucky shuts off his engine and goes in.

Without asking, Doris hands him his coffee and a slice of strawberry-rhubarb pie. "Everyone's out," she says. "Won't be any lobsters left for you."

"I'll give them a half-hour start, that way we'll all arrive at the same time."

Ronette looks up and pouts her lips at him, her body bent way over behind the counter to pull up a jar of pickled hard-boiled eggs. Her skirt lifts up so high he can see the shadow of her ass darkening her upper legs. As the father of a daughter he wants to grab hold and pull it back down, as a man out on his own in one of the mornings of the world he'd like to raise it the rest of the way. Talk about miscarriage of justice, an asshole like Clyde Hannaford sleeping every night alongside a woman you should have to be twenty-one to even look at. Without glancing up she says, "That's you, Mr. Luck, faster than the eye can see."

Doris is breaking coin rolls into the cash register but she's got her ear out. "Don't get near him, Ronette, he's so fast he'd do it and you wouldn't even know it was done."

"Wouldn't know till the Fourth of July," Ronette says.

"You'd know before that, dear." Doris slams the register shut, takes the key out and pockets it. Just then a truck comes screeching in, brakes spray gravel on Doris's plate glass window: smell of diesel smoke.

Doris says, "Jesus, what a stench. Who's got a diesel *truck?*"

"Blair Alley," Ronette says. "Watch out. Don't that thing smell." Blair and his brother Frank weigh a good six hundred pounds between them, about three ounces of it is brain. They kick the door open with their boots and try to walk through the doorway at the same time, get stuck for a second then figure out that Blair was firstborn and Frank stands aside. Ronette stands up with the jar of hardboiled eggs and looks down at their boots and says, "Frank Alley, I have always wanted to know, what size shoe do you take?"

Blair says, "Frank don't reveal things like that. They're trade secrets with him."

"He don't reveal them," Lucky says, "he sells them."

Doris opens the cash register drawer with a big ring but zeros showing on the screen. "Frank," she says, "how much would that information be?"

Blair reaches into the glass-doored doughnut drum and pulls out a chocolate éclair and throws it in his mouth like it was an M&M. He slides another one down to his brother, who opens his huge jaws like a basking shark and the éclair is gone. "I guess that will do it," Blair says. "Go ahead, Frank, tell her."

Ronette leans over the counter to look down at Frank's feet, but his trousers hang so far over his boots that Frank's standing on the cuffs, and meanwhile the cleavage of his dark hairy asscrack is showing like Dolly Parton on Rogaine. One of Ronette's tits presses down on the how-to-eat-a-lobster place mat, the other presses on a fork and knife. Lucky wonders if she can feel things like silverware through the bra and the white waitress blouse.

"You're going to have to lift them trousers up," Ronette says to Frank, giving him the weird glance she has, as if one of her eyes was astray. He has heard the rumor that Ronette has a glass eye but he does not believe it. Both her eyes move when she looks around, just maybe one doesn't come at you quite as fast as the other, that's all. It's a sexy moment, waiting for the other eye to catch up.

Doris, who was a friend of his mother's and must be close to sixty, is pushing her dyed blond hair up in an interested way. "You know what they say, Ronette. 'Big feet, warm heart.'"

Frank says, "I wear a nine."

"Sure you do," Ronette says. "And your brother here is a ballet dancer."

"Belly dancer," Lucky says. The Alleys choose to pay no attention.

"I wouldn't shit you, Ronette," Frank says. "You gave me an ee-clair." He hoists the trousers back up over his stern cleavage and there's a boot two sizes smaller than Lucky's own. "It is a nine."

"Something must be wrong with that one," Ronette says. "Must be deformed. Lift up the other one."

Same size. Nobody knows what to say. Frank Alley is the big one too, he must weigh over three hundred and he's walking around on a size-nine foot. Doris says, "Whew, I don't know how you stand up on them. They must hurt at the end of the day. I know mine do, and I ain't got your weight on them."

Blair says, "I think Frank should get more than a fucking eeclair." He pulls a glazed honey-dip out of the doughnut drum and gives it to his brother and stands up.

Frank says, "Fucking daylight saving time. It ain't never going to get light."

"Just set your watch ahead an hour," Lucky tells him. "It'll get light right away."

Frank looks at him seriously and says, "No shit?" He starts frigging around with his watch as they go out, then looks east towards the sunrise like he's just caused it, pleased as piss. By the doorway he bends down to pet Doris's weird little Chinese dog and as he does his pants slip down again. His big white cheeks bulge out in the brightening air.

Ronette whispers, "Ain't every day you get a sight like that."

"Don't get all jealous." Lucky says. "Frank's had an implant. It ain't real."

The Alley brothers can't hear a thing, they're outside cranking the diesel over which won't start cause it hasn't been plugged in, but Ronette still bends close to Lucky to whisper. The steam rising off his coffee forms a little ridge of moisture on her chin. "Would you of believed that?" she says. "Frank Alley. Size nine. What size are you, Lucky?"

Doris hears. "Why don't you call Sarah up and ask her? Lucky never buys his own shoes. How's he supposed to know?"

"You don't know your own size?" Ronette says.

"Eleven."

"Makes sense," she says. "You're a few sizes bigger than Clyde, he wears an eight."

"Small feet, cold heart," Doris says. She walks to the jukebox and plays some Garth:

> *Parked on some old backstreet*
> *They laid down in the backseat*

"Clyde does have a cold heart," Ronette says, suddenly serious, like the song. She hums along as she loads the hard-boiled eggs into the small jar. "Coldhearted Hannaford."

"Treats *you* nice," Doris reminds her. "You got that Ford Probe or whatever it is, you got that hot tub."

"Money ain't everything," Ronette says. "There's a few other things."

"Damn few," Doris says. "You get where I am in life, you see all the other things were daydreams."

"Money's a daydream," Ronette says. "Tell her, Lucky."

Lucky says, "I wouldn't know. Never seen any."

"You ain't going to," Doris says, "if you don't leave the help alone and get on your boat."

Ronette sticks her tongue out at her boss, just a quick flicker not meant to be seen, and puts the big egg jar back in the floor cooler. Lucky pays up and leaves her a buck tip for a sixty-eight cent coffee and heads for her husband's wharf, where he keeps his skiff.

Turns out he's not the last boat, the ones that didn't pick up their gas and bait the night before are still crowding Clyde's wharf at the pump float. Lucky just has to take the skiff out to his mooring and cast off. Rowing past the gas pumps, he calls, "Good morning, Clyde, just had breakfast with your old lady," and gets nothing but a wicked glare. Then he remembers his radio. Clyde also handles electronic repairs, not that he can do them himself, but he takes the units to Chubby Burke in Norumbega, supposedly to save you the trip but now Clyde's got it so Chubby won't take your repairs if they don't go through him. Chub gives him a volume discount that does not get passed on. That puts another wing on the hot tub so Ronette gets to stretch out her tired little body to its full length. One good thing you can say about the Commies, they would have eliminated the middleman. Guys like Clyde Hannaford would have got reformed in a labor camp. Too bad. "Hey Clyde," he shouts, "you got my radio?"

"Chubby says another wait. That thing's so old he's got to get parts from Illinois."

"At least they ain't coming from Tokyo."

"You probably got the last working radio made in the U.S.A. That thing belongs in the maritime museum. Chubby says it uses *crystals.* You could get two Apelcos for what those crystals are going to cost."

"Damn good radio," Lucky says. "You can hear the fucking thing fifty miles away. They don't make them like that anymore. Know where they make them Apelcos? Malaysia. Wherever the fuck that is."

"No doubt. But those crystals are going to be another three weeks."

"Don't need a fucking radio anyway. I ain't going out to talk. I'm going to fish."

It's now a brightening mackerel sky over Orphan Point. The snow has stopped. The underbellies of the eastern clouds are stained blood-red the way the floors of the old fishhouses used to look before the government shut the tuna fishery down. Lucky rows Downeast style, stern first, so he can see where his ass is going, not like the summer folks who row out blind as quahogs into the fog. Moving at half speed in memory of his operation, he rows down the west shore of the harbor, towards the Money side, where the seasonal residents have their estates and stables on spidery dirt roads that don't even get plowed in winter so some of them have a foot of snow on them even now. That's the way they like it, the summer people, they think it keeps the vandals out but nowadays kids break in anyway using their Ski-Doos. Lucky himself got caught once poaching a couple of bottles of Canadian whiskey out of one of those places when he was right around fourteen. He was detained and interrogated by Officer Arden Jewett, who accepted one of the bottles for evidence and let him go. The owners of those places have three or four homes, couple of Lexuses in the garage, helicopter pads on their lawns so they can step right onto their yachts, rich bastards, they ought to open their mansions after Labor Day and let people come take what they want, instead of having to break in at the coldest time of the year.

After rowing past a couple of these mansions to stay out of the current, he turns out towards his boat, heading for the east side, where the fishermen live, their old black-shuttered white-clapboard Capes still insulated with newspapers from the Civil War. Same families that built them are living in them now. Lucky's great-great-grandfather funded their place with a Union Army bonus — that's how his mother told it — became a fisherman, and they've been fishermen ever since. Not one of the Lunt men knew how to do another god damn thing. That's what they say, a Lunt can smell his way to Nova Scotia through the fog but he needs a compass to find the grocery store.

No different for Sarah. The Peeks were a fishing family since anyone could remember. They had a house with gingerbread trim, just below the Orphan Point cemetery, on Deadman's Hill. The Peeks and the Lunts had been marrying off and on ever since lobsters sold for three cents a pound. When the state came to town and set up that office of genetic counseling, they called Lucky and Sarah to come pay a visit, but it was too late, Kyle was on a tricycle and Kristen was on the way. They came out all right, five fingers on each hand, what the fuck. The GC office is a waste of taxpayers' dollars, except for maybe the Gross family, and all the genetic counselors on earth couldn't have stopped the Grosses from breeding in. They just don't have an eye for anyone else.

He can see his own house among the others, all the lights on now. Sarah will be fixing breakfast. Kristen will be pacing in the hall outside the bathroom for Kyle to finish, which takes an hour now he's shaving his whole fucking head, it's a wonder they let him in the school.

The *Wooden Nickel*'s riding low in the water, lower than she should be even with the traps on board. She's been a leaker since they put her in this March, no two ways about it. He put a few new strakes on her while she was hauled over the winter and he thought they'd swell in, but she must have half her bilge full cause the waterline stripe's a foot under even in the bow. Under the traps the stern's pretty near submerged.

He fixes the skiff to the mooring and pauses a minute to let his heart catch up. Everything looks right and smells right: fresh engine oil, black polysulfide seam caulking, bait bucket full of nice ripe herring in the stern. Just a whiff of that stuff brings women to his mind. When he was a kid he was scared to kiss them below the waist, then one day he recognized that aroma and realized he'd been working in it his whole life. After that, he never hesitated to plunge right in. He'd do it now if Sarah would give him half a chance, but she pulls his head back if he even gets close. "Lucas," she always says, "that *tickles*."

He sticks his head right in the opening of the bait bucket and takes a deep pungent inhale until his mind goes blank, he's back under the covers and Ronette Hannaford is in the bed, her whole body smelling like a beautiful smoked trout. He slides the cover off the engine box, just like opening a coffin lid, and there's a fresh-painted, reamed-out Chevy 454, cold as a corpse till he touches the electric fuel pump for a second, hits the starter and it comes to life, a miracle that could be in the fucking Bible if you think about it, yet it happens every single day.

He lets her run out a bit at 1300 rpm, then he switches the power takeoff to the bilge pump because half the harbor has slipped into the cracks of his christly hull. Another hour, she would have been up to the flywheel with the traps washing off the stern. Once he gets offshore and the sea works the hull a bit, she'll swell and settle in.

He tunes the stereo back to High Country 104, they've got a female DJ now with a nice raspy sunrise voice that makes him think of the Marlboros he's got stashed behind the radar screen. He flips the box open and eases one out with his teeth. Nothing about a cigarette he doesn't like, including the filter's crisp dry asbestos taste. They pick the best of life, every time, and take it away from you.

Dr. Burnside made him quit after the operation — right when he needed it most. Those first nights home from the Tarratine hospital, he'd wake up seasick from the medication, withdrawal pains worse than the angina, cold turkey after two packs a day for almost thirty years. He'd stand in the bathroom before breakfast those dark and frigid mornings with his hands shaking like an addict and tear up Kleenexes one after the other till Sarah came in and walked him to the table.

But Dr. Burnside left a loophole big enough to sail a supertanker through. He didn't say anything about smoking offshore. Outside the three-mile limit a man can do anything he wants, and in ten minutes that's where he's going to be. He jams the unlit Marlboro between the wool cap and his ear. He revs the engine to finish pumping the bilge, and soon as the hose sucks air he switches the PTO to neutral, then goes forward up on the high prow, pulls the heavy eye splice off the bitt and steps back to the wheel, backs off a bit so he won't catch the pennant, and in a moment he's clocking fifteen knots on the loran, stern down and throwing a rooster tail behind the prop with a nice wake forking off astern. He detours east across the harbor so he can pass by his own house with Sarah and Kristen waving from the kitchen window, steering so close to shore he can hear the prop echo off the bottom and see his family's breath steaming against the glass. Kristen turns away and it's just Sarah, not waving anymore, looking out to sea like a widow over the yellow Fisher snowplow and the snowy lawn. He slows to an idle. If he had his radio he'd ask her to meet him back at Clyde's and go out lobstering. She wouldn't have to do anything, she could sit and sketch the islands like she did in the old days. He goes to the port side to wave her towards the wharf with his orange glove, but by the time he gets there she's turned from the window and then she's gone. He speeds up and cuts sharp to starboard to avoid Little Sow Ledge with the three black shags perched on the daybeacon looking just like the shapes of death.

He'd like to max out the rpm and get right out to the three-mile limit and light up, but he's got a rebuild and she's got to be run gentle the first few hours. On High Country 104 Wynonna's singing "Heaven Help My Heart," which reminds him to take it easy on the engine. He turns up the radio and throttles the V-8 down to give it a break. He doesn't even have to look outside the wheelhouse to know where he's going in the light dawn mist, just watches the fishfinder trace its cardiograph across the screen and feels his way along its contours like a crab. As long as he can see a fathometer line he has his location in this world. He knows every rock and crevice on the ocean floor for ten miles in all directions. If he had to crawl home dead drunk on the bottom of the sea he could grope his way among the sunken dories and ghost traps right to the shore of his backyard.

The fishfinder deepens from six fathoms at the harbor mouth to nine off of Sodom Head, then it shallows up in the Sodom Ledge channel, so he eases her westward to clear the invisible killer shoal with its beacon missing and the pole bent crooked from winter storms. Once he's past that it drops off and he turns twenty degrees south without looking at the compass, steering by the contour line alone, because on the route to his spring territory he knows the seabed rock by rock.

Most of the boys will be two or three miles out already, going for the April lobsters, which are still creeping in from their deep winter grounds between Red's Bank and Nigh Shag Ledge. Lucky figures on going just inshore of them with his first string. He'll drop them around the fifteen-fathom line that runs south and east from the Sodom bell. No lobsters inside of that, not yet.

Now the fog thickens like a sudden eclipse, white dew coating the windshield as it steams into invisibility. He swings the glass open but it doesn't make any difference, so he switches the radar on, gives her a minute to warm up, then another minute, but it's still blank. He bangs his fist on the top of the screen housing and she glows green, the raster swings around, and one by one the Orphan Point boats form a circle of green blips, his own at the center. Fucking Raytheon, built right in New England. Maybe.

The fleet's setting their traps out past the twenty-fathom line, half a mile into the fog bank. But one blip is close by, pretty soon he's up to them and out of the salt mist appears the *Abby and Laura*, skipper Alonzo Gross. They say Alonzo's father married his father's niece, and Alonzo went and did the same thing: chip off the old block. His old lady's got the same name as his mother. If old Stubby and Abigail Gross had gone to the genetic counselor with little Alonzo, she would have counseled them to throw him back. Yet there he is hauling traps with his daughter as sternperson, who looks just like him: big square head, square face, squared-off body. Xerox copy, just like that sheep clone over in Finland. By now all the Grosses, male or female, look exactly alike. She's a big girl with a big orange lobsterman's apron around her waist and just a jersey on top, a contender in the wet T-shirt contest, sumo division.

Lucky waves at the *Abby and Laura,* slows down, yells out, "Hello Alonzo!" then follows the track of his bottom machine into the fog, leaving father and daughter back on the twelve-fathom curve, old Lonnie leaning right over her as they raise their string of empty traps. They say Alonzo gives it to her every chance he gets. Of course the world would be a fucking zoo if you believed everything, so you have to sort out the truth from the rumors, which are all mostly true in the case of Lonnie Gross. Back in high school Lonnie would grow these curly black hairs on his palms from too much jerking off. He'd stand there in the locker room, proud as piss, hands open for everyone to see.

He switches the fishfinder to high resolution and watches the bottom grow in contour and detail. He has to think like a crustacean now, not a hairy-assed air-breather but an armored and camouflaged creature that lives to hide. He fixes on the contour line with the eyes of a green-black lobster moving from deep winter water to medium-depth spring water, groping and searching for a place to lurk and feed. He slows the *Wooden Nickel* to half a knot, just about the speed of a lobster in high gear. The fathometer shows rocks and drop-offs, ledges and crevasses and canyons in the blind kelp-coated underworld. His body starting to outgrow its shell, driven by cold lust and raw anger, the lobster man feels his way forward with his sensitive antenna and arrives at the chosen spot. He turns her south-southwest to lay the trapline along the current flow. Back at the stern, he pushes over the first of a triple, uses its fall to pull the other two over, and casts his buoy over last of all, painted Day-Glo orange and green with a delicate white intermediate strip by his wife Sarah, an artist in everything she does.

Just as the pot buoy goes over, a small fluttering charcoal-colored bird comes by, circles the boat as if dazzled by the sight of an object in the fog, then settles on the water not ten yards off the stern. Good omen: birds know where the lobsters are. Maybe they can stick their beaks in and look straight down.

By the third string he's sweating and exhausted and has to sit on the coiled pot warp and have a smoke, his heart pounding the floor of his chest like a basketball, twenty-six thousand dollars down the fucking drain. He goes to pop another heart pill, then realizes he left them back in the truck. He opens the lunch pail. She's wrapped the crab salad sandwich in a penciled note: *Be careful out there. We love you.* He picks the sandwich up with shaky fingers but feels better after the first bite. Maybe it's just hunger and not the heart.

He kills the engine while he eats and lets her drift. He turns the radio up at first for Deana Carter's "If This Is Love," then turns it off. It's hard to swallow the word *love* out here in the fog: cold sea wind, no sound, no color, like one of those dreams where the earth is all water like it was at the beginning and you're the only person alive. He tries to taste love in the crabmeat salad Sarah mixed up at 4 A.M., but if there is any, the Miracle Whip covers it like a deodorant. He's not sure he loves any of them. They were all accidents, even Sarah, it was a shotgun wedding though they moved fast and they were the only ones that knew. Now they're all turning away from him. Kyle's got his own boat, he's not even lobstering anymore. He's diving for whore's eggs, that's what they called sea urchins before they got discovered by the sushi crowd. Kristen's three years younger than her brother. She was so smart she skipped a grade and now she's graduating a year ahead. They started Kyle late and kept him back a year in the third grade like you're supposed to with boys, then the school kept him back another in junior high. Kristen thinks her college roommate's going to be some lawyer's daughter and she'll have to confess her old man fishes with his hands. Sarah's a celebrity now with her little sea glass sculptures, all of a sudden the summer people think she's Polly Picasso. Come June she'll spend more time up at the art school than she will at home. All of them dykes and homos, that's what Stevie Latete says, he lives just a half-mile down the road.

He throws the sandwich crust to the gray seabird, who shows no interest, but two big gulls that have been trailing him all morning swoop down and fight for it. He lays the last string right where he's drifted, too tired to locate another perfect spot. The boat's riding higher with the traps off, and it seems to be swelling in so the leak is down, he hasn't run the bilge pump for half an hour. He's about seven miles from Clyde's wharf. The *Wooden Nickel* can do thirty-one knots in flat water when she's in tune, but there's no use risking the engine with the Stoneport races a couple of months away. Lucky got fourth in class at Summer Harbor last year. The guy who took third, Sumner Ames out of Riceville, has moved over to diesel, at least that's what they say. This year, if the heart behaves itself, he's got a chance to place.

Should be fifteen minutes at twenty-four knots. He takes the last sip of decaf from the thermos, lights his last Marlboro, turns up the radio and puts the hammer down. It's the first time he's opened her up since the rebuild. The 454 whines like a banshee, it throws a rooster tail, it pitches luminous spray over the bow onto the windshield and dumps green water back in the cockpit on every wave. It's a big Saginaw engine with a ripped muffler and it silences everything else around, including the rebuilt heart.

They eat supper watching CNN, it's President Clinton on with some lie about Whitewater, then he's holding hands with his Lesbian General, Janet Reno. Sarah sees her husband about to go violent and reaches up to switch the set off. "Thanks," Lucky says. "Saves me from throwing a Rolling Rock through the screen."

"Your first day out, Lucas, after the surgery. How did it go out there?"

"Finest kind."

"You smoked, didn't you? I can smell it in your hair. You're like a twelve-year-old, sneaking off with a cigarette, but it's your own body, you can't run away from it."

"I didn't inhale," he says. "That's one thing I got in common with that son of a bitch."

"Yeah," says Kyle over his third bowl of cod head stew. "You both lied about it."

"Who you calling a liar?" He pushes his chair back, stands, leans over the big chowder caldron on the table. Kyle's out of his chair, Sarah poised to move between them if it gets physical. They're almost the same height though Lucky's heavier, twice as thick in the neck and shoulders, not to mention the waist. He could still take him, bad heart or not. The kid looks like a terrorist with the shaved head and the shadow of an X cut into it and the T-shirt with the arms ripped off. A twenty-year-old high school junior: maybe they shouldn't have kept him back.

His daughter Kristen says, "Don't just stand there, *fight*. You're males. That's what we learned in biology. Males fight till just one of them is left."

"He ain't worth the trouble," Lucky says.

Sarah stands behind Kyle and runs her hand over the shaved head. "Lucas, it's your own son. Can you imagine *your* father saying that?"

"He wouldn't of said nothing. He would of cocked me one."

Kristen pulls her Walkman out of her backpack, jams the earphones down over her blond hair. "Thank God I'm getting out of this in September, I won't have to hear it. *EVER AGAIN.*" She cranks up the earphone volume till you can hear it in the room.

Kyle yells at her, *"WHAT'S THAT?"*

"Smashing Pumpkins." She closes her eyes and pegs the volume all the way.

He turns to the shaved head. "You got that shitheap in the water yet?"

"*Lu*cas."

"Just wondering if he's planning to race this year."

"Racing's a waste of time."

"You got third last year. Play with that Merc a bit, you could take it."

"That was then. Now's now. I got business."

"What kind of business? You're supposed to be in fucking school."

"Private business." He rubs the X on his shaved head like it's a sign saying *keep out.*

Sarah stays close beside her son to protect him, the top of her head level with his nose. She's done the same thing as Kyle, two weeks ago she came home from Shear Heaven with her hair chopped and spiked up like a gray-blond porcupine. It gives her a homeless look, though she's spent the last twenty years in this house, every single night. "I'm going to my studio," she says. "Send someone up when you guys have worked things out."

He turns his back on all of them and switches the TV back on to a Merrill Lynch commercial and turns the volume up. "Finally," he says, "an ad for bullshit."

Forgetting himself completely, he reaches into his shirt pocket for the Marlboros he should have left on board, sticks one in his mouth, looks around with his hands for a light. His wife says, "Lucas, if you don't care whether you live or die, think of the budget, twenty-six thousand dollars for that hospital to clear the tar out of your veins."

Kristen's got her earphones off now. "And the fat," she chimes in sweetly. "Remember what he used to *eat*."

"Money we don't have, with the home equity gone into the boat, Kristen's tuition coming up."

"Too poor for insurance," Kristen says, "too rich for welfare. We had a social studies unit about us."

It feels like he's in the parlor of a lobster trap, cornered crustaceans going at each other with both claws, might as well build a house of steam-bent laths, let the wind blow right through. He crumples the cigarette and puts it on his plate. "Jesus H. Christ, this place a home or a church? I'm going to bed. I got to set sixty traps tomorrow."

Sarah says, "Lucas, come to the studio on your way up. I'd like to show you something."

He doesn't want to get near the studio, it raises his blood pressure till his neck veins ache. Three years ago Sarah and Kristen said they didn't want him smoking in the house anymore. He built himself a den out in the attic of their three-door garage, deer head on the wall, nice little fridge, couple of windows overlooking the water, a man could take his boots off and tune in High Country 104 and light up without his family coughing like they'd been teargassed. Then after the operation, when young Dr. Burnside laid down the law, Sarah asked for the den as a studio for her beach glass ornaments that are supposedly works of art. She argued the case like a lawyer with Kristen beside her all the way. She'd been making them up in the bedroom, which hardly left them a place to sleep. The den had a north window with some special kind of light. And in conclusion, she might one day sell one of the christly things and help the cash flow. In the long run they caved him in, a den is pointless if you can't have a fucking smoke. Just before Christmas, Kristen and Sarah moved the workbench and soldering tools in. "You have the third bay of the garage," she would say. "You have the basement. You don't need the light the way I do." His response was a three-week reign of silence that included Christmas and New Year's Eve, when instead of taking her to the Grange party he got drunk at the RoundUp with Travis Hammond.

He still makes it a point not to set foot in his former den, but tonight he feels pretty good having set forty-eight traps without dropping dead at the helm, so he ducks his head for the low passage leading to the second floor of the garage. It smells of butane and soldering flux and something else, like clam flats, an odor you can never quite get off glass that's been salvaged from a beach. He misses the cloud of tobacco and spilled beer. She's got fringed lilac curtains and the big braided Peek family rug that still smells of her mother's dead cocker spaniel, Rufus. He spends all day in the stench of lobster bait, you'd think his nose would numb out, but it's keen as a drug dog. Every article in her room speaks to him with its own repellent scent, his back hairs are stiffening, he's in the lair of another species. She's got two long tables with mounds of sea glass stacked up by shape and color, she's got a tray of brass wires to hang them from, she's got another table with her vise, her low-heat butane soldering torch, her lead strips, and the diamond saw he got her Christmas before last when she still worked on a Black & Decker Workmate at the foot of their bed.

There's several of them in different stages on the workbench and a couple of finished ones hanging from the ceiling in front of the window, *his* window, that looks across the harbor to the old lighthouse which is now a yuppie bed-and-breakfast down on the tip of Sodom Head.

"I want to show you something, Lucas. These are the ones you've seen, from the group exhibition last year that you refused to go to. And this is the one Yvonne Hannaford wants for her gallery this summer. If I can make more like it, she *might* give me a one-person show."

"You'd be the first person that fucking family ever gave anything to."

"Well, it's not totally a gift. Dealer gets fifty percent. It's the one thing art and lobsters have in common."

Now she says "art" like the summer people, *ort,* like there's an *r* in it. Something wrong with their tongues. He picks the thing up by the top wire and holds it under the workbench light. She frames up chunks of different-colored sea glass with lead moldings like the windows in the Episcopal church showing Jesus H. Christ and the sheep, except in hers there's no story. He turns it around, squints at it, raises it and looks from below like he's staring up a girl's skirt, but he can't make out what it's supposed to be. "I give up," he says. "What is it?"

"It's not a puzzle, Lucas, it's an abstraction." She lays her glasses on the workbench. Her face is thin under the chopped hair. The outlines of her eyes are red, like she's been crying or leaning over the butane torch or staying up too late. Who knows when she goes to bed now that she's got the studio, he never hears her, yet she's up with his clothes and lunch fixed before he's even awake. She's got classical music going on his radio too, all of it sounds like a funeral, she's worse than Kristen.

He hits the preset for High Country 104, Reba McEntire's singing "How Blue." He puts the sculpture down, kicks the footstool out of the way, puts an arm around his wife's slender waist and waltzes her slowly from the workbench to the skylight across the den. "Remember her first one?"

"Lucas, it was a thousand years ago. I never listen to country anymore."

"'One Night Stand.' Jesus, we had a one-night stand, lasted us twenty years."

She gives in, lays her head on his chest even though his sweatshirt's crusted with green algae like a mooring spar. Then she pulls back and says, "Your heart sounds different."

"I got machinery in there."

"All the more reason to take care of it. You can't keep going out alone. Remember your father, everyone told him to take a sternman after his first."

"Won't be Kyle."

"It doesn't have to be Kyle."

"Lot of the guys are using their wives. Think about it. Working together, wouldn't be no overhead, we'd get the hospital paid up, Kristen's school."

She stops and looks up with the blue, red-lined eyes. "Lucas, I can't be a sternman. I've got another life. It's April. In another month I'll be starting school again." She takes his huge hand in her thin birdclaw hands, the two of which together don't weigh as much as his thumb. When they first got together, her hands were a mass of tiny cuts from picking crabmeat at the cannery. Now they're the same way, only it's from the workbench, and she's repeating, "I'd love to, Lucas, but I can't."

It's late, he's got to be up an hour before sunrise. He leaves her soldering another piece of sea glass and goes down to catch a few laps of the Coca-Cola 600 on ESPN2.

Even with the studio visit and a fiery stock car crash that takes ten minutes to clean up, he's in bed by ten-thirty. He takes a couple of heart pills with a shot of black rum. In no time at all he's dreaming of Ronette Hannaford in orange Grundens oilpants ten sizes too big so you can look right inside them but there's nothing down there, no hair, no pussy, not even legs. She has an oilskin top stained with fish blood which he strains to remove so he can see her tits, but he can't get his arms to move. He's yelling at her, or someone, *It's my fucking dream, I can get the coat off if I want,* but it won't work. He hasn't had a hard-on since he mixed all the heart pills in the same bottle, but now he wakes up stiff as a propeller shaft. He hears Sarah coming to bed, quietly so she won't wake him. The red digital clock says 11:30. He turns over so she won't notice the hard-on and ask him what he was thinking of.

She slips in beside him, quietly, then whispers, "Lucas?"

"Pretty god damn late, isn't it?"

"I've been talking to Kyle."

"Can't it wait till morning?"

"It's serious. He wants to move out and get his own place."

"He ain't even finished high school."

"He wants to quit. He's afraid to tell you."

"He *should* be fucking afraid. I'll kick his ass."

"Lucas, you didn't finish high school yourself."

"Things was different, them days we had lobsters knocking on the door, asking themselves to dinner. You didn't have to know nothing, any dipshit could make a living. Now there's technology out there. There's competition. There's guys setting twelve hundred traps. They got them on their computers, they don't even have to steer the god damn boat. Kid wants to go lobstering now, he's going to need a fucking brain."

"You tell him, Lucas, he won't listen to me. He feels bad too, his younger sister graduating before he does."

"I ain't going to tell him tonight," Lucas says. "It's almost twelve."

"You listen to the weather?"

He reaches over and pushes the button on the NOAA radio, but they haven't changed the tape. "I'll check it in the morning. It ain't going to blow too bad."

He thinks he can get back in the same dream where Ronette Hannaford has the oilskins on and this time he can get the top off and see what she's got. Then his wife puts an arm around him under his flannel sweatshirt and puts her hand over his heart. She's been working and her skin smells of the butane torch. "Lucas, you asleep already?"

"It depends."

"On what?"

"Depends on who wants to know."

He turns slowly, so he can have time to put Ronette Hannaford back where she belongs, and while he's turning Sarah switches her clock radio on and it's the Garth Brooks song "The Red Strokes," soft and easy, she couldn't have picked better if she'd punched the numbers into a jukebox.

Steam on the window, salt on a kiss

The outside air has gone tropical with the east wind, the last of the snow is dripping off the roof. The easterly must be bringing the fog in; even with the song playing he can hear the Split Point horn, sounding and echoing off the granite cliffs of Sodom Head. He reaches over his wife to turn the bedlamp on so he'll be certain who he's with. It's a mistake though. They're less than a foot apart but he can't find her. He squints his eyes twenty years into the past, there's a skinny blond kid jumping up beside him in the truck with cuts all over her hands from the cannery, four of them in the front seat, with Art Pettingill and his girl. Now Alma Pettingill would have to be weighed on a truck scale, but Sarah's got the same body she came with, so thin she's forever shivering from the cold.

When he opens his eyes again she's studying his face like a meat inspector. "I hear that Rhonda Hannaford's planning to leave home."

"I ain't heard anything to that effect." The news brings his dream back in full living color. He's face to face with his wife under a reading lamp but his mind's wondering what another girl looks like under an oilskin coat. It's not right and he knows it. But when he tries to put Sarah's body into the yellow jacket, it won't fit.

Then the front door slams. A truck pulls up outside, idles. It's a Ford six, not too new either, wicked knock, but he doesn't recognize the exact vehicle, must be from another town. "What the hell, Sarah. You hear that?"

"It's nothing, Lucas. Just one of Kyle's friends."

"It's fucking midnight." He gets up, yanks his sweatshirt down and his long underwear up, pulls the fishing boots on which are always by the bedroom door. He glances at the Winchester .30-30 in the open closet, just to make sure it's there. Kristen's light is still on. She's on the floor with her homework, feet up on the desk. "Where's your god damn brother going?" he demands.

"Hey, I'm not the criminal. Don't yell at me."

He opens the front door and there's his son talking to three guys in an '88 Ford half-ton that he's never seen. They've all got cigarettes and Kyle's lighting one up too. The Ford's on idle, missing a cylinder if not two and passing oil, he can smell it in the air. Whoever it is, they're on his list already for neglecting a decent truck. When they see the door open, the Ford crunches into first and takes off.

Kyle's startled to see his old man under the porch light, in trawler boots over his long johns. "Bit early to start out, ain't it?"

"Who the fuck were *you* talking to?"

"Friends."

"School friends?"

"Yeah."

"They ain't from around here."

"They're from Burnt Neck."

"What the fuck you hanging out with Burnt Neck kids for? Every one of them bastards ends up in Thomaston."

"I dive with them, that's what."

"You don't dive in the middle of the fucking night."

"We're just talking business, that's all."

"Business."

"Yeah, Dad. Business. We're in the urchin business together."

"Whore's eggs. Them are the garbage of the sea," he says. "I wouldn't bait a trap with them. Even a fucking lobster won't touch them things."

"Dad, the Japanese pay three dollars and fifty cents an *ounce* for that stuff. Darrell and me got it figured. We hold them back a while into the off-season, they're going to be paying us by the gram."

"Might as well sell cocaine while you got the scales out," Lucky says.

"Yeah, well maybe we'll do that too."

"I'll kick your ass. I need a sternman and you're out in the middle of the night playing pussy with the Chinese."

"I got my own boat, Dad. And I've got my own dealer. I ain't chained to that asshole Clyde Hannaford like some I know."

"Yeah, well at least Clyde ain't Chinese. The money feeds right into the U.S.A."

"The money feeds right into his wife, that's what I hear. You see the car she's got?"

"I wouldn't know," Lucky says. He stops in the kitchen to wash down another heart pill with a shot of Wild Turkey in a glass of double-strength mint-flavored Mylanta. He stomps upstairs past Kristen's bedroom with the light still on, some horrendous screeching coming out of her stereo. He pokes his head in, yells, "What's all that *noise?*"

"Nine Inch Nails!"

"Jesus H. Christ, you got the headphones on, shut the damn speakers off."

"I'm listening to *Brahms* on the headphones. I like the combination. Besides, it drowns out the cacophony in this house."

Cacophony. What the fuck. He kicks his boots off by the door. He gets back under the blanket and says to his wife, "Burnt Neck. Bunch of degenerates. Never should of consolidated the fucking schools."

She doesn't answer. He knows from her breathing that she's fast asleep.

2

I T ' S   A L M O S T   M A Y   and Doris has changed her opening hour
to four-thirty, but Lucky's early as always, sitting behind the wheel
in the parking lot. That's where he smells the weather, figures
how much he can get done out there before the wind comes on, what
can be learned about the day ahead from the lisp of the tide rip
and the fading moon. He's fishing a hundred and fifty traps at this
point, a respectable number for a handicapped guy working alone
in spring. The *Wooden Nickel* may be running cool and sweet since
he reamed the tubes out, but his own heart starts knocking after
the first string of traps and he's got to sit down and have a smoke and
a Rolling Rock to settle it down, which means he can't haul
half what he used to in a day. He's got to hire a sternman or cut
back. And cutting back is out. The home equity loan for the boat
rebuild left them with payments on a house that had been Lunt

property free and clear for a hundred years. Then they can start on his twenty-six-thousand-dollar hospital account, going up 18 percent a year. Already he's missed two equity payments and Les Bernstein called Sarah from the Tarratine Trust Company to find out what's going on.

His own father died of a heart attack at forty-eight. He was three weeks in the hospital before he finally went, it took five years to pay off the medical bills. He doesn't want to leave that legacy to his own kids. Fine way to go: cast off and leave them fifty thousand in the hole.

Mortgaged or not, the *Wooden Nickel* looks good out there, just the shape he goes for, boat or woman: high-stemmed, low freeboard amidships, good broad stern so she'll ride easy in a following sea. White hull, blue wheelhouse, Red Hand bottom paint the color of a baked lobster, American as the Fourth of July, she sits surrounded by hulls made from plastic resin sucked off the dregs of the Arab oil wells, diesel engines built in Stockholm by Turkish wetbacks. She is a thirty-six-foot bilge-keeled sweetheart built by the Alley brothers down in Moose Reach for his old man Walter Lunt. Nineteen seventy, the year before he got too sick to fish and passed her to his only child. In those days Fred and Stan Alley were the best boatbuilders on the coast, no relation to fat Frank Alley from Burnt Neck, who couldn't build a fucking herring crate. When Lucky took her for a total rebuild twenty years later, everyone had gone to glass. Fred and Stan Alley were raising turkeys down in Moose Reach. Their tools were rusted, their old boat shed was falling down. *Redraw the lines,* he told them. *Make it faster.* Stan Alley said, *Set you back more than a new one.* He hauled like a bastard that summer, mortgaged the house, and trucked her down to Moose Reach in November for the reconstruction. They ordered old-growth cedar from up in the Allagash wilderness and hackmatack frames out of the Canadian border swamps. Stan Alley keeled over from a stroke just after New Year's, but Fred and his son Junior saw her through, then they closed the boatyard down for good. He paid them forty thousand dollars and they moved right to Sarasota, father and son.

He had Harley Webster in Riceville rebore a factory-new Chevy 454 and custom fit it to an oversize Hurth transmission on a two-inch stainless shaft, not a cunt hair of torque lost passing through the hull. When he took delivery on *Wooden Nickel* that June he brought her right to the Summer Harbor races, broke it in on the way and took third in gas unlimited though there were three 502s in that race from as far away as Kittery Point. Thirty-six miles an hour on the radar gun, the only wooden hull in the top ten. That's what they clocked him at. Cocksucker was paid for and now it's the bank's again.

He notes one strange boat lying in the dredged channel just off of Clyde's wharf: the *Rachel T,* a big steel dragger out of Shag Island with rust streaks weeping down both sides. He knows them, the Trott brothers. Half of Shag Island is named Trott, the other half's Shavers. The genetic counselors make three flights a month out to their office at the Shag Island airport, which is this grassy field with a weather sock at one end and a graveyard at the other, that's where they get laid when they're young and buried when they're old. Captain Anson Trott and his boys must have brought Clyde a load of shellfish, then got drunk at the RoundUp and now they're out there sleeping it off on the *Rachel T.*

Moment he thinks of Clyde Hannaford, here comes Ronette herself, cruising in with her lemon-and-lime Probe, little white kitten on the rear shelf whose eyes glow red when the brake's on. The two of them get out of their vehicles at the same time, Lucky and Ronette. She's tying the lacy waitress apron around her waist as she goes in, so he's forced to hold the door open for her, and she brushes against him a little more than she has to to get past.

"Sleep late?" he asks as she disappears behind the counter.

"None of your business, Mr. Lucky Lunt. If you are. You look like bad luck to me." She reaches a hand out of the pantry with nail polish the same color as the blueberry syrup. The purple fingernails tune the radio to Big Country, they're playing Lorrie Morgan's "Go Away, No, Wait a Minute." Ronette's got black tights under the white waitress outfit, little fringed white cowgirl boots with waitress-shoe bottoms. He tries to see under her clothes but has no more success than he had in the dream. "See anything you need?" she asks, flicks her tail and ducks into the pantry again.

"Driving your own car now," Lucky observes. "What color they call that, anyway?"

"That's chartreuse."

"Chartrooz," Lucky tries to say.

"It's a *French* color, you wouldn't know." She's back out now, she had been opening a big five-pound coffee can on the industrial opener and now she's throwing the jagged top in the recycling box.

He likes the way the black tights tuck into the cowgirl boots, it makes his pulse beat in his eardrums like he was back to normal and not a medicated fucking cripple who may never get it up again except in his sleep. "How come you work here, anyway, Ronette? With all Clyde's money you could sleep late every morning and watch the Oprah show on TV."

"A woman's got to have her independence. This woman anyway. I ain't living off no one."

"Why don't you go ahead and tell him?" Doris says from behind the register.

The tinny radio over the coffee urn's playing a Garth Brooks song:

> *Little café, table for four*
> *But there's just conversation for three*

"I ain't staying at Clyde's," Ronette says. She sticks her chin up for a minute, then she lets her face fall and her mouth goes down and she starts crying, right behind the counter with the big open can held in her two hands and the drops making little craters on the surface of the coffee like rain on a dusty road. Tears have always silenced him, so he just looks at her with her mascara eye-rings breached through and offers his big hairy paw over the counter but she doesn't take it so he feels like a fool and pulls it back. "I ain't going to be able to get by," she says.

"You're working here."

"Three mornings a week. Way you guys tip, it don't buy cigarettes."

"Summer it'll get better," Doris says.

"Wicked long time till summer."

"Clyde ain't helping you?" Lucky asks.

"That son of a bitch ain't giving me a dime. He says I walked out on him so I can pay."

"Did you?"

"I couldn't go in the door of that place no more. It was like a frigging igloo in there."

"Thought you had a hot tub," Doris says.

"I mean the *emotional temperature.* Clyde would sit there without saying nothing days on end. It ain't walking out if you can't bring yourself to walk in."

"You did get the car," Lucky reminds her.

"What the hell use is it? The insurance was in his name. He ain't even paying the premiums. Just stay away from me, I'm an uninsured motorist."

"You know," he says, "I might be wanting a sternman. Didn't you used to fish with Teddy Dolliver at one time?"

"It was his brother Reggie," she says, with some pride, though Reggie Dolliver is currently up in Thomaston serving two to five for aggravated assault.

"Reggie then. He ain't going to need you in the joint. How about working every other day for me?"

Doris gives out a choked little laugh followed by a spasm of cigarette coughs. "Good idea, Ronette. You ought to consider it. Your husband would get a kick out of that. Hey Lucky, didn't Clyde date your old lady once upon a time?"

Ronette looks up. "He didn't do nothing of the kind."

Doris says, "How would *you* know, honey? It was before you were born."

Ronette lights a cigarette off the one she was smoking, stabs the spent butt in the dishwasher to put it out, throws it in the garbage. "Clyde is a jealous fool. He was born in the Year of the Pig, that's what it says on the Chinese place mat up at the Tarratine mall. Jealousy is the *main quality* in the Year of the Pig."

"You must mean horse, dear," Doris says. "There's no pigs on those Chinese place mats."

Ronette says, "I bet the both of you never ate a Chinese meal in your lives."

Lucky says, "Bullshit. I was in Vietnam. We used to eat stir-fried dogmeat over there. Tell me that ain't Chinese."

"It ain't. Dog's Vietnamese, not Chinese. Anyone with half a brain knows that. Rat's Chinese."

"How'd you come to know so much?" Lucky asks Ronette.

"Clyde used to take me out."

"So how come you left him?"

"It wasn't what happened when he took me out that was the reason, it was what didn't happen when we got back home."

"None of that talk," Doris says. "This is a family place."

"It's true, Doris, and my lawyer says that's grounds. Nonconsummation, he put it right down in black and white."

She starts crying again into the five-pound coffee can, which she's still holding.

"All them tears," he says, "ain't going to do the coffee any good."

"Hell with you, Lucky Lunt. I'll pee in it if I want." She shoots a guilty look over towards the cash register but the boss lady doesn't flinch.

"Flavored coffee, Doris. That'd bring the yuppies in."

"Why don't you take the morning off," Doris suggests. "I can handle things on my own. If I can't, I'll get Lucky here to help out. We'll put an apron on him, he'll make more here in tips than he makes off that old lobster boat."

Ronette puts the can under the counter where it belongs and wipes her face once more with the white waitress apron. Then she takes the apron off, throws it in Lucky's lap and says, "He'll look real cute in this. Thanks, Doris, that's exactly what I need. See you tomorrow."

Without a word more she waltzes out.

"What's that all about?" he asks Doris, who has taken over the job of brewing the new coffee. He gives her the waitress apron and she ties it around her waist.

"Guess you know as much as I do. She's right. Clyde's not planning to give her a cent either, that's what they say."

"Where's she staying?"

Doris gives him a dark suspicious look. "Wouldn't *you* like to know."

"Guess I ain't going to get *her* for a sternman. Doris, you mind if I put a note up by your door?"

"What do you want a sternman for? You always liked working alone."

"Sarah don't want me out there by myself, account of the operation."

"Can't say as I blame her. Considering your father, how he went, and his father too, didn't he? Working alone. Everyone else got a sternman anyway. What about your boy?"

"Kyle's got his own boat, he's a big urchin diver now. He fishes the underutilized species for the Asian trade."

"Urchin season's over this week," Doris reminds him.

"Don't bother him none. He'll go down after something. Sea cucumbers, squid. If it's got tentacles, them Asians will eat it. No questions asked."

"Afro-*dee*siacs," Doris says, "that's what they called them on 20/20. Barbara Walters, so it's not bullshit. They are highly regarded as a marriage aid for men."

"Well, they must have some pecker problems over there, cause they finished off the fucking tigers and now they're buying up everything in the sea."

"You wouldn't think so from the population," Doris says. "I heard the other day there's five hundred billion of them. Think of that, five hundred billion."

"Lot of god damn sushi." He tries to think of the number, but the picture that comes is not a land teeming with human beings but the darkness of outer space.

Doris says, "What about Sarah, can't she go out? She used to fish with her old man, back when she was a kid, before she worked at the sardine plant. And your daughter, Kristen. Jesus, Lonnie Gross takes *his* daughter out." They both break out laughing at that one, then Doris doesn't pursue the subject.

"Kristen gets sick from the bait smell, Kyle don't want to be on my boat. Period. I ain't going to force him. I asked Sarah but she's got her arts and crafts."

"She's quite the celebrity, I hear. Got those mobiles or whatever they are up at the art school. But you two are man and wife, and if you've got a condition she ought to be by your side."

"Well, she ain't. Print out a sign for me, will you, Doris? I ain't such a neat writer."

She prints on the back of her own business card and sticks it up with the others, right under the S&P Septic Service card.

STERNMAN WANTED. TWO DAYS. 222-2714.

"Thought you already asked Ronette. Trying to lure a good waitress away, better watch your step."

"You only hire her three days."

"She can go full-time in the summer if she wants. Lots of money in the dinner trade. She can earn a living off of tips, that one, she just flicks her tail at them, they leave her fifty percent. I let her keep all of it too. Some's don't."

"You are the employer of the month, Doris."

"Knowing her, by summertime she'll have somebody else paying the bills. *If* she doesn't go back with Clyde."

He borrows her pen to circle the phone number and starts to leave. Just then this decrepit Ford F-150 four-by-four drives up, solid rust, muffler dragging sparks, grille stove in like a guy smashed in the mouth. Two bullet holes in the windshield. No fucking license plates on it, front or rear. The Trott boys from Shag Island are in there, all three of them in the front seat, it's a miracle they can pull the doors shut. It must be the vehicle they keep on the mainland. Nice bumper sticker too:

IF YOU CAN READ THIS, FUCK YOU

It's clever and it makes a point about education.

The driver's door won't open, so they all three come out the passenger side. The driver's a giant, he'd outweigh Frank Alley, the bald-headed one that's only around five-six has a neck like a gorilla, and the third one's a wiry son of a bitch with a carved-up face and an artificial arm all the way up past the elbow. He's wearing a sleeveless black shirt so you can see how the thing's attached to his shoulder stump. Harvey Trott: they say his sleeve caught in the dragger winch, he had to chew his own arm off to get free. He's holding the cigarette in the hook of his artificial limb, with all the cables so he can twist it around like a robot and poke the filter between his lips. Out on the island he scooped a guy's eye out with that hook, that's what Travis Hammond said. Close relation too.

He asks the last one in, the driver and dragger captain, Anson Trott, "Them two come up in the net?"

Lucky stands six-one or -two, weighs two twenty-five, but Anson Trott looks down at him through his beard like a Civil War statue. "Kiss my ass, Lunt." The way he says it, sounds more like he's calling him "Lint." Licky Lint. You can hardly understand them, they talk a foreign language from not coming off of that island for three hundred years. "Hey Lint. Take at look at this." Big Anse unfolds a roll of cash the size of a horseshoe, all brand-new hundred-dollar bills with the big Ben Franklins that look like large-print money for the blind. "We just sold twelve thousand pounds of scallops to your cousin Hannaford."

"He ain't my cousin," Lucky says.

"We heard you was all cousins in Orphan Point." The Trotts all laugh like it's a big joke. Their mouths have some teeth, some black holes, some false teeth that look like wooden lobster pegs green with mold, there's not many dentists on Shag Island. They're all millionaires, though, that's what Noah Parker says, he's out there all the time with his pilot boat.

The Trotts order breakfasts of creamed chipped beef on English muffins, which Doris is gleeful to sell since she's had the stuff simmering in there for a month.

"You boys planning to race this year?" Lucky inquires. One of the Trotts is looking at his creamed beef like he's having a second thought, then decides it's all right and forks it in. The bald-headed one says, "Sure, we'll enter the dragger and sink the whole fucking fleet." Har, har, har, laugh the other Trotts with their mouths full of wooden teeth and pink-and-white creamed chipped beef.

Lucky's not going to let it drop, you don't get a chance like this every day. "I heard there ain't any fast boats out to Shag Island since Alvah Greene died."

"We got a couple," the skipper says. "Carleton Trott just got hisself a six-hundred-cubic-inch Deetroit Diesel."

"I heard he had a Deere."

"He did. After a week he didn't like it, pulled the cocksucker out and threw it overboard. Low tide, you can see that son of a whore right off the ferry wharf in eight feet of water, bright fucking John Deere yellow."

"Brand-new thirty-thousand-dollar engine," his brother echoes. "Put the dock crane to the son of a whore and dropped her over the side."

"He any relation?" Lucky asks, fishing in his pocket to leave a decent tip.

"Not that I know of," the Trott captain says, at the same time fingering a piece of chipped beef off one of his huge wooden molars, spearing it on his fork, and eating it again. He spits something else out of his mouth, holds it out, looks at it. "Jesus H. Christ, Doris, what do you put in this shit?"

"It's kind of a secret," Doris says.

"Looks like a fucking tooth. Don't that look like a tooth, Harv?"

Harvey Trott puts his cruller down with his hook hand, reaches for the thing with his good one, looks it over, pops it in his mouth and chews it down. "Nothing wrong with that, Anson. Just a bit gristly, that's all."

Anson gets up off of the stool, his head just about touching Doris's acoustic ceiling, and goes to pay her with a brand-new hundred-dollar bill.

When Lucky goes to take care of his own check, she says, "Coffee's paid for. The Trott boys picked it up."

Lucky runs right into Clyde Hannaford on the gangway leading to the skiff float. He can't avoid him. "Sorry to hear about things at home," he says.

Clyde answers, "Fuck you too," which Lucky doesn't know whether to take personally, or if it's just what a guy might say to anyone after his wife takes off.

"It ain't my fault, Clyde. Could happen to anyone."

"I'm going to close this fucking place up and sell it," Clyde says. He's got a bit of a whine in his voice, same whine he uses when he's jawing your dock price down five cents a pound.

"No you ain't, Clyde. We all need you. Get drunk after work, jerk off, give her a while, maybe she'll come back."

"I can't get drunk," Clyde whines. "Only place to get drunk is the RoundUp, and she's going to be there. Sure as shit. I'm moving to Florida, live with my folks down in Coral Gables."

"You ain't. Who would run things around here? Nobody knows diddly shit except how to fish."

"You boys could take over the wharf, buy me out, make it a co-operative like they got over to Split Cove."

"Won't work. There ain't one of us that can keep the books."

"No problem," Clyde says. "It's not hard. Just take what I pay you guys and add on fifty percent for yourself."

"That's simple," Lucky says. "I could even do that."

"Then take her, she's yours." He squints over at Clyde, who adds, "I mean the wharf."

"I'm sure you do," Lucky says. "I'm sure as shit sure you do."

He leaves Clyde turning the prices up on his fuel pumps and rows towards the *Wooden Nickel,* hugging the shore at first to avoid the channel current. A ways down he can see a construction crew renovating one of the old mansions for some Philadelphia son of a bitch, well-drilling rig in there, backhoe digging for a huge septic tank the size of a garage. That's what Dwight Lord tells him, he's the honey-wagon driver from Burnt Neck, *Nobody shits like the rich.* Dwight claims they stuff those big tanks full three or four times a month — just one family, plus a few other big shitters that show up for weekend visits in their corporate jets. He has to come down and ream the drains out twice a week. Eat and shit, that's how Dwight puts it. And the fucking contractor is from Massachusetts.

He ties the skiff to the pennant and lets it drift back aft where it's easier to climb on, not jumping up on the prow as he might have ten or fifteen years ago. You don't go leaping around when you're a forty-six-year-old medical experiment, proud father of a kid bound off to college and another one bound for jail. He climbs in, flips the radio to High Country and reaches behind the radar screen for a Marlboro. On the way, though, his hand encounters something else. Hey. A bag lunch. Sarah must have come out here and stuck it on the boat. That would be a first. Anyhow, he's already got Sarah's lunch right in his hand. He puts Sarah's sandwich on the engine box and opens the new bag. There's an éclair in there from Doris's with its cream interior oozing out and the chocolate topping stuck to the paper bag, and a banana and a Reba McEntire cassette and a note. The note is printed like the way Kristen used to print in about grade four. It reads, HAVE I GOT A DEAL FOR YOU, which is the name of one of Reba's songs. On the other side it reads, JUST A SNACK. DINNER SOME TIME. And on that side it is signed, Rhonda *(Astbury)* Hannaford. He barely remembers Ronette was an Astbury before she married Clyde. Her old man Ivan runs Astbury's Wrecking out on the Burnt Neck Road. And another thing, as a high school freshman Lucky played JV football for Orphan Point when Ivan Astbury was a senior on the same team. He must have had Rhonda first thing after graduation. Sarah would know.

Sixteen years difference. She could pretty near be his kid.

He throws the banana in the bait bucket, thinking he might bait one of the traps with it, lobsters might go for something new. He eats the éclair, wipes the cream smears off the cassette so it won't fuck up the stereo, and puts it on. It's cued right to the song too.

> *Have I got a deal for you*
> *A heart that's almost like brand-new*

Her old man Ivan Astbury lives over on the Split Point Road, right near the RoundUp so he can find his way home when he's drunk. That's where she's probably gone, home to Daddy, all the way across the harbor from the hot tub of her frozen home. He looks over eastward as if he could see Ronette Astbury standing on the Split Cove wharf, but it's a good two miles and his eyes aren't what they once were either, not anymore.

When he starts up, instead of steaming past his own house on the eastern side, he steers her down the Money shore and doesn't turn eastward till he's opposite the Split Cove entrance buoy, a red nun half sunk because the Split Cove boys like to take a shot at it as they go by. He doesn't go in exactly, it's been a long time since an Orphan Point boat crossed the Split Cove line. He does come close enough to make out a figure on the dock. He picks up the binoculars. It's not Ronette, just the blubbery outline of Chub Washburn, the Split Cove co-op manager, inspecting his lobster cars. It's a well-known fact that Chub takes a leak in them now and then, gives his product that special Split Cove taste.

He puts the throttle up and swings way over to avoid Split Rock, used to be big lobsters right in those shallows in his old man's day, but they're long since gone. He's going eighteen knots by the time he reaches Sodom Ledge, which at this tide is lined with seals, big fat cocksuckers, every one of them's got a hundred pounds of lobster digesting in their stomachs. The Eskimos have the right idea, kill them and eat them just like anything else. It would improve the environment. You cut up seal blubber in thin strips, dry it in the sun, it tastes just like a fried clam.

He slows and swings close to Sodom Ledge so the color fishfinder comes right up in a big red splash. He pulls the twelve-gauge out from its bulkhead rack, feeds a shell into the chamber and takes aim at a couple of big bull seals dozing off on a rock after pumping their harems all night. Take a look at those females, every one of them's pregnant, all they do is bellow and fuck out there, there's more seals than the sea can support so they have to raid traps, lazy fucking parasites, living off the sweat of other people's brows. It would be a good deed to kill three or four of the greedy bastards.

The seals take one glance at the *Wooden Nickel* and its bloodthirsty captain and slide off their deck chairs into the surge. Too late. He puts the gun away and hauls ass out to sea.

End of the day, he's made his gas and bait, he's got maybe fifty pounds aboard and a bucket of rock crabs from the line off Ragged Arse Ledge that will return to the water in Sarah's deluxe crab sandwiches. He's moving a line inshore that didn't catch anything out by Red's Bank, carrying twelve traps on the stern, motor purring easy at 1600 rpm, clouds breaking up after a gray spell, nice George Strait song on the radio. Though his heart's jumping a bit from the skipped medicine, it feels pretty decent to be alive. He takes Ronette's note out of his oilskin bib pocket and reads it again.

Just a snack.

What the fuck does she mean by that? He crumples the note into the bag and throws it off the stern. Then he notices one of his traps has the vent hatch missing so the lobsters can walk right out. And another. No wonder this string didn't produce. Fucking seals rip the vents right off the trap and help themselves. The state makes you use these escape hatches that turn every christly lobster trap into a seal feeder. Might as well forget about fishing and just throw pieces of meat off the side all day long. Fucking government can't help itself, it pisses out welfare every chance it gets.

He sees one of their brown bald heads staring at him from the water right off the starboard beam, with a dumb satisfied look like he's got two or three lobsters in his throat right out of some poor man's. trap who's. trying to make ends meet. He slows down and grabs the shotgun off the radar shelf and fires a twelve-gauge load right in the seal's skull.

BOOM.

The shot echoes off the sharp granite ledges and a flock of seagulls jumps into the air flapping and squawking like a hippie protest. Though the top of its head is sliced off at the eye line, the seal flashes a look of hatred, then goes down for its last dive. *"Fuck you too!"* he yells. Only this time it won't be ripping up anyone's trapline when it gets down there. Another Orphan Point family is going to have food on the table as a result of Lucky's quick thinking and steady aim even in a cross-running sea. Not to mention the lobsters already feasting on hot bloody seal. Scavengers, just like us.

Half the seagulls are circling the water where the seal went down, looking for what they can get. The other half are crowding over his stern for a free lunch, bunch of parasites worse than the seals. There's one big blackback cocksucker flying right over the bait barrel like he owns the fucking sea and every fish in it. He pumps another round into the chamber and blows the seagull into a cloud of bloody feathers. The minute its head hits the water another gull gives off a cannibal scream and dives down to peck the eyes out. He puts the gun down and backs up till he can gaff the dead gull and bring him over the side. He slices the left wing off with a rope knife and throws the carcass to the other gulls. He stands up on the rolling side deck and duct-tapes the bloody wing to the loran whip. Soon as it's up there, the other gulls back off like they've seen a ghost. He'll leave it up all season, teach them a little respect for the workingman.

He steers with one knee on the bronze wheel spoke while he runs a wad through the shotgun barrel, rubs a little Watson's gun oil on the untarnished surface, and puts it back. It's a dog-eat-dog world. Survival of the fittest. It's them or us. They've got the Marine Mammal Protection Act and the Greenpeace submarines and the financial backing of the Rockefellers and the IRS. Whereas we, the people, what does that leave us but our guns and our own two hands?

Or one, in the case of that Shag Island guy with the robot hook. A whole fucking government against one human hand.

He sets his trapline in five fathoms right where the seal went down. Free bait. He'll be back to get them in a couple of days.

He's coming in by Sodom Ledge now with a couple of other boats in sight. There's the *Bonanza* running a foot low in the water from what must be three thousand pounds of lobster, Art's kid steering while Art throws shorts over the side like he's trying to reseed the inner harbor.

There's Damon Peterson, he always took second in class C diesels till he got himself a vasectomy. Since that day he hasn't risen above sixth place.

Coming up on Damon is the *Trudy P,* Chucky Peek's boat, throwing off black smoke the way a boat does when it's in its death throes. Chucky's a relation of Sarah's, he's got six kids, his wife's pregnant, they have one with spina bifida so they spend half their time at the Ronald McDonald House, and now his diesel's going. They told him he was crazy to race the fucking thing, that 260 Isotta-Zucchini was a piece of shit right out of the crate. He came in dead last and burnt her out to boot. Guy like that's not going to survive, but where's he going to go? Ought to be a way to help out, chip in, keep it a secret, get him a new engine or something, but you can't. No way he wouldn't know it, and he wouldn't take a cent. A man would go under first. But there's no under, when you think about it. And nothing under that.

Now a Split Cove boat crowds the *Wooden Nickel* coming up to the narrows at the Sodom Ledge bell. It's a little black plastic diesel called the *Bad Trip,* there's about four Split Cove guys aboard. It's clear they've been hauling all day and have nothing to show for it, they're riding high and passing a joint around, all huddled grimly about the wheel. They've got a bottle of that fruit-flavored brandy they like so much, Split Cove life expectancy's around twenty-six. One of them pulls a Red Sox cap down low over his eyes, another one gives Lucky the finger, low and sneaky, but no mistaking it. That boat belongs to some Astbury cousins if he recalls, all of them dark-skinned like Ronette, dark-haired, there's Indians in the next town over. The Split Covers like to fish with the whole tribe aboard and they're now trying to crowd the *Wooden Nickel* into the bell buoy, which is not allowed. He puts the throttle up hard and the stern drops, his four-blade Michigan prop grabs solid water and the wake rises behind him like a waterspout. The loran takes a minute to figure it out, reads out twenty-one knots, then twenty-four, then twenty-seven. He sneaks past Ronette's Indian cousins before the bell. They're straining her. It sounds like a little Isuzu 650 in there, kerosene vaporizing from the stack and all six injectors strangling in oil.

Then, because he can't stand bullshit, he spins the wheel to port and cuts dead across their bow at top speed with about three yards to spare. He looks back to see them drenched and pounded by his wake, all four pumping the finger up and down, taking their trawler boots off to drain the water out. Fuck them. He slows down and lets them pass, falls just astern of them, floors her again and crawls right up their asshole with the *Wooden Nickel* throwing off a bow wave full of crystal stars and rainbows from the afternoon sun.

He parts company with the *Bad Trip* after Sodom Ledge, fast-forwards the Reba McEntire cassette to the next cut, "He Broke Your Memory Last Night." That lady is one fine musician. He throttles back so he can hear the words.

> *Like a rare piece of crystal*
> *Like a fine china cup*

Which leads his thoughts to Sarah's sea glass ornaments, the delicacy of leadwork that makes his hand seem as gross as a backhoe, so he's afraid even to touch them. Yet Reba's talking about sex, if you think about it. That's the thing about Reba McEntire, she's full of hidden meanings. You have to listen more than once.

The *Bad Trip*'s oriental whine has faded to the other side of the bay. He'll sell these lobsters, maybe take Sarah out to dinner at the Irving Big Stop, though if she makes him order the Petite Chicken Breast again he'll put a fork through her hand. Fuck her. He only had three cigarettes today. He's going to order the Prime fucking Rib.

He spots his son Kyle's dive boat in the shoal water west of Split Ledge, it's an old pop-riveted aluminum derelict that had been relaxing on the bottom for at least three years. *Metallica,* numb name for dumb music. Kyle spotted it one day on the *Wooden Nickel*'s fishfinder and floated her up with inner tubes. He borrowed five hundred from his old man and put a 60-horse Merc on the transom so it planes in a flat sea though it pounds like a bastard if there's any chop. On a calm day he might have a chance in class B outboards but the kid's too lazy to sign up. He's got one of his Burnt Neck buddies with him from the other night, half Indian probably, schoolmate of Kyle's but he looks about thirty with his skull shaved like George Foreman along with a snake's head tattoo on the left arm and two or three earrings in each ear. They're taking their dive tanks off, smoking cigarettes, pawing through a big black plastic bucket of urchins.

"Ain't you supposed to be in school?" he shouts.

"School got out at noon today."

"Bullshit."

"Bullshit, nothing. Ask Darrell. It was teachers' day."

Darrell looks around and shoots a big weasely grin earring to earring but he doesn't say anything.

"You ain't going to graduate," Lucky says. "That guy Leavitt called your mother. You're flunking two courses. I don't give a shit myself, but you got your old lady all wound up."

Kyle stands up in the boat, grabs an urchin and cuts it open with his dive knife, rubs the meat of it between thumb and finger, then spreads the eggs out on his palm. "Black gold," he says. "Price is going through the roof. Urchin divers don't need no diploma. Besides, when'd *you* drop out? Eighth fucking grade?"

"Another thing," Lucky says. "You ought to watch your language. Your mother heard you talking like that, she'd lock your ass right in your room. You wouldn't see your friend here for a fucking week. Wouldn't *that* be a shame."

The Burnt Neck kid, Darrell, picks an urchin out of the bucket, stares into the cunt end of it, then takes the dive knife off his belt and jabs at it like he's testing a clam. He brings the urchin up to his face and touches his tongue to it, makes a face, spits in the bilge and throws the urchin over the side. He looks into another one and throws that up to Lucky. "Here, Mr. Lunt. You want some lobster bait?"

Lucky catches it and smells it. It stinks OK, but it's got a different stink to it than lobster bait. "They ain't going to go for that," he says. "Might as well put a bag of horseshit down there."

"Never know till you try," the kid says.

Lucky kills the engine, takes a quick hitch around the midship cleats to raft onto the urchin boat, which they've got anchored with light line. "Hey Kyle," he says to his son, "you giving all them urchins to Clyde Hannaford?"

"We don't give," Kyle says. "We sell."

"Well, Clyde ain't going to buy none after this week. Urchin season's over. He's got the sign up already. Starting Monday, if you ain't in school, you can come out as sternman."

"Clyde ain't the only guy that buys them," Kyle shoots back. "There's others."

Down in the bilge, Darrell gives him a kick on the ankle to shut him up. "It don't matter, Darrell. He's my old man. He ain't going to tell no one."

Darrell cuts a rotten piece off an urchin and throws it over the side. "Don't say nothing about it."

Lucky feels his heart missing a beat, then pumping to catch up. He puts a hand on the pot hauler to steady himself, then says to Darrell, "I don't give a shit what you do. Half your fucking town's stamping license plates, other half's on welfare. Just don't drag my kid into it or I'll kick your ass."

"Too bad," Darrell says. "I hear they're paying top dollar for lobsters too."

"Top yen," Kyle adds.

"Go ahead, tell him," Darrell says, "Tell him about Mr. Moto. He might be interested."

"If it's Italian I ain't dealing with them," Lucky says. "They got the fish mafia up to Boston, frig around with them, they don't give a shit, they'll cuff you to the wheel and set your truck on fire."

Darrell squints down into the *Wooden Nickel*'s tank, couple of four-pounders in one corner, shakes his head. "Mr. Moto wouldn't have nothing to do with them. Too fucking small."

"Right up at the legal limit," Lucky says. "You put the gauge to them."

"No doubt." Darrell keeps shaking his head like he doesn't believe something. "You see them urchins, Mr. Lunt? The price of them suckers is going to double next week. Only we don't sell. We hold out. Week after that, closed season, Japs starving for sushi, the price is going to double again."

"You ain't going to play that kind of game with the mafia," Lucky says.

Darrell says, "Mr. Moto ain't Italian. He happens to be from oriental extraction."

"And he's buying off-season?"

"Oversize lobsters too," Kyle says, trusting his old man now that Darrell has trusted him. "How about eight dollars a pound?"

Lucky has to stop on this one. He's had a couple of jumbos in the outside traps over the last week, five or six pounds apiece, which he throws back by instinct, not even bothering to put the measure to them. Forty-eight pounds of lobster at eight bucks a pound would be close to four hundred bucks a week, on top of what he gets off Clyde. Kristen's going to college next year, mailbox full of bills all winter when the boat is hauled, nothing coming in, he hasn't the dimmest fucking idea where he's going to get the money.

Another voice comes in, it's his old man Walter Lunt: *Don't take no shorts, Lukie, and don't take no breeders, you got to leave something for your kids.* A brief little length of tape inside playing his old man's voice. Just like the shorts and the females, big offshore breeders are the future, like his house and his fishing grounds, a legacy to save for his own flesh and blood, whether they give a shit or not. If lobstering was a religion, that would be the first commandment. "I ain't going to do it," he says. "I don't care nothing about sea urchins, but them big deep-sea lobsters ain't going to Tokyo. They're the breeding stock."

"Don't worry," Darrell says, "you ain't going to catch them all."

"Don't matter, I ain't doing it. And Kyle ain't either. There's things besides money."

"I'd like to know what," Kyle says. "I didn't learn none from you."

"You won't learn none from him either. Or that gook dealer of yours."

Kyle gets sullen and looks down but he doesn't answer back. He takes up a cracked urchin and throws it on the other side. Darrell goes to cast off the *Wooden Nickel* but Lucky beats him to it. He idles out so as not to rock them too bad, then after a few yards he runs up the harbor to bring his legal lobsters into Clyde's.

3

HE'S GOT HIS FEET UP after supper on the big stack
of *Commercial Fisherman*s in the TV nook. One eye's checking out
the boat photos in the new issue, the other's watching the *K-Mart
Kountry Talent Show,* which is not showing much talent, couple of
Christian crotch-scratchers from the county, a commercial for the
Tarratine Monster Truck Show, then a pale wrinkly woman that
looks like Dale Evans out of the grave. It's supposed to be her debut
performance but she's sixty if she's a day. They used to have a good
show with real talent but now it's mostly freaks. They're bringing
the Lemieux Brothers next, a ghoul act with two dead-looking
teenagers stuck together like Siamese twins, when the phone rings
and he lets Sarah get it. She sings sweetly, "Lucas, somebody for you."

She hands him the cordless and waits listening as if it's a business
call that concerns them both. Must be some son of a bitch pushing

bank cards, they like to call you when your mouth's full, even though when they actually run his credit check, they turn him down. But god damn if it's not Ronette Hannaford answering the sternman ad.

"Don't like calling you at your home like this, I know you're with your family, probably finishing up supper, but I didn't want you to give it to no one else. You ain't, have you?"

"Not yet," he says. "I had it up awhile and no calls come in. That ain't to say I'm going to hire *you*. You already passed it up."

"Things are different. That bastard Clyde's cutting me off completely. I need the money. I got to have a better lawyer. I got to have car insurance."

"Insurance ain't that much," he says. "It's twice as cheap for females."

"You don't know, honey, I flunked so many breath tests, I got to go with a special company." He hears the tears in her voice, imagines her holding an open coffee can with the other hand.

"You got references? You say you worked for Reggie Dolliver over in Split Cove?"

"That's right. Reggie'll tell you how good I was. He was highlining when I worked for him."

"How am I supposed to get a reference off of a man in jail? You think I'm going to pay him a visit in his cell?"

"He ain't in no more. They just paroled him. Come on, Lucky. I need the money. I ain't forgotten how."

"I don't want no trouble with Clyde Hannaford. Clyde don't care for me much anyway but we do have a business relationship. Live and let live, that's where it's at. Don't step on nobody's fucking toes."

"Clyde don't own me," she says. "He maybe used to but he don't no more. I don't get you, Lucky Lunt. You dangle this job in front of me, then I get serious and you back off."

"Don't expect to get rich out of it," Lucky says. "You get a tenth of the gross."

"Reggie gave me fifteen percent."

"You was going out with him at the time, if I remember."

"Was not. Don't make no difference anyhow. Business is business. He started me at ten, like you're trying to do, then he moved me to fifteen."

"What'd he do that for?"

"Cause I was good. I work hard, Lucky. I learn fast. I pay attention."

Sarah's over by the TV pretending not to listen, but he can see her ear straining in the direction of the phone.

"I'll call you back," Lucky says. "I might have some other applicants."

"You ain't got no more applicants. Just me. Here's my number, I'm at my uncle Vincent's in Split Cove, I'm living in this trailer he's got on the Back Cove Road."

He writes the number down and says good-bye. Sarah looks right at him over the tops of her little wire-rimmed glasses. "I take it that was Rhonda Hannaford looking to work for you."

"I put an ad up at the Blue Claw," Lucky explains. "Can't find no one around here."

"Well you can't find her either. You better hope somebody else turns up."

Up to this point he's been backing out of this one like a shrewd old hardshell who knows what a trap funnel looks like, but when Sarah sets out the bait he has to take it. "I suppose," he says, "I could hire her if I want."

"I suppose you could, Lucas, and I suppose you could move right into that trailer park over in Split Cove. That's where she's staying, isn't it?"

"Where'd you hear that?"

"Lucas, I've known Rhonda Astbury's mother since high school days. Clyde Hannaford and Ivan Astbury were the same year. Don't you remember? That was the big scandal. Clyde Hannaford marrying his classmate's daughter. He has to be eighteen years older, no wonder they have problems."

That was back when Orphan Point had its own high school, now it's a municipal garage where the snowplows and road graders are kept. Kyle and Kristen have a fifteen-mile ride to the regional high in Norumbega, yuppietown, half the kids drive to school in BMWs.

Then he hears a Toyota four-by-four in the driveway, front end groaning on the turn from bad shocks and too much lift. The door slams and Kyle bursts in, head still shaved and now he's got a gold ring in his ear. Lucky shakes the TV remote at it as if it could not only remove the earring but change the channel of history, which is filling up with slackers and fairies including his own son. "Jesus H. Christ, mister, I hope they can stitch up that cocksucking hole again, cause you ain't going to wear no earring in this house."

"Go to hell, Dad. It's my own ear. I can do what I want with it. I'm getting my tongue pierced next week. Darrell's already got his done."

Kristen has wandered down from her room, headphones around her neck with the plug dragging behind her feet. She steps right in between son and father, then goes up to her brother, feels the earlobe gently, examining it with an expert's eye. "Keep some Neosporin on it for the first few days," she advises. "Remember what happened with me?"

"Yes, I do," Lucky says. "We had a hell of a hoedown on that one."

"You got over it, Daddy. With the passage of time."

"Time ain't going to make him into a woman," Lucky says.

"Dad," Kristen says, "half the guys in my class are pierced."

"That's right. The half with their old man gone so there's no one to set any limits in the house."

"Well you can't undo it," Sarah says.

"You sure as hell can. He leaves that god damn earring out, it will grow back like it's never happened."

"That's the problem with you, Daddy, you don't want anything to have ever happened. You want it all to grow back, just like the wooden ship days." Kristen gives her father a big wraparound hug, then takes a step back, still holding his shoulders. "Hey," she says, "you'd look cool with an earring yourself, let that beard grow out a little, maybe a ponytail . . ."

"It's true, Lucas," his wife says. "That would give you the real pirate look." The three of them have him cornered now, every one of them with earrings: Kyle's new gold stud and Kristen's little silver musical notes that she got for her seventeenth birthday and Sarah's handcrafted ones, chips of blue sea glass framed in lead.

All of a sudden he has a rush of claustrophobia right in his own house. "I'm going out."

"Out?" Sarah says. "Where are you going to go at nine o'clock?"

"I'll drive around," he says. "I'll think it over."

"What are we supposed to say if anyone else calls about the job?"

"Ask for one reference. If it's someone we know take the name down. Don't take nobody if they been in jail."

In the dark friendly truck cab, High Country 104 is playing Tanya Tucker's "Complicated."

Heads he loves me, tails he loves me not

The RoundUp's dead quiet on a Tuesday night. The old bowling lane that Big Andy converted to a racetrack for belt sanders is dark and covered with a green plastic tarp. The big stuffed longhorn steer head over the bar is the liveliest thing around. The stage where they have western music Fridays and Saturdays is empty except for the electric keyboard and the drum set. The small green-tiled dance floor in front of the stage carries a coat of sawdust without even a footprint on it. Wallace the bartender is on his stool watching the WWF Smackdown on ESPN: the Undertaker's throwing a couple of long-haired albinos out of the ring, twins it looks like, each one of them the size of a polar bear. They say the WWF breeds those guys out in Wyoming on a human farm.

There's a few sullen-looking Split Cove couples in the dark corners, all quite grim like they're discussing custody issues. Three or four guys sit by themselves at the bar, leaving a space beside them in hopes a woman might sit down. One of the guys is Reggie Dolliver himself, the inmate Ronette gave as a reference. Reggie's looking good for a guy that's served eighteen months on an aggravated-assault charge, having shot somebody's car windows out while the guy was in there with a girl Reggie thought was his. It turned out he didn't even know her.

Reggie's got his hair greased back a bit, a crucified dragon tattoo on his right arm, an empty shot glass and half a beer.

"Thought you was out of town," Lucky says. "Buy you a drink?"

"What'd you do, Lunt? Just cash your welfare check?"

"That's right. Taxpayers' money. On me."

Reggie orders a shot of Seagram's and another Rolling Rock. "I been living on taxpayers' expense for eleven months."

"They let you out early?"

"I kept my pecker clean."

Lucky looks down with technical interest at Reggie Dolliver's socks. "Hey, you got one of them ankle radios on?"

Reggie pulls up one pant leg but not the other. "I'm a free man," he says. "Just have to meet with my PO once a month and I ain't sup-

posed to have a gun in the truck. Made some money too, off of the
crafts store up there. I made ships in a bottle. Know what them cocksuckers sell for? Hundred bucks apiece. I could make three in a
week." Reggie pulls one out of this leather bag he's got over the arm
of his chair. It's a three-masted warship like Old Ironsides with half
the sails rolled up and a few men and cannons scattered around the
deck. The men have blue uniforms, and faces with pretty good detail.
He must have had plenty of time on his hands to paint every little
frigging gold button like that.

"Shit, you might as well keep doing it, now you're out."

"No. If an inmate don't make them, they ain't going to sell.
Anyone can make a ship in a bottle. But if it's genuine con art, the
tourists will suck it up." Reggie takes this long set of tweezers out of
the bag and sticks it through the bottle neck so he can play around
with the rigging, which does look a bit slack for a hundred-
dollar ship.

"Hey, why not go back in?" Lucky suggests. "You'll make more
in the joint than you will on the water."

"I already got a deal," Reggie replies. "Listen to this. I make the
things and we sneak them back into the prison and the cons retail
them for me at the prison store. Half that stuff is made by guys on
the outside. Not many people know that."

"You still own that black boat with the Lehman diesel? What
was she called?"

"*Diablo.*"

"Yeah. *Diablo.* That was a swift little boat."

"It was a piece of shit. I sold it to my brother."

"Want to go sternman on the *Wooden Nickel?*" Lucky feels good,
a man's down and he can offer something that would help him up.
As a sternman, even a con would be more acceptable to the family
than Ronette Hannaford. They'd haul some lobsters too. Reggie's a
good fisherman, it's not his fault he's from Split Cove where there's a
lot of criminal blood. You can't judge someone just by the place
they're from. They say old man Dolliver used to get drunk and put
his wife in a coffin, down in the cellar. The boys would sneak down
and see them there, the old man drinking and their mother lying in
the coffin like she was dead, only every once in a while she'd sit up
and old Dolliver would give her a sip of Gallo Red. Background like
that, you can't blame a man for going bad.

"I seen your ad," Reggie says, "but I ain't lobstering no more."

"How come?"

Reggie leans close so even Wallace the bartender won't hear him. "When I was on the inside," he whispers, "it was just like a fucking lobster trap. That's what I'd think of, looking out of them christly bars. I'd crawled in the wrong hole and I was fucking in there like a one-pound shedder."

"Locked in," Lucky says, with a rush of sympathy.

"It ain't just that. You know what it's like when you got a lot of lobsters in one small place, so it gets overcrowded. They turn on each other. They go cannibalistic. There was guys beating each other up, guys fucking each other in the ass. Man's in there awhile, he don't exactly want to set traps for a living."

He imagines Reggie Dolliver with a big hairy con on top of him, dog style, another one waiting in line. He shoots him a curious look but doesn't ask, and Reggie's not about to tell.

"Besides," Reggie says, "the government's going to retrain me in computers."

"No shit." Lucky is surprised a guy like Reggie Dolliver can even read the screen. "You didn't finish up at school, did you?"

"Don't need school for computers. That son of a bitch Gates dropped out of school. The computer prof we had, he was from the voc tech in Rockland, he told us Gates never finished the eighth grade, now he's got more fucking money than the sultan of Brunei. You know what? All them beautiful women he's got in Seattle making websites? They say he can fuck any one of them anytime he wants. Just goes up and asks them. They have to."

"No shit?"

"It's part of their job. The eighth fucking grade. You tell me a man's got to go to school."

"There you go." Lucky says. "Sure beats jail."

"Jail ain't what you think, man. It's where I learned. I took a computer repair class on Interactive TV. I got so I could take one of them son of a whores apart with my eyes closed. Course inside all they gave us was old junkers the kindergartens didn't want anymore so they dumped them on us. But they got a federal reeducation program up in Tarratine, train on the latest stuff. Windows Ninety-five."

Wallace the weekday bartender is still glued to the WWF, where the Undertaker has thrown some long-haired fairy wrestler into the crowd and the fairy's weeping and refusing to go back into the ring. Lucky pries Wallace away from the action long enough to order another shot and a beer. "Reggie," he says, "remember you used to hire Ronette Hannaford — used to be Rhonda Astbury — a few years back?"

Reggie starts rubbing this big pink scar under his left eye as if he's trying to scratch some feeling back to the dense numb flesh. "She only worked for me a couple months. Then she went and married up. She didn't need no work after that."

"Well she does now."

"I hear," Reggie says. "She want to come work for you?"

"Well, if you ain't going to do it. She's the only one that answered my ad. You think she can handle it? She didn't give you no trouble? I ain't sure I want a woman out there."

"Far as lobstering goes, Ronette Astbury was all right. I'd take her back if I was going out again. Which I ain't."

Lucky glugs his shot down. "You kept it strictly business out there?"

"What the fuck's that supposed to mean?"

"Nothing," Lucky says. "I was just wondering."

"A man makes a crack like that on the inside, he can get himself sliced."

Lucky looks him over. Reggie's a short little fart like all the Dollivers. He could have kicked his ass a year ago, though now he's not so sure. Reggie's bulked up his arms from lifting weights. He hasn't got any fucking stents in him either. Lucky puts the palms of his hands up. "No offense," he says. "Just curiosity."

"Me and Rhonda Astbury's related," Reggie reveals. "Her old man Ivan Astbury is cousins with my mother. That's how come she was working on my boat."

"Jesus, I guess if she's a relation of yours, she knows how to fish."

"I guess she does. I also guess if you hire her, old Clyde will put a bullet through you both." He leans back in his chair, folds his hands behind his slick prison-haircut head and cracks his knuckles while the dragon tattoo squirms on his forearm.

Lucky feels a little jump in his chest and realizes he didn't take his pill. He steadies both arms on the square black table carved up with phone numbers, initials, lobster and drug deals whose obsolete prices are etched into Formica forever. "Fuck Clyde," he says. "He's up there with the door locked crying in his office. He ain't going to shoot no one."

"Well," says Reggie, "why don't you take her on?"

"Sarah don't think much of the idea."

"She want you out there alone? I heard you was sick."

"She don't want me fishing alone, she won't go out herself, I get one applicant and she don't want me to hire her."

"Hey, if your wife and kids won't go out with you, you got the right. That's the way I see it."

"That's how I see it too," Lucky says.

"Might's well give her a call," Reggie suggests. "She's just sitting up at her place watching TV."

Lucky gives him a look. Reggie starts rubbing the scar again, the way he does when he's nervous. "How the fuck do you know what she's just doing?"

"We're all related. We ain't got no secrets around here."

He leaves Reggie Dolliver going into the bottle with his long tweezers to reef the sails on his ship model and goes to call Ronette and tell her she's on. The phone is located beneath the stuffed head and shoulders of a good-sized palomino horse, though both its eyes have been gouged out by drunks. It looks blind like a horse in a bad dream. The jukebox is playing a nice George Strait ballad but it's too loud. He reaches around the back and finds the volume control and turns it down, then pulls Ronette's number out of his pants and uncrumples it. When she answers it after the sixth ring, she sounds asleep.

"Where you calling from, Lucky? Thought they didn't allow country music around your house."

"I'm at the RoundUp. Your old boss says you're all right, so it looks like you've got yourself a job."

"Doris?"

"No, Reggie Dolliver."

"Oh Jesus. He's really over there, huh? I thought he wasn't supposed to drink. Don't hang around with *him*. He'll get you in trouble sure as shit. He's on parole. Reggie ain't supposed to leave the house after dark."

"I ain't prejudiced," Lucky says. "He's paid his debt to society, he's as good as you or me."

"Speak for yourself," she says, "don't drag me into it."

"Listen, you want to work?"

"You sure it's all right with your wife? She didn't sound none too happy when I called your house."

"If she ain't going to do it, I got the right. That's what Reggie Dolliver says."

"Well, right's one thing. Wrong's something else."

"You want me to ship Reggie instead? He's all eager for it but I told him you was first."

"No, I want to do it."

"We'll start at five tomorrow. You ain't planning to meet me at Clyde's, are you?"

"Not quite."

"I'll swing by the town wharf right next to Doris's and pick you up. Be there at five or you ain't going."

"I'll go down there right now and wait all night, that way I won't be late."

Kristen and Sarah are on the couch watching *Ellen* when he comes in. Ellen DeGeneres is hugging some woman, he doesn't even want to see it. Clinton's got fairies everywhere, Janet Reno on down. They say he's one himself, he puts up a front with all those Paula Joneses, just like J. Edgar Hoover.

He averts his eyes and goes to the kitchen for a beer. During the commercial he says, "Anyone else call about the sternman job?"

"No."

"Well, it's a good thing, cause I gave it to Ronette Hannaford. She's getting divorced and she needs the money."

The two of them look up like he's come home from the RoundUp with the clap. Sarah says, "She's not the only one that's going to be getting a divorce."

"Hey, I'm in business. I got a family to support. I got a mortgage on the house, I got a problem with every piece of electronics on that boat. I got medical bills. I need to haul more lobsters, and I ain't supposed to be doing it by myself."

"Well, if you want to haul lobsters you better get to bed," Sarah says. "I'll be up when *Ellen*'s over."

He's three-quarters asleep when she comes in, bringing a breath of the night's chill with her under the covers. He turns and puts a big arm around her and she doesn't resist. She unbuttons the top of his union suit and nestles close. Her chest is so thin and fine-skinned, it feels like their hearts are in direct electrical contact and if anything happened she could jump-start him without even waking up.

He pries open his left eye to read the time. Instead of nudging her to get some eggs going and make sure he doesn't forget to put on half his clothes, he slips out of bed like he used to when they were just married and he would watch her sleeping in the first fog-colored light of dawn. He knew her face to the bone, by touch, like working on the inside of a carburetor in the dark. He'd stare at her so long and hard he'd have to go look in a mirror to remember who he was. But now, in the reddish glow of the digital clock, his wife's face looks dry and papery, covered with restless markings he can't read. They could be depth contour lines on a sea chart, only there's no numbers. Who knows how far down somebody is when they're asleep.

He splashes hot water on his face and shaves in the dark, he never gives the mirror a second glance. He used to try and look like a mean son of a bitch that you could never fuck with and live. Now it doesn't matter, he could look like anyone who jacks off for a living. He'll brush his teeth with baking soda and salt water when he gets on the boat. It's pointless to stare yourself in the face when the problems are down in your fucking heart.

This morning he skips the Blue Claw and goes right to Clyde's wharf. Clyde isn't even there yet. Even Art Pettingill is just pulling up, climbing down from a brand-new Ford F-350, looks like fucking leather seats inside. He's got half a cigar in his mouth, smoking away, big fat fifty-year-old Mormon son of a bitch that lives on Pepsi and salt pork and still his heart keeps going like a herring pump.

He says, "Art, where's your boy? You by yourself today?"

"Boy's in school. Alma's going out."

He looks down and there's Art's skiff with Alma Pettingill already aboard, a substantial woman in the same size orange oilskins her husband wears. The both of them together displace a quarter ton easy, maybe more. The skiff is a good-sized lapstrake dory built to hold a day's catch, but she's practically shipping water from the uncompensated weight of Alma Pettingill in the stern. "You might want to get down there in the bow, Art, and balance her out."

Art heaves a big wire trap with two stones in it onto his shoulder and starts down the gangway, then turns and asks Lucky with some concern, "You ain't going to keep on going out alone, are you?"

"Nope."

"Who'd you get? Sarah?"

He looks over his shoulder to see if Clyde's there yet. "I got Ronette Hannaford."

Art reaches his free hand under the lobster trap to take the cigar out of his mouth and throw it in the water. He looks at Lucky for a moment like he's planning to say one thing, putting that away, and planning to say something else. Finally he says, "I guess she's gone out before."

"I guess she has."

A small orange-suited figure waits on the end of the public wharf. It's Ronette Hannaford in what looks like a brand-new Grundens oilsuit, size too big for her, and with her is some kind of animal. He pulls up closer and it's a god damn red-haired dog. They haven't got the float in yet at the town wharf, so he has to edge right up to the pilings and Ronette has to use the ladder to clamber down. He doesn't bother to tie on, just sets the stern in and she jumps off the ladder onto the narrow side deck, skids a bit on the bait slime but recovers herself with a grab first at Lucky's shoulder, then the pot hauler.

"Wait a minute," she says. "We have to bring Ginger."

"You'll have to wave good-bye to Ginger," he says. "We ain't bringing her." Ginger's the office dog that was always gnawing a rubber bone under Clyde Hannaford's computer desk. Clyde's pride and joy, it's a wonder he doesn't have a court injunction on the thing.

"We gotta bring her, Lucky. Clyde will have her kidnapped if I leave her home. He bought her for me and now the son of a bitch wants custody."

"The dog can't climb down a ladder." Meanwhile Ginger is leaning over the pierhead, whimpering like a seal pup and looking down, but her feet aren't built to grab the seaweed-covered rungs.

"She'll swim and meet us," Ronette says. *"Ginger, go around!"* She makes a sweeping motion with her hand and Ginger romps back up the wharf, charges onto the beach and swims for the boat. In a minute she's dogpaddling alongside, panting and whining at Ronette to get her aboard.

"What the fuck. How we going to get that thing up over the rail?" He guns the engine in neutral, hoping to scare the dog back to shore.

"Throw her a rope. A thick one."

He goes to the chain locker for a length of inch-and-a-quarter yellow poly mooring line. "This do?"

"Ain't you got any natural rope?"

He goes back for some tarry old hemp, bends a figure-eight into the end, give her something to grab onto, and heaves it over. Ginger sinks her teeth in and he puts the rope over the pot winch. When the dog's raised a couple feet off of the water, the two of them haul her up over the trap boards with Ginger pawing away to help out. She leaps all over Ronette, licking her face, clawing at her Grundens like she wants to rip the pockets off, then takes a look at Lucky and does a low guard-dog growl deep in her throat. The hair on her back stands up. "Easy," Ronette says. "You know Lucky. He's your friend from Daddy's office." Ginger goes over by the live well and shakes herself off like a vibrator, trots around the cockpit a couple of times, and comes back whimpering by Ronette's side.

"Never took no dogs aboard," Lucky says. "Dogs spook the lobsters."

"Ginger can come with us every time. Can't you, sweetheart?" The dog nuzzles her snout under the flap of Ronette's orange jacket, licking away, makes him wonder how the two of them might spend their evenings back in the trailer park. Then he recalls the one fact of life that ever came out of his old man's mouth, back in '63 or '64 when the *Twilight* went down off Three Witch Ledge. The crew of that big scalloper had picked up a couple of whores in Riceville and all eight of them went down, including the girls. His old man's voice again: *If you want to get laid on the water, Lukie, use a canoe.*

Ginger finds herself a place on the coil of spare pot warp and lies down. Soon as he's past the Sodom Ledge bell he grabs for a cigarette, forgetting the three-mile limit. "How about me?" Ronette asks, coughing, rubbing her hands together in the cold. He takes another one, lights them both off the red-hot exhaust.

"Got gloves?"

She pulls a pair of nice orange work gloves out of the bib pocket of the oilskins. "Like the outfit?" she says. She throws her chest out so her tits make themselves known despite the oversize oilskins and the layers of neoprene. She turns around with a little step to show the stern view, then turns back. "They ain't the latest fashion."

"They'll do," he says. "What matters is keeping your ass dry."

She looks at the trap load and whistles: "Jesus, Lucky, I didn't know anyone was still using wooden traps. Where do you even get them things?"

"There's one guy left that builds them, Luther Webster down the Riceville Road. Luther's about eighty years old, he builds one trap a day. Them things cost me twice what a wire one costs."

"Why bother? Reggie never used wooden traps."

"You take them metal ones, half them vents don't work, you lose that cocksucker and it don't rot out, it keeps on collecting lobsters, pretty soon they're gnawing each other to death."

"Gives me the creeps," she says.

"What?"

"All them lobsters in one place. Trapped like they can't get out."

"That's what your cousin Reggie said about the cons, he said they was just like lobsters in a trap."

"It don't take a prison," she says. "You can get nice and trapped right in your own home. There ain't no escape vent either."

"Guess you found one."

She says something else but he's got the throttle up now and there's too much engine noise to hear.

They clear the Sodom Ledge whistle and turn southwestward, edging the throttle a bit higher in the open water. The bow of the *Wooden Nickel* cuts the chop like a knife going through margarine, with the spray's arc breaking the sunlight into all the colors of an oil slick as it falls. It's colder now in the sea wind, so Ronette moves behind him to cozy up by the exhaust stack. He has to make himself heard over the engine roar. "Where'd you find a place to buy foul weather gear in the middle of the night?"

"It ain't mine," Ronette shouts. "It's Reggie Dolliver's. He ain't lobstering anymore so he let me use it. Brand new Grundens, he never even put them on."

"That was just last night," he says. "How'd you get his gear?"

"He brought it over."

"By Jesus, I bet he did."

She has to yell back over the engine noise, the exhaust is loose and rattling against its collar through the wheelhouse roof. "Fits decent, don't you think? Reggie ain't too much bigger than I am. I mean, he's fatter but he's about my height."

"He's a thoughtful guy," Lucky says. "Brought them right over last night?"

"Get your mind out of the gutter. Reggie and me, we're history. Ancient history."

"You're related, that's what he said."

"Honey, everyone's related. I'll bet you and me's related, if we dug up the family tree." She throws her filter overboard and reaches into her little tote bag for a cassette. "I'm tired of Reba, she's always whining about something. I brought Lorrie Morgan. How do you put this on?"

"It's down in the cuddy, works just like a car." Pretty soon she's playing "Go Away, No, Wait a Minute." She's also got the jacket off from her oilskins so there's just the bib front flopping over a purplish turtleneck sweater so tight under Reggie's overalls her tits look like they'll pop out and strike him blind. He turns quick and pokes his face into the radar hood even though it's clear for six miles around. The screen is round and greenish, contoured with shoals and shallows like Sarah's face in the sea-green morning light.

> *I want out*
> *Then I want in it*

"This ain't a Sunday picnic," he says. "We got eighteen traps on the stern that has to be baited. You remember what to do?"

In a minute she's back aft with a skewer stuffing the bait bags full of herring quicker than he could. If she works like that while he runs the boat, he's going to be able to set two or three more strings. If she can throw baited traps over while he hauls, band the claws up while he steers, he can double his cash flow, get the house unmortgaged, maybe even pay up on the operation. He may be uninsured but he's not on welfare. It doesn't matter if his arteries are cleared, until those bills are settled his heart's not going to fully heal.

"You're fast with the bait bags," he says.

"Ain't much different from restaurant work. Both of them's stuffing food into something."

"Least at Doris's the food ain't rotten."

She stuffs another mesh bag with ripened herring. "What you don't know won't hurt you," she says.

He lights a Marlboro for her off the exhaust stack and sticks it in her mouth so she won't drown it in fish guts. They're passing the big green RB flasher that marks Red's Bank, shags all over it, the buoy's covered with birdshit so it's almost white. He slows it down a bit and turns south to pick up the first of his green-and-orange pot buoys when it comes in sight. "Too bad," she says. "I like the speed."

"Can't haul no lobster traps at twenty knots."

"Hey Lucky, where would we of ended up if we just kept going?"

"We was heading south-southeast. Would of been Africa, I guess."

"We'd run out of gas," she says. "But I'd like to keep going just the same. Africa sounds nice. Put a few thousand miles between me and that dickhead Clyde."

"We got to haul traps," Lucky says. He's at the first one already and he eases her in reverse to cut his way. He gaffs the buoy, puts the line over the winch drum, and hauls the first trap of a triple. Practically no lobsters, nothing but brown kelp and starfish. They're set in eighteen fathoms and the lobsters have gone in by now. Only in the seventh trap he gets a five-pound female dripping with eggs. Even Ginger gets up from her rope-coil bed to sniff the big breeder and draw back when a claw snaps shut an inch away from her nose. She whines like she's in pain and sticks her face under Ronette's oilskin apron. "Whoa," Ronette says. "That will make us a few bucks."

"Won't make us shit." He notches her tail and throws her overboard. "First off, she's too big. Second off, she's an egg-bearing female, got to throw her back. Didn't you learn nothing from Reggie Dolliver?"

"Reggie used to keep them things. He'd scrape the eggs off them and sell them right from his house."

"Yeah, that's the criminal mentality. That's why he spent the last year stamping license plates. Ain't legal to take them that big. Ain't legal to take them with eggs on them."

"Since when are *you* so interested in obeying the law? I always heard you was a renegade."

"Ain't the state's law I'm following, it's fishermen's law. We make it, we keep it."

They both watch the massive five-pound female flail and spiral down through the deepening water and out of sight.

"She'd of been good eating," she says.

"You been hanging out with your cousin Dolliver too much. There ain't no right and wrong with a guy like that."

"I didn't mean sell her. I meant keep her for ourselves."

"There ain't no ourselves," he reminds her. "Especially with you hanging around with cons."

"Watch your tongue, Lucky. Reggie's a relation."

"I hear Clyde Hannaford's got spies over in Split Cove, seeing who you go out with."

"Let him spy. I ain't got nothing to hide. Job's a job." It's warm now and she drops the bib front of her orange overalls so there's just the purple sweater with her tits trying to tear the fabric through. He looks but has to turn away, it confuses him how such big ones can grow on a small little body, like a short female lobster all berried up thick with eggs.

A boat passes nearby, the *Gloria T,* which is Howard Thurston's boat. One of Howard's kids is on the stern, Howard's steering. They both wave and smile, friendly and everything but nosy at the same time, just drifting close to see what's going on.

"Hey, Howard," he calls out, *"want to buy some lobsters?"* Howard guns the *Gloria T* and heads for his territory, which is almost a mile to the east.

She's poking her head down in the cuddy hatch. "You got a ladies' on this thing?"

"Down below, forward of the engine, in the wooden box under the storm anchor."

She disappears, Ginger jumps up and follows her right down, good loyal dog. Then she shouts up. "How am I supposed to move this anchor? It weighs a ton."

"Can't hear you." He cuts the engine back down to idle.

"I said it weighs a ton. The anchor."

"Lift."

He can't see what's going on down there because the companion-way's on the port side, but he hears the scrape and crash of the big fluke anchor sliding onto the portside bench. "What the hell, Lucky, this is a *bucket.* I ain't going to sit on this thing."

"Well stand then. It's good enough for the rest of us. You ain't got time to read anyway, we got traps to haul."

"What do you mean, no reading?" she yells up. "What's this? *Hustler.* Didn't think you was the reading type. Hey, this looks like a good story. 'Up the Bow-wow Highway.' We're dog lovers, ain't we, Ginger?"

"Put that away, for Christ sake."

Next minute she's back up the companionway, hitching the big suspenders up under the oilskin jacket. She's got the *Hustler* in one hand, then she leans over the bait well and throws it overboard, good-looking blond too, high heels, shaved pussy, blurring down beneath the waves. Ginger's whining over the rail, eager to fetch it, must think it's a newspaper. "Good riddance," Ronette says. "That's it for porn around here. Next time I'm bringing some fabric to fix that downstairs up."

They haul another string. Reggie was right about one thing, she's good. He winches the trap up over the rail and she does the rest, diving right in, pulling the shorts out, dropping the crabs and urchins in the trash bucket, checking the doubtful ones with the state measure, quickly banding the keepers and tossing them in the seawater tank. Another string, then one more, and Lucky's got himself the biggest haul so far this year.

"Lady Luck," he says.

"Lucky Lunt and Lady Luck. Say that five times without stopping." She holds her hands up, they're all cut and bleeding around the nails.

"Better keep them gloves on," he says. "I ain't got no workman's comp."

"I'm faster without them." She rinses her hands off in the circulating water of the live well and lets Ginger lick them dry.

"Dog looks hungry," he says. "Let's eat." He kills the engine with a trapline on the winch to hold them in one place.

"We could eat downstairs if you kept the place clean. We'd have some privacy." She opens the yuppie little JanSport pack she brought and takes out two sandwiches. "One for you. Liverwurst and bologna. Did I guess right?"

"Can't eat them." He hangs his head.

"How come?" She twists her face underneath his and looks up into his mouth. "You got teeth."

"Can't have no organ meat."

She busts out laughing. The dog takes advantage of her thrown-back head and snaps for the sandwich. "Might as well let her have it, OK?"

"Might as well," he says. "I ain't going to eat it. I brought my own."

Ginger scarfs up the sandwich in two bites.

"Never figured you for a vegetarian. Always thought you was supposed to be a man."

"After the operation, they clamped right down."

"Poor baby, bad doctors took the cattle right out of his mouth." She pats him on the shoulder and he pulls away, goes forward to fetch the tuna sandwich his wife put up after the *Ellen* show.

Right in the middle of lunch, engine shut down and the tape playing a quiet Tracy Byrd ballad, something breathes in the water off to starboard. Ginger's ears perk up and she leaves her resting spot to lean over the side and whimper. A couple of fins break the surface.

"Porpoises!" Ronette cries.

Lucky yells, "Hey Ginger, you want to eat one of them puffin pigs?"

"The Indians eat them," she says.

Lucky's surprised she knows something he's never heard. "No shit. How'd you hear that?"

"My uncle Vince told me. He's part Indian, he knows all this Indian stuff. Ain't supposed to tell you, though. It's a tribal secret."

"You got these Indian uncles," he says. "You must have some Indian blood."

"Uncle Vince ain't related. He's Rosie Astbury's husband."

"Thought you was all related."

"Better watch out, Mr. Unlucky Lunt, you might be related too."

She ducks down and switches to a Vince Gill tape. It sounds nice with the light hum of the wind on the radio antennas, the chop's rhythmic hammer blows on the hull.

Take your memory with you when you go

Ronette's been working without her rubber apron, and even though her purple sweater is soaked through with trap slime and fish guts, it's still sexy cause it's shrunk even more and it looks like there's nothing underneath. Then he recalls Sarah saying, *Lucas, don't let her freeze out there.*

"It's cold," he shouts. "I got an old sweatshirt down there somewhere, look around for it."

She comes up with the big barnacled sweatshirt bagging over her, it's still covered with bird blood from when he shot the gull. Her hair's stranded with seaweed, lipstick and mascara smudged off, her cheeks and forehead red from the salt spray. She looks less like Paula Jones now and more like a kid that's never been out of Split Cove in her life.

"You ever been anywhere?" he shouts.

"I've been to Fenway Park. And Clyde took me to Quebec City for our honeymoon. We rode a horse and carriage and everyone spoke French. I ate a rabbit."

"That's it?"

"I ain't ashamed of it. No need to go anywheres anyway. You can get everything you need off of the TV." She lights a Marlboro and gives him one. "You been anywhere, Lucky? You have, ain't you? You was in Vietnam." She looks up when she says this like he's a figure from history, a big bronze soldier statue in the park.

"I was."

"You ever been to Washington, to see that monument to all the dead? You know anyone on there?"

"I was in a motor pool," he yells over the engine noise. "I didn't see no action. Ain't no mechanics on that monument. Lester Seavey got himself killed, he might be on there."

"You're *old*." She laughs. "My *mother* went out with Lester Seavey. Back when she told me the birds and the bees, she used to say, 'There was this boy Lester, he used to try and feel around.' So I always thought Lester Seavey was Satan incarnate or something, then I found a picture of him she kept right in her drawer."

"Guess she didn't mind too much."

"People like stuff they ain't supposed to like." She lights another Marlboro off the manifold. The fleet is converging on the Sodom Ledge whistle, everyone putting on a little steam as they get within earshot of each other. He throttles up to nineteen knots on the loran, the wheel drops and digs in, Ronette sticks her face out beyond the pot hauler into the wind and grabs his arm to hold on. They're all gawking, so he shakes her off.

"Sorry," she shouts. "Didn't want to fall in."

He steams up close to the Money shore to stay off his own house, then cuts her sharp in towards the town pier to avoid Clyde's wharf. Soon as he pulls up to the ladder beneath her lemon-and-lime Probe, Ginger dives in and swims for the little patch of beach. He waits for Ronette to climb off, but she doesn't, she just stands there with a hand on the ladder and her foot up on the port rail. He revs the engine to hold the stern in against the current. The harbor chop scrapes his hull up against the barnacle-covered piling. "Ain't going to be coming in here again."

She lets her chin drop and sniffles to herself the way she did in the Blue Claw when she said she was moving out. "Guess you don't want me working for you no more. I tried my best."

"You got the job, Ronette. Only from now on I'll just swing over to Split Cove. Easier on you that way."

"Easier on you too."

"Ain't so easy. Your relations don't like Orphan Point boats."

"They like you better than Clyde and your wife like *me.*"

She slings the backpack over one shoulder and hauls herself up the ladder, in Reggie Dolliver's orange pants and trawler boots, the red dog waiting for her at the top.

When he takes his catch into Hannaford's he's the last boat in. Clyde's waiting on the lobster float with his dim-witted dockman Albert. Clyde's got a green Heineken can in his hand like the workday's over and there's nothing left to do. "Hey Clyde," he says, swinging his stern in so Albert can tie onto the aft bitt as usual, but Albert doesn't move either, just stands there with his mouth open like a funnel, as if he's waiting for his boss to pour something into it.

Lucky jumps back and ties on himself. "What the fuck, Albert?" he yells. "You in a coma?"

Clyde takes another swig of the Heineken and says, "Dock's closed. Try tomorrow morning."

"The fuck it's closed. I got a hundred pounds of lobsters in here and in the morning half of them will be dead."

Clyde hands the Heineken to Albert and wipes his mouth. He comes over and looks into the lobster well where the big doomed crustaceans are crawling all over each other looking for a way to get out. "Why'nt you try over at Split Cove. I hear they got a co-op over there."

"Listen Clyde. I'm sorry about your troubles. Your wife answered an ad and I hired her. It's strictly business."

"It's pretty fucking sneaky to drop her off over at the town wharf then come over here like you was working all alone."

"You want me to bring her in here every day so she can help unload? I'll do it if that's what you want. I thought I was doing you a favor. It ain't going to hurt you, you know, if she's got her own income. If a woman looks broke the judge'll ream you up the ass."

His dockman makes a grunting sound and Clyde looks up to see him shaking his head in agreement. Though he looks like he wouldn't know what hole to put it in, even old Albert Doane has been married and divorced, he's got a couple of kids over near the Indian reservation in Burnt Neck.

"It ain't easy," Clyde says, "thinking of her out there with you. You hear the boys referring to it on the VHF?"

"I ain't got a VHF, remember? You're supposed to be fixing it."

"Just as well," Clyde says with a grim little laughing sound. The fact is, his mouth is so tight it's pursed up like an asshole and it always seems like a miracle when he laughs.

"You going to give me a price and unload them fucking things? I got to get home for supper."

"Two fifty-nine."

"That ain't what you're paying today. I know that."

"I got too many already. I ain't going to be able to sell them all."

"Fuck you."

Clyde writes him up for two sixty-five. The minute the pen hits the paper of his little money book, Albert's into the well scooping the lobsters out. It's late and he wants to get home too.

4

A SHARP CLEARING NORTHWEST BREEZE shakes the rooftop antennas and drags him from Vietnam dreams: rattle of helicopters, smell of perpetual oil slick on the backwater by the motor pool. A trough of bad weather has kept the *Wooden Nickel* on her mooring, the traps will be full. What did Reggie Dolliver say, four or five cons in a two-man cell? Anyone could turn animal, no wonder they cornhole each other up there. Same for lobsters. You'd think the ones in the trap would tell the others not to enter, but the dumb bastards keep on coming in.

On the way out Sarah hands him a lunch in the thermos pail that seems heavier than usual. "I made two." It's too dark to know if she's being bitchy or generous, when it comes to the sternman situation she's been known to go either way. She has calmed down some since the beginning, seeing that he's hauling more lobsters and the help out there seems beneficial to his heart. She's got her own world too. Her summer art school's starting up again, she's helping Yvonne Hannaford open some kind of museum next to the lobster wharf, then she's sawing and welding and filing till midnight in his ex-den. She's home for breakfast and supper, rest of the time she's in Volvoland.

He checks out the two identical sandwiches in their Baggies, side by side. "Thanks," he says. "But she brings her own."

"Just thought she might like one of these."

"What is it?"

"Moose. Your favorite, the tongue."

"Hey. Surprise. Thought tongue was off the menu."

"I won't tell."

He hefts the pail of coffee, moosemeat and bulkie rolls with one arm and with the other waves good-bye, as he has done every predawn morning for the last twenty years. Only this time she stops him. She takes her glasses off and tries to wrap her thin arms around him for a squeeze, though with his girth and the gear he's got on she can't reach anywhere near around his back. "I'm glad you're not working alone out there. Take care, though, you're still recovering."

"Always do."

"Be sure and don't hog the moosemeat. Give some to Rhonda. Now that I think of it, it would be healthier for you if you gave her the whole thing."

He's picking up his sternperson deep in her own territory, at the Split Cove wharf. As he follows the markers at half speed through the tight dredged channel he meets up with a couple of Split Cove boats returning at 5 A.M. from God knows where, evil-hearted bastards, nothing but dark colors on their hulls. These two are the *Shadow* and the *Night Runner*. The sun shines just as much on Split Cove as Orphan Point, but from their boat names you'd think it was some Eskimo village in year-round night. Weasely bastards, they can't catch fish so who knows what the fuck they do. Kyle was a good kid till he started hanging out with those cocksuckers. Ronette too, she's probably got something up her sleeve. Nobody's blameless, it takes two to deep-six a marriage. Good thing Sarah's a saint, otherwise he'd be jerking off alone just like old Clyde.

He spots the lemon-and-lime Probe in the parking lot before he sees her on the wharf, she picked a good color for piercing through the fog. She's got her orange Grundens and a black seaman's watch cap forced down over all her chocolate-colored piled-up hair. She's also got the christly dog again, which leaps aboard before he's even up to the float. The instant Ronette steps over the rail, he turns back into the channel and opens her up a bit, he'll leave a little wake for the Split Cove lobster fleet. They're just climbing aboard now, lazy dipshits, maybe he'll wash a few over the side. Course every frigging one of them's cousins of Ronette. She's waving and shouting to this and that uncle, they've all got big fish-eating Indian dogs on board so Ginger is pawing the gunwales and yawping like a circus seal. He gives the dog a slap on the ass and says, "Jump, Ginger, go for it," but Ronette grabs her collar and holds on like it's a drowning kid. "What do you mean," she says, "telling her to jump off? What if she did? You'd have to go in and get her. You'd be responsible. She's half Clyde's, you know."

"No doubt. Who was the lucky mother?" She kicks the ankle of his trawler boot. He yells, "Christ, we're all half Clyde's," and right in the narrowest part of the channel, Split Cove boats on every side of him, he puts up the throttle all the way. The bow spurts up, the stern squats, and the big Michigan prop chews water as the *Wooden Nickel* wipes out four black-hulled boats like they're in reverse. She throws a twenty-foot-high rooster tail that catches the May-morning sunrise and rains down a plume of oily Split Cove water on men and dogs alike. They're all rocking and pumping their middle fingers and goosing clouds of black smoke out of their pathetic oil-furnace motors in an attempt to catch the swiftest wood-hulled lobster boat on the coast, being let out for the first time since back in February when she was reamed.

"*Bunch of cunts!*" he shouts back over his typhoon wake. He pulls a Marlboro pack from behind the radar, but it's empty. He flings it into the propwash and glances up at the speed digits on the loran: twenty-six point two. He's through the channel and the Split Rock passage and approaching the Sodom Ledge bell by the time his stern-lady can smuggle a fresh pack out of her yuppie knapsack. The engine noise forces her to stand on tiptoe and yell into his ear.

"Here, I'll light if for you, but I don't want you to talk like that. Them guys are family."

"Whose family, Ginger's?"

"Fuck you."

"Jesus. Clean the airwaves."

"Another thing," she shouts. "We're going to fix up the downstairs room. You got a potentially decent boat but it looks like shit."

On the fishfinder Red's Bank rises up to eight fathoms from a twelve-fathom trough, so he just bites the cap off a Rolling Rock and follows the sounder curve till the first orange-and-green buoy heaves into sight, then slows her down.

Ronette says, "Good, now we can hear the radio." She's got her arm in the hatchway fooling with the dial, trying to get Classic Country from way over in Vermont cause she likes the good old stuff.

"Ain't got time to play with the radio. You're supposed to be sternman, ain't you? Get back and start stringing bait. We're going to have traps busting with lobsters."

She sticks her tongue out at him but obeys. "Might's well work for Doris as for you. She's just about as much fun."

"Work for Doris, I don't give a shit. What's she pay you? Three bucks an hour?"

"Three twenty-five. Plus *tips*. I don't see many tips on the table out here."

"This works out, you'll clear eight, nine bucks an hour. Tax-free. You'd have to work naked to make that off of Doris."

"Wouldn't you like *that*? What would you leave? Ten percent, up from your normal five?"

"Christ, I leave you a dollar for a fifty-cent cup of coffee. And that's with your clothes on."

He rounds up to gaff the first warp and throw it around the winch. The line's got weed on it from not being hauled enough, the stone-ballasted traps are so heavy the boat leans halfway to the gunwale when the strain comes on. Just as he thought, eight or nine decent ones just in the first two traps.

"Two culls," Ronette says. "Two breeders. One short." She throws the short and the breeders over after notching the tails, puts the culls in, and holds up a nice two-pounder with claws intact. She deftly secures it by one claw as she slips a blue rubber band around the other, then lets the free claw snap around in the air a bit before she bands it.

"Survival of the fittest," he says.

"It ain't, though. He's the fittest and he'll get boiled."

"Well then we're the fittest."

"No, the fittest was them two breeder females I threw back. They're down there on the bottom, free, white, and twenty-one." She bands the second claw. "And pregnant."

"Free, pregnant, and twenty-one."

"And they're going to survive."

He's got twelve more traps on the stern, which he puts down in four sets of three. Working their way inshore, they haul a couple more strings off of the boulder-strewn ten-fathom plane west of Red's Bank, then it's past eleven and they stop for a break. He runs the warp forward and loops it once around the bitt for a lunch hook. He's about to go back to show her the contents of Sarah's pail when he catches sight of a big cocksucking bull seal diving on his trapline and goes for the shotgun instead. This time he's got his double-barrel, empty, so he has to open the box of green twelve-gauge shells, and by then it's gone.

"What the hell, Lucky. What's the gun for?"

"Son of a bitch raiding the traps. He'll come up."

"Who?"

"Big bull seal."

"Bull seal? You mean a *seal*? You fixing to kill a seal?"

He puts the second shell in and closes the barrel and snaps one hammer back. "Son of a whore's got to come up before long. They ain't got gills."

Just then the seal surfaces right above an unhauled trap and gives Lucky the royal eye, like he's saying *I'm going to flip open them trap doors down there and eat every fucking lobster you got.* Arrogant bastards, ugly as a bald-headed dog. He sights down the left barrel straight into its earhole but it goes under. He's keeping his aim on the spot where it went down when Ronette steps out in front of the muzzle and stands up on a lobster crate so the shotgun is pointing just over the bib front of her orange oilskin pants. "Go ahead, shoot," she says. "Put it through me first, then that poor animal."

"Ain't supposed to step in front of a loaded gun, you're liable to get hurt." He moves the gun barrel up and over her shoulder so it's pointing at the seal again. She leans her forehead right on the cold steel muzzle and keeps it there. "What the fuck, Ronette."

"Don't fool around with me, Lucky. I ain't going out with no murderer."

"It ain't murder, cause they ain't human. It's survival out here. It's them or us." He lowers the shotgun.

"They *are* us, Lucky. They're mammals. They got hair, they nurse their kids same way we do. Besides, I just threw enough lobsters back for ten seals. The seals don't care if they have claws on them. They can have the culls."

"They don't eat culls. They like them with two claws."

"Jesus, Lucky, seals can't count."

"They like the breeders. Ain't going to be nothing left for us."

She's trying to rub off the two red circles left by the gun barrel on her forehead, makes her look like she's got two pairs of eyes. "You're so full of shit," she says. "It's a big ocean, there's plenty for everyone."

Not taking the two twelve-gauge shells out of the chamber, he puts the gun back down on the bulkhead rack. "Let's eat," he says. "Sarah's fixed us some lunch."

"Oh yeah? What is it? I just brought tuna."

"Moose."

"Wild moose?"

"Hell no. Sarah bought it up to the moose farm."

"You eat it," she says. "I've got my tuna roll."

"Well, she fixed two. One for you."

"Your wife fixed me a sandwich? I'll be god damned. It's probably poison."

"You got to say one thing about Sarah," Lucky says, "she always provides."

"Always has, always will. That's an old-fashioned marriage, don't make *them* anymore." She pulls the bread apart, looks at the moose tongue slices, neat as a row of shingles. "I hear you got it pretty cozy at home. You ever strayed off the reservation?"

"Nope."

"All these years? Don't tell me you ain't had the opportunity. You two must be wicked in love."

"Ain't seen nothing better."

"That's the thing about marriage, makes you walk around with your eyes closed. Course then you're likely to run into something."

As she hands Sarah's sandwich back to him, one of the tongue slices falls on the cockpit floor. Ginger's off her perch in an instant and the meat is gone.

They pull up two upside-down bait tubs next to the lobster well for lunch. The mid-May sun is coming out strong, Ronette unsnaps Reggie's bib-front oilskins and peels off the gray sweatshirt. She's there for a minute in just a blue tank top with no sleeves, the orange bib hanging to her knees. She looks down at herself as if kind of embarrassed, then smiles at Lucky at the same time that she pulls the oilskin straps over her shoulders and snaps them up. "Ain't supposed to get too much sun at first. Melanoma. That's what my momma has." She goes into her purplish-pink yuppie backpack and hauls out a hunk of something wrapped up tight in aluminum foil, then she draws back: "Jesus, will you take a smell of them hands?"

"They smell OK to me, just a little lobster bait. Hey, what happened to your ring?"

She rubs a finger on the pale circle where it used to be. "Took it right back to Fishbein's where we got it, no questions asked. Twelve hundred bucks, less thirty percent restocking. Half-carat diamond, fourteen-karat gold."

"Got to say one thing for Clyde. He does something, he goes all the way."

"Yeah, well he didn't do that much going all the way with me." She unwraps the tuna roll and bites into it. "Tastes like lobster bait." She throws the rest of it in the saltwater tank.

"Christ sake, you'll wreck the balance of nature in there."

"Eat your frigging mooseburger," she says, "packed with ten pounds of love from your ever-loving wife, and me with nothing but a rented trailer and a sub from the convenience store." She looks pretty sweet like that, red in the face and mad, lips pursed tight and tears starting in her eyes, it goes nice with the blue tank top and her chest heaving under the orange bib overalls. She's lost weight over this divorce everywhere but the tits, so they stick out all the better on her shrinking frame.

Ginger reaches a paw into the live well, drags the floating sandwich to the side and slurps it down, salt water dripping from her jaws.

"I ain't got it that good," he says.

"Oh yeah?" She calms down a bit, sits on her bait tub again, curious. "You ain't? Everyone thinks you do. Couple of good-looking kids, nice caring little wife."

"She ain't around much. And you seen my kid? Fucking skinhead, hanging out with them Burnt Neck cocksuckers. Nothing but Indians down there."

"We got a little Indian blood in Split Cove too."

"A little's different. That kid with the earring is a fucking criminal, sure as shit bound for jail and he'll drag Kyle with him. Like your cousin Reggie."

She puts a hand over his on the gray fuel filler pipe between the bait tubs and pats it. "Jail ain't so bad," she says. "Maybe your kid will like it. Reggie learned a trade."

"He ain't going to go far building ships in a bottle."

The way she's sitting, he can see right down the front of her tank top. She's got a small tattoo on the top of her left tit, right over where the heart's supposed to be. She knows he's looking. "You're worse than the customers." She gives him another moment, then adjusts the stray strap on her shoulder.

"You got a tattoo."

"I bet your wife don't have a tattoo."

"She don't," Lucky says. "But I do."

"Where?"

"My chest, same as yours."

She looks intently at his chest like she's trying to see right through the sweatshirt and orange lobster apron. "What is it? Your wife's name?"

"It's a truck."

"A *truck?* I never heard of that."

"I got it over in Vietnam. Everyone in the motor pool got trucks. Mine's an M-thirty-five six-by-six military troop carrier. Workhorse of the marines."

"I thought you'd have it saying Sarah or something."

"I wasn't married then," he says.

"Thought you was born married. Let me see your tattoo. I don't believe it's a truck. It's probably a girl's butt and you don't dare say it."

"It ain't a girl's butt. It's a truck."

"You can see mine," she says. "It's a sea horse." She slides the tank top and bra straps to one side and there it is, right where the hollow under her collarbone starts to swell up and become a tit. His heart stops cold. It's not going to catch again. They'll find him stretched out on the cockpit floor just like his old man, only Ronette Hannaford will be leaning over him with her shirt half off and her little sea horse breathing the open air.

She pulls the straps back and the heart starts up again, too slow to too fast, just like a partridge drumming in the woods.

"So," she says. "Where's yours?"

"I'd have to take the whole damn sweatshirt off, and the vest, and whatever else she put on me this morning."

"She put on you?" Ronette busts out laughing. "Your wife dresses you in the morning?" She's hitching her suspenders up, laughing, getting ready to go back to work.

"She don't dress me," he says. "She just lays the clothes out, depending on the weather."

"And you dress in the dark, so you don't even know what color your underwear is."

"It ain't that bad."

"It ain't that bad. It's worse. That's what's wrong with marriage, Lucky. That's why I had to leave, you get so frigging close to someone you don't even know what you got on."

"That why you left?" He's curious now. She had a split-level ranch with hot tub and sunken swimming pool, now she's in somebody's mobile home. It's not enough that Clyde Hannaford is an asshole. There's got to be something else.

"It ain't the only thing," she says shyly, not laughing anymore. She tilts her head to one side and pulls back the permed-up curls over her neck. "Take a look at that."

A dim blue line runs diagonally across the back of her neck. He reaches over, pushes more of the curls up to follow the mark as it fades into her hairline. "What's that?"

"Son of a bitch tried to strangle me."

"Jesus H. Christ. Clyde Hannaford. Didn't know he had it in him."

"Yeah, well he had it in him. And I was out the door. There's some girls I can name that put up with it, including his little brother's wife Yvonne. I could put *that* cocksucker in jail in about three minutes. I'd rather go on welfare than get treated like that. Clyde's a weak little bastard too, I could stand up to him, but I ain't going to have that kind of marriage."

"Maybe Yvonne had it coming," he suggests.

"I ain't saying she did or didn't. But *I* didn't have it coming. I was behaving myself like a choir girl and getting nothing in return. I don't stay if I get slapped around. Ask my old man."

"Ivan Astbury? Ask him what?"

"Ask him what I do when I get beat up, I don't even stop to say good-bye."

She's crying now, pausing to listen to George Strait singing "I Know She Still Loves Me," then crying again, though both the song and her sadness are drowned out by Siggy Winchenbach's big diesel pilot boat, the *Gretchen and Irene,* which passes a little closer than he has to, then steams over to lay a string into the boulder canyon stretching north off of Red's Bank.

"Nosy bastard," he says. The first wave from Siggy's wake slams the side of the hull, sprays them both, then the wake hits and they rock hard up and down, splashing a few gallons right out of the circulating tank.

"You ain't showed me your tattoo," she says.

"I ain't taking my shirt off with them assholes hanging around."

"Take it off down in the cuddy, then." She ducks her head in the companionway for something to dry her cheek but she can't find anything cleaner than an engine rag. "Jesus, Lucky, what a mess down here. But let me show you what I brought."

She reaches into the backpack and pulls out two strips of flowery blue fabric.

"What the hell's that? A bikini?"

"It's the curtains. First thing you need to make it decent down here."

"Ain't got nothing to put them up with."

"Look, I brought these." She gets out a box of pushpins, scoots down the hatchway and starts stabbing the curtains along the cabin windows. "Gives us a little privacy too. Now you can show me the damn tattoo. It better be a good one after all this work."

She's not going to be quiet till she sees the truck, which is a very nice piece of art though Sarah's tired of it and makes him take his shirt off in the dark. He folds down the front of his big rubber lobster apron, so thick with grass and barnacles it's got green crabs breeding on it, and pulls up the layers of shirts and sweatshirts so Ronette can have a look at his chest.

"Christ sake, Lucky, it *is* a truck. I don't frigging believe it. A truck with hair!"

"M-thirty-five A, six-wheel drive. Cocksuckers could roll through anything. A Chinese guy did that on R and R in Manila. The truck don't look too oriental, does it?"

"Hundred percent American," she says. "You can see mine again if you want. Tit for tat. I got it before we was married."

She pulls the strap down, shudders her shoulders so the little sea horse comes to life. Down here in the dark curtained cabin he feels like a shark at a nude beach, all the forces of nature pushing him up to take a bite, except for one voice in his ear saying, *Lucas, this is the worst kind of activity for your heart.*

"Can you believe it," Ronette's saying, "that bastard Clyde wanted me to have it removed."

He stands up, as much as he can under the low cabin trunk, and speaks with authority. "Can't really remove them. You're always going to have a shadow, it's going through a lot of pain for nothing. Specially in a soft-tissue place like that."

"That ain't the point, Lucky. He thought he could own me. He was afraid that skinny bitch Yvonne would see it and not invite us out to her precious *cunt*ry club. It's my frigging body, that's what I told him, and I can do with it as I see fit."

"You sound like one of them pro-choicers," he says.

"I am a pro-choicer. Only with Clyde I didn't have to make no choice, you know why?"

"Why?"

"Cause you know what his sperm count was? Zero. Point oh oh oh. So we didn't have no choice to be pro *about.* And you know what? That dickhead knew it all along. Only he never let on till after the honeymoon."

He's struck with a rush of sympathy for his dealer. "Jesus, Ronette, how was he supposed to know that? Ever take a good close look at sperm? Can't hardly see them little bastards. A normal guy don't go around counting his sperm all the time."

She lights another Marlboro, leaves her strap down so the sea horse jiggles around when she pounds the cigarette pack and flicks the lighter. He can't quite see the nipple but he's sure it's in there. "That's just it," she says. "My husband is not a normal guy. He had an undescended testicle till he was thirty-one years old."

He chews on that term for a minute. "No shit," he says. "Undescended. You think you know someone your whole life, it turns out you don't know them at all. The boys are going to look at old Clyde some different when this gets out."

"So he had to have an operation to bring it down, and afterwards, that's when they did the sperm count and he found out it was zero. He knew that and he married me anyway. You don't know what that means to a woman. And you know what he wanted? He wanted to get me artificially inseminated, just like a frigging cow. It's so embarrassing, I never told no one, not even Doris." She leans her head into the weed-encrusted folds of Lucky's sweatshirt and seems to shrink, like a kid or something dying in his arms. Then the boat starts to rock a bit as the late-morning southwesterlies pick up strength, and she calms down, wipes her eyes, and goes over to the stereo at the wheelhouse end of the cuddy. "I also brought my new Reba tape," she says. "*Starting Over.* Good name, huh? Get it? Just like me."

> *Three o'clock in the mornin'*
> *And it looks like it's gonna be another sleepless night*

He stretches and starts up the hatchway to finish hauling, but Ronette puts an arm out and blocks his path. "Your crew don't feel like hauling, Lucky. They ain't in a working mood." Under a coil of pot warp she spots a brown beat-up slab of foam he hooked one time on a mackerel trawl. "That all you got for bunks in this place? Reggie's boat had a whole bedroom down below."

"Portholes even had bars on them, made him feel right at home."

She drags the foam out and plunges her face in it. "It's *wet,*" she says, "and it smells like fish bait." She tosses the foam on the workbench and sniffs the air. "It don't matter, I smell like fish bait too. But you know what, Lucky? It ain't the best time of the month for me."

"I don't mind fish bait. Lived with it all my life."

"I don't mean *that.* I mean the time ain't safe. You got something out here we can use? We don't want to have no accidents."

"This ain't the Rite Aid Pharmacy," he replies. "This is a lobster boat. And we ought to be hauling lobsters, afternoon wind's coming on."

"Too bad. I guess you're all married up and everything."

"My old man used to say something, and I always stuck by it. Ain't supposed to mix fish and flesh."

She grabs his face in both hands and looks right at him but she goes blurry, he can't focus that close. "Jesus H. Christ," she says. "You got your wife dressing you, you go by your old man's sayings like they was the book of God. Who am I out here with? You're like one of them giant clams. It would take a crowbar to pull them shells apart, see what's inside."

"I ain't got a crowbar. It's in the truck."

"Bet we could find one on board, Mr. Lucas Lunt, if we look hard enough." She's standing now, her head almost touches the roof beam. He's sitting on the engine box, so she looks down on him like a mom undressing a kid for bed. "She probably takes everything off for you too, home from a hard day's work." She undoes the suspender snaps of his grass-covered orange apron and lays it on the chain locker. A couple of green crabs scuttle off it and make for the bilge. Then comes the sweatshirt that says ORPHAN POINT V.F.D., then his old man's red plaid hunting vest. When "Ring on Her Finger" comes on she listens to Reba for a moment.

In a three-bedroom prison I tried to make a home

She finishes pulling down the top of his one-piece union suit and stands back to view her work. "No shit, Lucky, you're a good-sized man. Clyde's such a little fucker, I used to call it Snow White and the Seven Dwarfs. Now unhook me, will you? This dumb thing unfastens in the back." She turns around and bends her head down so he can see the bruise again while his huge fingers fumble with the hook. He's hoping for the voice to stop him, Sarah's or Clyde's, but there's only a dog whimper from the hatchway and Ronette saying, "Be a good girl, Ginger, we'll give you a Milk-Bone when we're done."

She lets the tank top slide all the way down on one side, there's no more bra in the way, the nipple puckers and sticks its little tongue out under the sea horse riding the wave crest of her tit. Under Reg-

gie's big oilskins her pants slip down to her knees: nothing but some
kind of bikini bottom left, curly hairs peeking around the edge.
"Clyde's crazy," he says. "You ought to get a couple more of them
tattoos."

"Bet we could find a couple more on *you*." She pushes him back
on the wet foam, rolls down his oilskins, canvas pants, union suit.
"She's got more layers on you than a wedding cake." He tries to stop
her before she gets to the camouflage boxers he got at the ammo
store, but she's got him backed up against the foam and she keeps
pushing things down. "Whoa. Camouflage shorts. You sneak up on
the moose in them things?"

She has no trouble peeling the boxers down, but underneath he's
limp as a garden slug.

"Must be them heart pills, it ain't been working right all year."

She's looking down, shaking her head like her dog died. "It ain't
the pills, it's your loving little wife. She owns you, her and your old
man. If you ain't interested, we better go back to fishing. No hard
feelings, Lucky Lunt. I know true love when I see it." She slides the
blue tank top over the sea horse and goes to stand up, then gives him
one last glance with her big kelp-colored eyes. "Before I go, I'd love
to give that little guy a kiss. I bet he don't get half enough attention."

All those long winter nights under the covers with Sarah Peek,
all the truck-seat midnights of their courtship, that was always
where she drew the line. Her mouth got anywhere near it, she'd close
up tight as a quahog, so finally he gave up hope. That's what they
say, girls don't do it north of Boston. Now all of a sudden he's watching the pile of brown hair crawl down his stomach just like a deep
throat video. He glances once more at the blue bruise on her neck,
closes his eyes, and leans his head back onto an old moldy seat cush-
ion that smells like blue cheese. Ronette mumbles something like,
"Like that?"

"Ain't polite to talk with your mouth full."

She releases him for a second but he can feel her warm breath as
she speaks. "Clyde couldn't stand it. He was scared I'd bite it off. I
should of, too." Then she plugs him back in. His wife's face appears
on the screen of his eyelids — *You can still stop, Lucas, and it will be all
right* — but down below it's another story. When she finally comes

up for air and looks at what she's done, her eyes grow wide. It's a foot and a half long and glowing red in the shadowy cabin like an electric eel. He tries pulling his clothes back up but it's too late, she's got one leg of her oilskins off and she's on top of him saying, "It's too big, Lucky, it ain't going to fit." She has to grab onto his arms to pull herself down tight, then she's got him surrounded, she's rowing him homeward like a lapstrake dory and all voices of the past are drowning in their foamy wake. Then out of nowhere there's an engine roar and a big six-cylinder Mack diesel passes close astern. Jesus, if it's Siggy Winchenbach he could peer down the companionway just like an aquarium. Siggy's wake rolls them right off the engine box onto the starboard bench as she slides in under him on the foam pad soaked with bilgewater and herring juice where she'll be crushed flat, he's the size of a walrus and she's so tiny with that little patch of fur, just like Alfie when he was a kitten from the pound. But no, she's still alive and laughing and pulling at his union suit to try and bring him deeper in. There's still a few inches that won't fit, but she's working on it, then all of a sudden she screams like a fish hawk and seizes his chest hair with both hands like she wants to pull the truck off and cram it inside her with the rest of him, the veins stand out of her neck like a weightlifter, her face and chest turn bright red, the sea horse is a dragon with eyes of fire saying, "You got me, Lucky, I ain't never," then she clamps him like a live warm oyster so even though he doesn't want to he can't hold it, he's the bull seal up on both flippers roaring his nuts off and spraying inside his female like a fire hose. A thousand-volt electric shock runs from his dicktip right up his spine, jumps into his heart and cracks it open, only it's pain now and he can't stay up, his shoulders and elbows buckle and he collapses like that moose in the October sunlight, .357 hollowpoint dead center in his chest.

He manages to roll off to one side so he won't squash her, ends up flat on his back on the bilge-smelling foam with his heart fibrillating uncontrollably like a fish on the cockpit sole.

She's up now and her eyes are bugged out, she thinks he's dead. "Jesus, Lucky, are you OK? What the hell's that *noise?*" She lays her head on his truck tattoo and clenches her eyes shut like that's going to help her hear.

"Heart," he says, his voice up high like a little kid's.

"Sounds like you've got two of them in there."

"That's right. I keep a spare handy, just in case."

"No shit? That's what they did at the hospital? They put in another one? If I'm going to be with you, Lucky, you have to tell me how to switch it on."

The heart's calming down now, but he still feels the blood swirl like transmission oil through his wire-mesh stent. He ought to reach for the pills in his lunchbox — he brought them this time — but Ronette's cheek pressing on his chestbone seems to have the same effect.

"Better not try *that* anymore," she says, lifting her head up gingerly. "We don't want nobody dying out here, least of all you. I wouldn't know how the hell to get us back."

He swallows a couple of pills and claps another under his tongue. They sit there naked and quiet, just listening to Reba, while his heartbeat settles down, her body pale as a flounder except for the purple sea horse and the big brown nipples, his own body a hairy skinned-out whale.

You shouldn't of done it, that's what his heart was trying to tell him. But it waited till it was too fucking late.

Ginger's sitting on the floor beside them with her tongue hanging out, she could be spying for old Clyde. Ronette disentangles an arm, reaches into the backpack and feeds her the Milk-Bone. Outside, the light little waves slap up against the hull as the current pulls them broadside to the wind. Reba McEntire has reversed herself twice over the last hour.

I had a ring on my finger and time on my hands

He rests a fingertip just under the sea horse, and the brown nipple tip wakes up and stirs, just like touching the neck of a clam to see if it's alive. She looks down, curious, like it belongs to someone else. He traces a letter on it, up and over the stiff little bud, ending on the sea horse tattoo.

"What'd you write?"

"F."

"F for *what?*"

"Finest kind."

She blushes so much her whole face and neck turn red. "I got saline in them."

"What?"

"Saline injections. You know. They used to do silicone, but they don't anymore. Saline's just salt water. It's natural."

"When'd you do that?"

"It was a wedding present from Clyde. The health plan don't cover it. He wanted them bigger. He used to compare me with that bitch Yvonne. Yvonne had hers done when she was fourteen years old."

"I wouldn't of made you do it, if it was me. Bet they was nice enough as it was."

"Well, you ain't Clyde Hannaford. Clyde was always wanting more more more. Not that he could do nothing when he had it."

He touches the other one and she shivers and pulls away. From the new angle he can make out the little scars under each tit where they put the salt water in and sewed her up. "Little bit of the ocean," he says, rubbing the scar tissue gently at first, then a little harder, thinking he might erase it with a fingertip, but it won't come off.

"You too," she says. She traces a fingertip around the incision scar on his left thigh where they went in with the heart balloon. "That won't come off neither. What's it feel like when I rub it? Numb like mine?"

"There's times when it feels like they left the whole fucking tube in there, but it feels pretty good right now."

It's a fine mid-May evening when he drives back from his errand at the Rite Aid drugstore. A yellow dust of pollen has settled over the cars and driveway, the roofs of houses, it's so thick in the air he has to put the wipers on, just like driving through a fog of piss. Then when he gets there his garage door is blocked by a rusted-out Toyota four-by-four longbed which he's never seen. He parks up close behind it to check it out. The Toy's got thirty-five-inch mud tires and big yellow Hurst lifters that raise it so high a dog the size of Ginger could walk beneath. Its cab stands taller than his full-sized GMC, and he's got five inches of extra leaf on that. There's dive tanks and weight belts in the back, must be one of Kyle's pals from Burnt Cove. He whistles his way in from the truck with a tune from the Reba McEntire tape that played and replayed through the lunch hour and etched itself into his mind.

Lord, I'm still five hundred miles away from home

"Somebody's happy about something," his daughter shouts as soon as he gets in the door. "Must have been a good fishing day." He's looking around for the guest that would explain the unknown pickup truck outside. Usually Kristen's locked up in her room studying or listening to church music, but now she's got all her brochures and pamphlets from the university spread out on the living room rug, because, as she says ten or twelve times a day, "September tenth and I'm getting another life."

Sarah gives him a big welcome too. She lets her wire-rimmed glasses slip onto their neck cord and puts a thin hand on the back of his neck, though he can't actually feel it because it's a spot where Ronette Hannaford touched him and the skin seems numb. "We were concerned," his wife says. "You're unusually late."

"Busy day out there. We brought in pretty near a hundred and twenty pounds. That's better than I was doing in a week, working alone."

"I guess we were wrong, Lucas. Your sternperson's paying for herself. I hope she's taking some of the physical strain too, for your health's sake. I hear Ellis Seavey's got a girl working for him too, they're all doing it these days."

Kyle looks up from the TV and says, "You can't *get* no guys to go sternman anymore. That kind of money, might as well go up to Norumbega and work for the Pizza Hut."

His wife pops into the warm chowdery kitchen and returns with his earthly reward for a hard day's work, hot tea with a shot of prohibited 101 black rum and a light kiss on the crown of his head, a spot where the scalp can feel the direct touch of her lips. "Kristen's got some good news too. She's got a job."

"Where you working, Princess? Down to the cat food plant?"

"Don't you wish. Then I'd smell like you when I walked in."

"*Kristen,*" her mother says.

"I'm only teasing. Daddy can take it. He's tough." She hops up and gives him a whack on the shoulder, not with all her might like the old days, more of a heart-patient pat, then a big bear hug, rubbing her nose right in the mossiest fold of his sweatshirt. "Big fragile bear. We have to take it easy on you now."

"Don't have to do nothing different. I'm fixed."

"I don't know what I'm going to do without you up at the U."

"You'll think of something," Kyle says. "You can hang some bait bags around your room, they'll remind you of home."

"You still ain't told me what your job is. One of them topless dancers Andy's hiring for at the RoundUp?"

"*Lucas,*" Sarah warns. "Keep this up, you'll be sleeping out in the garage."

His daughter covers his eyes with both hands. In her palms' darkness he sees a little sea horse in the circle of a lipstick kiss.

"I'm going to be an au pair."

"Oh pear? What the hell's that? You going into the fruit business? Not a bad idea, when the summer trade shows up."

"It's French, Daddy. It means someone who takes care of children. And no more slurs on the summer families. I'm working for one now. They're from Baltimore."

He asks Kristen, "Which family you working for? You happen to know what they drive?"

"You wouldn't know them, Daddy. They're called the Hummermans, and they're new. They're fixing up that big old Victorian down from the Point Club, on the shore road, it's the one with the turret. You could see it from here if the air were a little clearer."

"I don't have to see it, I know which one it is. Half this town out of work and the son of a bitch hired foreigners."

"*Lucas.* It's your daughter's employer."

"They're not foreign," Kristen explains. "The architectural firm is from Salem, Massachusetts. It's not like a local contractor could do a *historical restoration.*"

"Local contractors was good enough to build the damn thing in the first place. Them shingle jobs was all built by old man Lurvey, Wendell Lurvey's grandfather."

"Restoration is different, Dad. You can't dig up Wendell Lurvey's grandfather. You have to know history. I've met them. They were there when I interviewed. The head of the construction crew has a Ph.D. Can you imagine how much someone like that *knows?*"

Lucky's back has a quick spasm and flash of pain like he'd thrown it out hauling a trap over the side. He tries to recall how it happened, then he remembers. Suddenly he's back in the cuddy with Ronette Hannaford squirming beneath him and his spine arched upward like a sea lion.

Sarah says, "Oh Lucas, did you strain your back today?" and adds a second splash of black rum to the half-full tea. "Maybe you *should* have hired a man, he could have taken on the strenuous part." She then tries to massage his back and shoulder but her thin fingers aren't strong enough to get through the layers of body hair, blubber, muscle and cartilage down to where it really hurts. "I suppose I'm failing you, Lucas, not to be out there, but look at my hands, they don't have the strength for a proper backrub. I wouldn't be much help on a lobster boat."

"Them Ph.D.'s," he asks Kristen, "how many kids they got?"

"Well, with Dr. Hummerman's old wife he has a son in college, and with his new wife, who is the one that interviewed me, they have a girl eight and a boy five. And I know the Hummermans let local people work on their dock project because Billy Thurston's working there too, so there'll be someone I know."

"I heard. Doug Travis has got three men on that job full-time and they've been there all spring long. Doug's crew put in a granite pier and a float made of Tibetan redwood, they must be putting half a million into it."

"The Hummermans *need* it, Daddy, for their new yacht."

"I'm sure they do. And another thing, why can't the college boy take care of their kids?"

"Lucas," Sarah says on her way out to the kitchen, "a college boy doesn't want to baby-sit for two small children. It's a perfect situation for an au pair. It will get her ready for college too. These are the kind of people she'll meet in her new life. They've already stopped in at Yvonne's gallery. She says they have excellent taste."

"Hey Mom," Kristen says, "one of your mobiles would look nice in their house."

"Don't be pushy, darling. I'm not good enough yet."

"Not true. You're the best. And Dad, did I tell you, I'm going to have my own room there. Right in the old servants' quarters over their carriage house."

"Slave quarters," he says. "They lost their fucking plantations down in Dixieland, now they come up here. Confederates should of won, this country'd be a damn sight better off."

"Daddy, they're not Confederates. They're Jewish. Mrs. Hummerman's going to teach me all their customs, like eating by candlelight on Friday night."

"Jesus H. Christ, our customs ain't good enough anymore?"

"*Lu*cas."

"No, let me explain to him. Don't you see, Daddy, we don't *have* customs. We live in a cultural vacuum. The Hummermans can't watch any TV after sunset on Friday. It's very refined."

"Can't be Friday," he says. "You must of heard it wrong. Friday's World Wrestling night on TNN."

"Daddy, if you think like that you'll never get anywhere, you're just going to *rot* here in this old house that hasn't changed since the Civil War."

Sarah's just arrived back at the table with a full steaming bowl of mussel stew thick with diced turnips and onions and what looks like tofu but he prays to God is big chunks of salt pork. Even Kyle shuts the TV off with his foot and sits down to slouch his half-shaved head over his food. Now it looks like some kind of writing's carved into his hair, probably Chinese.

Sarah serves her daughter first, as the person of honor. "We should all try to have some positive feeling for Kristen's achievement. I heard there were a dozen girls applying for that job."

"They didn't hire Lenore Hannaford," Kristen says. "And she goes to private school."

"No shit? Clyde's niece, huh? That's decent. Sounds like this guy Hummerman really stepped in shit. What did he do, win the Maryland Megabucks?"

"He's a doctor," Kristen says. "He's a cardiac surgeon at Johns Hopkins University, and you know what his wife told me? Nobody's supposed to know, only members of the family, so Kyle, don't say anything to your dropout friends. If anything ever happened to the president's heart, Dr. Hummerman would be on the team that gets called in."

"Hey. He could fix the whole frigging country with one little slip of the knife."

"You know, Lucas, you might not be here eating this food if it weren't for the miracle of heart surgery."

"That would be OK with me. A man ain't good enough for his own family, he might as well be fucking dead."

"*Lucas.*"

His son stands up from the table and flips a set of keys in the air. "I don't have to listen to this shit. I'm going out."

"Out? Where? Ain't this a school night for you?"

"Maybe I'll drive over to Split Cove, see what's happening."

"Drive what? You ain't using the GMC, you got a ticket last time. You going to use the Lynx?"

"Don't have to. Got my own."

Lucky had forgotten about the truck. "That ain't your Toyota blocking my door, is it?"

"Sure is," Kyle says proudly. "Bought it this afternoon."

"Bought it with what? You ain't got any money. You ain't even paid me for your outboard motor."

"I bought it on credit. Mr. Moto lent me the money."

"Mr. *Moto?*"

"That's right. Mr. Moto. At least I got *somebody* that trusts me."

"You don't know about economics, do you? You don't know the Japs have been buying up the United States ever since V-J Day and one day they're going to show up with a piece of paper and we're going to be *theirs.* The whole cocksucking country. We will be serv-ing them cold jellyfish and shining their fucking shoes. And you're going to deliver us right to the gates of Tokyo with that god damned truck."

"Well you don't have to worry about it none," Kyle says, "cause they ain't going to want *you.*"

"They ain't going to want you either, you and that fairy boyfriend of yours. He's been in jail already, ain't he? I'd like to know what *he* does in his spare time."

Kyle was on his way out but now he turns and faces his old man head-on, swinging the Toyota keys in his face like a hypnotist. "I'll tell you what he does in his spare time. He FUCKS DOGS."

Lucky goes blind with rage. The whole room shrinks and darkens in his narrowed eye. All he can see is that cocksucking shaved head with the gold earring hanging off of it like a drop of piss. He leaps up and goes for him. "You got it coming now, you little bastard!"

Sarah shrieks, "Lucas, your *son!* Your *heart!*"

Kyle ducks fast and breaks for the door at the same time. Then he turns and spits: "Fucking loser, at least I ain't going to end up like you."

Lucky leaps forward and lets one fly right at the earring just as Kristen dives between them and knocks Kyle aside so the fist of authority meets empty air. His arm wants to slug Kristen but she looks him right in the eye and says, "I *dare* you," so he backs off shouting, then lunges around her to face Kyle again. "We're going to have some fucking discipline in this house." He's got a hold on Kyle's denim vest and he's lining him up for another try when Kristen screams and slides in front of her brother again. "Mother, it's *happening*. He's going be*rserk*. You better dial nine one one."

Kyle doesn't go anywhere either. He stands right up there in the doorway beside the open closet of sea boots and oilskins, Kristen beside him, and grinds his teeth at his old man. Lucky is six-one in his lambskin slippers and Kyle's just under six and still growing, he pumps iron in the cellar too, though Lucky's got maybe eighty pounds on his son and forearms like a hardshell lobster, thirty years lifting stone-ballasted wooden traps. Kyle turns his head and spits out the open door onto the welcome mat, which has a couple of worn-out mallards on it and now says THE   UNTS. "I ain't putting up with this," he says.

"You ain't going nowhere in that fucking Toyota."

"Who says?"

"I say. And I am blocking the driveway so you can't get out."

"Give me the keys, then, I'll move that broken-down piece of Deetroit shit."

"Keys my ass." He makes damn sure the key ring is deep in his left front pocket, then sits down in his chair and flips the remote to *The Bowling Hour.* It's a mixed doubles championship out in Wisconsin somewhere, nothing but fat white midwesterners in white shirts and black bowling pants like an indoor dairy herd, but they are pretty decent bowlers and fun to watch. Just as he turns up the volume and settles in, Kyle grabs the remote out of his lap and shuts it off. "Now I'm going to fucking kill you," Lucky shouts, but just as he's going for the weasely bastard he slips out the door and he's gone.

Sarah's crying and breathing like her asthma's come back again. "I don't know which of you is worse. Thank God they'll be in college in a couple of years."

"Kyle's not going to college," Kristen says sweetly. "He's going to move in with Darrell Swan over in Burnt Neck. He *told* me."

Just as he's getting back into the bowling match, he hears this tremendous engine roar and a scraping noise like a steel boat grounding on a half-tide ledge. He runs out to look at the garage. Even though his truck was in park, Kyle has backed up against it in his granny gear and he's pushing it backwards down the driveway and right out into the street, which means the pin's been ripped out of the transmission and chewed up in the fucking gears. *"Son of a bitch!"* he yells, but Kyle's engine is so loud he can't hear anything and he's off towards Split Cove. The last thing his father sees is the white rectangle of his son's cardboard ten-day plate.

He walks out in the road and climbs up to his driver's seat to check the transmission. Everyone's forced to drive around him, honking. Fuck them. The shift lever's stuck fast. He starts the engine, puts a little muscle to the lever, it snaps and flaps free like a broken arm. Then there's this moment of high-pitched turbojet whine and a final complicated crunch like turning on a blender full of spoons and forks.

His truck. Useless. Its rear end is half out in the roadway and he can't even move it back. He stands there looking down the road towards Split Cove as if expecting to see the slant-eyed headlights of the Toyota returning to strike again. His heart pounds so hard he can hear his stent whistling and the valves opening and closing in his ears.

Sarah and Kristen are watching from the front steps. "Come finish your supper," his wife calls. "We'll get Alan Ashmore to come over with the wrecker. He's Triple-A."

"Triple asshole," he says. "We ain't covered by them no more." He stomps upstairs for the bottle of heart pills in the medicine chest.

When he comes back his daughter has brought him a straight black rum, without the tea, balanced on the Naugahyde arm of his recliner. "I know Kyle will feel bad about this," she says. "Course he'll never admit it."

"I'll wait up all night if I have to. When he comes home I'm taking a crowbar to that fucking truck."

"I have another idea," Sarah says. "I'll ask Kyle to lend you his truck till yours gets fixed."

"I ain't driving it. He won't be lending it to me neither, cause I am going to convert that son of a whore to a mooring block."

She moves quietly behind him, massaging his shoulder blades to calm him down. "Lucas, I'm just trying to think of how you can get to work. You're welcome to my car but you won't set foot in it. Or maybe Rhonda Hannaford can pick you up."

"Great idea. We'll stuff ten lobster traps in the trunk of her Barbie doll Probe. That ought to hold it to the road."

He's in his socks already, ten-thirty at night, just listening to the weather before going to bed, when he hears the Toyota pull into the driveway. Sarah and Kristen are up in the studio over the garage, so they can't stop him. He gets into his mud boots by the doorway, grabs a crowbar from the workbench and goes out to start on the grille and headlights, then work back to the windshield and the doors. When he gets out there, though, it's not Kyle but some other cocksucker with the same kind of truck, just stopping to see why the GMC's sitting there with its rear end in the street. Alan Ashmore never showed up with the wrecker. He almost runs out and bashes in their grille, just for driving that Asian shitheap, but he stops short and stands there in the night waving the crowbar while the strange truck flees down the road in terror. Serves them right. Another year or two and there won't be anything else on the road. Hondas, Hyundais, Accuras, Lexuses, Nissans, Daewoos, amazing they don't make a Mitsubishi Zero with a bloody fucking sun on the doors, just like Pearl Harbor only this time the suicide pilots are us.

He unspools the electric winch on the front of his truck and hooks it around a spruce tree alongside the garage and with a terrible grinding noise winches it forward enough to get the poor thing off the highway. He lays out his own clothes for the morning, makes his own sandwich of cold moose liver and Miracle Whip, mixes up some tuna salad for Ronette, and, with the crowbar under his side of the bed, finds the way to sleep all by himself.

In the middle of the night he hears the Toy again and gropes for the crowbar below. In his union-suit pajamas he creeps downstairs. The truck just idles there with its beady low beams on and shakes with the four-cylinder twitch. He walks up to the driver's side head-light and puts the cocksucker to sleep with a single stroke. Then his son steps down and puts his hands up like a prisoner, only one hand is full of money, fifty- and hundred-dollar bills, and Kyle extends the bills towards his old man like you'd offer your bare wrist to a rott-weiler. "I've sold it, Dad. I've got five hundred dollars to fix your transmission." Lucky drops the crowbar and throws his arms around his son, who doesn't have an earring anymore either, and he's got his curly brown hair back like he used to wear it when he was a kid. It's not Darrell Swan beside him in the Toyota either, it's a dead body, and when it turns around he sees it's Ronette Hannaford, staring at him through Sarah's wire-rimmed glasses. His heart starts palpitat-ing and he wakes up sweating in his bed, he reaches for the woman beside him but she's not there.

From the bedroom window he can see her studio light's still on. His truck is in the driveway with the winch cable still attached around the tree. He opens the dormer window and cranes his neck around to view the whole neighborhood, but the Toyota is nowhere to be seen.

5

VIRGIL CARTER'S STILL GOT Lucky's pickup in the garage and he's stuck with one of Virge's old beaters, a '74 Ford half-ton six that's locked in low range so it drives like a road grader. He heads for Luther Webster's place on the Riceville Road to buy some traps. Luther's deaf wife meets him at the mailbox. She's standing three feet away from him but she yells nevertheless, as if he were the one that couldn't hear. "He's *worming.*"

"Worming?" Lucky yells. "Best trap maker in the state ain't ought to be worming."

"It's worm or starve," she screams back. "Nobody wants wooden traps."

Lucky buys twelve from her and loads them in the back of the loaner, then adds a couple more, till it looks like the Ford's rear springs are going to snap. Seven hundred bucks. Then on the way out he notices the brand-new satellite dish on a steel pillar cemented into Luther Webster's back lawn. Well fuck it, now they can buy a thirty-two-inch TV.

When he gets back to the smooth black asphalt of the Riceville Road, he puts the old loaner to the floor, valves slapping the head, bone-dry transfer case grinding itself to death, full of traps, sparks flying off the low-slung rear. Fucking Virgil Carter, he'll never sell this cocksucker to anyone. Serve him right.

When he gets home Sarah's Lynx is already in the driveway and she's waiting for him in the breakfast nook with a cup of Red Rose tea.

"Lucas the Loner." She smiles like she's looking to make up. The house has been cold as a meat locker since Kyle left home after the truck duel. He doesn't give a shit, he's not going to hear or speak the name of his son till he gets his pickup back.

"I'm driving a christly loaner. She's right out there." He gestures out the window to the Ford six, which has a puddle of purple fluid rapidly forming underneath the crankcase and a plume of green smoke pissing straight out from the grille.

"That's right. You *are* a loaner. Only thing is, *I* don't get to give you back."

"Ain't nobody'd take me."

"I can think of some that might. They don't know you like I do, though. How was fishing?"

"Halfway decent, for a crippled old fart and a professional waitress. Price is up too, now Clyde's got the cooker going out front. Even that cheap bastard is paying three-fifteen a pound."

He switches on the stock car channel. Ricky Craven is supposed to be driving in the North Carolina Dura-Lube 400 but there's a huge pileup with a couple of cars on fire and the yellow flag's up so there's no action, just cruising around slow like they're looking for a place to park. He sits down and watches it anyway.

"Lucas, why don't you shut the TV off? We don't get to talk much these days."

"We're hauling lobsters sunup to half past three. Don't leave much time for talk."

"I don't imagine," she says. "Why don't we go out for supper? Just the two of us. Kristen can look after herself. It's been a while."

"Where at? Doris ain't open yet for supper. RoundUp's nothing but beef, they ain't had a vegetable in there since Prohibition, what are you going to eat?"

"How about the Irving Big Stop up at the Narwhal Mall? You always like it there."

"Only decent thing on the menu's the bacon cheeseburger, and the prime rib on Thursdays but it ain't Thursday. Where's that leave you?"

"They've put in a very attractive salad bar," she says. "My art class stopped there once when the Salad Patch was closed. Anyway, you've had your meat for the week."

In the Irving Big Stop restaurant he goes to order the bacon cheeseburger with double blue cheese but she covers the row of glossy burger photos with her hand. "We're both having the salad bar. Remember, I promised I'd look after your diet."

"That was way back in March."

"No, Lucas, it was forever."

"Don't know why we bother," he says. "Might as well eat what we want and die."

"That's not what you said last winter. I should have made a tape of you promising young Dr. Burnside you'd reform your eating habits."

"Well, that was then. Now it don't seem worth it."

"What do you mean, worth it? Lucas, you're only forty-six years old."

"My old man Walter, he was just turned forty-eight."

"That was a different generation, Lucas. The technology that's made you able to work again was not available to Walter."

He gets the old image back of the *Wooden Nickel* as a brand-new boat, found adrift off Toothpick Ledge by the Thurston boys, trap wide open, Chrysler slant-six idling away, his old man unconscious on the floor. Howard Thurston said the lobsters had already crawled under his oilskins, greedy bastards, they couldn't wait for revenge. The Thurstons got him to the hospital but he never fished again.

"Sometimes I'll be out there," he says to his wife, "the days I'm alone . . ."

"Which aren't very many," she reminds him. "Your sternperson's with you almost every trip."

"Seems like half the time I'm alone, and you know how many smells there is out there, the bait and the hydraulic oil, and the kelp and eelgrass off the bottom, the rotten trap wood, gullshit and salt air . . ."

". . . cigarettes, Wild Turkey. Lucas, I think your self-discipline melts away when you leave the mooring, and I don't see Ronette Hannaford offering much support."

"This ain't a church, Mother, it's just a gas station, and I'm trying to tell you something. I've been picking up another smell out there, it ain't the bilge or anything I can put my hands on."

"Might be something your sternlady's sprayed on herself. Those colognes have a way of lingering."

"Tell you what I think, I think it's the smell of death, mixed in with everything else. What worries me, it don't smell half as bad as I thought it would."

She shivers and draws the hand-knit sweater around her shoulders. She's always been cold, her whole life, there's not enough flesh on her to keep her warm even on the first of June. "It doesn't matter what you want or don't want for yourself, Lucas, there are those of us who care."

"Who? Kyle's gone. He ain't coming home. Kristen? She's got the oh pear, then she's off to college and she ain't looking back. You? You're out every night now over to the art school with the stained glass, think you was a monk."

"I'm not a monk, Lucas. And from what I hear these days, neither are you."

"What's that supposed to mean?"

"Let's make our trip to the salad bar, then we'll talk about it."

He realizes why she chose the Big Stop now, they don't serve alcohol. He's got half a pint in the glove compartment, he's thinking how he might get out to it, but she's already handed him his three-inch Formica bowl and she's steering him towards the lettuce bin, there's no escape. He moves through the Irving Big Bar feeling dry and clumsy as the first fucking fish learning to walk on land, groping through the vegetables for edible food. Lettuce is too much like rockweed. Tomatoes are all right in spaghetti sauce but he doesn't eat them raw, especially the little cherry ones you can't even cut into with those blunt plastic knives so they go rolling off your plate. They got carrot slivers, celery slivers, big black olives the size of a guy's balls. He grabs a tongload of red onions and goes to pile on a cheese slab and a few slices of hard-boiled egg. "No eggs," she reminds him, "and no cheese. You're way past your quotas for this week."

"Christ."

He comes back to their booth with a bowl of onion chunks and green peppers smothered in skin-colored Lo-cal French under which he's concealed a few chunks of boiled ham. "What's that you've sprayed on there," she asks, "bacon bits?"

"Jesus, they're just chemicals, they ain't real bacon."

"Lucas, do you want to know why I spend so much thought and energy on you? Because I care about you. That's what marriage is, remember. Death do us part. Till then we have to keep each other alive."

"OK."

"But I don't particularly want to preserve you for the enjoyment of someone else. Remember the other part, *forsaking all others?* You know, I had a couple of admirers back then. As you well know, one of them was Clyde Hannaford."

"Well, here's your chance. He's all alone in the hot tub."

"Lucas, the last thing I'm interested in is another man. One is enough, I assure you. I'm only recalling his name to tell you I had a choice back then. I chose you, and I still do." The tear bulging in each eye makes it look like she's wearing contacts under her glasses.

"I don't get it. Why dig up the past? Them days are gone."

"I ran into Rhonda Hannaford the other day, while I was delivering some much-needed supplies to your son in his new home. Or Rhonda Astbury, as she's starting to call herself again. God knows why she would want to claim relation with that Burnt Neck crowd. She caught my eye and turned green like somebody seasick. I never saw anyone look so guilty. She spun right around and went back to that ostentatious little car Clyde gave her."

"It's got the sixteen-valve overhead-cam six," he reminds her. "Ain't a big engine but she torques up."

"I'm sure she does. I walked right over and leaned on her car roof so she couldn't just drive off. I said if she's working for you, I'd like to get to know her a little better. It's almost like she's in the family, spending all that time on the *Wooden Nickel,* which as you well know is legally half my boat. So I said, 'Why don't you stop off for supper one of these days after hauling, and get acquainted?'"

"You did, huh? And what'd Ronette say?"

"She said something like, 'Me and him's already acquainted.' You know her grammar, it's worse than yours. I said, 'Does that mean what I think it means?' and she said it could mean whatever I want. She looked at her watch and said something about going home to feed her dog. Lucas, I felt as if I'd been condescended to."

He can't quite look her in the face at this point, so his glance drifts towards the plate glass window behind her. His eyes would like to check out the vehicles in the parking lot, but the view is blocked by the June forsythias in violent yellow bloom under the mercury-vapor lamps. He can just make out the twilight sky and the first star, on which he makes a wish to be the fuck out of there and not going through this, when suddenly a brand-new forty-five-foot fishing boat pulls right in front of the window, ten miles from the nearest shore. He can't see its lower half because of the shrubbery, and the thing's so big it looks like the Big Stop restaurant's moving and the boat is standing still. He's caught off guard for a moment.

"What the hell, Sarah, take a look at that."

His wife turns around and says, "Heaven's sake, Lucas, it's just someone with a trailer hauling a boat. Try to pay attention. I'm doing my best to talk with you."

"But the trailer don't show, so it looks like she's steaming right through the parking lot. Ain't that the optical illusion?"

She's got a stainless steel tuna pulpit up front, full controls on the wheelhouse roof, cabin closed on both sides so she'll never haul a lobster trap. The boat stops right there in front of the Irving door, so new he can see the mold wax clinging to the sides. He hears the idling diesel of the hauling truck but he can't see it, so it appears like the boat has docked up in the Irving parking lot to unload the catch.

In a moment the door swings open and in struts Wilfred Beal with his arm around Clyde Hannaford's brother Arvid, both of them with big cigars. Sarah's got her back to them, but right away they spot Lucky in the booth. "Hey Lunt, which way's the smoking section?"

"It ain't here," he says, his nose hairs trembling from the whiff of smoke. "Don't wave them god damn cigars over the salad bar."

The two men wheel around to view the new boat through the window. "What do you think?" Wilfred Beal asks. "Trucked her up from Point Judith, Rhode Island. Pequod Boat Corporation."

"No need to buy local," Lucky says. "How come you didn't get a Mexican one?"

"They ain't got the technology around here. This one's an off-shore rig, turbocharged diesel, refrigeration, Satcom, monel tanks, sixty-four-mile Furuno radar."

"She don't have no pot hauler," Lucky observes.

"Ain't going for lobster. Four, five years, lobstering's going to be dead. Government's going to move in, start the trap-limit squeeze, guys like me and you won't haul ten christly lobsters in a week. That there boat's for the twenty-first century. The good old days has peaked. They ain't coming back neither. She's full tuna. Total refrigeration, right to the airport: Sushi Express."

"You going to drag with her in the winter?"

"Ain't going to be here winters. No more iced-up fuel lines, no fucking frostbite. You know my brother lost a toe off of his right foot."

"Still got five left, don't he?"

"*Luc*as."

"No, that's all right, ma'am," Wilfred Beal says. "Your husband's got a right to be jealous. This thing's going to get me a condo in West Palm Beach."

"No investment like local talent," Arvid Hannaford says. He's got those same little pig eyes like his brother, fat cheeks and a tight wrinkly little pursed-up mouth like putting a pair of glasses over someone's asshole. Arvid looks at the boat again, takes out a calculator, pokes in some numbers with a soft pudgy jointless finger that looks like a dick. It's pretty clear Wilfred Beal won't be seeing any Florida condos, but Arvid and Yvonne Hannaford might buy a few.

"My man," Wilfred Beal says, laying his arm on Arvid's shoulder.

As the two of them head for the smoking section, Sarah turns around and flashes a quick smile, not for domestic consumption. "Arvid, say hello to Yvonne for me. Tell her I'll call her tomorrow about the fabric."

"Finest kind," Arvid Hannaford says.

"We're getting real cozy with the Hannafords," he observes.

"I'm helping Yvonne redecorate her gallery. She might hire me part-time when it gets busy."

"Wait a minute. You wasn't available when it came to lobstering. Take too much time from the studio."

"Things have changed, Lucas. I might need the money. In case I find myself one day supporting a household."

"What's that supposed to mean?"

She leans forward across their uneaten salads, speaks low so Yvonne's husband won't hear. "Lucas, just because I'm finally getting a life of my own does not mean our marriage is over and anything goes. That afternoon in Burnt Neck I asked Rhonda Hannaford right out if there was anything she wanted to tell me about your working arrangement, and you know what she said?"

"No."

"She said, 'Why don't you ask around back home?' Which is what I'm doing. I want to hear it one way or the other straight from the horse's mouth, not whispers and rumors and certainly not from a woman who is practically young enough to be your daughter. *Our* daughter, if we'd married like the Astburys, right out of high school."

The Irving Musak system is playing a Vince Gill song and he goes to look in the direction of the speaker, but she reaches for his cheek and turns his face towards her, looks him right in the eye without blinking with her face so thin and solemn and hurt-looking that it can't be lied to and he starts to forget everything but the truth.

"Ain't nothing happening," he says. Then, after a long pause, "Anyways, not anymore. Maybe one time early on . . ."

"Lucas, I don't need the details. I understand that woman is going through a divorce, I know what things can be like for someone under that strain. With your size, and the age difference, you must be a refuge for her in a stormy time. And I can only guess what it must be for a man, exposed to temptation out on the solitude of the ocean. I even take partial responsibility because I know you asked me to work for you and I refused. But Lucas, for twenty years I've submerged myself in your life, and the children's lives, and now I'm determined to find my own. Do you know what this means to someone like me, who never got a day of education beyond high school, and has never traveled more than a few miles from home?"

"It ain't what it used to be," he says. "You been away a lot."

She starts crying when he says that. He looks over at Wilfred and Arvid's table. At the first sob the two of them stopped talking, and now they're staring over at the Lunts, Wilfred's blowing a smoke ring and Arvid Hannaford has his cigar stuck straight in his mouth like a turd in a dog's ass. Sarah's saying, "I *have* been away. I'm trying to cope with an empty nest, in my own way, and maybe take some of the financial burden off your shoulders. But it's not worth all the money on earth if it tears down what I wanted to support."

The tears are crusting on her cheeks, as if a damp easterly fog blew over and salted them down. She looks younger than when she was knocked up with Kyle and he proposed to her that summer evening in the cab of the '68 Dodge Power Wagon with the old small-block 318, toughest truck he ever owned, and despite its carburetor icing problems he can't separate it from his memories of early love. He has the impulse to lean forward over their salad bowls and take her face in his hands the way he did twenty-one years ago, but there's Ronette's brother-in-law staring right at them with a fried clam dangling from his tight little asshole mouth and the impulse to kiss anyone is lost.

"I'll fire her tomorrow," he says, "if that's what you want."

"Lucas, you've already claimed whatever was happening is over and I will take your word for it. I don't want you out there all alone. If you continue to keep it strictly business you can give her two weeks' notice, but meanwhile, for everyone's sake, I want you to be looking for someone else."

"That's pretty white of you," he says. "Don't know's I would of done that if it was me."

"There are women who wouldn't let you back in the house, but I believe in a second chance. Just this week Dr. Nichols's sermon was on the Prodigal Son."

"Speak of the devil."

"I will. I'm going to try and get Kyle home too."

"Jesus, Mother. Don't go overboard."

"I *am* going overboard. You know, I've been thinking of Hillary Clinton. She is a role model for all of us on turning the other cheek."

"Hope she don't turn it too fast," he says. "She's liable to rip his nose off."

"*Lucas.* We can start off by talking like civil human beings. Hillary Clinton is an admirable woman, and she's been a source of strength in my working through this. What she's had to put up with — that Jones person, who I must say does look a bit like Rhonda Hannaford on first glance."

"Nose is different," he points out.

She looks at him with her eyes angled up after this remark, like he's not her husband but a vinyl siding salesman she's never laid eyes on in her life.

"The nose *is* different," she says. "And I'm different from the first lady too. Because she seems to put up with repeat offenses. But you better listen carefully, Lucas Lunt, because you are not the president and you can't expect your wife to be part of a harem. If you have not completely separated yourself from the Hannaford woman, and hired a new sternman, two weeks from today, June fifteenth, which will be Kristen's graduation, I'll have no choice but to open our rainy-day fund and retain a lawyer."

She turns up the volume on those last words, like she's dragging in Arvid Hannaford as a witness.

"Ain't no need to," he says. "We'll get her straightened out."

The waitress refills their coffee to the halfway point and shoves the check under his saucer like she wants them to get out now before they cause a scene. The overhead speaker's still playing the Vince Gill tape.

> *Why can't I forget it*
> *Why can't I admit it*
> *There ain't no future in the past*

Arvid and Wilfred are sitting on the same side of their table poring over a list of figures when they leave. He swings out of the way to avoid them but Wilfred yells, "Hey Lunt. Check out the tuna rig on your way out, you may want to order one. Japanese pay nine thousand for a single fish."

Outside, he studies the big hull on its Brownell trailer. "*Miss Butterfly,* what kind of fairy name is that?"

"It's a nice name, Lucas, I think it's a Japanese opera."

"They ain't going to catch no fish with a name like that."

Then he sees the shafts. The props are five-bladed Michigan Hi-Torqs on three-inch stainless shafts. Behind each screw, halfway up the exposed shaft, something else glistens in the orange mall lot light: spurs. That son of a whore has put razor-sharp stainless steel cutting blades on each shaft. When he plows his way through a trap zone on the way to the tuna grounds he'll just slice off any pot warp he happens to encounter. Wilfred is going to leave lobstering with a vengeance.

"Got your eye on a new one?" Sarah asks. "Thought you were going to be loyal to *Wooden Nickel* right to the end."

He turns his head and spits in the direction of the tuna boat. "Wouldn't take one of them things if the government gave it to me."

He gets into the loaner and turns her over. Battery's so weak it's got about one flip left to it before it catches. His wife's looking up at him from the little Lynx. "Till death do us part," she says. "Remember."

Then she pulls out and leads him back to Orphan Point. He's still stuck in low-range four-wheel drive, however, and before too long the navy blue Lynx is out of sight.

When he reaches his house there's a red Mazda Miata in the drive, top up, Maryland plates, blocking his way to the garage. It would be a beautiful act to drive the big bald thirty-one-inch Wranglers right up and over the back of it just like the way they do it at Ben Schmidt's Monster Truck Show. Society, however, has a visegrip on his nuts just like everybody else's, and he stops short with one front tire about a half inch from the Miata's plastic bumper, the bow of the F-150 hanging like an aircraft carrier over its little trunk. Whoever it is, they'll need his permission to get out.

Sarah's waiting in the doorway with a grim tight-lipped whisper. *"For heaven's sake, Lucas, at least try and be nice."*

Inside, Kristen stands proudly in the door of the den with some classical thing playing behind her on *his* stereo, which is wired for country music and nothing else. "Thought you was only going to play that stuff upstairs," he reminds her. "It's bad for the speakers."

"Daddy, I'm entertaining. I want you to meet Nathan Hummerman. Nathan's from the family I'm working for."

Behind her is a red-haired little college boy with thick-lensed glasses that pop his eyes out like a haddock. The kid jumps from his own chair, looks up at Lucky, who's a head taller, then gropes for his hand like a blind man. Lucky plants both arms behind his back so the kid can't get at them. "Only shake hands when I buy something," he says.

"That's a good principle," the kid says. "I'll have to think about that. I've heard so much about you, Mr. Lunt. Kristen says you're totally unique. Believe me, I wanted to be a fisherman till I was twelve or thirteen."

"Oh yeah? What made you change your mind?"

Kristen steps between them same as she does with Kyle. "Nathan goes to Brandeis," she says. "He's premed."

"That your car out there, Nathan?"

"Yes, it is, sir." He stands straight, pushes the glasses right up against the meat of his eyes.

"How come you didn't get a Corvette?"

"I thought of a Corvette, but they get about ten miles to the gallon."

"What the hell," Lucky says, "there's plenty of oil down there. Ain't you heard? The whole fucking center of the earth is filled with oil, making more of it every day."

"It's OK, Daddy. We'll take the Brahms upstairs and finish listening. You can have your den back."

"Nice to meet you, Mr. Lunt, I'll remember what you said about shaking hands. About the oil reserves too. It's reassuring to know we'll never run out."

When Kristen leads him across the dining room towards the stairs the kid's arm jerks out and snakes itself around her waist. Lucky was just turning the Sox game on, but when he sees that move his spine freezes in place. "Just a minute, Kris. I got to go to bed anyway. Why don't you two stay down here."

The ball game is the Sox and the Orioles. The kid takes his arm off of Kristen's body and stands next to Lucky as Tim Wakefield shakes off a call and winds up. "Hey, there's Cal Ripken," the kid says. "I have a ball signed by him."

"What was you, in the stands?"

"No, my dad's one of the team's consulting physicians. He's their heart man. Cal Ripken came to dinner once, that's when he gave me the ball."

Both males are intent on the game now, with Kristen standing in the doorway saying, "Nathan, I'll be outside."

"Guess we're going to go, Mr. Lunt. Sorry I couldn't watch the whole game with you. I know some of the other players too."

"No shit," Lucky says. "Guess I'll go outside and move my truck."

He wakes for no reason at half past one. The house feels empty. Kristen's not home yet, her absence is like an open window. He lies there listening to Sarah's asthma, every spring it gets worse with all the pollen around. A truck passes on the road, Dodge Ramcharger with twin pipes, probably Stevie Latete weaving home from the RoundUp at closing time. A boat leaves the harbor, way too early for lobstering; that would be Noah Parker's pilot boat heading out to meet an offshore tanker bound up the Tarratine River to offload at the Exxon dock. He hears the sheriff's cruiser, a Chevy Caprice with a well-muffled 350 V-8 under the hood, snow studs still whining cause the town didn't vote any money for summer tires. His ears are silenced for the next two minutes by a deep-throated Harley twin coming down the hill from Norumbega, downshifting when it meets the cruiser, then racing off towards Burnt Neck, making sure nobody's going to hear anything for a while. He hears Bobby Whelan's Mercedes reefer truck, heavy with shellfish, starting off on the Boston clam run.

Then he hears the Miata accelerating out of the village and downshifting as it gets near, four little cylinders but he has to admit they've got them tuned. It turns into the driveway and stops and he can relax. But then the doors don't open. What the hell. They must be talking, and he hears some kind of rock and roll filtering his way. He thinks of the old pickup he had in high school, not his really but his old man Walter's, '61 Chevy stepside with a bench seat you could lie right down and fuck somebody on if she was short enough. The night he took Dolores Thurston to the Riceville Fair, it was the first time he ever saw a girl's tits in real life, she was smoking a cigarette and blowing smoke down across her chest so the nipples stuck out in the saltwater moonlight like a couple of brand-new pencil erasers. Just a blink of time's gone by and now she's a wrinkly Mormon grandmother with snow-white hair.

Sarah turns over and says, "Lucas, are you all right? What time is it?"

"I'm all right."

"You were breathing like you were going to die."

"Dreaming, I guess."

"Are Kristen and Nathan back?" She sits up, draws the blanket over her chest and listens. The cruiser goes by again.

"I heard the car," he says, "but she ain't come in."

"Well call her in, Lucas, it's a school night and that girl has final exams. Besides, aren't you worried? You didn't even want them to go upstairs."

"What the hell?" he says. "They ain't going to do nothing in a Miata." He goes to the window and looks down. Sarah gets up and draws the top blanket off and joins him, wrapping the cover around her thin shoulders like a nun.

"Cold," she says, "for this time of year."

They both gaze down on the foreign vehicle that looks too small to contain two grown human beings. It's not rocking, at least. He can see one of their arms on one side, one on the other. "Just talking," he says.

She lets one side of the blanket fall and puts an arm gently on his back. "They do a lot of talking, Lucas."

"They ain't like us." He lets himself put an arm around her shoulders, looking down at the little car.

"You had me pregnant before we had a conversation."

They hear the door close as they're getting back in bed. Downstairs the refrigerator opens, closes. The lights snap off, Kristen's footsteps climb the stairs. With the sound of a furious Chinese locust the Miata heads off for the head of the harbor, and pretty soon he hears it on Summer Street, all the way down the Money shore till it comes to the Hummermans' house on the point directly across from them. There it dies and the night is quiet again. In an hour and a half he'll be rowing out to his mooring in the fog.

6

B ACK AT THE STERN, Ronette looks like she's yelling at something halfway to the horizon but no sound's coming out of her mouth, then come these little squeaks, then, "Holy shit, Lucky, it's a *WHALE!*"

She's got an unbanded lobster flapping in one hand and Ginger's collar in the other to hold her back, looks like the dog wants to jump in and retrieve the fucking thing. With her rubber bib down and no bra and a snapping lobster in hand, his sternperson stands a very good chance of losing a tit. Now she's climbed up on the washboard with the dog beside her, and she's pointing straight at the horizon so he can see right down the armhole of her top, a nice-looking woman he's not allowed to fuck. He hasn't told her yet, but for the next few days she's just a sternman, then she's gone. "This ain't a nature cruise, Ronette. See one of them things, you've seen them all." He pulls the *Wooden Nickel* up to another trapline, in four fathoms, gaffs the buoy and slings the warp over the davit. Ronette's saying something, though, so he pauses before throwing her in gear.

"Yeah? Well, I never seen one. When I went with Reggie, he never let me look at nothing. Hope it comes up again, they get me right in the stomach."

"Scared?"

"No, scared ain't it. Something else. I used to get that stomach feeling when I was a kid in church. Only other time, might of been right here on this boat . . ." Her tanned face turns a little red, she walks over to the trap hauler and leans on him. "Church and you, Mr. Lucky Lunt, them's the only other times."

"Well, it ain't Sunday, and we ain't after whales. Take a good look, then get back to work."

"Ain't you the crab today? You biting?" She takes his hand and moves the thumb in and out like a lobster claw. He pulls away, kicks in the pot hoist and grinds up a double. The first one's full of rock crabs and a big green eel that he tries to grab but it squirms off and over the side. The second one has a clawless pistol and two culls. He slides the traps back to her on the side deck, she baits them and wipes her hands on the oilskin bib, grabs the two bandits and slips the elastics on. The pistols always disgust him a bit, like a girl with no legs. He throws it to a big blackback seagull following behind. Funny thing, that bloody wing on the antenna keeps the regular gulls off but not the blackbacks, though it came off one of their own.

It's hot. Lucky's got his shirt off under the Grundens oilpants, his flesh is bulging out through the side openings between bib and suspenders. Ronette can't resist giving him a squeeze like she's kneading a loaf of fresh white hairy bread. He knows there's nothing but a pair of cutoffs under her orange Grundens, which are hanging down in front with the straps astray. Her purple tank top's soaked from the salt water and herring guts. High Country 104's playing Tracy Byrd's "Don't Love Make a Diamond Shine," only song on the airwaves this week. Howard Thurston's hauling maybe half a mile off to starboard in the big calm seas, his boat going mostly under a swell when Ronette yells, "Whale! There it is again!"

He thinks of the shotgun under the wheelhouse deck, his hand trembles a bit like whenever he sees a moose feeding alongside the road, old itch goes back to when men were hunters at the start of time.

"Wonder what would happen," he says, "if you shot one of them son of a whores?"

"Jesus, Lucky, they wouldn't even feel it. They got skin a foot thick. You know what I heard? A whale's heart weighs more than a Volkswagen. Think of it, Luck, just the heart. How could you shoot something with a heart that big? They ain't bothering you."

"I don't trust them bastards. One of them things could cruise through a trapline and eat the whole fucking business, pots and all. That guy Moby Dick was on the right track, stick a harpoon in every fucking one of them."

"Lucky, I think Moby Dick was the whale."

"Jesus Christ, Ronette, didn't you learn nothing over in Split Cove? Moby Dick was this one-legged skipper out of New Bedford, he killed so many whales the government shut down the fishery. And them bastards was just warming up. Few more years and we won't be able to catch a god damn thing, we'll all be working for Bill Gates. The Japs have a good thing going with whales."

"What's that, Lucky?" She's baiting traps fast now, not even looking up.

"They grind them into cat food."

"One of them things would feed a lot of god damn cats."

"They eat them in sushi too, that's what I heard. They just don't talk about it, they're scared them Greenpiss hippies will drop another atom bomb on them."

"Lucky, did you ever think of going back and finishing up high school?"

"What for? A lobster don't ask if you got a fucking diploma."

"I was just wondering, that's all. I mean, you got all this knowledge, you ought to have something to show for it."

"I know one thing. One of them cocksucking whales will take more lobsters than a herd of seals."

"That ain't what I heard, I heard their mouths was so small they can't even swallow a sardine. If that's true they sure as hell ain't going to eat any lobsters."

"Shows all you know. Some of them has small mouths, some of them don't. How the fuck are they supposed to know they got small mouths? They don't give a shit, they trash your gear anyway. One of them things goes through your gear, you're fucked. It's them or us. Survival of the fittest." He reaches into the cuddy door and feels for the familiar oiled wood of his shotgun stock, just to be sure it's there. He's got a twelve-gauge slug that would stop a rhinoceros. "Son of a whore comes up again, I'm going to shoot it. Millionaire Greenpiss activists fuck the little guy every time."

"Lucky, you ain't the little guy. What are you, six-two, two-fifty?"

"That ain't what I meant. The world ain't physical no more, Ronette. That kind of size don't mean nothing."

"Means something to me." She quivers her tits like blueberry Jell-o under the purple tank top, gives him a little smile that harpoons down his spinal column almost to the dicktip before it runs into a voice saying, *Lucas, look but don't touch.* All of a sudden the whale's in closer and it sticks its fin up again like some government bureaucrat giving you the finger. The dog goes crazy, leaping up and barking like she's about to swim out and bite it. Ronette says, "You got one on your side, anyway."

"You ain't exempt," he says to Ginger. "We'll eat a few of you too while we're at it."

After a couple more strings Ronette steps right out of her oil-skins from the heat and shakes her hair out from under the red kerchief she uses to keep it out of the winch. Everything's in motion under the tank top. "Like what you see, don't you?"

"I might but I ain't looking."

"Ain't for you anyhow. Cruelty to animals don't get to first base with me."

"I didn't do nothing, did I? Let's haul some traps."

"It's wicked hot, Lucky. How about cooling off below instead?"

He turns to her with a big rock crab in one hand, the other on the bronze spoke of the wheel. "Ronette, there's something I got to tell you."

"There's something I got to tell you too, Lucky, but it can wait till we been below. It's been a week at least, ain't it? I lose track of time out in the sun."

He hoists a trap over the rail and slides it aft to Ronette. Right when she's got her hand in the parlor end pulling the culls and starfish out, he tells her. "The arrangement don't seem to be working out. I got to get somebody else as sternman, after today."

She finishes pulling a big two-pounder out of the hole and turns to face him, her kelp-colored eyes wide open and the lobster snapping away in her right hand. "What the hell, Lucky. Ain't I been good enough?"

"It ain't that, Ronette. You're a good worker and I'll tell anyone you want to go sternman for. Finest kind. But I ain't had no peace since you went and told Sarah out at Kyle's."

"I didn't say nothing to your wife."

"She thinks you did."

"Thinks I said what?"

"'Go ask your husband,' something like that. Anyway, it got her full of piss and I got to let you go."

"She's a smart one," Ronette says, going for another lobster. "Why?"

"I didn't say nothing like that. I never even talked to her. She got suspicious and she trapped you. You're like a god damn pea-brained lobster, you crawled right into it."

"Maybe she trapped me, maybe not."

From one hand she's dangling a small green cull that's not even struggling. It hangs there limp as if it's dead. "Don't I mean nothing to you, Lucky?"

He lights a Marlboro but the first puff tastes like creosote and he spits over the rail. The sky's graying over with high fog. A big black rusty Shag Island trawler crosses their path, close enough to read the name off her stern: *Black Angel.* He lets the warp slack over the winch drum and braces for the wake. "I can't leave Sarah," he says. "She ain't up to taking care of herself. Other day, her right-hand wiper blade come off and she couldn't even fix it, she let the wiper arm carve a groove into the windshield."

The trawler's wake comes through and kicks up the port quarter so high that Ginger slides off into the saltwater tank and leaps out vibrating and spraying. Ronette has to grab Lucky's apron and hang on, the cull coming to life and snapping at her hand.

On High Country 104, Garth Brooks sings "It's Midnight, Cinderella."

I gotta few new magic tricks
Your godmother can't do

Ronette stands there holding the lobster with Ginger beside her and says, "Lucky, it ain't going to be that easy. I been sick the last three mornings in a row."

"What do you mean, sick?"

"I mean sick, that's what I mean. What does it mean when a woman takes her first sip of coffee and throws up? I ain't been this late since I was twelve years old. Three weeks."

"I thought you said Clyde couldn't have no kids."

"It ain't Clyde."

"What do you mean, it ain't Clyde?"

"I ain't even seen Clyde except to swap off Ginger and at the lawyer's office. I ain't seen no one, Lucky. Outside of you."

He turns away and puts the pot warp around the davit and hauls a deep one up from seven fathoms. It's got two nice keepers in there and a bonus of three or four fat-clawed crabs hanging from the bait bag. She stands there waiting for some kind of answer, not laying a hand on the trap, so he does her work of pulling them out and banding them as if she isn't even there. He takes the watch out of his apron pocket. It's one-thirty. He's got to get in, get unloaded and get to his daughter's high school graduation, first Lunt that ever made it through. "What do you mean, outside of me?"

"This ain't no Hannaford, Lucky, and I sure as hell didn't clone it. It's a Lunt."

"What do you mean, it? It ain't nothing. I ain't even known you that long."

"Five weeks tomorrow. That was the first time, remember? You about had a heart attack. That must of done it. I got one of them Dewline home pregnancy tests at the Rite Aid and it came out green as grass. It's a wonder you ain't got seventy-eight kids like Saddam Hussein, cause you're like the Burpee seed catalog. Guaranteed to sprout. Won't Clyde have a big surprise."

"Clyde don't need to know, does he?"

"Well he's sure as shit going to know when I drive past with a baby seat in the back. Damn creep. All that stuff coming out of him and nothing in it. Might as well been Ivory Liquid. Fake. Like the whole damn family. You know his brother Arvid's kids are adopted? I never told you that. That skinny bitch Yvonne got herself laid by one of them surrogate doctors, that's what Clyde told me, and when that didn't work they bought them kids in New York City. Ever wonder how they got that Puerto Rican look? The whole christly Hannaford line, it's a dead end."

"Well you still got a few weeks to decide," Lucky says.

"Decide on what? There ain't no deciding to do."

"Ain't going to be easy, raising a kid by yourself. You got no money to speak of, you're never going to get nothing off of Clyde."

"I counted on working for you, Lucky. You and Doris. Doris will be the godmother. She was kind of around when things got going."

He baits the last trap himself and throws it off the stern. "I got to get back now," he says. "It's Kristen's graduation. She's the first Lunt in history that ever finished up."

"And she's going to college. You ought to be proud of her."

"She don't need college. She's too god damn smart already."

He reaches behind the radar screen for a Marlboro and lights it with a Bic lighter, as the manifold has gone cold with all the idling. Then he puts her in gear, points the bow for South Sodom Ledge, east-northeast, and shoves the Morse lever almost to the stop. The big Chevy V-8 explodes with a message of power and freedom that erases the word *pregnant* like it was never spoken. In ten seconds she's stern down and the loran's reading eighteen knots, taking the long way around so he doesn't disturb Howard Thurston, who's still working traps, and Lonnie Gross just beyond. Lonnie's daughter's throwing bait off the stern with a cloud of seagulls around her like she's the most attractive creature in the world. Shows what the fuck birds know.

He's got her slowed down after the Orphan Ledge nun where it gets shallow and there's a raft with a divers' flag in the cove. He stays slow at the narrows, where he's squeezed in by Noah Parker's pilot boat with the big numbers on the coach roof: 772503. What a racket, Noah gets a thousand bucks each for bringing the cocksuckers in, he doesn't even do the work, just watches over the shoulder of some Liberian captain with a row of silent Arabs on the foredeck, not a word of English between them so Noah doesn't even have to talk. A thousand bucks just to stand there guzzling his rum and coffee on the bridge.

He gives Noah the finger as he goes by, Noah gives him a big wave back and steals a long look at Ronette Hannaford perched up on the washboard in her cutoff shorts, knees crossed, already scraping barnacles off the rock crabs. Their two wakes meet in the narrow space bounded by ledges and tide rips, causing a confusing little chop, but he throttles her up a hair and she cuts right through. Ronette comes up behind him as he steers, lights a Marlboro off of his, reaches over his shoulder to turn the radio up for Reba's "I Won't Mention It Again." In the rush of V-8 speed, she presses her belly up against his back and a deep shock goes through him like she's carrying an electric eel. "What about tomorrow?" she shouts.

"If I want you tomorrow I'll call you at half past four."

He lights another Marlboro off the hot engine stack. They're inside the ledges now and the water is calm and smooth. Off to the westward, ranging north from the big Johnson estate, there's a string of dark-shingled mansions with turrets and hidden porches that look like Dracula's castle. Anyone ever spent a winter in one, they'd hang themselves.

"We used to call that Kotex Point," he yells. "Guy that ran the Kotex company lived there."

"I wish I'd of known you back then, Lucky, you must of been an interesting kid."

"You wasn't even born."

"I was an angel, waiting to come down. That's what my momma used to say."

"You're still an angel, Ronette."

"A pregnant angel. They don't show those ones on the Christmas cards."

Most of the moorings are still empty because the summer people have not really arrived yet, but there's one big new dark blue sailboat out there, still got the hull wax on, two million in her easy, satellite dome on the spreaders so he can chat with his broker in the Cayman Islands, big chrome windlass on the foredeck so he won't get a hernia hauling chain. Think of the poor bastards breathing fiberglass dust over to Bunny Whelan's boatyard, emphysema, workman's comp for a few years, then so long Sam. Glass lung. Place is worse than a coal mine, all so some rich bastard can go nowhere at five miles an hour.

He says out loud, "Every one of them things is some son of a bitch screwing the working man." Then he slows down, edges a point to starboard so he can see behind the canvas dodger and there they are, five or six of them in the cockpit not doing a god damn thing, getting drunk while the money comes gushing down the mast from the satellite. Look at the bloodsuckers, three in the afternoon, swilling martinis like a bilge pump. Come suppertime they'll reach over and pull up some poor lobsterman's trap and steal a day's catch, living off the labor of others, worse parasites than a colony of fucking seals. "Son of a whores," Lucky yells and heads right towards them, turning the throttle to 2200 rpm.

"Who? You still ragging on the whales?"

"You talk about whales, take a look at them fatass pigs, you think they ever done a day's work?"

"Christ sake, Lucky," she screams over the engine, "they're on *vacation*. This is supposed to be Vacationland, ain't it?"

"Ain't no vacationland for the ones that live here, it's Work Your Ass Off for Nothingland. They should have the cons stamp *that* on the license plates." He heads right for the stainless steel barbecue grill smoking off the stern rail, no doubt full of stolen lobsters.

"Lucky," she screeches, "what are you *doing?*"

He steams the *Wooden Nickel* right at them till he gets about fifty feet off their stern. He comes so close he can read the name off the transom in big gold metallic letters, probably fourteen-karat leaf like the church steeple. *Zauberflöte,* whatever the fuck that means. Then he swerves hard to starboard so they'll catch a nice fat quarter wave and turns away. "Fucking Krauts. Should of finished them off when we had the chance." He pins the throttle so they won't be able to read his boat name in the cloud of spray, smokes eastward across the harbor towards the Split Ledge beacon at twenty-two knots on the loran. Ronette has got the binoculars and she's looking back over the stern. "Jesus, Lucky, you destroyed them, their table's fell over, they look like they're drenched, and now they're all going down below."

"Fucking bloodsuckers, it's a good place for them."

He gooses the engine and swings east, they're past the Split Ledge can in about two minutes, out of sight of those bastards, so he throttles down now to thirteen knots as they pick up the Split Cove channel buoy sequence. Then he spots a plastic lobster boat he's never seen before, little one, looks like a Vern Eaton twenty-two with a Merc outdrive and a pink-and-white buoy speared on the radio whip. "Ain't that cunning," he says. "Pink and white."

"What's the matter with that?"

"Ain't a fisherman's color."

"It is now."

Not only that, they're setting traps in two fathoms just north of Split Ledge. Vern makes a decent boat, ruins it with a stern drive, then he puts a little bathroom in them so they can wash their hands after handling the catch.

The name on the transom is:

ALICE B. TOKLAS
Split Point

"Don't seem like a name from around here," he says.

There's a couple of squared-off rugged figures on board setting and hauling, both of them women. They've got matching yellow aprons so new they still have the factory creases in them, they're waving at Lucky and shouting what sounds like "Ahoy!"

Ronette waves back. "I know them, Lucky, they're the two summer ladies from down on Eastern Head."

"But how the hell are they setting on Split Ledge? That's neutral territory between Split Cove and us, been that way for fifty years. Nobody sets there. It's all sand anyway, ain't no catch to speak of off of sand."

"I heard they *bought* Split Ledge."

"Jesus H. Christ. Split Ledge is a *landmark.* Can't buy a fucking landmark."

"Money can buy anything, Lucky. You ought to know that."

"Couldn't buy you."

She leans up close to him and whispers, "Want to know something else? I hear they're lesbians. That's what Reggie Dolliver says."

"How would he know? He inclined that way himself?"

"Course he ain't. Reggie's a man."

"Spend a while in the joint, anything can happen."

"Reggie wired their home for a security system. That's how he knows. That's Reggie's new job, residential security."

"No shit. Ain't that the fox in the henhouse?"

"He can wire your whole house and connect it direct to the sheriff's office. He was telling me."

"He's connected direct himself, ain't he?" Then he looks over and one of the women's pulling a big snapping lobster out of the trap, then another, even bigger, flapping its tail, bending ass backward trying to bite off her hand. They're pulling them in as fast as they can band them. "Bottom must of changed," he says. "Didn't use to be no lobsters on Split Ledge."

Ronette stands close to him now and takes his hand down by the fuel switch as if she didn't want it to be seen. She puts the other hand on a wheel spoke, so they're both steering in. "I ought to learn to drive this thing, case anything happens to you."

"Ain't nothing going to happen."

"Watch your heart, then. Don't get so mad at things. And stop smoking. We may be needing you around."

"What the fuck. *You* smoke."

"Not anymore. I thrown them away. From now on, I'm breathing for two." They're in the channel now, Split Cove boats all around, they're all giving him the finger from under the gunwale where he can't see it, otherwise he'd blow their fucking windshields out. Then she says, "Hey Lucky, we're almost home. We ain't even talked about it yet."

He lets her steer and backs off to lean up against the hauler so he can give her a long hard look, he's getting farsighted. He can see the horizon sharper and sharper but when he gets close onto something it blurs up. "You spend considerable time with that Reggie Dolliver," he says.

"What's that supposed to mean?"

"Means what it means. Something could be his, well as mine."

Slap.

With no warning she lets go of his hand and whacks him so hard across the ear he has to hang on to the pot hauler so he doesn't go over the side. When he opens his eyes and looks at her she hits him again. "You are lower than a snake's asshole," she says. "You're even worse than that fucker Clyde."

Then with his good ear he hears a double horn blast like it's right on top of the boat.

"Christly fuck." He grabs the wheel out of her hand and jams it hard over. The *Wooden Nickel* just misses bashing a big rusty Split Cove scalloper with four screaming bastards on the rail, every frigging one of them pumping the finger at him while the huge black-

haired captain dives down below for his deer rifle. Then they realize Ronette was steering and they double up laughing and turn back on their course. The scalloper's wake throws half the water out of the saltwater tank. Three or four nice lobsters splash onto the wash-board, bounce off and they're gone. Ginger's barking like she's gone rabid, Ronette tries to grab the exhaust stack to steady herself and backs off with her hand smoking, everything slides off the radar shelf: cigarettes, lunch pails, socket wrenches, crashing onto the cockpit floor. He turns back from the wheel to read the name *Big Lizzie* on their stern as they steam off. All the Split Covers are still on the transom, three of them doubled up laughing and the fourth one hanging onto the drag vanes while he takes a leak over the stern.

"You ain't going to steer no more," Lucky rules. "That's it."

"Don't be so nervous. We didn't hit them, did we?"

"We came pretty god damned christly close. Cunt hair closer and we'd of been stove in."

"What was you saying about Reggie Dolliver?"

"Nothing," he says.

"That's cause there ain't nothing to say. You may think I been running around, Lucky, but I ain't. I exercise Ginger, sleep, listen to Rush Limbaugh, watch a little TV. That's it. Couple days I work for Doris. And I work for you." She pauses. "Only it's going to be different now. I don't give a shit if Clyde gets the dog or the Probe or whatever the fuck he wants, cause I'm going to have me a little family of my own."

"A woman don't have to have no kids if she don't want them. It ain't like the old days when me and Sarah had to get married. Whole matter could end right here."

"What do you mean, end?"

"You know what I mean. End. Like it never begun."

"Jesus H. Christ, Lucky Lunt. Mr. Pro-Life himself. He sure had us fooled, didn't he, Ginger?"

"Don't get me wrong," he says. "I ain't for them partial births. Them kids are already alive, got a brain and everything, right in the hospital dumpster."

"I got news for you, Lucky. This one's already alive too. It's half you, so's I don't know about the brain part, but it's in there and it ain't coming out till New Year's Day."

"New Year's?"

"That's right. It's due in January but they come out faster if you drink in the last month, so we'll make it the New Year's baby and we'll get a trailer full of stuff, they give you everything, crib, toys, diapers, most of what we'll need for a whole year. Come December I'll just start having a beer or two a day, they say that loosens them up."

"You ain't supposed to," he says. "It could get deformed."

"It ain't going to get deformed in the last couple weeks, it's all done by then. Anyhow, what do you care?"

"I don't. I'm just saying it, that's all. If you drink, it could come out deformed. It says so right on the fucking bottle. Then would you feel like shit or what?"

"OK. Only if I don't drink, we stand to miss on the New Year's stuff."

"You're saying 'we,'" he says, "but I ain't decided nothing."

"You don't have to," she yells. "I decided for both of us."

He swerves quick to port to avoid a couple of wet-suited scuba divers in an outboard with the striped diver's flag. He looks twice to see if it could be Kyle and Darrell Swan, but it's a pair of long-haired Split Cove guys that look like Navahos. He gives them the finger. "Right in the fucking channel, nice place to park."

"I got you figured," she shouts over the engine noise. "You're pro-life for everyone with one big exception. You."

"It ain't me," he shouts back, "it's a medical condition. I got a bad heart."

"I got news for you, Lucky. You don't even know it, but you got a good heart. One of the best."

"The fuck I do. This thing last winter, if that don't work I may be going in for a valve job. And if *that* don't work . . ."

"I ain't talking about *that* heart, Lucky."

"I got news for you. I ain't only got but one."

At this point they're through the Split Cove thoroughfare and throttling down as the *Wooden Nickel* comes up on the waterfront. The sun's still high and the tide's down. The summer algae bloom hasn't struck yet so the water's still clear. As it shallows up near the float he can see under the surface, big square granite pier blocks with blasting scars and starfish all over them, three or four old engines rusting on the bottom, a railroad wheel, an outboard, a toilet, a snowmobile, a refrigerator, a couple of bikes: god damn Split Covers just drive up and throw their lives off the fucking pier. Over on the co-op's stone wharf a big Oregon-style trawler is getting its hold sucked out by the vacuum pump. It's from someplace down east, Cape Maliseet. He's never seen her before, it's probably a one-time fling cause Split Cove's paying a better price. He's heard they don't pay shit for nothing down there, fog all the time, Canadians steal your lobsters, nothing but French TV. "At least we ain't there," he says out loud, but she doesn't know what he's talking about.

"You still going to fire me, Lucky?"

"I'll figure that out when I call you. Four A.M."

"Don't call, cause I ain't going to be home. I'm going to be down here waiting."

Up on the pierhead a rusted-out Mazda B-200 pickup sticks its tailgate over the side, big red bumper sticker saying,

UNLESS YOU'RE A HEMORRHOID
GET OFF MY ASS

"Hey Lucky. Check that bumper sticker out. Tell me they ain't clever around here."

"They just *bought* the god damn thing, Ronette, they didn't write it." On second thought, it would have been a good one to slap on the loaner before giving it back to Virgil Carter, but it's too late now, he's got his GMC back.

Before leaping off, she puts her arm around him and gives him a wet kiss right on the mouth. Her hair smells of lobster bait, her purple tank top is soaked with fish guts, but inside she tastes like a warm live strawberry and for a moment he forgets graduation, pregnancy, the wrath of Sarah, his lost children, the staring brain-dead Split Cove fishermen, and just lets his head dive below the surface for a while.

Then he hears a bunch of the local unemployed, which is most of them, gagging and giggling at the scene. He puts his finger up in the direction of the biggest one and kisses it. Ronette grabs the finger and folds it back into his fist. "You got to act civilized around here," she says. "Them's your relatives now."

Except for a funeral or two, he hasn't had a tie around his neck since he stopped going to church after his prayers were finally answered and Reagan sent Jimmy Carter back to the peanut farm. He can tie a sheet bend between a one-inch hawser and a piece of fishing line, he can tie a rolling timber hitch, he can tie an anchor bend under water, a tugboat hitch with one hand in pitch blackness, but right now he's standing in front of the mirror bloody from three shaving cuts, one end of the necktie in each hand and he can't figure out how to make the fucking knot. No matter how hard he tries, the big end is up around his collarbone and the small end dangles down to his crotch. Finally his wife comes in and says, "It's not an eye splice, Lucas. It's just a necktie." She takes the two ends in hand and in two or three strokes she's tucking the short piece where it belongs under the JC Penney label and he's ready to go. "Remember, we're meeting the Hummermans tonight."

"I know that. But how come? They ain't got kids in that school."

"Kristen has invited them, that's how come. She and Nathan have grown quite close, and I think it's good for her, he'll give her a little taste of college life."

"Hope that's all she tastes."

"*Lu*cas. They are a very refined family, so for God's sake try and put a leash on your language, especially at the table. And just because the Hummermans made the reservations, be sure not to let them pay the check."

"Why the hell not? They already got all our money, they might as well hand some back."

"Lucas, they don't have our money."

"Thing about you is, Sarah, you ain't got a head for economics. Once you start giving to the medical profession, they all share the pie."

"You haven't given anything, Lucas. All those cardiology bills are still unpaid. You are a tax write-off as far as the medical profession goes."

"Fucking vultures." He digs out the black wool sport coat he got for Stubby Gross's funeral, but the moths have got to it and it looks like he got shotgunned in the back. "Surprise, surprise," Sarah says. She's got a box with a brand-new size 48 blazer in it, and it fits his chest and shoulders smooth as shrink-wrap. She pats the coat into place and pulls the collar out over the tie. "No two ways about it, you're still a very handsome man. You ought to dress up more often. Too bad you stopped going to church. Dr. Nichols has some very thoughtful sermons, not boring like Reverend Platt."

"Biggest god damn racket in the history of the world. They're up there telling you how to live, next moment they're in the back room with the altar boys."

"Lucas, there aren't any altar boys in the Methodist church."

He drags his wristwatch out through the blazer sleeve. "Let's go. I'll follow you, cause I ain't even sure where the damn place is."

"Lucas, it's your children's high school."

"They should of kept the school right in Orphan Point. Ever seen the cars around there? Range Rovers. Audis. They wouldn't let a fish truck in the parking lot."

"At least you don't have that awful black one that Virgil Carter lent you, with the muffler scraping the road. Say, maybe you could get your sternperson to lend you her little Mustang or whatever it is."

"Come on, Sarah, let it alone. We got a daughter to graduate. We ain't going to see it if we don't haul ass."

He wakes up to this huge noise like a ship is holed and there's water roaring through the bulkheads both fore and aft. He clears his eyes and steadies his spine in the folding metal chair. He's not at sea, he's in a high school auditorium and everyone's clapping so he starts clapping too, Sarah right beside him with Nathan Hummerman on the other side of her, then Mrs. Elsie Hummerman, a cute little lady with rust-stained hair and diamond earrings and nice plump freckly tits peeping out over the rim of her summer dress. It's not clear to Lucky how such a bald owly little guy is married to that red-haired sexy low-cut woman. Maybe it's money, you can see she's a spender. Kristen says she's remodeling her whole kitchen in polished granite. Tonight she's got more jewelry on than Princess Di.

He whispers to his wife, "What'd I miss?"

"It was a very good speech," she whispers back. "He talked about global warming."

He puts his hands in back of his head and stretches, cracks his knuckles, tries to glance sidewards around his wife's neck and get a better angle on Mrs. Elsie Hummerman's sleeveless dress. You can see a lot of cleavage any Saturday night in the RoundUp but it's mostly on fat women, which doesn't count. This one has skinny tan arms, probably from tennis, and bony shoulders like Sarah's but she's built like Ronette on top, maybe her husband slipped some of the saline in. Then for no reason his heart misses a beat, just stops in midair, waits about three seconds, then kicks in hard. He remembers he skipped his pill this morning because he was getting ready to fire his sternperson and that medicine can soften his will power like ice cream in the sun. Now he could use one but the pills are in the truck. He closes his eyes and thinks of taking a carburetor apart, step by step, till the heart rhythm goes normal and he can breathe. Hummerman squints over at him for a moment, then straightens around again. Short guy like that, hands like a little kid's, he doesn't look strong enough to saw your chest open. He must use a power tool.

Up on the stage, which seems a long distance away, the procession of graduates is filing towards the center, couple of wheelchairs in front ramping up beside the stairs, then the short kids, then the middle ones, including Kristen, who smiles towards the sea of parents and takes the diploma from the principal and lifts her long white gown off the floor so she can make the steps. He's glad he woke up for it. Grandpa Merritt Lunt didn't go past the sixth grade. Lucky's own father, Walter, back in the Depression, only made it through the eighth. Walter Lunt was fishing full-time by the time he was fourteen. Lucky himself dropped out right near the end of junior year, not much of a family for the books, but now a Lunt is walking off the stage with her diploma and sliding the tassel to the other side of her square graduation cap. College track too, course that's the easiest, they don't have to do anything but read.

On the chest of her white gown Kristen displays a small red loop ribbon, probably some kind of award. She did win a bunch of them, she got the scholarship from the Kiwanis and split the one from the Odd Fellows with some kid who was supposed to be the smartest one in the school. A few others in the line have the same decoration, mostly girls, not that they're smarter but they do have less energy so they can study more. He asks Sarah, "What's the ribbon for?"

She whispers, "It's for AIDS."

A chill goes through him. A bunch of them have those ribbons, and every one of them looks sick. No wonder she's been acting strange this spring. He feels the sweat of fear breaking out on his face, then a spike of anger at the perverts and radicals in that degenerate town. They should have home-schooled her, they never should have put her on the bus. He looks at Sarah with the sweat flowing over his collar where the shirt is suddenly so tight it's strangling him. "Goodness," she says. "What's wrong?" She turns and flashes a look over to Dr. Hummerman like she's glad he's near.

He manages to whisper, "All of them got it?"

"All who, Lucas?"

"All the ones with ribbons. They all got the AIDS?"

A big smile breaks out on her face and she goes right to work loosening the tie and unfastening the top button while she speaks close into his ear so he can feel her breath. "AIDS *awareness,* dear. They're members of a support group." She gives him a squeeze on the arm as Kristen returns to the rows of seated graduates. "Aren't you proud of her, Lucas? Our little girl."

Dr. Hummerman flashes Lucky a thumbs-up and a big smile like it's *his* daughter graduating. Then she's back in her seat and the last of the basketball freaks are striding across the stage and it's time for them all to hit the Chinese restaurant, which is okay with Lucky because his child is cured of AIDS and he's suddenly starved.

Out in the school parking lot, Dr. Hummerman congratulates him and shakes his hand. In the grip of delicate small fingers that can slice your heart open and stitch all the little veins back up, Lucky's own hand feels stiff and useless as a lobster claw. "This must be a gratifying event for you," the surgeon says. "She's a poised and accomplished girl. We already think of her as one of the family."

In the Mei Lai Pavilion restaurant, Mrs. Elsie Hummerman orders Moo Shoo Gay Something, her husband orders Straw Mushrooms with Bean Curd, Kristen orders Tofu Kung Fu, Sarah orders a General Sow's Chicken but her daughter clears her throat and says, "Mother, what did you promise me about meat?" She changes it to something that sounds like Bow Wow Fried Rice — and it's his turn. The little Chinese waitress stands over him tapping her pencil on her order pad. The menu's fourteen pages long, mostly in Chinese, and he's got to choose, good thing they put pictures beside the drinks. He points to a Fog Cutter that Sarah lets him order because it's graduation night. He points to the lobster image and the waitress says, "Lobster Kowloon."

He's been handling lobsters all his life but the Lobster Kowloon is like nothing he's ever smelled or seen. He keeps ordering Fog Cutters till the food blurs enough so he can approach it. Sarah whispers in his ear, "Try using the chopsticks, Lucas. You're the only one at the table using a fork."

He whispers back, "It's like going after a dog turd with a pair of oars." She turns her head away and starts talking to freckly Elsie Hummerman on the other side.

Kristen, who's seated on his right, puts the two sticks between his fingers and shows him how. He manages to haul up a small poisonous mushroom shaped like the umbrella in his drink, not to eat it but to shove it under his dinner plate, but it hits the rim and falls into his lap. He says to Kristen, "No wonder they're all starving over there. They can't pick up their christly food."

"They're not starving," Kristen says. "Chinese babies learn to use chopsticks at the age of two. Look over there!" Sure enough, there's a Chinese family across the room with five or six little Chinese kids, chopsticks in hand, every one of them scooping up the fried rice like a backhoe.

Lucky's poking around his plate looking for something to eat, without much success. "Ain't no lobster in here."

"Don't be silly," Sarah says. "It's not our kind of lobster. It's *Chinese* lobster. There's a world of difference."

He manages to pick up a dark stringy little knot of something, and with Kristen's hand beneath it all the way, he raises it to his mouth. He hails another little Chinese waitress walking past in a red dress. "Excuse me, miss. This ain't lobster. It tastes like cocker spaniel."

"*Lucas.*" Sarah hisses at him but the waitress didn't seem to notice at all.

Dr. Hummerman reaches across the table and puts his hand on Sarah's to calm her down. "I was in Seoul just a couple of months ago," he says, "and I did get a taste of man's best friend. It was an option on the appetizer list. I didn't expect I'd like it but the tenderness surprised me. Like everything else, it's all in the preparation."

"See?" Lucas turns in triumph to his wife.

This Hummerman may be all right after all.

Elsie Hummerman says, "Really, Mr. Lunt, it's a delight to have Kristen working at our house. She's worth her weight in gold. We can't wait till she moves in. We've fixed up the old servants' quarters over the garage."

"You can call me Lucky," he says, speaking right to the low-slung diamond of her necklace like it's a microphone.

"Oh, yes. Very much so, to have a gem of a daughter like Kristen. You are a very lucky man."

Nathan's on the other side of Kristen and he's about to ask him about the Miata when Dr. Hummerman stands up, lays down his chopsticks, and raises his wineglass in a toast. "To our extraordinary young graduate, Kristen Lunt."

Hear, hear. Glasses go up. A wandering Chinese photographer slides up to the table and takes a flash shot: that'll be another twenty bucks on the check, but what the hell, Hummerman's paying, few hundred on his platinum, he probably doesn't even read the bill.

Kristen doesn't have a wineglass but she lifts her orange juice and speaks in a voice he can hardly recognize, like she's some summer tourist out of Massachusetts. "Thanks, Dr. Hummerman. Here's to your new boat!"

With a beaming smile like she's his own daughter, Dr. Hummerman clicks glasses with her. "To the *Zauberflöte.*"

Lucky takes a big slurp out of his Fog Cutter but his throat closes up and it won't go down.

"She nearly came to grief this afternoon," Hummerman reveals.

"Oh no," Kristen says. "What happened?"

"While you were at the beach with Jason and Becky, we were anchored off the point for a little christening. Phil Good — he's my naval architect — was up from Sag Harbor. Dave Wong had come all the way from Taiwan, where she was built, and we're sitting around the cockpit table when quite out of nowhere a lobster boat headed right for us at full throttle. I honestly thought the poor fisherman had died at the helm and the bow was going to cut us in two, then he veered off at the last minute, but the wake knocked the hell out of us. Food went everywhere, Dave Wong got a minor scalp gash on the awning frame. Phil — who was up on the coaming — practically got knocked overboard. Luckily he caught himself on the lifeline. I had to check Dave for concussion, so I didn't even get to see the name on that fellow's stern, or I would have called the Coast Guard in a minute. Glass all over the place"— he says directly to Lucky —"Lucas, you'll laugh at us for having real glass aboard ship, which we rarely do, just for special occasions."

"I don't know," Sarah says. "Lucas can always find a bottle or two on board."

"But who *was* it?" Kristen insists. "Can you describe them, even if you didn't see the name? My father knows every boat in Orphan Point, don't you, Daddy?"

"Wasn't an Orphan Pointer," her employer says. "I'm glad to say. That boat headed straight east into Split Cove. Full throttle. They were throwing a wake so high we couldn't even see the stern."

Lucky's chopsticks open by themselves and drop a big chunk of stir-fried dogmeat onto his lap. He shifts his leg and lets it fall to the carpet between his shoes. "No telling what them Split Cove boys will do," he says. "Most of them's pretty much bottom-feeders over there."

"Anyway," Hummerman says, "by the time I got Dave Wong's skull patched up, the culprit was long gone. But Lucas, you're a lobsterman, what would get into someone to pull a stunt like that? Aren't we all sharing the same ocean?"

"There's some of them's don't care much for pleasure craft, since they see themselves as out there working for a living, and there's some of them's think their lobsters get stolen by the summer crowd, and there's always some that just don't give a god damn."

His wife says, "Lucas, it's not funny. Someone might have been seriously hurt."

By this point Lucky has long since given up on the chopsticks and he's just forking in the Lobster Kowloon, though it's got no more lobster in it than a can of Alpo.

Finally their little waitress shows up with the check in a folder whose gold Chinese letters say *Guess who **really** won World War Two?* He leans back and studies the mushrooms and dog chunks on the floor around his chair, so he doesn't have to see Hummerman reach for his platinum card and snatch the check. Beside his plate are four little umbrellas in a row, all that's left of his Fog Cutters, and when he gets up he has to hold on to a red lacquered column because it feels like he's back at sea.

"Good thing you brought your designated driver." Hummerman laughs. "But you deserve it. It's not every day a man sees his daughter graduate."

Out in the My Lai parking lot, Kristen heads off in the rattly Mercedes diesel to her new family's house. Then Mr. and Mrs. Lucas Lunt walk to their vehicles, which are parked side by side, and stand between them. "How many little Chinese umbrellas, Lucas?"

"Three."

"Think you ought to be driving home?"

"Hell, dear, I steered through thicker nights than this."

"And also, we have a date to talk about your sternperson."

"Ain't no time to bring it up, right after Kristen's graduation."

"You made a promise, Lucas. She's all graduated, now we have to talk about ourselves."

He's glancing around to see if maybe their Chinese waitress is going to float across the parking lot with another Fog Cutter on a cocktail tray. Then he's looking at his feet in their funeral shoes, head down, a kid that forgot his homework in front of the teacher. "I ain't found anyone else."

"Lucas, have you been *trying?* That's what the two weeks were for. You should have hired someone by now. Have you been asking around? Did you put your ad back up? I mean, I haven't mentioned it because I trusted that you'd get it done."

"Can't find no one. If they ain't out lobstering, they're working at the boatyard. Bunny Whelan's giving them Blue Cross and a dental plan."

"Lucas, this has been embarrassing and humiliating beyond belief. I have had lifelong friends avoid me in town. People hear things, and they talk. And this spring what they are talking about is the Hannaford girl and her husband, and although no one would ever say it to my face, I'm sure they're also talking about the time she spends with you."

This conversation is rapidly sobering him up. He's ready to drive. He wants nothing more than to take himself right home and sit down in his own chair and watch Ricky Craven in the NASCAR Pepsi 400 on TNT. "It ain't that easy," he says.

"I understand your sympathy for someone you've been working with all these weeks, but Rhonda Hannaford will not be allowed to starve. She has a job, Doris Twitchell treats her like a daughter, she has the whole Astbury clan over there, she's young and attractive. Lobster fishing is a dead end for her, Lucas. It's not like a young boy going out sternman, saving for his own boat. I don't see why you find it so difficult. You might well be doing her a favor."

He pauses, then blurts it out. "She's going to have a kid. That's why."

"Well, she's a married woman. She's got a right to be pregnant. Maybe this will settle her down."

"Maybe it will. Only she says it ain't Clyde's."

"What do you mean, not Clyde's?"

"You figure it out. It ain't Clyde's."

"Lucas, you're not trying to tell me you're in trouble with Rhonda Hannaford? The woman's not even divorced yet. Not to mention *you*. A man who has two legitimate children of his own."

"That's what she says."

For a moment she just stares at him through the round librarian glasses that give her eyes an underwater look. She's got her face pointed up, of course, there's half a foot difference in height, but to Lucky it feels like it's his mother and she's looking down. She takes his two huge hands while she asks him a question. "Lucas, whatever happened to us?" She doesn't even wait for an answer. She lets go of his hands, slides in the driver's seat and slams the door. She pokes the lock shut and collapses with her face on the steering wheel. He looks in the windshield to see if she's crying but it's too dark to make out. He goes around to her passenger door but it's locked too.

"I'm sorry," he says through the safety glass. "It wasn't nothing I ever planned."

She just stays there with her face in the wheel dish like she's been in a head-on collision and she's dead. He stands over her car till he feels cold and foolish, and she still doesn't move. She's like some kind of a snail that's sucked itself inside, little muscle of snailmeat tightened in her coil of shell. He kicks her left front tire but she doesn't move. Her hands are on the bottom of the wheel, her face squashed up against the hub.

He thinks he might chain onto her and tow her home, but he couldn't get her into neutral and it would wreck her transmission, same as the pickup. He climbs into the cab and starts the engine up and waits. The radio's playing Deana Carter, "Did I Shave My Legs for This?"

> *Well, it's perfectly clear, between the TV and the beer*
> *I won't get so much as a kiss*

He's been married to Sarah Peek for twenty-one years. He knows she's capable of waiting in that position all night until he leaves. It's happened a couple of times before, once when her mom died, once for no reason at all back when Kyle was in diapers. She went to bed in the daytime and curled up tighter than a boiled shrimp and the county nurse had to give her a shot to get her uncoiled again. No permanent damage, and life went on. But she never curled up in a parking lot like this, and he doesn't know what to do. Well, he's the root cause of it, he figures. If he disappears she'll straighten herself out and drive on home.

He keeps his headlights low and carefully navigates the nine foggy miles to Orphan Point. He's tired and he'd like nothing more than to park himself in front of the races with a beer, just like the song. But if she sees the truck in the driveway she may fold up again. They've got a big-screen TV down at the RoundUp, so he keeps on going and pretty soon he's sitting under the steer head clearing away the Fog Cutters with a Rolling Rock. He's just finished persuading Wallace the bartender to switch to the NASCAR races when in walks Travis Hammond with two or three huge bastards in oilskins and trawler boots. Travis is a scrawny dark-haired guy with a black little Hitler mustache and the biggest god damn truck you ever saw, an F-350 with car-crusher mudders and a two-foot lift, it's a wonder he can even reach the pedals. He was a couple of years behind at Orphan Point High, just coming in ninth grade when Lucky dropped out. One night they were all getting drunk and pissing on tires in the junkyard behind the old Ford garage, there was Howard and Lonnie Gross and the Jenks brothers that were a couple of years older, and all of a sudden one of the Jenks boys told Travis Hammond to kneel down and suck his dick. Just like that. The Jenks brothers held him down one after the other and he blew them both. Later on one of them got fucked up in Vietnam and the other tried to kill somebody in prison and got life without parole. Thirty years and that's what he thinks of when he sees Travis Hammond. *Kneel down and suck it.* Nobody paid much attention to him after that.

The guys with him are not exactly familiar, but not strangers either. They walk like they've never been on land. They come past the bar surrounding little Travis Hammond like bodyguards, pass the band and the dance floor, and take a table near the blind stuffed horse head on the far side of the room.

He asks Wallace the bartender, "Who the fuck's Travis got with him?"

"Got me. Some of them Shag Islanders don't come to the mainland but every four or five years, get their teeth pulled and get laid and it's back to sea."

Tonight's Montana Night at the RoundUp so they've got a live country band, the Sundowners, big banner behind them: THE BLUE GRASS BOYS FROM ATHOL, MASS. He takes a look over at the dance floor, which is mostly full of old-timers waltzing their wives in full western outfits with cowboy boots and string ties. They're playing a scaggy mutation of Marty Stuart's "Burn Me Down" when Travis Hammond spies him staring at the future and shouts across the dance floor, "Hey Lunt, come over and join us before you get yourself in trouble." He's got no choice but to take his Rolling Rock over and sit down.

"Band sucks," he says.

"That's right," Travis Hammond says. "That's why we're sitting over here. Hey, how come you're solo? I thought you had women up the ass."

"That's exactly where they are. They ain't much use up there either."

"Know what you mean," Travis Hammond replies. "Know what you mean."

Meanwhile the three fishermen with him are drinking shots and beers as fast as they can put them down. Even to Lucky's sea-hardened nostrils their clothes stink of herring and diesel fuel, and one of them's talking about blowing an 800-horsepower Caterpillar engine just out of the crate. "Son of a whore cracked open like an oyster. I sunk her for a skiff mooring."

A second one turns to Lucky and says, "Don't I know you from someplace?" He's a big black-bearded guy bald as a dick on top with his long gray-black side-hairs pulled into a ponytail in back.

Lucky says, "You ain't a Trott, are you? Thought you was all Trotts out there."

"No, we ain't Trotts." The three of them grin at each other and laugh. "We're Shavers, the Trotts is up to the north end."

"You ain't married into them, living out there all them years?"

"Nobody'd marry a Trott woman, they're too fucking ugly."

The black-bearded one does look familiar, he's been at the lobster boat races, though he never wins. Small boat, big diesel, but he's afraid to let it out. "You was at Summer Harbor last year, wasn't you?" Lucky recalls. "You had that black Goldwing that jumped the gun."

"How about you, you still running that Model T?"

"Fourth place, gas unlimited," Lucky reminds them. "Swiftest wooden boat in the race."

The guy with the sunken Caterpillar is a big orange-bearded fisherman with one wide brown spade of a tooth in his upper jaw. He must have had a good haul, because he buys Lucky what they're all drinking: shot of Wild Turkey and a Rolling Rock, it settles down smooth on top of the Fog Cutters. "Thanks," he says. "You guys come to the mainland for dental work?"

"No. We come in to make a bank deposit and get some local pussy, if you don't mind, then we're heading back. You fellows got any spare daughters?"

"That ain't what I heard," Lucky says. "I heard you boys wasn't much interested in women."

The orange-bearded one holds up a middle finger that's just a one-inch stump, a big raw scar on the end that looks like he sewed it up himself with his other hand. "I heard you was interested in this."

"Seriously boys, I hope you're coming in for the races next month. We always enjoy watching you get towed back home."

Travis Hammond says, "These guys was saying the lobsters out their way is getting scarce."

"No fucking wonder," Lucky says. "Greedy bastards fishing a thousand traps apiece, you caught everything on the bottom, now you're whining they're gone. You might try giving them a rest, we'll sell you some starters, you can let the stock build up."

The black-bearded guy wears a studded Hells Angels vest over a black T-shirt with the sleeves cut off and a tattoo with the head of a pit bull in a black star. He has so many spaces between his teeth his mouth looks like a piano. He throws back his shot and looks at Travis first and then Lucky. "We was thinking we might want to expand our territory a bit."

"Well," Lucky tells him, "you got three thousand fucking miles of clear water the other side of you. Go for it."

"They ain't no keepers that side of us. You know it and we know it. It's too fucking deep. Course that don't stop them Taxachusetts cocksuckers coming up and dragging it clean. We was figuring we might move inshore a bit. Heard you guys got more lobsters than you can handle, ain't that so, Travis?"

Travis takes a sip from his Wild Turkey and a slosh of Rolling Rock. He looks very serious, which he should be, because these guys are basically asking if he and Lucky would like to bend over and get fucked. Just like ninth grade. "We got a lot of pressure," Travis explains. "We got Split Cove on one side and them Tarratine River bastards on the other. We're squeezed bad as you."

The third of the huge Shag Island figures turns out to be a woman, at least he thinks so since they're calling her "Priscilla." Maybe she's a Shaver too, she's got the size and shape. She must weigh in at one-ninety, she's got an anatomically correct heart tattoo on her bicep with blue sliced-off arteries coming out of it, black pirate scarf around her forehead, on her chin a quarter-inch of kinky purplish beard the color of dulse on a stone, and now she's addressing Lucky in a low chain-smoking female voice. "Think of it, sugar, all them boats fishing off of this point, you ain't even going to notice a couple more."

Lucky throws back the rest of his Wild Turkey and looks the meanest one of these bastards right in the eye, the bald piano-toothed one, and says, "There was a guy out of Stoneport, he set a couple traps on Toothpick Ledge back when my old man fished it. Next day they come out to haul, they found four boats waiting for them with a dozen men. Last we seen of them son of a whores."

The black-bearded guy says, "Them was the old days. Things has got a bit more flexible now. It ain't so fucking uptight anymore. People ease off, they get along. Them territory lines ain't written in stone."

"Can't write in water." The big female laughs. "The ink don't take."

Then Travis is craning his neck to see past Lucky in the direction of the band and the bar. He looks like he's trying to get more drinks, then he says, "Hey Lucky, ain't that your boy over there? Ain't none of my business, but I can't see why he hangs out with them fucking retards over to Burnt Neck."

"He ain't in here," Lucky says, "he ain't even twenty-one. Anyway, I ain't in charge of his life."

"You're his old man, ain't you? That fucking Swan kid, his old lady is a whore. I heard she sucked off a whole Halifax trawler crew after the Stoneport races. One after the other. Ten bucks apiece, Canadian."

Sure enough, it's his son Kyle and his Burnt Neck buddy, the two of them in sweatshirts with the arms razored off, showing off their steroid biceps and their tattoos. He doesn't want to run into them, he's had enough fucking family for one night.

"I don't know him," Lucky says.

Travis Hammond says, "I heard you two wasn't getting on."

Behind Kyle and Darrell a dozen geezers are waltzing around with their arms around their partners, old dried-out bodies hanging on each other like stuffed animals, nothing inside them anymore but Dunkin Donuts and All-Bran. They all used to be fishermen, now they can't even find the hook, death's climbing up their stern pipe but they hang on to their wives and waltz away. They come from Orphan Point and Split Cove, Burnt Neck and Riceville and the closer islands like Hadley's and Cleftstone, and some from as far off as Norumbega and Stoneport, which was a dry town till the last decade and they still don't have a dancing spot except for the public pier. The old men look like they've been flaked down and shrunk, big eyes stare over the shoulders of their wives at something nobody else can see.

Kyle and his buddy are standing at the bar being guarded by Big Andy himself so they don't try and order a drink, though Kyle's got less than a year to go. Liquor police must be on hand. His son looks like he's put on another inch or two since he left home. His eyes are up to the level of Big Andy's mouth. He's growing a mustache too, make up for the shaved head, only it's not his color. Looks like he's dyed it blond. He's still got the earring. On his left shoulder he's got a new tattoo but it's too far off to make out what it is. His friend

Darrell's a shorter, skinnier, weasely type with a crotch-hair mustache, just the kind they love in prison.

Travis Hammond says, "Hear your boy's living over to Burnt Neck."

Lucky spits on the floor. "I wouldn't know. I ain't been to see him."

The orange-haired islander stops talking to his buddies and asks Lucky, "That kid yours?"

"Used to be. I don't know who the fuck he is now."

"He lobstering?"

"No. He's urchin diving."

"What about you?" the guy says to Travis Hammond. "You got any kids?"

"My kid's in the service," Travis says. "And I got another one . . ." He pauses. ". . . in the community college system."

"The fuck he is," Lucky says. "He's in the juvenile detention system."

"That's exactly my point," the bald black-bearded guy argues. "Your kids ain't lobstering, why make such a big fuss over a few traps?"

"Them territories ain't going to change," Lucky says.

Travis turns to Lucky. "I don't know, Luck, we might be able to accommodate a few more sets, way out south, southwest of Sodom Ledge."

"Shut the fuck up, Travis. They ain't getting nothing. Think what your old man would say, he'd piss in his fucking grave, same as mine."

"We was thinking we'd just try it out," the orange-haired guy says, "like an experiment. Lay some traps along south of your traps, then you could add up and see if you was getting less lobsters, keep everything nice and scientific, and if you was, like your friend says, we could back off."

"You can back off now," Lucky tells him, "save yourself a whole lot of trouble."

The orange-haired guy gives Lucky the big shit-eating grin with his shovel tooth and the purple tongue poking out of his mouth like a liver-colored eel. He takes a slug out of the bottle of Rolling Rock and pushes his chair back. He takes off his wristwatch and slides the expansion band down over the bottle, like he doesn't want it to get hurt. Though this guy must spend his life in the open sun, his face is white as a slice of cusk and his hands are huge and pale with large moldy freckles on them like blue cheese. The guy says, "Who you telling to back off?"

The woman puts her tattooed forearm on the guy's sleeve. "Let the poor man alone, Cyrus. He don't mean nothing."

Lucky feels his heart beat nice and strong and regular in his chest, just like the old days, no jumping around. "Fag Island," he says, "that's what we used to call it."

The orange-bearded guy sits there a moment with his eyes bulging out of his face like a flounder, then he stands up and leans over the table to grab Lucky by the throat, his hands knocking down bottles on the way, but they never get there. Lucky plants his ass in the chair and gives the table a good forward shove and it makes contact just over the guy's knees. The big son of a bitch grabs the air for support and goes down backwards, knocking his chair over and breaking the legs off it as he crushes it to the floor. He lies there a minute, parts of the chair all around him, then starts picking himself up with one hand while the other hand's grabbing at his eye like he can't see. The other two Shag Islanders get up to help him, though not too swiftly, like they've never seen this guy down and they want to enjoy it for a while. Meanwhile the band has stopped and all the old geezers are closing in on the action while Big Andy charges through the crowd with one hand stiff out in front of him to clear the way and the other holding an aluminum baseball bat. Along with him's a guy in a sport coat who was up at the bar drinking, now he's letting his coat slip back and there's a badge on his shirt, he must be the liquor cop. That's why they gave Kyle a hard time.

Lucky's still holding the table edge, then takes the opportunity to remind Big Andy, "I told you not to let them cocksuckers in here. They ain't nothing but trouble."

The orange-haired guy's still got his hand over his eye and the big woman hisses at Lucky, "Jesus, you blinded him," but the black-bearded one says, "Cyrus ain't blinded, he lost his fucking contact."

The big black-bearded guy yells, "Don't step on it, for Christ's sake. Somebody get a flashlight."

"Maybe it's up under the lid," the woman says. She's pulling on his shoulders, trying to bring his head down to her level and calm him so she can look and see where the contact is. "I'll need a flash-light to look up in there," she says. Big Andy goes back to look for flashlights. The liquor cop has his arms outstretched to secure the area where the contact was lost so nobody walks on it. The woman yells after Big Andy, "See if anyone can find a Q-Tip!"

It seems like the perfect time to leave. He gives Travis Ham-mond a twenty and says, "Leave a good tip, Travis, we want to be asked back."

When he gets home the garage doors are closed, the house is quiet, and the lights are out. He did the right thing by instinct, killing a little time at the RoundUp while Sarah got calmed down. He knows her to the bone, she gets all excited over stuff, then she cools off and comes around. They're closer than Siamese twins, that's why they've lasted all these years. He peeks in the window and there's the navy blue Lynx in its place right beside the ATV. He has to be very quiet so she doesn't wake up and start going again about Ronette. He won't even turn on the TV, though the Daytona replays start at 1 A.M. Maybe he could put it on mute and just watch them go round the track, in hopes of glimpsing Ricky Craven in number 25, his Budweiser Chevrolet.

He steps into the breezeway and can't open the kitchen door, first time in history the Lunt house has ever been locked. He fingers the big key ring hanging from his belt loop. He's got the truck key and the snowmobile key and the key to the ATV, a key to Clyde Hannaford's ice locker that Clyde gave him in earlier days, a key to the Lynx, two boat keys, engine and cuddy hatch, key to the chain padlock for the punt, key that Ronette gave him to her trailer though he's never yet set foot in it, key to the gun cabinet and the gun rack in the pickup, and that's it. He does not possess a key to his own house.

He tries the front door, which they only use for company. Locked. Garage door too. He gets the crowbar out from behind the truck seat and tries to jimmy the roll-up doors but they're down tight from the electric opener and the only remote control is in the Lynx. He takes the crowbar around to the rear window of the garage and pries the sash up, cracking a pane in the process because it hasn't been opened in years and the salt dampness has swollen frame and sash into a single piece of wood. He pries it about halfway up and there it jams. He has to force a couple hundred pounds of human meat and bone through a half-open garage window: part by part, leg first, balls over the threshold, ass and belly as a one-piece structure, then bring the other leg around so he's half in, backwards, and the rest is easy. Coming in like a burglar, he trips over his own lawn tractor, feels his way to the light switch, and he can see.

His heart gives a little flip of fear. What if something's happened? He peers into the Lynx looking for a woman slumped over the wheel the way she was when he left her, but the car is empty. It takes a while to penetrate that she's locked him out. She locked the car doors back in the restaurant parking lot. She locked her body into the steering wheel. She locked her car even in the locked garage. No problem, she's a free woman. But the house is different. The car is hers and the body's hers, but the house was built by a Lunt and Lunts have owned and maintained it since the Civil War. It's his. He was born in the big upstairs bedroom, same as his father was. In the years since his old man's death he has roofed it and plumbed it and dug the sump out and scarfed in new sills and rafters where the ants got to them. Evenings, after a full day's lobstering, he built the three-car garage and her studio over it with his own hands. When Kyle and Kristen came, he framed the bedrooms out of the raw attic where he himself had grown up under bare roofboards with the nailpoints sticking through. He has passed through these doors without question for forty-six years. As far as he knows the house has never been locked, and though he once owned a house key, he can't remember when he saw it last.

He knocks hard on the kitchen door and waits. No answer. It's possible she's sound asleep and doesn't hear him.

He goes outside through the breezeway and knocks hard on the central front door of the house, which she has to hear. No light appears in the south bedroom and no footsteps sound on the stairs. He looks at his watch dial under the yard light. One-thirty. In four hours he has to be in Split Cove picking Ronette up for the day's work. He yells up to her window. "Sarah. What the hell?"

No answer. He rips a clump of grass and sod out of the lawn and underhands it up towards the bedroom windowpane. In the silence that follows, he remembers once up at her folks' house when they

first met, he'd been out shrimping and they filled the boat by midnight so they all came in early, maybe one or two in the morning,
and all he could think of was seeing Sarah Peek. He went to the old
Peek house on the Deadman's Hill Road and lobbed a fistful of live
shrimp at her window and the light came on. She came to the window, thin as an elver in some kind of white nightdress, and whispered down, "Lucas, my *folks*."

Now he's throwing things at her window again, and finally it
does slide open, the light still off but she sticks her head out in the
dark and says, "Lucas, I told you that night in the Irving Big Stop
and I meant it. You can't come in."

He yells up, "Christ's sake, Sarah, I've got to be fishing at
five A.M. We can settle this out tomorrow night."

"It's settled, Lucas. You've violated everything this house stands
for. You show no sign of remorse. You don't have the right to live
here anymore."

"What do you mean, the *right?* My family fucking built this
place, my old man framed the window you're looking out of, and I
laid the floor you're standing on. A hundred and fifty fucking years
this has been a Lunt house. Now get your ass down here and unlock
the door before I kick it in."

By now there's a car stopped on the road watching this man
yelling at a woman in the window. Nobody he knows, though. Not
a cop.

Then she cries down, "Lucas, don't you see? Nothing is yours
anymore. Not me, not this house, nothing. You don't even own
yourself."

She shuts the window and the house stays dark. He heads back
into the garage and finds the chain saw on its shelf over the little
summer pile of fireplace wood. It's a McCulloch Pro 20 that he
swapped even for a crate of lobsters two years ago, it wouldn't cut
dogshit when he got it but since then he has filed every sawtooth
razor sharp. As always, it starts on the first pull. The sound is high
and clean at first with the choke on, packing the garage with the
noise and fumes from its rich mixture, then with the choke off it
warms and idles to a smooth burpy two-cycle purr. He carries the
idling saw over to the kitchen door, the locked one, and touches the
blade tip to the door panel just above the knob. The clutch isn't
engaged yet so it doesn't make a cut. This is a door his old man put

in, back in '71 when he was too sick for lobstering and too restless for just sitting around so he rebuilt everything in the house before he died. A door could have been bought all built at the Tarratine Housing Supply, but his father grooved and rabbeted it out of raw white oak, a month of Walter Lunt's silent devoted labor. The door has four panels and he could easily make a cut in one of them that would allow his hand to reach in and slide the bolt. Then he hears her behind the door. "Lucas, what's that noise, what are you doing? What's that noise?"

"I'm coming in."

"You're not. You're crazy."

He squeezes the trigger and raises the saw tip to the high point of the door in the upper right corner, above the knob. The instant the moving tip starts smoking through the paint Sarah screams. *"Lucas, for God's sake!"* The saw makes a vertical pass right down the door, pausing only for a second's resistance where his old man had grooved in the hardwood panel. Apply a little more power and she's through, just like cutting the crust off of a slice of whole wheat bread. Free of its lock, the cut door swings open on its hinges. He walks over the threshold in triumph, holding up the chain saw like a sword. The little two-stroke is purring smooth as a house cat, eager for more work.

Sarah leans against the refrigerator with her arms folded, eyes just as steady as if he came in that way every night. She's not ready for bed at all but still dressed for her daughter's graduation. She says, "You may have cut your way in but I'm leaving. Are you going to keep standing in that opening or are you going to let me through?"

"Where are you going? It's the middle of the god damn night."

"It doesn't matter, Lucas. You have no right to ask. Just get out the way so I can get to my car in the garage."

He hears the electric garage door open. The tinny Lynx engine starts and backs out past his GMC, then she's gone down the pitch-black road. He's left looking at the sawed-off kitchen door, like a cross section sliced through his old man's life, the deep channel grooved to receive the two door panels, the whole thing watertight as a ship. If all that glacial warming bullshit ever came true and the tide rose a hundred feet up from Orphan Point harbor, this door could have kept the floodwaters out of his father's home.

He turns on the NASCAR races but Ricky Craven spins out on

the seventh lap. Everyone knows he's been having seizures since the New Hampshire crash, but he has a contract and he's got to race, world-famous son of a bitch but he's trapped like everyone else. The yellow flag's out for the pileup and they're just crawling around, so he grabs a Rock out of the icebox and takes it to bed with him but he still can't sleep. The house is empty. He can feel the sliced-up door like it's wide open, and for the first time ever he'd like to have it locked. Christ knows who could walk through that opening and climb the stairs. The late-rising moon is blasting in through the south window of the bedroom, the kind of thing that used to wake Sarah in the old days and she'd toss for a while, then she'd wake him in turn and anything could happen. Now she's got one of her sea glass mobiles hanging from that window and just as he's about to pass out, its vanes catch the moonlight and he's wide awake. He dozes and the thing swings on its string and he's staring at the red 3:30 display on the digital clock. From downstairs too, something's scratching and shuffling around, it sounds like one of the kids getting up for a piss or a snack, but they're both gone. He stands up and puts his boots on. He pulls the sea glass thing off of its hook but in the dark one of the vanes breaks off and falls on the floor. What the fuck, this is what started it, she starts welding broken glass together and suddenly she's an artist and it's all gone to shit. He throws what's left of the thing down beside the vane and smashes his heel on it, glass splinters and leading gouge into the clear pine floor.

There's still something scratching around downstairs, probably one of those son of a whores from the RoundUp, they'll grab his chain saw off the breakfast nook and come up to cut off his arms and legs. He keeps a loaded .30-30 right in the closet for just such moments. He grabs it and throws the bolt once to bring up a round in the chamber and heads downstairs. Before going into the kitchen he throws the light switch on to surprise them, but what he sees isn't a human being. It's Alfie, the coon cat, back from his disappearance on Christmas Eve. Six fucking months. He's thin and rangy, his fur is matted with burdocks in it, and he's got a bald scar on his tail. Lucky would hardly know him if it weren't for the broad six-toed paws, three black and one almost orange, that Kristen used to call "web feet." "Only cat that could swim across the harbor," she used to say.

The minute Lucky comes into the room with the deer rifle Alfie goes to where his food bowl used to be and starts sniffing around like he's just been out overnight. "We ain't got any cat food," Lucky explains. "We thought you wasn't coming back."

Alfie hops up on the sink in a quick leap that he could have never made when he was a house cat and licks the water drop off of the faucet like he always did. It's Alfie all right, that's the only way he would ever drink. He gets a can of human tuna from the shelf, White Diamond select, cats love it cause it's mostly dolphin meat. He puts the electric opener to it and gives Alfie the whole can. No sleep tonight. In half an hour he'll be rowing out to the *Wooden Nickel* in his skiff.

7

His sternman is pregnant, his wife has moved in with a bull dyke welder out at the art colony, neither of his kids will talk to him, every few hours his heart flops like a mackerel, and he's having breakfast alone on a Sunday morning at 5 A.M. Every Sunday of his married life he came downstairs to a stack of buttered blueberry pancakes, now he's listening to Tanya Tucker's "Ridin' Out the Heartache" on High Country 104, having a cigarette, and sharing a can of King Oscar sardines with Alfie the cat.

Hey there, where you headed?
I told him I don't really know

Neither does he, but this is one morning when it doesn't matter, he's traveling to the Stoneport races and he's not worried about anything but speed. "You got to concentrate," he says to Alfie at the breakfast table. "You can't think of nothing but the engine or else you're fucked." He'd take Alfie with him for luck but the cat goes wild and starts throwing up hair balls the minute he's aboard a boat.

He opens a fresh can of Norwegian brisling sardines in olive oil. Alfie doesn't go for the local ones anymore since he came back, some yuppie must have been feeding him on the back porch and spoiled his taste. Lucky puts the whole can in the food dish, who knows what hour he'll be coming home. No doubt about it, it's an omen of victory that Alfie showed up the night she left.

The Stoneport lobster boat races start at 10 A.M., he's got to travel the twenty-five miles of open water and show up by nine-thirty to register with the race committee. Over the weekend he got Harley Webster up from Riceville and traded two crates of lobsters for Harley installing a secondhand turbocharger on the 454. Now the engine box cover won't clamp down so it's loud as hell, but they took it out off of Sodom Ledge and when the turbo cut in, it jumped her up five knots on Harley's portable GPS. While they were working on it, he asked Harley if he could thread the turbo unit to take a propane fitting on the air intake. "Wouldn't *that* go like shit," Lucky said. Harley answered, "What the fuck you want to do that for? It ain't legal, and you could blow your frigging boat up." He installed the propane fitting, though, and by the looks of how quick he did it, it wasn't the first time Harley had put one on.

It's 6 A.M. now and all around him they're starting their engines up. Usually Sunday mornings they take it easy on the volume, in case God is nearby they don't want to bust His eardrums, but this is race day and every fucking lobster boat is revving up to 3000 rpm, half of them with their mufflers off, not that they're all going to be racing, just to remind the summer residents whose harbor it really is. Howard Thurston won't be entering because his son Danny would whip his ass, but Howard went up to Burke's Diesel and got himself a four-thousand-dollar overhaul anyway, just so his Detroit 501 would sound right on the way down east. It's easy on the ears, the noise of motors coming back to life, just like a choir of hard-core smokers hacking and coughing themselves awake, then breathing easy as their lungs get going. One engine puffs a black cloud and sings its note, then another, finally they all throttle down or up to come in tune so it sounds like music in the lifting fog, only engines are better than music because they're real. It proves smoking is natural when you see marine engines doing it. Same with the Indians, they didn't give a shit, they invented tobacco, they crawled in their tepees buck naked and inhaled till they dropped. He finds the Marlboros and pounds the pack on the radar housing till one comes out, then lights it off the exhaust stack, already cherry hot. One thing about living alone, no one tells him what to do with his own body. He keeps the big sea-clam ashtray right in front of the TV and the refrigerator's so full of green Rolling Rock bottles it looks like a Christmas tree farm. Twenty pounds of mussels in the vegetable storage bins and a freezer full of salt pork that Sarah would have never allowed anywhere near his heart.

Art Pettingill's got his wife and boy aboard the *Bonanza,* ballasting the stern. Art races in the diesel 600–800 class, then big Alma takes the helm for the powder puffs. She's let him replace his old rusted-out Cat with a new Lugger 610 that must have cost him forty thousand, just for the Stoneport race. Howard Thurston's kid is coming down with a whole new hull, it's called *Perpetrator* like all Danny's boats. This one's an ink-black custom AJ-28 with a 315 Cummins turbodiesel and dual side exhausts like a formula race car. He took his new H&H four-bladed prop and had it CAT-scanned just like at a hospital, make sure every frigging atom was in the right place. One pass through the MRI tube cost him a thousand bucks, same as a heart. The hull's made of Kevlar, he's got a fake pot hauler of lightweight aluminum and no glass in the windshield, he races with ski goggles on against the spray.

There's Travis Hammond in the *Pisscat,* off to the eastward's Lonnie Gross and his wife and daughter in the *Abby and Laura,* which is leaking so fast Lonnie's got the bilge pump squirting steady out the back like a fire hose. The man oughtn't be allowed to take his family in that wreck, but there's the three of them fat and happy in the wheelhouse, already diving into the beer. Behind them their kid Norton's coming on strong in his outboard, the *Li'l Snort,* it's faster than his old man's boat but Norton stays behind since he hasn't got a clue where he's supposed to go. The whole fleet is traveling to Stoneport for the 10 A.M. start, though those first events are only the kids' races, sterndrives and outboards like the *Li'l Snort.* The serious racing won't get going till noon.

They don't look competitive, bunch of boys out for a good time, but every boat intending to race has been stripped of all gear except the required pot hauler and the life ring. Danny Thurston's even dropped his antennas and unscrewed the radome off the wheelhouse roof. Lucky and all other racers have left behind their saltwater live wells, washdown pumps, and of course cleaned the cuddy of loose gear, anchors, wet mattresses, pot warp, six-packs and piss buckets. He was almost going to leave his guns and ammo at home but he thought better of it. Even on race day there's assholes everywhere you look.

Off Sodom Ledge the Orphan Point fleet usually turns west, to fish the territory bounded by the Sodom Ledge whistle and the Graveyard bell off of Graveyard Point, which is the boundary of the Tarratine River gang, mostly crude country bastards and dope runners that couldn't tell a lobster from a crab louse. But today they'll pass by their fishing grounds and travel eastward in open water beyond the Split Point gong and the crooked number three daybeacon that marks Three Witch Ledge off of Burnt Cove. Most days an Orphan Pointer could get himself shot passing through Split Cove territory, but today's race day and the boundaries are off, whole fleets will be crossing each other's waters, trying fairly hard not to slice any lines as they steam by.

Lucky's not out to pussy around with his motor today, what the hell, he's been holding her back all summer, so when Brent Plummer passes him in his forty-two-foot Volvo-powered Moody shitheap he lets her out a little, the turbo cuts in, and she moves up so fast he has to hang on to the wheel to keep from getting dumped right on his ass. This is what men and boats were built for, letting her out offshore in smooth early-morning water, no traps on the stern, unending rainbow tunnel of spray over the *Wooden Nickel*'s bow. He pulls alongside the *Pipedream* and plays with her a minute right at the Narrows where you're squeezed between two buoys, so he can look right into Brent Plummer's eyeballs and give him the friendly finger as he opens her into the turbo's full thrust and wipes him clean. He hears a tremendous roar from the Volvo, too much noise for a marine engine even with the muffler off, he looks back and there's black smoke pouring out of the Moody's dual stacks and Brent's slowed to a crawl. Too bad, that's how the dinosaurs went extinct, too fucking big for their own good. Two boats behind Brent are slowing to see what's wrong, they're cousins and they have to help him out.

Lucky backs her to 1800 so he can hear the new Tracy Byrd tape he bought for the trip: *Big Love.* Side two starts off with "Don't Love Make a Diamond Shine," the only candyass track on the album but you can't blame Tracy, he's got to put food on the table too.

> *Tommy and Janey hardly eighteen*
> *Holdin' hands at the jewelry store*
> *Eyes open wide starin' inside*

He reaches in the cabin hatch and feels for the program switch to wipe that bullshit and track to the other side. This cheap Sony does not have the amps to make itself heard. They're paying five hundred bucks for class winners at the races. If he can do it, with Harley's help, that would get him a down payment on a stereo that could crank up over the engine noise, if he can ever find one that's U.S. made.

Running ahead of schedule at an easy eighteen knots, he lets himself cruise southwest away from the fleet for a minute to graze the edge of his fishing territory and check things out. He finds the slim channel they leave between the thick sets of traps and runs past the broad, superproductive Thurston area, you can hear the fucking lobsters under there wondering where Howard and his boy are, then Art Pettingill's special turf, a ten-fathom canyon that supplies Art with seventy pounds a day, eighty or ninety of Art's white-and-maroon buoys, set a tad farther apart because Art's got five or six traps under each of them. He's coming in sight of Toothpick Ledge, his own six-fathom family ground amidst his own orange-and-green pot buoys, with Danny Thurston's banana yellow off to the east, when his eye catches a foreign buoy set right over the dropoff of Toothpick Shoal, on the far southern edge of his own gear. He looks back to see the gang rounding the Sodom whistle, bound east for Stoneport, they're letting it out in the chop with whoops of spray. They'll get ahead of him but he's got to stop and check this out. Alongside the familiar Orphan Point colors is a black-and-white zebra-striped buoy he's never seen. It's got a toggle, too, floating ten yards to windward of the zebra float. Orphan Point boats never use toggles on their summer grounds. He looks around for strangers. Except for the fleet steaming off a couple of miles eastward, the sea is clear. Whoever it was, they must have come at sunrise, maybe on the way to the races, and dropped that cocksucker before the Orphan Point boats came out.

There's lots of ways you can fuck around out here, but that one's not allowed. A fisherman's territory is a matter of life and death. Lucky has fished this ledge in summer for thirty years and his old man Walter before that and old Merritt Lunt before him under a canvas sail. Lunts, Pettingills, Plummers, Grosses, Gowers, Thurstons have mixed and shared in here, traps rubbing up against each other the same as their houses on shore, one's garden back up to another's garage, kids going to Orphan Point schools, mixing and marrying for pretty much a century; but there's never been a zebra-striped buoy on this territory and he hasn't the faintest fucking idea whose it could be.

He could just tie a gentleman's knot in their line but that would be a candyass route under the circumstances. He could slice the pot warp in two but that would leave a ghost trap on his own grounds sucking up good lobsters. He could put one of his own orange-and-green buoys on it and get a new trap out of the exchange. But he has to send a message to make it clear, because he does not want this happening again. Bend over just once, like Travis Hammond, and get fucked the rest of your life.

He didn't expect to be hauling traps on race day. He disengaged the hydraulics for a little more speed, now he has to reengage, then gaff the toggle and sling the line over the pot hoist and haul it up from six fathoms down. It's a brand-new green wire trap marked only by the manufacturer's name: *Tanous Trap Company 1997,* no tag number visible. The trap's got a nice fat shedder and a couple of stringy culls in it, but Lucky's cleaned his boat and taken the sea well out for the race, so he just pulls them and sets them free. Leaving the trap on deck, he goes below and gets a .30-caliber cartridge and a rubber condom from the Magnum box hidden under the old RDF shelf. He drops the cartridge in the rubber and puts his mouth on it and blows it up like a balloon, big enough so it won't float out the trap vent, and ties it off. It looks good in there, the brass sheen of the cartridge shining through the pink latex condom, like a sunset at the end of a misty day. He doesn't know whose the fuck it is, but a word to the wise and if their brains are somewhere above their assholes they'll check this trap once and they won't come back.

Everyone else is miles ahead by now. The ocean belongs to the *Wooden Nickel,* a boat built for the open sea and bilge-ballasted with a half ton of cutup gravestones from the Orphan Point Funeral Home. He catches sight of the fleet when he's climbing a sea swell and loses them when he's in the trough. He powers up a bit, and soon he spots the *Abby and Laura,* which is now towing the *Li'l Snort* with the whole family in the wheelhouse drinking beer, then he's coming up Travis Hammond's tail cause the *Pisscat* wouldn't go over fifteen knots even when she was new. The big Chevy's cruising at seventeen on the loran with power to spare. He cranks open the windshield pane and lets in the sea air, lights another Marlboro and almost lights a second for Ronette, he's got so used to her on board. Off to the southward, Shag Island lies there dark and low on the horizon, and after that's Bull Island, which is nothing but sand and rock, the navy uses it for a target range, and beyond that is the open Atlantic, sparkling nearby but on the horizon dark as a pool of spilled oil, or blue wine.

> *I've got a love full of wide open spaces*
> *I've got a big love*
> *Wild and free*

He cranks up the volume to hear Tracy over the engine noise.

> *Deep as a river in raging flood*
> *As endless as the stars above*

Tracy Byrd may have the Texas desert and some wetback river that's dry sand half the time, but if he came out here he would see what wide open spaces really means. The horizon's so far off you could steam all day and not come to the end of it. That's what a boundary is, air on one side, water on the other, you can't frig around with it, nobody dragging their zebra-stripe buoys across the line. There's a whale out there too, he's scratching his back on the air like a big wet dog, then he takes an outlaw piss into the sky and slides under and he's gone. If Ronette was here she'd go crazy and they'd have to chase after the fucking thing, but what does she know? Whale's just another homeless fisherman, looking out for himself like anybody else.

He spies Danny Thurston's fast little black-hulled AJ-28 running way offshore of the pack and wings out to starboard, see if he can catch up. The AJ's a lightweight Kevlar diesel and the swells are going to set it back. He pegs Danny on the radar and opens up to nineteen knots, going faster than the swells now, diagonally across them, cutting the tops off, sharp spray knifing through the windshield so he has to close the screen and put the wiper on, but there's nothing like being out here with the throttle open, bronze spoked wheel straight and steady in his right hand and a Rolling Rock in the left. Wide open, the way it was at the beginning before everything got fucked up. A man, an engine, and an ice-cold beer.

They are almost to the Bull Island whistle going twenty-one knots on the loran when the *Perpetrator* has to slow down cause the seas pound its short plastic hull. It's only six fathoms along here and the surge mounts up before it crashes in pillars of breaking foam on the long granite tongue of Deuteronomy Shoal. Gas and diesel trying to harmonize their different voices, just like Charley Pride and Willie Nelson in the old Tarratine auditorium, he comes in with Danny Thurston side by side.

After the Virgins gong they meet the rest of the fleet that took the inside route north of Three Witch Ledge and the Pope's Nose, and ten or twelve Orphan Point boats squeeze in together past the fish factory and the barberpole lighthouse on Jacob's Point. Jackoff Point, that's what they called it when they used to pick up the Stoneport girls and take them to watch the red light through the evening fog. Three red flashes equals *I love you,* numbest line on earth but it always did the trick. Three little words and they'd be nibbling on your tongue like a hungry trout. They were hot tickets and they fucked like minks, not like the Orphan Point girls that were all spines and prayers and tougher to feel up than a spider crab. The Stoneport girls were pregnant by seventeen and their daughters were pregnant by seventeen, so the ones he used to know are grandmas now, sweet little saltwater cunts that would dive in the backseat for a beer and a cigarette and a lift back home.

As they pass the Stoneport breakwater the harbor narrows down to barnacled seal ledges and lobster-shack islands and gray shingled fisherman's cottages, where the Stoneport girls are sitting up there on their aluminum beach chairs, out of the race now, gray-haired spectators with binoculars watching the boats steam past the lighthouse on Jackoff Point. Who knows what's in their memories, maybe a kid named Lucky, long ago.

The Orphan Point boats raft up in a line alongside Stevie Latete's big green dragger, the *Orphan Queen.* Stevie's always saying, "I got a million five in the bank so don't call me La Tit anymore," but it doesn't help. You get these names in grade school and if there's any truth to them they don't just go away. Stevie brought all the wives down and they're up on the *Orphan Queen*'s foredeck with lawn chairs and thermoses full of margaritas, one radio tuned to High Country and another to the race channel on the VHF. Every year since he can remember Sarah was up there with them, and he looks the group over just in case her thin body's mixed in with the heavier ones, but she's not there, she's over to the art school eating finger cookies with her New York friends.

Since his radio's still not working, he cruises up to the committee boat to find when he's racing. This is a big Bruno 42 out of Stoneport called the *Heather and Valerie,* parked at the finish line and packing a radar gun to measure the final speeds as they rip across.

"*Wooden Nickel,*" he shouts. "Where am I at?"

The race committee guy is one of the Hallett brothers that control this stretch of the coast. They're all big bald-headed guys with piss-yellow mustaches and tight little dog-ass mouths. This one's got a Red Sox hat on and a portable VHF squawking in one hand. He points to the radio and yells, "Race info's on channel seventy-five!"

"Ain't got no radio!"

The guy has to yell louder over the sound of a hundred souped-up lobster boats revving their engines as they jockey around for the best view. "Lunt. You're in race four. Antiques!"

"Fuck you, antiques. This boat ain't even paid for."

"We put all the wood ones together this year, give them a break."

"Don't I get to race nobody fast?"

"Christ sake, that thing'd just be in the way. What's in there, gas or diesel?"

"Chevy four fifty-four. Turbo. She'd kick *your* ass."

"There'll be a free-for-all at the end. Winners of each heat, throw them together, fastest boat on the water. Race number ten. *If* that shitbox can win its class."

He heads over to the Orphan Pointers rafted on with Stevie Latete. He ties up alongside the *Pisscat* to see if Travis Hammond wants to come racing. Travis is scared to burn his engine out and catch hell at home, but he enjoys a fast ride. Now he gropes into the *Pisscat*'s cuddy and comes back with a cooler full of Rolling Rock and a hot thermos of cod head soup. Lucky takes a Rock and downs it in about two swallows, then takes another to nurse while he tells Travis about the striped buoy on their fishing ground.

"Bet it's them fuckers from Shag Island," Travis says.

"I didn't notice you telling them not to, the other night."

He takes another one of Travis's beers and they sit on the *Pisscat*'s paint-peeling washboard to watch the first two races, for youngsters and the smallest craft. "Ain't no use getting worked up till it happens," Travis says.

"Well it's happening. It wasn't no drifter I saw out there. I pulled it. Some son of a whore set that fucking thing right where it's at."

"Pre fucking meditated," Travis agrees.

"That's right."

Now they're on race one, outboard-powered, mostly kids that don't have their first real boat yet. Travis says, "Hey, ain't your boy racing this year?"

"He ain't got time to race. He's got an urchin boat. He makes a thousand bucks a day selling sushi to the Japanese."

"No shit? Hey, I hear you're all by yourself over to your place. How's that?"

"Finest kind. Eat what I want, jerk off when I please. Nobody asks no questions."

"I'd like that," Travis says.

"I bet you would. Hilda still beat the shit out of you every night?"

"Finest kind," Travis says. "Least she's to home, she ain't living in Dyke City."

"What's that supposed to mean, Travis?"

"Don't mean nothing." Travis gets himself another beer and another cupful of the cod head soup with a fish eye sticking out of the milky surface, staring right at him.

The high-pitched insect whine of six small full-throttled out-boards drowns conversation for about two minutes. Two or three motors go up in smoke, one snaps a shear pin, and four of them cross the line. The time comes over the *Pisscat*'s radio: DONNIE WASHBURN, BOAT NAME HOMER SIMPSON, POWER MERCURY FORTY-FIVE, TOP SPEED TWENTY-THREE POINT SIX. Before the racers have wound down in the runoff zone, there's a different sound, one- and two-cylinder inboards revving up, working their way to the starting area for race two: small diesels. These are a bunch of retirees and summer lobstermen, nobody to take seriously, they'll come farting across the course like a flock of golf carts, but Lucky's race is two slots away and it's time to go. Travis jumps aboard with a six-pack in each hand, they cast off from the *Pisscat* and head for the starting line. Cruising through the clear water back of the spectator fleet, he turns up *Big Love* on the stereo and looks around for an open straightaway so he can give Travis Hammond a little foretaste of Harley's turbocharger. It comes on with a high-velocity blistering roar that sounds so good he points her ninety degrees off the race course and takes her up to 3000 rpm for a few seconds, right out to sea. Travis uncaps a couple more Rocks with his big shit-eating grin, yells "Finest kind" over the turbo howl, then he throttles her back down towards the start.

Tracy lays down the guitar line for a V-8 engine in perfect tune.

> *Let's forgive and forget and start over*
> *We all make mistakes now and then*

At first he was pissed when they threw him in with the antiques. Now he's got a plan. He'll bury the cocksuckers in the first race and end up in the final free-for-all with the winners of all classes. He'll hook the propane tank to the turbo intake, just for the one minute of that race she'll be turbocharging pure propane with high-test gas, she'll smoke out the best of them and maybe take the whole fucking thing, he'll get the five hundred and buy two new stereos, boat and truck. Ronette will love it when he cranks those up.

By now the small diesels have plodded across the line — top gun went nineteen knots — and they're up to race three, adult outboards and sterndrives, light enough to get up on a plane and clock some speed. Race three is running a full six-boat field, the most the race committee allows in the narrow passage between the spectator boats. The thoroughfare along the Stoneport harborfront is a mile-and-a-half-long channel marked for the race by rows of orange and green balls two hundred feet apart. That means each of the six boats has to race at top speed within a thirty-foot lane, and it pays to get ahead and stay ahead because they are all throwing big wakes and if you catch one at open throttle you can flip or get thrown off into the spectator fleet, which is lined up five or six deep on either side of the course. Every harbor and island on this part of the coast has a string of boats rafted up along the race course. Right by the finish line there's also four or five mega-yachts, they're chartered by big-shit diesel corporations that sponsor these races and want to be there if their engines win. Couple of years back Dennis Ingalls from Moose Point took diesel unlimited with a Mack 740 and the losers went back home and pulled their engines out with dock hoists and dumped them right off the end of their wharves. Mack sold a hundred units the next month.

Lucky circles in back of the starting area with the other antiques, waiting for the sterndrive race to run. Some of those little bastards really get going, they whine like hornets and throw so much spray you can't even see the field. They're all over twenty-five by the time they hit the finish line. Course they're not really lobster boats, they're more like Ski-Doos. If Lucky was in charge of things they wouldn't even have a class.

Now it's time for race four and the antiques are shouldering each other for a good running start. Travis is up on the cabin trunk cranking the windshield open to cut resistance, then he settles himself on the stern where he belongs. The procedure is to follow the pace boat to the start and cross the line all together at fifteen knots, then open her up for a mile and the first one across the finish line wins. They clock each winner with a radar gun, and at the end of the day, top gun speed is the boat that gets remembered, whether she wins the free-for-all or not.

He checks out the competition as the other antiques move from their circling approaches into the starting line. The *Jenny L* hails out of Woodpecker Cove up the Tarratine River. The owner's an old fart that can't see anymore, but he's got one of his grandchildren helping him steer and you can see his old brown wrinkled face through the windshield, proud as piss. He's had twelve heart attacks, strokes, cancer, everything they carry up at the Tarratine hospital and they still can't keep him off the water. Death doesn't want him, so he's going to race another year.

Off to port of the *Jenny L* is the *Peg Leg* out of Riceville, Morris Ashmore, he's been racing against Lucky all these years. Morris is the only serious competition in the wood boat class. He's got a cedar-and-oak downeaster built by the old Cherrylog Boat Shop right on the Canadian border in Shackle Cove. Morris raced a 501 Dodge hemi last year but it ripped his transmission apart and he failed to finish. Now he's running something a bit smaller. Lucky listens intently through the noise of a half-dozen engines: sounds like a Chrysler 440 conversion with a deep bass tone because Morris has tuned the muffler for the race. He can also hear a new Hurth reduction gear in there and down on the shaft a titanium four-bladed prop. They say Morris hires a diver to go down and sharpen the prop blades with a rat-tail file. They are the only guys left that give a shit about wooden boats anymore, and as he draws alongside Morris he gives him the friendly finger and Morris comes back with a thumbs-up. Let the best man win. Morris got shot up in Vietnam and he's lobstered all his life with a left leg made of green bronze and hackmatack. He's a competitor. But when he hears the turbo cut in on the *Wooden Nickel* he is going to shit.

The fourth antique in the four-boat field is called *Bottom Dollar,* out of Burnt Neck, and he can see why they called it that, it looks like they raised it off the sea floor just for this race. One side of the windshield is peppered with bullet holes and the other side has its glass held in with duct tape. The hull has red streaks bleeding out of the scuppers from the machinery rusting out, the engine is an oil-burning GM 350 rattler that's pouring blue smoke out of the stack like a refinery. He'll give it one minute of race time before that thing swallows a valve and dies. The driver is a young long-haired Burnt Necker with his shirt off and his girlfriend right beside him with one hand on his dick, her other hand holding a cigar-size joint you can smell from here. Stiff competition.

The pace boat shepherds them into line and speeds up to twelve knots or so, then gets out of the way and the four antiques approach the start in pretty good form holding steady at fifteen knots, Morris on his port side and *Bottom Dollar* to the right. Travis is at his elbow with another Rock but he pushes him back. "Get your ass on the stern, Travis, far back as you can get. Don't sweat it if you fall in, she'll go faster without you." A split second before the line Lucky puts her up to three-quarters and his whole year of trials is justified the minute that four-bladed prop digs into the water and takes root. Can't be anything wrong with your heart if your engine throttles up like that. Way off to port the old blind guy is already falling behind. To starboard the Burnt Neck kid is yelling *Yahoo* like he's got a horse under him, his girlfriend's hunched up behind him with her arm in his pants up to the elbow. Lucky's got the Chevy wide open already, he's pouring the gas into her and he moves ahead. On the other side Morris Ashmore moves from three-quarters to full throttle and he keeps up with the kid, Lucky a bit behind at the midpoint, not torquing the engine yet, then a ripping noise comes from the Burnt Neck boat and a spurt of black flaming smoke splits their exhaust open and it's just Lucky and Morris as it has often been before. Morris opens the 440 and Lucky can feel the Hurth gearbox vibrating right through the water. He stays ahead. Lucky's at 3600 rpm, the loran says twenty-four knots but it can't keep up, he knows from the green water surging over the bow they're breaking twenty-nine. The turbocharger howls as the tach climbs right to 3900, and without even overheating he buries Morris Ashmore in a plume of spray.

Travis comes forward with a Rock and he chugs it in a single swallow while Hallett's voice comes over a hundred radios at once, all at different distances so it sounds like the resonant voice of God. *LUCAS LUNT, BOAT WOODEN NICKEL, ANTIQUE CATEGORY, THIRTY-FOUR POINT FOUR.* Morris Ashmore gives him the finger and revs his Chrysler a few times to make sure it still works. He can see him mumbling *Next year,* but he can't hear the words. Who the fuck knows about next year? Maybe he'll grow his leg back like a lobster. Maybe we'll all be dead.

He idles off the turbo and checks the Chevy to see if she survived the race. It's overtorquing the valve shafts, he can hear one of the valves hit just a cunt hair off the beat. He won, though, so he will get to race again.

Race five is the powder puffs, women taking their husbands' and boyfriends' boats, for the most part, though these days some of them drive their own. Mostly the guys stay on board back in the stern so they can jump in if there's any trouble. These are slow races, the girls don't want to eat shit if they burn the engines out. Lucky usually takes his lunch break during the powder-puff race, now he's cruising behind the starting line, checking to see who's letting their wives race this year. He can't quite make out the names on the stern, but every boat carries its trap colors on the wheelhouse roof and Lucky knows most of them by sight. There's a Split Cove boat, Jason Astbury's *Red Dog*, it's a Walker Johnson 33 with a Yanmar diesel and a tuna bridge. That's a strong motor but they're carrying too much superstructure to go fast. Jason's got a young girl he wants to fuck so he's letting her drive the boat. Art Pettingill's old yellow *Bonanza* is in this race, new Lugger diesel's pissing out brown fumes cause it's not yet broken in. Art and Clayton are both in the stern to balance off Big Alma at the wheel, the three of them set the *Bonanza* down a foot below her lines like an oil barge. There's a full field in this race, he sees the *Big Mack* out of Norumbega with a whole family aboard, kids and all, and a Volvo-Penta Walker Johnson called *Hog Heaven*, this one out of Three Witch Cove.

At that point he grabs Travis's arm and says, "That's *them*." One of the boats crossing his bow to start the powder-puff event is carrying the zebra-striped buoy right up on its roof. The boat is a Wing Brothers Goldwing 29, fast little glasser, brand-new, running what sounds like a 230 Isuzu diesel, no smoke at all visible, dual vertical stacks tuned like a couple of organ pipes. Unlike the other powderpuff boats, she's not carrying a man aboard. He gooses the *Wooden Nickel* a bit and comes up close behind her so he can read the name. Doesn't look much like a woman from behind, but it has to be if she's in the powder-puff, unless they're using morphodites like the Chinese Olympic team.

Across the Goldwing's stern it reads

BAD PUSSY
Shag Island

Lucky says, "Who the christly shit is driving that island boat?" Most of the powder puffs aren't being pushed too fast but they're full race vessels making a lot of noise and wake. The *Bonanza* is wallowing back under the weight of its ownership, but the *Red Dog* and the

Bad Pussy are up there neck and neck, the *Pussy* showing that zebra buoy on the roof. *"That* one," Lucky repeats, "that's the cocksucking striped buoy that was on our ledge."

Before Travis can answer, the *Bad Pussy* is over the line and the powder-puff race is hers.

They tie up alongside the *Pisscat* to resupply. As Travis gropes into his cooler for a couple more Rolling Rocks, the *Bad Pussy*'s speed comes over everyone's radio at thirty-four point six. "Ain't bad," Travis says. "Art and Alma must have done around fifteen."

"Ain't bad," he echoes, "for a cunt that doesn't know where she's supposed to set her traps."

"What's that supposed to mean?"

"See that fucking black-and-white-striped buoy she's carrying? That's the cocksucker I found on Toothpick Shoal."

"Know who that is, Lucky? That's Priscilla Shaver, you slammed her brother the other night at the RoundUp. You met her. You don't even remember, numb peckerhead, you was drunker than shit."

"Sweet fucking Jesus, Travis. I thought we made it clear to them cocksuckers not to move in."

"I knew they was coming," Travis says, "just a matter of time. You cut their warp off?"

"I gave them a bullet and a rubber and set it back down."

Travis opens another Rolling Rock. "Tell you my opinion," he says. "Them fuckers are here to stay, like it or not."

"That's cause they're counting on chickenshits like you."

"This ain't the old days, Lucky. Things change. Them Gloucester son of a whores come up and vacuum their christly territory out there, what are they supposed to do?"

"What are you, their fucking PR agent?"

"No, Lucky. I'm a realist. So they don't set right on Toothpick Shoal. Maybe they'll set half a mile out. There's a shitload of fucking lobsters out there. Nobody's starving at Orphan Point."

"Nobody's starving on Shag Island either. That bitch has a brand-new Eye-zoo-zoo diesel, brand-new Wing Brothers boat. Hundred fifty thousand right up front. That ain't exactly the face of poverty. Greedy fucks, why should they need more?" He looks hard at Travis Hammond's narrow-set eyes and mustached little mouth, trying to see where he's coming from on this, but it's the same old hollow face that got a dick shoved into it back in the ninth grade. People don't change. "I ain't racing with you, Travis."

He puts his half-drunk beer on Travis's washboard, gets into the *Wooden Nickel* and casts off by himself. Stoneport's the one race they let you run solo, as long as you have a kill switch so your boat won't keep going if you flip off.

He can't go forward cause they're running another race and there's six high-cube diesels pissing right towards him, neck and neck. He backs up behind the spectator boats, wheels around, and cruises seaward for a minute; then he remembers he's got another race coming, the class winners' runoff, and the *Bad Pussy*'s going to be there too.

They run the last race in two heats. The winners of the slow and small classes start off first. Antiques, powder puffs, one-cylinder diesels, and sterndrives. Then the big glass gas and diesels finish the day, including the winner of the first runoff. He'd like to save his nuclear weapons for the second heat, but with the *Bad Pussy* running thirty-four point six he'll need to feed the propane to her in the first. With his turbo breathing pure gas he'll swamp that zebra-striped witch and join the serious racers for part two. That should end the antique category once and for all and get the wooden boats back in contention where they belong.

He has one quick second thought as he recalls for a moment the look on Harley Webster's face when he put the propane fitting in, then he thinks: *That's old age talking, don't pay no attention.* Harley used to burn nitro but now he's an old fart with a Taurus who guzzles Poland Spring water all day long. He digs the five-pound propane canister out of the life jacket box and screws the propane hose to the turbo intake so this time when that turbocharger calls for air it's going to find itself breathing LP gas. Surprise, surprise.

Six boats come into line at fifteen knots, including a fast little Volvo sterndrive that's up to speed and planing right away. On the other side he sees the Shaver woman, size of a cow moose, with a blue bandanna around her head, a cigarette in her teeth, and a whiskey bottle in the binocular rack next to her wheel. Jesus H. Christ, she won't even look his way. She's swift too. A half-second before the line she redlines the Isuzu, her stern drops, a tongue of purple smoke flares from each stack. She pulls ahead and goes for the Volvo sterndrive in the starboard lane. Lucky's turbo is screeching since it can't get any air from the screwed-in valve. Fuck it, you only live once, and some bastards don't even get to do that. He reaches down with his left hand and opens the propane valve and there's an instant smell of gas, his Chevy howls like an F-16, the tach goes up over the 5000 point and snaps off its needle at the pin. He blows past the stern of the *Bad Pussy* and buries that blubber-headed whore with the wake of an aircraft carrier, thirty-six knots on the loran and he's only at the halfway point. Off course to port he hears Stevie Latete blowing the dragger's horn to speed him on. He's in sight of the finish line when down in the cuddy there's a noise like a blown tire and a spurt of yellow flame out of the turbocharger, then the whole engine box fills up with black-and-orange fire like a volcano. Sweet fucking Jesus, he thinks, why *now?* Why me? There's less than a hundred yards to go. He doesn't give a shit, he throttles up to take her through the finish line on fire but the propane's not making her go faster, it's just burning in the cabin air. He backs down the throttle and dives for the fuel valves. He grabs the big old gas-fire extinguisher beside the helm and pulls the pin and throws that son of a whore down there like it's a grenade, while meanwhile the boat slows so fast the stern wave comes over the transom and everything's fucking drenched. That helps. The fire extinguisher has not been inspected since 1985, it could go in there and explode like everything else, but it does what it's supposed to do and the cuddy fills with brown steaming foam and the flames turn to black smoke that coats his lungs like boiling creosote.

Just up ahead he hears the *Bad Pussy*'s Isuzu screaming across the line, then it's the whole Shag Island fleet blowing their christly horns like a herd of elk.

His H&H cap is black and his hands are burned red by the blast from the companionway. His clothes are smoking and the hair of his arms is burned off. The mad-dog siren of the Coast Guard twenty-six-foot lifeboat is on top of him now, they've got a hose out and they're spraying the whole boat with seawater, including Lucky himself because someone has yelled, "That son of a bitch is on fire!"

He yells back, *"I ain't,"* and they stop spraying and come alongside. Pretty soon there's five or six coasties over the rail shooting fire extinguishers in every corner like they're fumigating his boat for bugs. They lash the *Wooden Nickel* onto the twenty-six's side, preparing to take him in tow. "Ain't nothing wrong with the boat," he tries to explain. "Scrub her down with some Ajax, she'll be clean as new."

The lifeboat skipper comes aboard and orders him out of his boat. "You'll have to ride with us, captain." He's about eighteen years old. Then he starts sticking his head into the engine compartment, which is still half filled with brown carbon dioxide foam. He looks right at the propane bottle and hose but they're so wet and blackened the kid doesn't know what they are. "These older vessels," he says, "no sense pushing them too hard."

Over the lifeboat's radio he can hear Shep Hallett on the race channel announcing the winner's time: *BAD PUSSY, WING TWENTY-NINE, ISUZU-POWERED, DRIVER PRISCILLA SHAVER, SPEED THIRTY-FIVE POINT ONE. SECOND PLACE, BODACIOUS, MERCURY-POWERED. THIRD, WHITE ELEPHANT. DID NOT FINISH: ONE BOAT, WOODEN NICKEL, DUE TO ENGINE TROUBLE.*

Then he hears the big diesels circling around for the final event.

The Coast Guard reads him their fire sermon off a printed card, and after he signs a paper saying he won't sue them for any damage during the tow, they give him back his boat and turn him loose. He grabs onto an old kelp-covered Stoneport mooring to check things out. Down below, the new turbocharger unit's cremated beyond recognition and the inside of the cabin is a black hole with a leftover stench like roasted cowshit, all the paint charred, gray sludge over everything, six inches of fire foam over the floorboards, coils of floating pot warp and half-melted mattress chunks drifting beneath the ashes of Ronette's blue curtains. Doesn't smell of gas, though, so he disconnects the propane hose and fitting and heaves the five-pound cylinder over the stern.

It seems impossible an engine would run after such punishment, but on a hunch he tries. He opens the gas line to see if she'll kick over, gives her a squirt of ether, and after a little cranking a couple of cylinders answer the call. Fucking Saginaw engines, they are a miracle, kick the living shit out of them and they ask for more. Running on three cylinders, he engages the mechanical bilge pump off of the power takeoff and watches a few hundred gallons of black foamy scum pour over the transom into the crystal-clear waters of Stoneport Reach.

He's with Reggie and Danny Thurston and Clayton Pettingill and some of the younger guys, waiting for the dark of the Stoneport evening to settle so the street dance can begin. Already the band is up on stage, they try a guitar lick, shorting out one amplifier with a clap of stage lightning, then try out some more amps and speakers. Their drumhead reads THE DEAD CRABS. Used to be decent country-western at the Stoneport races, now it's nothing but rock and roll.

Reggie's got a quart of Old Mr. Boston apricot brandy in a brown paper bag, he's passing it out to Travis Hammond and Danny and Clayton, then Norton Gross walks up and Reggie hesitates a minute because everyone knows there's something wrong with Norton, he gets some kind of seizures and he's not supposed to drink, but Reggie Dolliver says, "What the fuck, Norton, it's race day." Norton makes a funny noise when he slugs on it and his eyes bug right through his Coke-bottle glasses as the stuff goes down.

Lucky takes a hit for his engine and another for the woman with the Goldwing 29. "I seen this cocksucking striped pot buoy right on the south slope of Toothpick Shoal."

"Shag Island," Danny Thurston says. "I figured one of these days they'd be spreading out."

"Lunt gave them a rubber and a bullet," Travis adds.

Reggie Dolliver doesn't give a shit because it's not Split Cove territory, and he's not even fishing anymore, he's into home security. He's still urging them on. "Wouldn't be a bad idea to get them ass-holes, while you still got some territory left."

"Ought to go after them," says Norton Gross. He's reaching for the apricot brandy again, this time his eyes are popping out before he gets his hands on it. "Teach them a damn lesson."

"It ain't the old days," Danny Thurston says. "I got three hundred thousand sunk in this business. I can't afford to lose it. You guys see any trouble, call the Marine Patrol. Let the state handle it, that's what we pay our taxes for."

"What the fuck are they going to do about it?" Reggie says. "They're cops, they cruise around all day counting life jackets, what do they care who's fishing on whose ledge? Lobster territory ain't law any-how. It's tradition. You want to get something done, do it yourself."

"Them Shavers are trouble," says Art Pettingill's giant kid Clay-ton. He's around sixteen, but he's hammering down the apricot brandy like it's Prohibition. "I heard one of them bastards shot down the mail plane out there, just like they was shooting crows."

Lucky says, "It's the woman that's carrying that striped buoy up on the wheelhouse roof."

Norton Gross says, "I'm getting me a four-ten shotgun and keeping that son of a bitch aboard." Norton has a walleye like all his family on both sides. Just like a fucking flounder, one eye looks at you and the other's looking at something else. Old man's the same way. He's just a kid with his voice breaking but he says, "I see one of them cocksuckers setting inshore, I'll shoot first, ask questions later."

"Shoot with what," Clayton says, "your dick?"

"My four-ten. I'm getting it."

Lonnie Gross shows up now from out of the row of blue porta-johns, hitching up his pants. He's a square-shaped husky guy, built like a bear. Lucky's seen him lift a half-ton mooring block off the bottom with his bare hands, hooked her right over the cleat and reset her without using a hoist. Lonnie Gross grabs the brandy from his kid and slurps on it, then shows his hand around, same way he used to show the hairs he got from jerking off. Now he's got a whole thumb missing, not even a stump, looks like the hand of a fucking raccoon. They say the thumb is what makes us human, and Lonnie Gross has only got one left. "Dynamite cap," he says.

Norton Gross follows his old man with his straight eye like he ought to get the Purple Heart. The two of them look at each other with their good eyes, the wandering eyes meanwhile search the ground like metal detectors, looking for something else. "I'm getting me some of them dynamite caps," Norton Gross says, a chip off the old block.

Reggie Dolliver's got another bottle out now, getting the kids worked up over the territory. He loves it, reminds him of his convict days. Then he points behind Lucky with his big shit-eating grin. Lucky turns to see Reggie's old jailhouse buddy Ronette Hannaford driving right up to them in her chartreuse Probe. She rolls down the window and says, "Jesus, Lucky, look at them clothes. You look like you got struck by lightning."

She parks and hops out in cutoff jean shorts and Nike sneakers and a green tank top she could be arrested for. Reggie Dolliver turns to Lucky and says, "You let your sternman dress like that?"

Ronette says, "He don't let me wear nothing on that half-assed boat, but he ain't the captain on dry land."

He takes her over to the big Stoneport municipal wharf, where the Dead Crabs are into their first set already and the kids are starting to choose up partners and dance around. They get two beers and a plateful of chili dogs with peppers and onions and head out on the long pier. From there they can see the last rays of sunset over the lighthouse on Jackoff Point. The light switches on for the night while they're watching it, three red flashes just like thirty years ago, though he doesn't have to decode it like he used to with the Stoneport girls, it's already done. The sun sets fire to the Virgins for a moment, then it's gone and another race day is over, a year's worth of blown engines and broken dreams. He can't figure why anyone does it, except that when you think of it, nothing else matters. Once you know who's got the world's fastest lobster boat, everything else kind of falls into place.

Ronette separates their two hot dogs under the mound of chili, takes her own and scarfs it down. She's starting to eat for two. She looks him over as if something's missing. "Hey, you're not holding no trophy, are you?"

"No need to talk about it," he says.

Half the lobstermen are staying for the street dance, half are headed home, they turn on their running lights as they pass the Narrows and head out into the darkening water. Some of them have a three-hour ride, but they're used to it. They switch their radars on but don't bother to look in the hoods, they can all see in the dark. Most of their life's spent in the pitch-black hours before the sun comes up. They're off, drinking and laughing. In the dead calm of evening the sound carries all the way back to town.

Now the Stoneport girls appear from the crowded hilly little streets in packs of four or five but ready to be detached, sexy as ever, daughters and granddaughters of the girls they used to drag under the tuna wharf. Christ, one or two have a Lunt look to them, they could be anyone's.

"Hey Lucky, you're supposed to be staring at *me*." Ronette spins him around and gets a light off his cigarette.

"Fucked the boat up that last race," he says. "Might limp her home, but she ain't going fishing for a while."

"I heard. You was the talk of the town up at the Blue Claw. Racing some island woman and they say your boat caught fire. Deputy said you was burned alive."

"Bet you didn't give a shit when you heard that."

She kisses his ear with her wet chili dog lips. "I took off my apron and come right down. Somebody's got to give a shit, Mr. Luck, and I ain't seen Mrs. Lunt running your way."

There's a little breeze off the water now it's dark, and it does feel good on the singed skin of his arms and face. She edges up close to him on the tar-smelling pierhead and gives him the last inch of her chili dog. "I been thinking about it all the way down. I can take a second job at the RoundUp, Big Andy's always after me, then I can help pay for the boat."

"You got two jobs already. Anyway, you're the sternman. You ain't supposed to cover expenses."

"Lucky, look at me." She pulls his face around with both hands so he's right up close to her, he can feel the heat of her Marlboro on his ear. "I ain't just your sternman anymore."

"I know," he says. "I got to pay social security on you."

"That ain't what I meant. Don't you hear nothing I say?"

"Know what else, Ron? We got some fucking trouble coming up."

"Well it ain't going to happen tonight. Tonight we're going to forget it all and dance."

"Dance? I ain't danced since Danny Thurston's wedding."

"You been keeping the wrong company. You don't exercise, that heart'll go soft as an old tomato." She drags him past a bunch of Coast Guard men in their T-shirt uniforms, their eyes glazed over from testing the evidence, then through a clump of Stoneport kids standing in a fog of pot smoke, probably bought off the Coast Guard too, son of a bitches never waste an ounce. She drags him right past the Orphan Point gang, who are still huddled with Reggie Dolliver planning to shoot up a few boats. One of them whistles when Ronette starts to dance, and she is great-looking tonight in the green low-cut top with her tits peeking out over it like a clutch of wild duck eggs in the grass. Then he remembers why it is they're starting to look so big, it's not just Clyde's saline, she's going to be bulging all over before too long. The thought makes his hand reach into the deep back pocket of his work pants for the pint of 101-proof Wild Turkey. Nobody watches his habits anymore. He pulls it up and takes a slug and offers it to Ronette but she says, "No darling, I ain't supposed to, it says right on the bottle. Not yet. That's why I like them draft beers in the plastic cups, they don't have no pregnancy label."

Pregnant or not, she's dancing all over the place like it was the Rolling Stones up there playing "Brown Sugar" and not a bunch of clamdiggers that just met each other the night before. Lucky's big rusty eight-cylinder body is trying to recall what it was like to dance, but it gets mixed up with what it was like to fight, so he stands in one spot throwing long loopy punches in her direction while she's got her arms up in the air and her stern swaying and those big milky knockers sloshing around in a tank top that glows like a bug zapper in the mercury-vapor light. She's traveling and he's standing still. Pretty soon she's spun off towards Reggie's group to get another drink and he's throwing punches towards a woman he's never seen, a hippie tourist with blond hair and glasses and tired little city tits under a T-shirt that says LET LOBSTERS LIVE. He points at her chest and yells, "What the fuck's that?"

The hippie woman screams, "How would you like to be thrust headfirst into a boiling caldron?"

"Excuse me?" Lucky's not sure he hears her right, twists his finger around to drill out his good ear, the starboard one on the other side from the exhaust.

"Crustaceans feel *pain,*" the hippie woman shouts, "when they're *scalded.* Just like you or me." But she is dancing in a way he can keep up with, making deep swoops with her arms like she's swimming but staying in one place so he can throw punches at her till Ronette comes back.

Then he catches sight of Ronette dancing with Reggie Dolliver, they've both got beers in one hand, cigarettes in the other, and she's looking his way and sticking her tongue out since he's dancing with this animal-rights chick. Then she's getting too fucking close to Reggie and he stops dancing and works his way in their direction yelling, "Ain't you supposed to be on parole?" But suddenly there's the big zebra-stripe woman standing right in his path, and right behind her is the black-bearded brother with half his teeth. "What's your hurry," she says, "you going to a fire?"

"I would of sank you," he says, "if the fucking turbo was working right."

She laughs and takes a big suck out of something in a paper bag, wipes her mouth off with the back of her hand. "No doubt about that, captain."

He's about to get serious with her over the striped buoy when she takes one of his hands and says, "You dance as good as you race?" Before he can believe it he's dancing with this huge Shag Island pirate sow that looks just like one of those Russian female weightlifters that always turn out to have a dick.

Ronette comes up and looks about a foot up into Priscilla Shaver's face and says, "Ain't there no men where you come from?" and Priscilla purses her lips up like a monkfish and gives Ronette the finger, then the black-bearded guy says, "Ain't you the waitress over to Doris's Blue Claw?" and he starts doing this chicken dance in front of her, he's squatting down, clucking his Halloween teeth with his black tongue, his elbows are flapping, he's turning around and around and Ronette's not even trying to keep up with him, she's standing there staring. Well, she wanted to dance so much, what the hell. He turns back to Priscilla Shaver and shouts over the band, "You hauling many traps these days?" and she looks over towards her brother and shouts, "Looks like somebody's hauling your trap right now." Lucky spins around to crack out the rest of that son of a whore's teeth with the Wild Turkey bottle, but then Ronette busts out laughing and he doesn't have the heart to spoil her fun. He's getting into the Dead Crabs now, shaking the meat off his joints with both hands in the air like a revival meeting and the Bad Pussy right before him, eyeball to eyeball, same weight and height, saying, "You and me got together, we wouldn't have no boundary problems, would we?" He's trying to form the image of Priscilla Shaver in a wedding gown when Ronette comes up and cuts her away like a sheepdog. It's just skipper and sternman again, right in front of the Dead Crabs' amp. She's got both his hands and she's spinning the two of them back and forth, shouting, "Got to dance when you're pregnant, music's good for their *brain*."

"Jesus Christ, Ronette, this ain't music. It don't have a brain yet anyway."

"Speak for yourself," she shouts. "It does too."

The band's right in the middle of what sounds like "Satisfaction" and she's got him hopping up and down like a bullfrog, when all of a sudden he feels the twang of a busted guitar string, only it's not in the music, it's right in the center of his chest. He stands there rigid with his feet spread apart so he can stay upright, and when he gets his voice back, he says, *"Fuck,"* only it comes out high and croaky like a twelve-year-old.

She stops dancing and grabs both his hands and says, "What's the matter, sweetheart, you OK?"

"Ain't nothing," he says, "just my fucking heart. Twenty-six thousand dollars and they couldn't fix that son of a bitch."

"Sweetheart, your palms are all clammy. Let's sit down."

She takes him around the back of the chili dog stand along the wharf with the Stoneport skiff floats. No problem finding her car in the public lot, the chartreuse metallic looks radioactive in the mercury-vapor lamp. She opens the door for him and moves her waitress outfit off the passenger seat and tilts it so he can lean way back. The heart twangs once again but less so. His pills are back in the *Wooden Nickel,* moored up where the Coast Guard dropped him off. She feels under his blackened sweatshirt and work shirt and T-shirt and rubs his chest over the heart. "Jesus, Luck, you can't dance wearing all these clothes. No wonder."

It flips again, weaker but still random and noisy, sounds like the last flops of a mackerel on the cockpit sole. "Feel that?"

She puts her ear to it. "Yeah, it's scary. It stopped for about three seconds. Then it flopped. Now it's going again, just like a motor."

"Got to head out to the boat, get some of that stuff."

"Don't have to," she says. "I got some of your medicine right here." She reaches in the small lighted glove box of the Probe and comes up with an envelope of heart pills. "I took them off the boat," she explains. "Figured they might come in handy."

He swallows a few with a slug of Wild Turkey and things quiet down in there. "Ain't used to so much dancing," he says.

She takes his hand and holds it between her palms awhile, then checks the windows to see if nobody's looking and puts it on her chest, right on the little sea horse, which has grown bigger like it's painted on a balloon. "Maybe that'll warm it up. It's a heat wave and you got a hand like a Klondike bar." Then she pulls the tank top up and puts his palm down on her belly, low enough to feel the tickle of curly whiskers on his finger's edge. "It's *in* there," she says. "Sometimes I think I can feel it flopping. Just like your heart."

"Don't expect it's big enough to move around much."

"No Lucky, it is. I felt it. They're developing faster these days, it's on account of all the growth hormones in our food."

He rests his palm there awhile without feeling anything but drumbeats from the Dead Crabs, then he realizes where his hand is and starts feeling a little hard-on coming on. First it's the memory of a hard-on, since this is the very spot where he first got laid, sixteen years old, the far corner of the big Stoneport municipal lot, in the shadow of the icehouse, where he could feel the vapors of dry ice on his back like the cold tongue of death. The icehouse is still there, beneath the mercury streetlamp, its long shadow stretching almost to the Probe. "Hey Ron," he whispers, "the seats go all the way down on this thing?"

She says, "What about your heart?" but the windows are steamed up, it's dark outside, and one of her tits has already wormed out of the tank top, the end of it browner and bigger than it used to be.

"That's what I like about you," he says, "you're right up front."

"I'm an egg-bearing female, Lucky Lunt. You better notch my tail and throw me back, else you're going to be in deep-shit trouble."

"Too late," he says. She's already groping around the door panel on her side and pretty soon the driver's seat glides electrically down and forward, the seat back reclines almost to horizontal as if he's going to get drilled and filled. His heart pulses around like it can't decide whether to slow down with the medicine or run and catch up with Ronette. Then it takes a look at her tank top slipping down and just stops. For a second there's nothing happening in his chest at all, then there's a loud low thump back on the car's trunk and the heart starts racing like a timing chain. He turns fast and scrapes the fog off the window while Ronette pulls her clothes up and smacks the power locks down on her side and scrapes her window too. There's a huge towering figure blocking all light on one side of the low-slung Probe and a shorter, broader one on the other side. A weird, broken voice is calling, "Mrs. Hannaford!"

"Who the fuck?"

"It's me, Norton. And Clayton Pettingill. We seen your car. We can't find nobody from Orphan Point."

She lowers the window an inch with the power switch. "What do you kids want, a ride home?"

"No. Grind down your window. Hey, you got Lucky Lunt in there?"

"No, that's just a passenger seat dummy, keeps the perverts away." Ronette's fixing her shirt, patting her hair before she cranks the window down. Then she goes in the glove compartment for a cigarette. When the light goes on, he also notices a little .25 automatic, no bigger than a water pistol but it's real. Nice thing to have when there's a couple of guys hanging over your roofline, but these are friends.

Norton doesn't talk so great, and Clayton's shy, but between the two of them they get the information out. "Clayt's almost seventeen," Norton says, "and he ain't never been drunk before."

"Norton ain't either," Clayton Pettingill says.

"I have, you dumb fuck. I got drunk with my old man and my sister Laurie."

"Get it out," Lucky says. "What are you kids trying to tell us?"

"We found their *trucks*."

"Whose trucks?"

"The Shag Island trucks. When them cocksuckers come to the mainland they leave all their trucks in one spot, and we found it."

"You wait here," he says to Ronette.

"Lucky, don't be stupid. You just had a heart attack."

"I won't be a minute, I'll make sure these boys find a ride, then I'll come back." He hitches his pants up and follows them past the icehouse to a dirt-paved parking annex where there's about twenty-five vans and pickups, mostly big new four-wheel drives but some shitheaps too, there's dubs everywhere that can't find a lobster even if it's grabbing them by the nuts. The trucks are sitting in the moonlight quiet as headstones, all he can hear is the blood pumping in his chest and the far-off cacophony of the Dead Crabs.

The kids have stepped up from apricot brandy to a fifth of 151-proof Black Seal Rum that Reggie Dolliver sold them out of the goodness of his heart. Clayton Pettingill's already so big the fifth looks like a perfume bottle in his hand. It works, though, it's got him walking wide-legged and careful, looking down at the ground, like he's on deck in a heavy sea.

"You should have bought three of these," Lucky says. He hits up on the bottle too, hell of a lot healthier than those christly pills. Everyone knows alcohol's good for you, fucking doctors hold that information back. Clayton Pettingill stops to take a long piss on the back tire of a black Chevy Tahoe with a vanity plate that reads

SHG ISLD, no doubt where they're from. Beside the Tahoe is a brand-new Dodge Ram crew-cab whose metallic paint gleams in the moonlight like a kid's first dream of a red truck.

"That ain't what we want to show you," Clayton says after he zips up. The boys sneak him around behind the rows of trucks under the high three-quarter moon. His heart's fine now, his hard-on's gone, he feels like a young kid out to raise hell. It's women that slow you down.

The boys have a tough time crouching cause they're so big. Lucky doesn't bend so great either, his spine's stiff as a crankshaft from years at the pot hauler, but they're down on all fours by now, the two boys up ahead with their pants dragging down off of their asscracks like a couple of big pink pigs. Lucky brings up the rear, trying to keep from laughing because there could be people smoking and fucking in any of these silent trucks.

Clayton passes a white Dodge Ramcharger van with a black lab inside, curious but not barking, then stops at a Nissan King Cab shining lemon yellow in the moonlight, dark and empty inside but the bed full of lobster gear.

"King Crab," Lucky says. "So what?"

Norton Gross leads him around the back of the truck. There's four or five wire traps, a few coils of pot warp and about twenty zebra-stripe buoys, brand-new and still roped together in two bunches of ten, fresh from the painting shed. There's also a couple of jugs of outboard motor mix. Lucky takes out his rope knife and slices one of the buoys off. The three of them study the stripe pattern in the moonlight like it's a secret code. "That it?" Clayton asks.

"That son of a whore was setting right on Toothpick Shoal."

"Well," Clayton says to him, "you done this before. What are we supposed to do?"

"Norton's got the idea." He always thought Norton Gross had his wires crossed, but he's already back there with the gas flap open and the gas cap screwed off and he's got his dick down the filler pipe, taking a leak right in her tank. Meanwhile young Clayton Pettingill, who he always thought was a candyass Mormon despite his bulk, takes out his hunting knife and stabs it slow and deliberate into the front tire on the driver's side, the air squealing out like a stuck hog.

Lucky says, "Norton, when you're all done there, give me your T-shirt."

Norton hoists his trousers up, then starts to grunt and twist his short stubby arms around like he's trying to take his skin off, then he holds the shirt up so they can read it in the moonlight.

DON'T LIKE THE TIMBER INDUSTRY?
TRY WIPING YOUR ASS WITH A PLASTIC BAG

"What are you going to do?" he whines. "My mom bought me that shirt."

"Give me that jug of outboard mix," Lucky says.

They stuff as many striped buoys as they can into Norton's enormous T-shirt, then they splash on a decent amount of outboard fuel and set the bundle back in the bed of the Nissan, and top it off with a coil of poly rope. They scout around and find some newspaper and wad it up. He says to Norton and Clayton, "OK, I'm going back to Ronette's car, so she don't freak when it goes. You wait three minutes then light them papers and toss them onto Norton's shirt, then run."

Norton Gross takes out a Bic lighter and gets it ready by lighting up a cigarette but then he says, "Clayton should do it, it's his first time drunk."

Clayton reaches way down in his pocket, pretty near pushing his pants off in the process, and comes up with his own Bic lighter.

"Just wait three minutes and light the newspaper, Clayton, then set it on the shirt and run like hell."

Lucky walks back past the Chevy Tahoe that smells of new car paint and human piss, then stops to check out the toolbox in the bed of the Dodge Ram crew-cab next door. It's unlocked and he can stand on the running board and feel around in there till he gets his hand on a stubby little crowbar that ought to do the job. He tries it out on the left rear door, just soft at first, case anyone's around, then he gets going and whacks the passenger window on the crew-cab, makes a nice spiderweb on the second stroke, then moves up forward and takes out the two lights and the ram's head in the center of the grille. He turns and backhands the left headlight of the Tahoe, then takes out the windshield right above the wheel and brings the crowbar down on the center of the hood, nice strong Detroit steel at first, but a few sharp whacks and it's pretty much stove in. He'd dearly love to take out the Tahoe's grille, but he doesn't have the heart for that first whack on the Chevy emblem, too close to home, so he wedges the prybar in the driver's side door and bends it hard till he pulls the hinges out and leaves the tire iron inside on the floor: a little present from three generations of fishermen on Toothpick Ledge.

He crosses the uncut field between the main parking lot and the annex and joins Ronette in the Probe.

"I was so worried for you," she says. "I ain't even supposed to be smoking and look at this." She lights a new Marlboro from the one still burning and throws the half-smoked one out the window.

"You want to worry about something, look over there." He turns her head to stare into the darkness out of the left quarter window of the Probe. In about half a minute they see a pillar of glowing smoke in the next lot that makes him recall the old days before the environment, when they had such grand towering fires at the dump.

Ronette says, "Lucky, them boys set somebody's truck on fire?"

"No, ma'am. Just some pot buoys they wasn't ever going to use."

Then there's screeching and yelling from the Fag Islanders over in their parking lot, at the same time Clayton and Norton show up at the Probe smelling like smudge pots and they bang on the roof to be let in.

Lucky gets out on his side so the two huge kids can squish themselves in the back of the Probe. Norton Gross whines, "I can't fit, this fucking thing's in the way." He holds up a baby seat, brand-new blue padding and shiny chrome.

"Hey Ronette, I didn't know you had a kid." Clayton laughs. "You been keeping it secret?"

"Ain't none of your business," she says. "Be a good boy, Lucas, and stick it in the trunk."

But there's no time for that. Half the street dance is moving through the municipal lot, everyone's yelling *Truck on fire, truck on fire,* but they're not going to wait and see. He holds the child seat in his lap while Ronette backs out and maneuvers her way through the oncoming crowd. They're the only people going the other way.

Then someone runs past shouting *Orphan Point bastards* and Clayton says, "We better rescue them fucking boats."

They pass the municipal wharf with the Dead Crabs playing to an empty parking lot and a deputy's car flashing its blue strobe trying to open a passage to the crime scene. Honking, flashing her lights and nudging the crowd aside with her bumper, Ronette gets them down to the lobster dock where the Orphan Point boats are rafted up. Most have gone already, there's just the *Pisscat* and Danny Thurston's *Perpetrator* rafted up to the poor crippled *Wooden Nickel*. At least she's still afloat.

Travis Hammond and Danny Thurston show up running. They've got a quart of black rum and a couple of Stoneport girls. Travis's girl is this year's tenth-grade prom queen, Danny's got her little sister. The girls are begging to go aboard, but Danny and Travis fight them off and get on their boats so they can cast off before the lynch mob arrives.

He's still holding the baby seat when they climb aboard the *Wooden Nickel,* Ronette too, leaving the Probe right at the dock. He turns her over, hoping she's got enough cylinders to start. Fucking Chevy: two or three exhaust valves gone, carburetor black from the turbo fire, she turns over a couple times, thinks for a while, then remembers how to do it and starts up. Danny's got Norton and Clayton with him. Danny shouts over, "Hey Lucky, they rolled over the cop car!"

"Finest kind. Next they'll be coming after us."

"Don't worry, Lucky, we'll stay with you."

He shouts back, "You fucking well better, you got the bottle." Keeping it slow and quiet, not even the running lights, the three Orphan Point boats head westward past the band on the wharf, the red flasher off Jackoff Point, the green radar shapes of the Pope's Nose to starboard and the sharp dot of the Virgins gong buoy off to port. Now they're in open water, Danny snaps on his deck light so they can see him and Lucky puts on his red-and-greens so they can see him back. Travis Hammond's up between them with his lights blacked out but he's a nice fat moving target on the radar screen. Lucky's going only seven at full throttle, the smell of raw unburned gas mixing with charred cedar and extinguisher foam. Danny and Travis could be out of there in a minute, but they hold back and flank him side by side.

The radar shows a boat coming up behind, closing fast at a third of a mile. He looks back and can't see any lights. "They're coming," he says. "Only one boat. Anything left of them guns?"

She feels around below and hands him the twelve-gauge and a box of shells.

"Not that. The deer rifle. Look around for it."

"It stinks down there, Lucky." When it comes up, the gunstock smells like barbecue coal and it's covered with black soot like everything else down there. Good thing the ammunition didn't go off. He clicks the spent cartridge out of her and eases the helm to port so the oncoming boat is directly aft, then he hands the wheel to Ronette so he can turn around and aim. She says, "Lucky, what if it's the Coast Guard or the Marine Patrol?"

"It ain't. They'd show blue strobes like a cop car." There's nothing back there but the glare of the street dance off to the northward. He can't see the boat coming but she's still on the radar and he fires a shot over his wake into the area of blackness around the stern, but high. The blip keeps coming. He fires another one, low enough so it will whistle over their heads, then the blip turns and speeds back towards Stoneport harbor. "Hey, them stealth bombers got nothing on us, Ronette. We turned them with our radar-aimed missiles."

"Jesus, Lucky, put that thing away before somebody gets hurt."

The danger past and the rifle returned to its bulkhead rack beneath the shotgun, he can take back the helm and let Ronette snug up behind him in the chill. They're beyond the Jacob's Point light and the Virgin ledges now, in open water with the three-quarter moon dead in front of them on its way down in the southwest. In the flat calm, the sea looks like a bowl of light all the way to the horizon and they're steaming right into it. He's got the engine on full throttle but she's still doing only eight point one on the loran, farting and backfiring from the bad cylinders that got their valves sucked out when the turbo went. With that AJ-28 Danny Thurston could be under the covers with his wife by now, but he's hanging back for group protection, and Travis is staying with him, chickenshit though he is.

Ronette buries her nose in the small of his neck, presses up close to remind him of what they were doing when Norton and Clayton showed up. "You smell of gunpowder," she says.

"You like it. I ought to fire a couple rounds before I come to bed."

"We ain't got a bed," she reminds him. "You torched it trying to race that island slut."

The engine goes dead for a moment then catches again with a backfire that belches red flame up through the stack. "Ought to put one of them bullets through the block so she don't suffer so much."

She's left the wheelhouse to take a flashlight down into the cuddy and try to scare up some music.

"Lucky, there's fucking *water* in here."

He kicks in the bilge pump and he can hear the water slosh over the side. "That better?"

When she comes up she's crying. "You ain't got a stereo anymore. I wanted to play my new Tanya Tucker tape."

Number four cylinder has dried out and she sounds a bit better now, though it's loud as hell cause he took off the muffler for the race. She comes up the companionway and stands behind him and puts one hand on his shoulder, the other on the glowing radar screen. "I was getting pretty comfortable on this thing," she says. "It's close to all the home we got."

"You got your cousin's trailer. I got my house."

"I mean *we,* Lucky. I used to think it was our little nest down there. Now it's a black frigging hole." Still wearing the tank top and cutoffs from the street dance, she burrows into his sweatshirt to get warm.

"Put on some oilskins from below."

"There ain't any, Lucky. All the rain gear melted together down there." She comes up with a big mass of blackish-orange material that used to be bib overalls and aprons.

"I'll pull them apart back home," he says. "Might be able to salvage some of them things."

Soon as the moon goes down, a light damp southerly comes in and it starts clouding up fast from the west. There's a dull flash of lightning way to the westward, over the Tarratine River mouth, then right over the hills behind Burnt Neck. A little gust of rain comes through the open windshield and she shivers like she's standing in a fish freezer. "Ain't cold," he says. "It's July."

"It's cold for me."

He peels off the remains of his sweatshirt, which has a nice comforting smell, like brake fluid after a long summer drive. It hangs down below her knees like a dress, she pulls her hands up in the sleeves and puts her face up so he can tie the hood. By the time they follow the *Perpetrator* through the Split Head passage and into home territory the sky is glowing behind them and it's 4 A.M. Ronette spots two porpoises off the port bow in the dim light. "Look Lucky, bet them things been following us all night." He swerves sharp over like he's going to run them down. "You want me to get the gun, Lucky, so's you can shoot them?"

"They're good eating but they're too fucking hard to clean."

The child's car seat is still lying on the platform where they dropped it in their escape from Stoneport. She picks it up and hooks it over the bulkhead opposite the wheel and pot hauler, protected by the portside window. "That's where he's going to ride."

"What do you mean, *he?* How do you know what it is?"

"I just know, Lucky. But soon as I can, I'll get a sonogram."

"What's that?"

"It's like the fishfinder, only they put it on your stomach. You can see them. Only they don't look human yet, they look like fish."

"We was all fish once," he says. "Would of been nice back then." She yawns and closes her eyes on his shoulder as he's making the last turn around the Split Point gong. He flashes his spotlight to say good-bye and thanks to Travis and Danny and heads north and east into Split Cove. Then she gets excited when they pass the Split Ledge nun. "Hey, you going to let us go home and get some sleep?"

"Ain't no sleeping on this boat," he says. "I'm going to Split Cove to pick up bait. See if you can scrape off a couple aprons down there. Boat's running decent. We got some lobstering to do."

8

H E GETS UP LATE and shares with Alfie a long breakfast of microwaved eels and King Oscar Norway sardines. The sun's
well up there in a cool cloudless sky. A branch of the poplar out back
has gone yellow already and half its leaves are on the ground. Wind's
coming northwest, just like fall. The other boats pissed out of the
harbor three hours ago, today the *Wooden Nickel* is fishing late. The
Shag Islanders have set a couple hundred zebra-stripe pot buoys off
of Toothpick Shoal and they're hauling them after everyone's gone
home. He's heading out there armed like a helicopter gunship and
hope to Christ he'll catch them in the act.

The old Chevy engine went from bad to worse. Harley tapped an
eye into it and sank it for a mooring block, then sold him a little
Ford straight-six that had been rusting in the grass for twenty years.
She'd run better with a hamster wheel but what could he do, he had
to get out to his gear. A lobster trap is like a woman, you don't haul

her up off the bottom now and then, she'll gnaw herself to death. By the time he got out to his fishing ground they'd laid a minefield of zebra-stripe buoys that stretched southward towards Nigh Shag as far as the eye could see. Fuck that. He nukes another eel for himself, changes his mind and slips it into Alfie's dish. Going out at this time, eight-thirty, when everyone else has been fishing since sunrise, who knows when he'll be getting back?

He can't help slowing down as he drives past the window of Yvonne Hannaford's Wharfside Art Gallery, it's full of Sarah's sea glass, big sign in the bay window:

ABSTRACTIONS
MOBILES AND SCULPTURE
SARAH PEEK LUNT
OPENING AUGUST 15 4:30
WINE & BRIE

All that fucking money and they don't even know how to spell beer.

Art Pettingill's got the *Bonanza* up to the wharf already and he's shoving hard-packed lobster crates on the dock as fast as Albert can weigh them in. "I had too many goldarn lobsters," he shouts. "Had to quit early or we would of sank." Art's a true believer, he's got the Mormon Rock station going full blast, that's all he listens to. He wouldn't come out with a swear word if one of his twelve-dollar lobsters reached up and bit his dick off. It crosses Lucky's mind that Art's fishing success might be related to his faith in God, but he lets that one drop into the bilge of bad ideas. Plenty of atheistical bastards catch big fish. Besides, the *Bonanza*'s sporting a bullet hole in the port windshield, few feet on the other side and it would have ended up in a Christian brain.

"Hey Art, you putting some speed vents in that windshield?"

"I picked up one of them new stripe traps down south of Toothpick Shoal, just to see what they was using for bait."

"Hope you killed a couple of them bastards."

"I did not. Reverend Pingree addressed the matter Sunday and he said to turn the other cheek and that's what I intend to do."

"Then you ain't packing?"

"I am not packing nothing," Art says. "The Good Lord will provide enough for all. Besides, they're down on your end of the ledge. Har har." Art laughs like a fucking walrus, climbs stairs like one too, the way he snorts through his mustache and drags his three-hundred-pound body up one step at a time, you'd think the Good Lord gave him flippers instead of arms and legs.

Lucky's helping old Albert roll a bait barrel down the gangway when Clyde Hannaford comes limping down the outside office stairs like something's wrong with his leg. He's holding a box. "Lucky, I got your radio back."

"Finest kind, Clyde. I ain't got no money to pay for it."

"Hell, Lucky, your credit's always good with us. Ninety-four bucks' damage, and I'm not making a nickel off it. I'll show you the receipt straight from Neptune Electronics. For that price I could have sold you a new one that would have got all the channels."

"I like the old one, thanks."

Clyde looks down at the gun case. "Those pirates giving you trouble?"

"No Clyde, just thought I might spot a deer out there. What's wrong with your leg?"

"Nothing. My foot fell asleep at the computer."

"Jesus, Clyde, you got a hazardous occupation up there. Your insurance cover you for that?"

"It doesn't. It doesn't cover Rhonda anymore either."

"What's that supposed to mean?"

"Nothing. Just a point of information." Albert the baitboy, who's about sixty years old, is stopping close by with his ear hanging out. "Carry the man's bait over to his boat, Albert," Clyde snaps. "He's running late."

"You got any other information?" Lucky says.

"I hear they near put a bullet through Li'l Nort, out by Tooth-pick Shoal."

"They ain't very good shots, then. Li'l Nort's a hard target to miss. What's he doing out there anyway? He ain't got the boat for that."

"Slicing off pot warp, that's what I hear."

"Jesus. They take a fucking shot at me, they'll remember it."

"Don't kill them all," Clyde says. "They could improve the local economy." Under the tinted glasses Clyde's eyes look like a couple of squirts of gullshit.

"You ain't saying you're going to do business with them son of a whores?"

"Free enterprise," Clyde says. "Those Shavers are highliners. Ever seen the trucks they drive? They bring in three hundred pounds a day. They've been lugging it all the way to Sweeney's Seafoods in Norumbega, might as well let it pass through Orphan Point. Our school needs a new roof, our roads have more potholes than Bosnia."

"They're taking them lobsters right off my fucking ledge."

"Then you better go protect them. Better take care of your stern-lady too, it's a jungle out there. The world is changing, Lucas, the old boundaries are coming down."

He gives Clyde the finger and backs her out sharply under a cloud of screeching seagulls and blue smoke from the old Ford, pleasure craft scattering out of his way. Fuck sailboats. Fuck kayaks. He opens the throttle and heads for one black-haired yuppie kayaker that looks just like Clinton's boyfriend George Stepopotamus, then swerves at the last moment and pisses right through the school of them, only his new six-cylinder wake is so small they don't even notice him go by.

Ronette's wearing a pink T-shirt from the Burnt Cove Oyster Farm with a ripped-open neck that's falling off one shoulder and a big open oyster over each tit. She's got cutoff shorts and Nikes like they're going on a picnic, not to haul lobster traps and maybe digest some lead over the territory of Toothpick Ledge. Those slick brown legs would look pretty bad cut up with birdshot. Or worse. She swings down the ladder and over the starboard rail as Ginger performs her new trick of jumping off the pierhead right onto the wheelhouse roof.

"Ginger ain't coming today," he says. "Get her back up on land and send her home."

"How come, Lucky? She gets bored at home. Besides, Clyde could come over and kidnap her."

"I got two guns aboard today, don't want no animals getting hurt."

The dog hasn't learned to climb the ladder yet, so Ronette has to climb back up and call her from shore. Ginger leaps in and swims for the boat landing and Ronette slaps her on the tail and sends her home.

He looks her over when she gets on board. "How come you ain't dressed for work?"

"Aw, Lucky. It's wicked hot." She looks down and tries to fasten the top snap of her shorts but she can't do it.

"Eating too much," he observes.

"I ate too much back in May. I'm on the Lucky Lunt diet plan. Gain fifty pounds in nine months."

"Here, put these on." He tosses her the big spare orange rubber work pants he uses to keep the sun off the seawater tank.

"Too damn hot for them things. Maybe I'll work topless today, that'll scare them pirates off."

The whole time they had the *Wooden Nickel* over in Riceville while Harley dicked around with the Ford six, Ronette was coming aboard with her paintbrush and sewing box. She painted the bulkheads horsepiss yellow and the wood trim the color of windshield-washer fluid. The new foam pad has a flowery couch cover and a fringed pillow with an embroidered picture, smells just like Yvonne's Gift Shoppe. Pine cone soap. The picture is a six-passenger canoe entering a covered canal with bushes all around it, looks like the boat's steering right into a cunt. *Tunnel of Love,* that's what it says. They're paddling right back where they came from. She's got new blue curtains on the side windows. She's painted the old piss-bucket bright yellow and stuck a roll of pink toilet paper beside it so you no longer have to wipe your ass with the tide tables. He hollers up over the exhaust: "Looks like a whorehouse down here."

"I knew you was going to like it," she says. "But it ain't a whorehouse. It's a nursery."

They make the Sodom whistle and turn southwest towards Toothpick Shoal. Just north of Toothpick, on the four-fathom spot known as Gross's Bank, Lonnie and Laurie and Li'l Nort are pulling in keepers as fast as they can haul them. Danny Thurston's about a mile beyond, hauling off to starboard from the *Perpetrator,* his old man Howard a bit beyond him in the *Gloria T.* By this time it's getting choppy, they've all put in a seven-hour day, and they're pulling their last strings, boats full and fixing to go in.

It's so shallow at the center of Toothpick, the sunlit morning swell breaks over it in explosions of fourteen-karat spray. He's almost forgotten he's got a working radio till a voice comes in on the

Orphan Point channel: *HEY, WOODEN NICKEL, YOU GOING OUT FOR SOME NIGHT FISHING?*

It's Howard.

"Negative," he comes back. "I'm going to drag for some bottom-feeders. You might want to come along."

NEGATIVE, LUCAS. I GOT THREE CRATES OF LOBSTERS ABOARD, I'M TAKING THEM IN WHILE CLYDE'S STILL GOT SOME MONEY LEFT.

Ronette says, "You ain't getting much help on this."

"My old man's day, they'd of had a posse out here. Boundaries don't mean nothing anymore."

She gives him a big pregnant smile. She used to have an under-nourished look, now her face is rounding and widening like a belly. "You got a posse of one. One and a half, counting the unborn."

"Can't shoot too good when they're all balled up like that."

"Don't matter, loyalty's what counts."

They're steaming onto the north edge of his ground with no foreign boats in sight, though the radar shows a couple of vessels way offshore and coming on. The only thing on Toothpick Shoal is a red-hulled sailboat that's dead in the water with her canvas furled and heeled over like she's trying to winch up a trap. In the binoculars he can read the name on the stern: *Bull Goose,* out of Dover, Delaware. "They don't make enough off of their god damn stocks," he says, "they got to steal lobsters. Steer over, see what the fuck's going on."

They come up to starboard of the *Bull Goose* but they can't see any traps aboard. The crew are all hanging over the side looking down towards the rudder. Three men and three women with blotchy sunburnt legs and a tangled pot warp around their wheel. They should be on the golf course where they belong, bunch of rich ass-holes with a big red plastic bath toy frigging up five hundred dollars' worth of gear. Just one of their stainless steel winches would cost more than a man's house. His finger trembles for the bird gun but Ronette says, "Take it easy, Luck, they ain't got one of yours."

He takes the binoculars and looks again. The buoy tangled in their propeller has a zebra stripe. He steers upwind and brings her alongside on the lee of the sailboat and yells, "You drag that fucking thing from someplace or was it there?"

"Right on this spot," the skipper says. "It stopped us cold. I'm awfully sorry, if it's one of yours. We had no intention . . ."

"Finest kind," Lucky says. "It ain't one of mine. You want some lobsters?"

"Never pass up an opportunity," the guy says. "Course we can't afford an arm and a leg."

"I'm sure you can't." He slips back a bit and gaffs the zebra buoy and slices it off with the rope knife. "Here's a souvenir." He tosses the buoy over to the skipper, then spins the *Wooden Nickel* bow-and-stern alongside of the *Bull Goose,* gaffs the warp and puts it on his pot hauler. "Now turn your prop nice and slow in reverse," he yells, "slip the clutch, she'll peel the line right off." The captain starts his fart-nosed little toy diesel and the hauler pulls the line free off his shaft.

"How much do we owe you for the rescue?" Now they've all got their wallets out, big eager accountant smiles like a bunch of Arvid Hannafords.

There's more than one trap on the zebra buoy's line. He hauls the first one, then comes in close and throws four good-sized shedders right into the sailboat's cockpit, one after the other. The three wives are backing away and squeaking like rabbits, but the men corral the monsters into a corner with their boathooks and work all four of them into a nylon sail bag, then they pull the drawstring tight and throw the bag below. The wives squeal and applaud like they're married to a bunch of toreadors.

Free at last, the red sailboat is drifting downwind now in the breeze and tide. "Better watch it," Lucky shouts, "you'll pick up another one."

"How can we thank you?" one of the wives shouts. "Don't you want a bottle of scotch?"

Ronette yells back, "I can't drink alcohol, ma'am, cause of my condition."

"Oh dear, what a sweet thing. And you're still working all the way out here. Take care!"

By the time they turn around there's a foreign boat hauling traps right on the southern drop-off of Toothpick Shoal. He doesn't need binoculars to see it's a Wing Brothers hull and hear the same Isuzu diesel that smoked him at the Stoneport races.

"There's another one coming," Ronette says. This one he hasn't seen before, it's an identical Goldwing hull with the snub stern, but midnight black. "Let me have them glasses." It's coming on fast, in a minute he can read the name *Darth Vader* on the bow. The white one's the *Bad Pussy*. They've both got zebra buoys skewered on their radio whips. The two of them are stopped together now, right on the south fringe of Toothpick Shoal, and the *Darth Vader*'s just idling while the *Bad Pussy* hauls a triple over the side. The orange-bearded guy with the finger stump and contact lenses is alone on the *Darth Vader*. The ponytailed one is sternman on the *Pussy*. The traps are loaded and they're keeping everything they haul. "You think they don't see us?" Ronette says.

"Of course they fucking see us. But they ain't going to want to see us when I'm done."

Soon as they bait and drop the last of that string and cast the buoy off, the two boats head for another a hundred yards northwards. Lucky reaches behind the bulkhead and pulls the .410 out and hands it to Ronette. "Bird gun," he says. "Ever use one?"

"Old Clyde had me trained on the pistol range. He wanted me to defend myself, case anyone made a sexual advance."

He puts a hand down the back of her orange work pants but she slithers away. He steers up to the zebra buoy they just set two minutes ago, gaffs the toggle and slices the warp off with the rope knife, that's two traps they'll never see again. A man's voice instantly comes over channel 64: WATCH YOUR ASS, COWBOY. THEM AIN'T YOUR FUCKING TRAPS.

There's another zebra buoy a couple of hundred feet upwind. He puts the helm up and goes over and sets that one on the hauler to see what they've got. He sees the *Darth Vader* guy holding his mike, and the same voice comes over the VHF: I SAID, STAY THE FUCK OFF OF THAT TRAP.

He punches the mike button and says, "Clear off the fucking channel, this channel's Orphan Point."

Lucky cuts him off by going back to channel 16 — emergencies only — but there they are: YOU DON'T OWN THE AIR, COWBOY. YOU DON'T OWN THE WATER, YOU DON'T OWN NOTHING.

He punches the VHF mike and says, "Suck my dick, asshole."

A sugary female voice comes on and says, VESSELS CONVERSING ON CHANNEL SIXTEEN, BE ADVISED THAT CHANNEL SIXTEEN IS A CALLING AND DISTRESS FREQUENCY. THIS IS THE UNITED STATES COAST GUARD, OUT.

Now the two boats are coming right at him from the windward side of the ledge. He puts her in neutral and pumps a shell into the chamber of the .410. They're looking down each other's throats but the Isuzus make so much noise they have to use the radio. When he gets out the deer rifle and hands the .410 shotgun to Ronette, the *Bad Pussy*'s diesel queen comes on: HONEY, AIN'T YOU TOO SMALL FOR THAT KIND OF WORK?

A boat comes steaming up behind them. It's the *Abby and Laura*, manned by Lonnie and Norton Gross. Lonnie comes on the radio, WE AIN'T GOING TO LET YOU DOWN, then the *Darth Vader*'s skipper picks up a big hunting rifle and fires one right into Lonnie's hull less than a foot over the waterline. Cheap fucking glass must be about an eighth of an inch thick, cause the hollowpoint opens a hole you could put your dick through. He goes back on channel 64: "Lonnie, the son of a whore opened you up on your port side. You better stuff a sock in there and haul ass home."

Ronette's at the wheel idling the engine but when she sees the chop splashing around the hole in Lonnie's hull she says, "Lucky, why not get out of here and let the law take care of this?"

"Only law out here is us. We let them get away with this, they'll be handing this ledge down to their fucking kids."

He tries to reach Howard and Danny Thurston. "*Gloria T,* this is *Wooden Nickel.* You on here, Howard?"

Howard comes back, CAN'T HEAR YOU, LUCKY, YOUR TRANSMISSION'S BREAKING UP.

He looks at the radio and there's a film of blue smoke coming out of it like someone's smoking a cigarette in there. He rips the mike cord out of its socket and yells into it, "Fuck you, Clyde, ninety-four dollars to fix this sucker and it works for five minutes." He throws the mike towards the *Bad Pussy*, which is calmly setting a string of traps maybe a hundred yards away. It whirls around and lands in the waves. "Fucking lobsters can fix it better than your old man."

"Old *ex.*"

One of Lucky's green-and-orange buoys bobs off the *Bad Pussy*'s port side so close it's almost up against her hull. "Dumb cunt's setting them right on top of me. Steer over there."

As soon as the *Bad Pussy* baits her zebra-stripe and sets it down right next to his orange-and-green, Ronette shows up there with the

Wooden Nickel. Lucky hauls the single trap on his buoy and takes out a nice two-pounder. He cleans the crabs and starfish out, baits it and drops it back. The *Bad Pussy* is working a couple hundred feet to the west, the *Darth Vader* close in behind her but not working traps, just waiting in reserve.

At that point the Coast Guard lady comes on his radio, which can't transmit anymore but it can hear. *VESSELS ENGAGED IN TERRITORIAL DISPUTE, PLEASE GIVE YOUR LOCATION.*

He sees the orange-bearded guy pick up the microphone over in the *Darth Vader. WE ARE FOUR MILES SOUTHEAST OF THREE WITCH LEDGE.*

THANK YOU, CAPTAIN, WE'LL HAVE A VESSEL ON STATION ETA THREE P.M.

Ronette looks startled. "That ain't where we are."

True enough, the *Darth Vader* gave the Coast Guard a position twenty-five miles away. Anyone would have done the same. "Ain't government business, Ronette. It's them and us."

He reaches down and gaffs the zebra-stripe buoy they've just set down and slices the warp off below the toggle. Over in the *Darth Vader* the orange-bearded brother leaves the wheel and aims a rifle right at them. "Down in the cuddy," Lucky orders Ronette.

"What the hell, Lucky, I ain't scared."

"Ain't you I'm thinking about."

She takes one step down the companionway and stops by the engine box with just her head out above the hatch. In the face of that son of a bitch with his raised rifle barrel he steams over to the next zebra-stripe buoy and slows to gaff it. Right as he's bringing the toggle up to catch it on the drum, a shot breaks the safety-glass windshield over Ronette's head and a split second later the bang comes in, cunt hair's difference between impact and noise. Fucking bullets are faster than sound. Another shot, then the radar makes a couple of loud clicks like a sewing machine and the screen goes blank, just the raster line wheeling around. He can't see the radome up over the wheelhouse but they must have knocked it out. He pumps the lever on the .300 Savage and aims through the two-power scope sight to put a shot through the *Darth Vader*'s windshield from the stern.

Boom.

He got the shot off steady but a wave lifted him just as he fired, so it probably went over. Didn't kill anyone, anyway: the orange-bearded captain comes to the transom and flips that missing finger at him, a fist with a one-inch stump on it. If he wants to get the point across he ought to use the other hand.

He runs seaward again to pull another zebra buoy but before he can get the gaff on it the *Bad Pussy*'s black-bearded sternman buries a rifle bullet right in a hull plank aft of the stem, no .22 either, got to be at least a .30-30. Ronette says, "They *got* us," and grabs his leg like it's a life ring. The *Wooden Nickel*'s inch-and-a-half white cedar is sounder than the day it was cut, it didn't open up like Lonnie Gross's pulpy fiberglass, but still he feels it like it went into his own skin. He puts the crosshairs on the left shoulder of that black-bearded sternman standing with the rifle in one hand, scratching his balls with the other and smiling like a piano with his missing teeth. Just like aiming at a deer. His bald head is covered with a Hells Angels bandanna but the ponytail sticks out behind and in the scope the pit bull tattoo shows on his upper arm. With no one at the helm, they've gone beam to the wind so both boats are in the trough, causing the crosshairs to move up and down on the guy's body. The swell drives the sights down to the guy's knee, then up to the wheelhouse top. He's standing right in front of the big female captain, who is mostly out of sight behind his body, and that crazy son of a bitch, with a .300 Savage scoped right in on him, has now got his own gun butt down on the platform and he's raising his ball-scratching hand to give Lucky the finger. He doesn't know who he's fucking with, it's not just Lucas Lunt but his old man Walter and Walter's old man Merritt Lunt who fished this ledge under a canvas sail. Even so, Lucky would not pull the trigger on a man for his dead ancestors, or for Kyle either, he's a lost cause, with his Jap sushi dealer and his fairy boyfriend, but this other one that's already popping the buttons of Ronette Hannaford's shorts, he'll be a chip off the old block. He's still in the larval stage now, but one day he'll be a lobsterman and he's going to need this ledge.

So thinking of someone he can't even picture in his mind, he waits for the upswell to pull the crosshairs right under that fucking finger, then he shoots.

The deer rifle kicks his arm back so he can't see where it hit. The sound of it throws Ronette's head down into the companionway, but she comes up yelling, "Jesus, Lucky, what'd you aim at?"

Though he truly wishes the black-bearded guy's body would be jerking like a mackerel on the cockpit floor, he is still standing. He has dropped his gun and gone over beside the female captain at the helm. Lucky tries to see what's going on through the two-power scope but it's too weak and he can't hold it steady. "Give me them binoculars."

He missed the black-bearded bastard's finger and hit the woman. She's standing with a bloodstain on her sweatshirt, he can see that, then the black-bearded guy sits her down on the rail to take a look. The *Darth Vader* comes up close beside the *Bad Pussy* while the black-bearded sternman leads her below. There's no one visible for a while, then he comes up and takes the helm. They've still got a line on the pot hauler. The sternman slices the warp off the winch drum with a knife, so it must be serious. He watches the line clear his wheel, then he puts her in gear and jams it, the stern dips and they steam due south for Shag Island under full throttle, with the *Darth Vader* hammer down and following close behind.

Ronette's back in the companionway now, saying, "Lucky, what did you do?"

"I winged her."

"You shot a human being?"

"Depends how you want to define it."

"You don't believe in nothing, do you?"

"I believe them son of a whores are off the territory. Now we got work to do. Let's finish slicing off their christly traps."

By now the two Goldwings, black and white, have disappeared into the summer haze around Nigh Shag. He heads for another zebra-stripe buoy and gaffs it up onto the hydraulic winch and cuts the line. She's standing beside him at the pot hauler but she's not helping, just bitching about something over the power takeoff noise.

"It's gone too far, Lucky. It ain't funny anymore. What if something happens to her?"

"She's built like a fucking buffalo. Just grazed the blubber, ain't going to hurt her none."

Just then an official-looking dogshit-colored boat comes steaming from the eastward. Arriving just a wee bit late, the State Marine Patrol slows up and hits the blue flashing strobe. He empties the chamber on both guns, dumps the spent shells over the side and sticks the guns in the life jacket locker, then lights a cigarette to cover the gunpowder smell.

The radio clicks on: *WOODEN NICKEL, THIS IS ENFORCER. HEY LUCAS LUNT, THAT YOU? WHAT THE HELL'S GOING ON OUT HERE?*

He steps to the middle of the cockpit, points to the antenna and throws his hands out, palms up, to signal his transmitter's out. In a minute they're alongside, two guys in olive uniforms, one old, one young, and he knows them both. Ryan Beal is an Orphan Point native, Wilfred Beal's brother, he was playing cop and arresting kids when he was nine years old, whole family of righteous dickheads.

Ryan Beal yells, "Hey Lucas, your radio out?"

"It listens. It don't talk."

"You ought to take a lesson from that thing. Har har." Ryan says to the kid, "Looks like we might have a violation here."

Young Jason Reynolds stares like an owl at Ronette's outfit, he doesn't get to see much pussy in his line of work. Not caring for the smell of cops, she ducks down and comes back in one of Lucky's oilskin jackets that covers her like an umbrella tent. On top of the *Enforcer*'s wheelhouse their blue police strobe keeps flashing, though there's nobody to see it for miles around.

They put a couple of fenders over and tie up alongside. The afternoon chop sloshes the boats together like a couple of drunks. Ryan Beal steps aboard, followed by the kid Jason. They've both got the brown Marine Patrol uniform, green shirt, dogshit neckties to match the boat. Ryan's dead serious as always but the kid looks like he wants to give Ronette the body cavity search, see if she's carrying any drugs in there. They've both got notebooks and pencils and Ryan is snooping around the boat like he's Dennis Franz on a homicide. First thing he sees is the bullet hole in the windshield. He flips his notebook open and starts writing notes. "Have a little altercation out here?" he says.

"They was setting traps in my space, so we chased them off."

Jason, a tall skinny kid with a little black mustache and a weird deep voice like a radio announcer, says, "No one owns the sea."

Ryan says, "You carrying any weapons aboard?"

"Just a little .300 Savage, to scare the gulls away."

"Got any other damage? Anyone hurt?" He looks at Ronette, who's leaned back against the wheel in his big yellow Grundens jacket, listening. "You all right, miss?"

"Bit shook up is all. Never had bullets pass that close."

Lucky looks over his shoulder to see what Ryan's putting in the notebook but he can't make it out. "They took out the radar too, that will cost me four or five thousand, windshield will be a couple hundred if I glaze it in myself. Took a bullet in the hull too. Write that down."

"You were cutting their traps, huh? That's a violation. 'Intentional damage to fishing gear in or out of service.' Do any shooting yourself?"

"We put a couple over their heads, after they knocked the radar and windshield out."

"And they took off."

"Yeah."

"You didn't hit anybody? You didn't damage the other vessel?"

"Too far to see nothing. Soon as we fired back they took right off."

Ryan Beal turns to Ronette, who's lighting one cigarette off the other and leaning on the wheel like she can't stand up. "What about you, miss? You're the waitress at the Blue Claw, aren't you? You look like an observant person. Did you notice anyone hurt, any damage to the other vessel?"

Ronette shakes her head silently like she's deaf and dumb.

Ryan Beal goes on: "We're asking you cause we heard something on the scanner, somebody hurt out to the island. We was just wondering if maybe your warning shot might have come in a little low. Seeing as how it's pretty rough out here."

"Might of been hard to aim," the kid Jason adds. "I'd hate like hell having to shoot straight in a chop like this."

Ryan Beal writes something in his notebook. He says to Lucky, "You still living in your house?"

"Course I'm living in my house. Where the Christ you think I live? You pass it every day going to work."

"Just wondering. Place got a vacant look. Just so's we know how to reach you." He measures the windshield hole with a lobster gauge, pokes his head below, hops up on the rail to check out the holes in the radar dome, one on each side where the bullet went clean through. "Let's go, Jason, let these nice folks get back to fishing. We'll take a run out to sea, see what the islanders have to say."

"Finest kind."

Ryan Beal turns to him. "One other thing, Lucas. We're going to have to take your gun."

"Like hell."

"You want to see trouble multiplied by ten, you just try hanging on to that thing."

Ronette goes below for the .300 Savage and comes out holding it at arm's length, barrel pointing straight up in the air. "That's a good girl," Ryan Beal says. He takes it and hands it over to Jason, who opens the chamber and smells it like a drug-sniffing beagle. "Been fired," Jason says.

"Course it's been fucking fired. It ain't brand-new." They don't ask for any other weapons, so he doesn't mention the shotgun still left in the life jacket box.

The cops keep their light flashing and throttle up due south, tearing a path right through a patch of Travis Hammond's blue-and-white buoys, probably rip a few of them up, big government wheel wouldn't even notice them. In five minutes they're hull down and halfway to Nigh Shag Ledge.

"You're going to hear from them guys," Ronette says. "They was both taking notes like maniacs, and the young guy was drawing pictures of the windshield and the radar. He was kind of cute too, for a cop."

"He looks like one of them perverts that would put the cuffs on you before he did anything. Besides, I thought you was already notched."

She wraps her arms around him in the old oilskin jacket that smells of gullshit and herring guts. He stays long enough to feel the shape of her body fitting around him in a different way, then he unsheathes the rope knife, gooses the antique Ford and steams over to slice another Shag Island trap.

9

Ronette has to work both breakfast and dinner shifts at the Blue Claw, so she can't come with him to the State Fisheries Board hearing at the Tarratine County offices, where he must show cause why his lobster license should not be revoked. He's driving up there with his lawyer, Kermit Beal. At 8:30 A.M. Kermit shows up in a two-tone Eddie Bauer Edition Ford Explorer that still has the price sticker on the window. Thirty-three thousand, bit over the cost of a heart job.

It is the height of the tourist season now, the Norumbega Road's jammed with out-of-state Saabs, Lexuses, Range Rovers, BMWs, Volvos, humpbacked Mercedes Nazi SUVs. Kermit's looking at his watch and swearing under his breath.

"We ain't due till ten," Lucky says.

"Know how I got this car?" Kermit Beal asks. Lucky swallows

his heartfelt answer, looks straight ahead. "I got it because I have never been late to a god damn thing. Not since grade one."

"I was late all the time," Lucky says. "I used to get up at three and go out fishing with my old man for four hours, and when the tide weren't in our favor I'd miss the bell. One morning I reached the front door of the old Orphan Point High School around nine-thirty A.M. and just kept on walking and left her abeam. My old man was waiting at the dock like he expected it. I ain't been in a schoolhouse since, that's why I'm driving a piece of shit pickup and you're tooling around in this. They probably still got me counted late."

"That's a good one, Lucas. Thirty years late. And you haven't done bad for yourself. Up till now, anyway. He he he." He ends up his laugh with a big slurp from the Eddie Bauer coffee mug.

"You said them other guys been in already?"

"Cyrus Shaver gave his deposition last week, he's the one that was driving the third boat."

"That fucker fired the first shot, cause I decked him in the RoundUp."

"Maybe you should let me do the talking, Lucas, that's what I'm hired for. Anyway, we have to go in there not knowing what the hell he said. He could have been lying through his nose, but it's going to go better if your story squares away with his." Meanwhile Kermit is tailgating this white Taurus that suddenly slams on its brakes with no warning and swerves off into a shop that sells old wooden lobster pots fitted out with glass tabletops. The big Ford Explorer almost drives on top of them. Up on the dash, Kermit's coffee tips over and spills down the defroster holes. Kermit says, "Damn tourists, we're not going to make it."

"You could let me take the wheel, Kermit. I'd drop this thing in low range and drive over them out-of-state yuppies like the Car Crusher."

"Don't bite the hand that feeds you, Lucas. Every one of those out-of-state cars is a potential customer. Guys like you couldn't support their families without the tourist trade. You need them like I need criminals. Whip out your magic wand and whisk them away, we're eating off food stamps, simple as that. Another thing, you need to get in a serious frame of mind. No smirking, no grinning. They see one shit-eating grin on your face, you're toast."

"I thought you had it all arranged."

"What we arranged was that the state would drop the criminal charge because we have a case for self-defense. Lucky for you, these islanders don't trust the system. They prefer to take the law in their own hands."

"They should still get that other bastard for shooting first. He didn't have no self-defense. He also took a couple of shots at Norton Gross."

"They forget those little details when somebody gets hit. By the way, you know something? When I flew out to Shag Island checking things out, that woman you winged, Priscilla Shaver, she pulled me aside and asked if you were single. She's got hot pants for you, that's in your favor. They have some strange birds out there."

"You'd think a bullet in the shoulder would of cooled her down some."

"Some folks, Lucas, you kick them and they love you more."

"I got my limits," Lucky says. "That woman could enter the frigging horse pulls up to the Riceville Fair."

"I'm not saying she's Winona Ryder, Lucas. I'm saying she's got a soft spot for you and that can work in our favor. You *shot* her, for Christ's sake."

"I was trying to shoot that other bastard. He buried a hollow-point in my hull."

"Henry Shaver. I've represented him once or twice in the past. Not to mention his brother Cyrus. Know how Cyrus Shaver lost that middle finger?"

"I got a few theories," Lucky says.

"Cyrus was in a jailhouse fight with his cellmate up in the Tarra-tine lockup and the guy bit it off and threw it in the toilet. He had it flushed down before Cyrus could dig it out of there. Warden had three cons comb through the septic tank but they never found it. Hey Lucas, you see that Audi go by?"

"Missed it."

"I'm getting one of those soon as the ninety-eights come out. You can't beat the Europeans for safety. *Six air bags,* what do you think about that?"

Seven, he thinks, including the driver, but he doesn't say it because it's Kermit Beal that stands between him and a fisheries board that's drooling to send him to the worm flats with old Luther Webster.

Now it's starting to rain, big thick heavy summer raindrops that fall like transparent birdshit across the Explorer's dusty windshield. The lawyer puts the intermittent wipers on. Tourists are stopping in the middle of the road to raise their convertible tops.

"They fixing to pull them other guys' licenses too?" he asks Kermit Beal. "They was the ones that shot first."

"The other side's claiming they sustained bodily injury, so they shouldn't be punished."

"Well what the fuck? They shot my fucking radar out. There's four thousand dollars right there."

"Believe it or not, Lucas, in the eyes of the law, a human being is worth more than a radar set."

"Don't that depend on who it is?"

"It's the United States of America, Lucas, haven't you heard? All men are created equal."

"They teach you that at law school? That's bullshit. That son of a whore is a con. He's a repeat offender. Three strikes and you're out. Everyone knows that."

"He wasn't the one you hit, remember? Didn't you say you struck another member of that family over in the RoundUp? Remember to behave yourself in there, don't say any more than you have to, try and look sincere, and for Christ's sake try not to *swear.* Here, put these on." He flips open the glove compartment and there's about ten pairs of wire-rimmed glasses like the kind Sarah wears. Kermit pulls out a big pair and hands them to Lucky. "There's no prescription to them, it's just window glass. I put them on all my clients. It makes them look like they can read."

He looks at himself in the Eddie Bauer vanity mirror, and for a moment sees another life in there, Mr. Ph.D. Volvo with eyeglasses and bumper sticker:

REPEAL THE SECOND AMENDMENT

It scares the piss out of him. He takes the glasses off and puts them back in the glove compartment. "No thanks."

Kermit called him at 7 A.M. to tell him what to wear. "Dress like

church, Lucas. They might take it easy on you if you look contrite."
So he put on his blazer and necktie even in the August heat. The tie's
got a bowline in it but it hangs OK. Kermit's tan summer suit seems
a lot more comfortable but he's got the air-conditioning on anyway
and all the windows rolled up, like driving down the road in a meat
cooler.

"Let's get the story right, Lucas. After they deliberately put your
radar out, you fired a warning shot to keep them away so they
wouldn't hit you again. It was unusually windy and choppy at the
time, that's the way to put it. Both boats lurched and the shot came
in low. That's how Ms. Shaver received her injury."

"No problem. That's how it happened."

They're in the hearing room facing the fisheries panel over a long
wooden table in a room with barred windows and fluorescent lights.
There's a flag at each end — state and national — plus a few paint-
ings of white-headed old farts along one wall and that's it. The com-
plaining officer, Ryan Beal, all dressed up in his shit-colored shirt
and camouflage tie like he's going to stalk some game, stands at one
end of the table, by the state flag. The three panel members get up
and introduce themselves like they're interviewing him for a job. The
shortest guy smiles and says, "My name is Robert Fulmar, I'm the
acting assistant fisheries commissioner." Fulmar turns to a woman
about Lucky's age who keeps pulling her skirt down to cover her
knees, though with those piano legs she's got nothing to worry
about. She has a lot of nice gray-blond hair but it looks like a wig,
and he can't really get a clear idea of her tits because she has a very
loose-fitting high white blouse. She looks nervous and uncomfort-
able, like she's wearing somebody else's clothes. Fulmar says, "This is
Sherry Pintle, state representative from South Livery and a member
of the House fisheries panel." He finishes off with the third guy, a
downstate lobsterman he's never met but heard of, "Corliss Drummond, president of the Dead River fisherman's co-op and member of
the governor's seafood council."

"Heard of you," Lucky says. "Dead River's just about on the border, ain't it?"

"Mile from the state line. Heard of you too. Your name's on all
the race results. Gas-powered."

"Finest kind," Lucky says. This gets a little grin out of his lawyer. Kermit seems happy there's a real fisherman on the panel, but his client is not so sure. This Drummond has the thick brown scarred-up hands of a lobsterman but they're sticking out from the sleeves of a politician's dark blue suit. That's another thing his old man used to say: Fishing and politics don't mix. He can hear his voice over the old Pontiac six, first boat he can remember. *Lukie, good fishermen don't need no laws. Just leave them alone, they'll regulate themselves.* His old man couldn't even read a comic book, but he was right.

The panel members sag down into their heavy upholstered chairs. The two chairs for Lucky and his attorney are ketchup-colored plastic, the legs feel like they're going to splay out and snap right off. Fulmar starts off by saying, "The reason for this hearing is to give you a chance to show cause why your state fishery license should not be revoked. It is a state policy that any use of firearms against another fisherman will result in a suspension, from ninety days to a full year. In the case of an actual wounding, such as we have here, there is no maximum and suspension can be indefinite."

The Pintle woman adds, "Violence escalates, Mr. Lunt, as I'm sure you are aware."

His lawyer, at two hundred fifty bucks an hour, responds. "I want to remind the board that the shot was fired in self-defense. Striking the victim was an unintended consequence of justifiably defending life and property. The Shag Island parties had already fired on and hit an Orphan Point boat belonging to Mr. Norton Gross, so there was good reason for my client to carry a gun while he worked his territory."

Fulmar says, "A warning shot might be understood, but a gunshot wound is something else entirely. Both the bureau and the fishermen have worked hard over the years to civilize the fishery and it has paid off. We have no interest in a return to the mayhem of former times."

Next they have Ryan Beal give his version of what happened. "First of all, a false position was reported on the VHF so we were taken twenty miles out of our way. Deliberately, if you ask me. The whole business could have been prevented if the coordinates had been right."

"That was them." Lucky says, "My transmitter didn't work."

Kermit Beal whispers, "Hold it for now, Lucas. Anything you say will make it worse."

The Marine Patrol cop goes on. The whole time his hand's resting on his revolver butt and he's looking in Lucky's direction like he's authorized to shoot him in his chair if he feels like it. "We heard the call for Orphan Point vessels on the scanner, so we arrived on scene at fifteen-twenty hours and found the suspect boat with several bullet holes but no injuries and a freshly discharged weapon on board. You will find that in the evidence display. The accused claimed they had fired a warning after receiving gunfire that pierced the radar antenna and the windshield. Examination of the accused's radome showed damage consistent with a bullet passing from bow to stern. A thirty-caliber hollowpoint was also found in the hull of the accused. The other vessels departed the scene southward and we pursued. We followed them to Shag Island and ascertained that a thirty-four-year-old adult female, Priscilla Shaver, had received a gunshot wound in the incident and was taken to a local residence since there is no medical facility on the island. The victim refused to be interviewed without a search warrant so we returned to Stoneport base. Subsequently the victim declined to testify or press charges, so we have turned the matter over to the board."

"Thank you, Officer Beal," Fulmar says. Then he turns to Lucky. "Mr. Lunt, you may now take the opportunity to speak for yourself, or have your attorney enter your version of events, as you wish."

He gets up and starts to say, "We was just minding our own business out on Toothpick Ledge . . ." when Kermit Beal gives a secret little tug on his blazer hem that pulls him into the chair. The lawyer stands up and clears his throat. He looks like a near cousin of Ryan Beal no matter what he claims. They've both got the same Adam's apple full of shaving cuts and the same little black mustache blending in with some serious nose hair, but Kermit's got more weight on him from having a desk job. "My client has asked me to speak in his behalf. This being a clear case of self-defense, these islanders were admittedly encroaching on traditional territory that has been handed down in his family for over fifty years. They deliberately set traps on the southern tip of Toothpick Shoal while my client was clearly present in his own boat with his buoy colors prominently displayed. By this provocation, the victim and her family members had shown disrespect for the community codes that have civilized the lobstering profession. The wounding was accidental, the victim recognized this by refusing to press charges, my client will pledge to carry no firearms or alcohol . . ."

Lucky grunts out loud at this point. He can't help it. He never agreed to go dry, that's just Kermit Beal's plan to make him an altar boy. They all look at him but he just sits lower and heavier in the splay-footed plastic chair and sucks his tongue.

". . . or have any contact with the victim or her family."

The downstate lobsterman breaks in: "What if the Shag Island gang keeps setting traps on your client's territory? He willing to pledge he won't retaliate?"

"My client promises, if his license is renewed, not to commit any acts of violence, even if provoked."

Drummond looks directly at the defendant with one eye squinted like he's aiming a gun at him. "You go along with that one, Mr. Lunt? Them islanders keep setting traps on your ledge, you'll pledge to accommodate and not fight back?"

He's just about to kiss their ass and say yes, sure, I ain't got nothing against bending over and sharing my old man's ledge with them cocksuckers, then he gets an image of setting and hauling side by side with the *Black Pussy* or whatever it is, on the ledge his old man's father staked out under sail, no radar, no bottom machine and no loran, fishing not only for himself but his kids and their kids after. Merritt Lunt would shit in his coffin if his grandson went along with that.

With an infinite suspension resting on the question, he looks right at this fat hake with his thick fisherman's neck puffing out over the white collar and answers, "I can't do it."

"You might want to think that over," his lawyer quickly corrects. "I believe we may be able to reach a compromise."

"I thought it over. And I still can't do it. I ain't hauling alongside them bastards on my own family grounds."

"Is your client stating that under the same circumstances he would react in a similar manner?"

"I am."

"I think that will be enough from the defendant," Fulmar says.

Outside, while they wait for the verdict, the lawyer puts his arm around Lucky's shoulder like he's shipping him off to prison and says, "What are you going to do if you can't go lobstering?"

"I'm going to law school," he says. "I'm going to get me one of them Eddie Bauer Explorers and a couple of them Airbag sedans."

Before the next minute is up the door opens and Ryan Beal motions them back inside. Fulmar and the fisheries panel are sitting down while Lucky and Kermit Beal stand on the opposite side of the table, Ryan Beal beside them like a guard. Beyond the panel, in the free world outside the barred courthouse window, a long charter bus roars past in a cloud of diesel exhaust, big sign saying CADILLAC TOURS, full of old ladies pale as skates.

"Mr. Lunt," Fulmar begins. "I'm going to make this short and to the point. The panel has heard the sworn statement of an eyewitness, Mr. Cyrus Shaver, and has read the written version of what Mr. Ryan Beal reiterated here. Because the state construed this as an act of self-defense, and the victim did not press charges, a grand jury was not convened. However, since the bureau has a zero-tolerance policy toward violence in the fishery, the panel has issued a suspension of your lobster license for a period not to exceed five years, along with a five-thousand-dollar fine."

"You're taking my client's livelihood," Kermit Beal says. "And his children's too. If Mr. Lunt is kept off the water for five years, his territory is gone forever."

"The state has excellent retraining programs for men leaving the water. The retraining center is right down the street, in the state office building. Take my advice, though, Mr. Lunt, and don't go in there carrying a gun."

There's two cars in the driveway when Kermit Beal stops the Explorer at Lucky's house to drop him off. One is Sarah's navy blue Lynx and behind it is a brown-and-white police cruiser with a Tarratine County Sheriff's star on the side door, cage wire between front and back seats, shotgun barrel poking up over the Motorola. His GMC's in the open bay of the garage.

Kermit looks the scene over like a hunter stumbling on a whole christly herd. Big lawyer's grin: "Looks like you got company, Lucas. Sure you want me to let you off?"

"I live here, where the fuck else am I supposed to go?"

"You can retain me again if you want, it'd be just another five hundred up front."

He jumps down and slams the Explorer door and walks between the two vehicles into the open garage door. They must be in there getting her stuff. She always blows things out of proportion. He'll sit in the truck and smoke till they've had their fun.

He's just hauling his Marlboros out of the glove box when a brown-shirted deputy comes through the breezeway door, he's got sweat all over his bald head and a beer gut drooping over his ammunition. In the opening, behind the cop, he can see the long vertical line where he tried to epoxy over the chainsaw cut. It looks stitched up like a surgical scar.

Holding a big piece of paper, the cop walks past the snow sled and the ATV, right up to the open truck window and says, "Your name Lucas Merritt Lunt?"

"No," he says, "it's William Jefferson Clinton."

"Don't bullshit me, mister, or you'll be right in the backseat with the cuffs on. Your wife here's got a court protection order to keep you off the premises."

"The *premises?* These ain't premises. This is my own fucking house."

"Used to be, mister. It ain't no more. Judge Saperstein issued a restraining order on you. Domestic violence. You the one chainsawed that kitchen door?"

"My old man built it. I got the god damn right to cut it out."

"I got news for you, mister. You ain't got any god damn rights at all."

He's got his hand on his revolver just like Ryan Beal.

"OK," he tells the deputy. "Just one thing. I got my heart medication inside. I got to keep taking it or I ain't supposed to be on the road. While I'm in there, I'll grab some of my gear if I ain't going to be coming back, then I'll take the truck and leave."

"Do I look stupid? I ain't going to let you go inside with your wife in there."

"I'll be five minutes. She can stay with you out in the cruiser."

"OK, buddy. Five minutes. She ain't to have no contact with you, it states right here. She stays in the vehicle with me."

He lights another Marlboro off of the first one while the deputy brings Sarah out to the car. At first she keeps her head down like a criminal on TV, then she stops the deputy so she can give her husband this long sad look like she's the one getting kicked out of her family home, not him. He watches her mouth to see if it moves or tries to say anything but the thin pale lips stay tight as a razor clam. The deputy takes her arm and slides her into the backseat of the cruiser and she's lost behind the cage wire and the tinted glass.

"Five minutes. In and out. Judge Saperstein finds out about this, I lose my job."

"That'd be a shame," Lucky says. "You'd have to go back to breaking and entering." The deputy unsnaps the hammer flap on his holster and Lucky puts his hands up in the air and backs off, saying, "Hey. No offense."

In the upstairs hallway he walks past the painting of the original *Wooden Nickel* that she made for him when they were first going out, past Kristen's bedroom with the university pennant on the door and Kyle's with the Metallica poster covering a busted panel, straight through the breezeway attic to his wife's studio above the garage. Both doors are open. Just as he thought. She's already got a new piece under construction in the workbench vise, another half done beside it. One is a blue-and-white form, looks like a bird wing, framed in sharp splintery lead molding she hasn't smoothed down yet. The other isn't anything you could recognize, just a lead-framed sea glass panel, mostly greens and browns, old beer bottles tossed on the rocks before the nickel deposit law and worked over by the surf. *Abstractions.* He picks the blue-and-white one up in his right hand and feels the burrs of unfiled metal on the lead corners like the sharply filed teeth of a chain saw. He takes one long glance at it, gives it a last chance to look like something, then centers the force of his whole body into his right hand, imagining it not as a hand with skin and bones but a cold green crusher claw that collapses the wing just like Alfie pulling a nuthatch off the suet block. He's not even surprised when the blood jumps out between his fingers like bright red bird blood. He pulls the other piece out of the vise with his left hand and does the same thing, this time without even giving it a second look. Like the pincher claw, his left hand is weaker and the piece is more of a cube, so it is hard to crush and he has to bang his fist down on the spruce plank of the workbench to finish it off.

He hears the cruiser's horn bleat down in the driveway, she must be eager to get back to work. It's hard to pry the lead and glass fragments out of the palms of his hands because they're gouged in at several points, but he does it and lays the skeletons down on the workbench. They're bloody but they're not smashed enough. She hasn't even got a decent hammer. He takes a pair of tin snips and bangs the flat end on the remains of her sculptures till there's nothing left but a small pile of beach debris you could see on the tide line any day. That's how they started, that's how they'll fucking end.

On the way out, after raiding his side of the medicine cabinet, he detours through the kitchen and grabs an opened can of marinated cod hearts out of the refrigerator, just about Alfie's favorite meal. While the deputy is leaning on his horn out in the cruiser, he dumps the cod hearts into Alfie's dish and hears the quick padded pawsteps coming out from his bed behind the gun cabinet in the den. He could scoop Alfie up and take him, but he doesn't. This is his home, he's got a right to stay. He bends down to give the cat a couple of quick strokes that raise up its neck fur with static electricity and then dampen it down with blood. He grabs a pair of work gloves out of the hall closet so when he crosses the parlor he won't bleed all over his grandmother's braided rugs, they were her pride and joy.

Outside, the afternoon's starting to cloud up across the harbor, the sun dropping dark and mean behind the gold cross of the church on the other shore. The deputy has his parking lights on. Lucky steps up in the truck and lights another Marlboro with his gloved hands. He backs past Sarah's Lynx, cuts his rear end around the cruiser so he doesn't have to look inside, and heads into the road. In the mirror he can glimpse a figure passing from the cruiser across the yard into the front door. She's moving back in now, the house is hers.

He drives the back roads for a while, then heads for the Blue Claw.

The Claw looks like a different restaurant on a summer evening. No more friendly three-hundred-pound lobstermen at the counter with their asscracks smiling out over their wallet chains. The coffee counter is now a latte bar for yuppie tourists with sweaters tied around their necks in case the night should grow cool. Doris has set the tables with flowers and candles and black-and-white checked tablecloths and every one of them has four Philadelphians with bibs on like big sunburnt children, grinning at each other over dead red lobsters and cowpiss yellow wine. He looks for Ronette through the porthole in the kitchen door. Fat Charlie Bonsall, the dinner cook, is in there blowing his nose on his apron. Doris is playing hostess in a yellow dress with little brown ships sailing across it. She takes one look at Lucky and stands back from the cash register with her hand over her chest. "Look what the cat dragged in."

"You ain't seen Ronette, have you?"

"Your sternlady's back there getting her order. Take a seat at the counter, have one on the house. Ronette's so busy tonight, all by herself cause Jessie called in sick, which she's not. I'll get it myself." She pulls out a counter stool for him like he's the food inspector. "You look like one of those serial killers, with the suit and gloves. That a necktie you got on, or a noose?"

"I was up to the courthouse in Tarratine."

"I heard. You make out all right?"

"They got my license."

"You're not telling me they grounded Lucas Lunt. How long you been lobstering? Thirty years?"

"Time don't mean nothing to them."

"What will you do now?"

"I ain't thought that far, Doris. Maybe I could help Charlie there in the galley."

"I'm afraid Charlie takes up the whole space." Doris brings him a shot and a microbrew, he didn't even know they carried the god damn stuff. She puts the shot down on a little napkin with a red lobster on it inside a life preserver. The yuppie beside him stares at the work glove wrapping itself around the algae-flavored beer. Doris leans on the bar corner on his other side. "You know, with Ronette and everything, it feels like you're family around here." She looks down at his work gloves. "You need help or anything, don't be afraid to ask."

"What do you mean, help?"

"From what I hear, you could use a place to stay."

"Jesus," he says. "It don't take long."

"That deputy was setting in your driveway all afternoon, just waiting for you to come back from Tarratine. Everyone figured your wife would come back to claim the house. That art school's closing for the season. She needs a place to live, same as anyone else."

"It ain't hers."

"She raised two kids in there. Guess that gives her a stake, same as you."

Ronette comes swinging out of the kitchen in a low-cut black dress with gold ear hoops the size of mooring rings and her tits bubbling over like they're the Blue Plate Special. She's carrying a platter of four lobster dinners on her shoulder. The tray's so heavy she has to lean way over to keep it level so the melted butter bowls don't spill. Each lobster has the tail and claws around the edge of the plate and the body sitting straight up in the middle. Their eyes bulge like they're still looking around the trap for a way out. Back in the kitchen he gets a glimpse of Fat Charlie leaning his bare gut against the griddle, his stomach a road map of burn scars, cigarette hanging from his mouth, lining the lobsters up and whacking their tails off with a cleaver, three at a time.

When she catches sight of Lucky at the bar with his microbrew and the Sunday clothes with gloves on, she almost trips. She puts the platter down on the tray rack and dishes the lobsters to a table of four skinny queers with gray ponytails reaching down their backs, giggling and whispering and patting each other on the back of the hand. Sweet Jesus, he didn't think they ever reached that age.

Finally she comes over and rests the big empty platter on the end of the counter. She bows her head for a moment like she's too tired to keep it up, then gives it a shake and widens her kelp-colored eyes. "Lucky Lunt, what are you doing in here on the dinner shift? I thought they was going to put you in jail."

"Should of. At least I'd of had a place to sleep."

"Heard that too. Your wife's back, you're out. That's what Doris said. Hey, why in hell you wearing gloves in here?"

He pulls one of the work gloves halfway off and shows her the sliced-up palm.

"Holy shit. You been in a fight."

"Just doing some housecleaning," he says.

The front door opens and four more yuppies squeeze in. All the tables are full and there's people waiting at every seat in the bar. Ronette gives his bare hand a quick pat and pulls her fingers back caulked with congealing blood. "No shit, Lucky, I'd take off with you but I'm the only one on, and look at this place. You can't even stay, the dinner customers have to have a place to sit. That's the rule. No drinking if you don't eat. Otherwise it'd become a dive. Take care. You need a place, you got my trailer key."

"There's places," he says. "I won't be needing it."

"I'm sure there is. See you tomorrow, then. Five A.M."

"That's what I came to tell you. We ain't going out."

"What do you mean? We ain't hauled in four days. Them lobsters will be busting through the traps."

"We ain't hauling. I got five years."

"Five years in prison?" She bends her head down and her eyes look like they're getting ready to cry.

He likes that look and lets her hang there a second before he says, "A five-year suspension. Just as bad. A man can't fish, he might as well be in the joint making bottled ships."

"Lucky, you been working all your life. You earned some time. I got it figured out. I'll take another job. I got eight hours between shifts here at the Claw. I'll work down to Riceville at the cat food plant, my cousin Shane is a foreman. You just have to stay home and take care of little Luke."

Doris comes over to hustle Ronette back to work. "You're going to have to speed up, dear. People are waiting." By now she's got customers lined up beside the door just for seats at the counter so they can wait for a table. Standing room only. Every fucking one of them is having lobster and they don't even know where it comes from. This is what he lived for and his old man lived for and his grandfather drowned for, to stuff a butchered-up red shellfish in the mouth of these gossiping fairies who are pulling the assholes out of their lobster tails and laying them on the saucers of their butter bowls. All of a sudden he's getting a picture of Merritt Lunt on his last morning, he's seen it a hundred times, clear as a real photograph. The old man's slipping a trap over the transom, first of a double. A loop of pot warp catches around his ankle. He doesn't even see it. Puff of wind tips her and trap number two slips off the rail just as he's dropping number one. Silent movie, black-and-white photograph, bad dream. Soon as he's down there the lobsters are all over him, he had no pecker when they brought him up. They find his boat with the old four-banger jeep engine idling in circles north of Toothpick Shoal, loyal as a spaniel, marking the spot where he went down.

That was the first *Wooden Nickel,* her skipper perished so these fucking parasites could enjoy their meal.

He could take his work glove and sweep the lobsters right off their table, he could handle four fairies with one hand and smoke a cigarette with the other. But Doris is at his elbow saying, "We love having you here, Lucky, but you're distracting the help." She points the big stray lobsterman towards the open door. "Take care of yourself," she says. "We'll be here in the morning. You need anything then, just ask old Doris and she'll fix you up."

On the oyster-shell walkway to the parking lot, he runs into a crowd of Chinese tourists in red and white sweaters, cameras around their necks. They're pointing at Doris's sign, chattering, "Robsta, robsta."

"She's full up," he tells them. "Go eat someplace else."

One of the Chinese asks, "You take picture?" and hands him a Nikon. They line up in front of Doris's shiny blue claw sign and he squeezes them all into the frame, then pulls the trigger. He's pretending it's his .410 loaded with duck shot but it just flashes and they all laugh and clap, then the Chinese line up around him with some of their arms on his shoulders and the guy with the camera takes a picture: Lucky and the seven dwarfs. He's never been that close to a Communist in his life.

It's way too early for the RoundUp's parking lot to be full, but it is, he can't figure out why. No out-of-staters either, just wall-to-wall pickups, some he knows but many he's never seen. It's Wednesday, nothing special, no live band. Soon as he parks, though, he hears the noise and smells scorched hardwood and burned power cords. Now he remembers, it's Belt Sander Night, third Wednesday of the month, he should have known. He was hoping to have a few quiet shots and beers and get his hands washed and maybe get someone to put him up for a couple of days so he doesn't have to sleep in the truck. He also hoped to see what's around for odd jobs now that his work is gone.

Inside, there's a couple hundred guys with caps and beers around Andy's old birch-planked tavern bowling lane. The wood has two deep grooves laid in by the races, with deep brown burn scars on the side-lines and the median strip. The track is still smoking and smoldering from the last race. The racers are huddled with their belt sanders down at the starting end, they're tightening up the belts, checking the duct tape around the cords. Up at the finish line Big Andy has two clam hods full of ten- and twenty-dollar bills. To bet on one sander or the other you have to throw your money in the right- or left-hand hod, then the losers' cash gets dumped into the winners' hod and the winners take double. Honor system, people trust each other around here. There's so many guys he can't even see the bar.

"Lunt! You coming home from church?"

It's Reggie Dolliver, last man he wants to see. But Reggie's right alongside of the bar so he's got access. "Get me something," he shouts.

Reggie comes over with a shot and a Rolling Rock. "Guy from Riceville's smoking everyone. Hey, what're you all dressed up for? Somebody die?"

He takes the shot and beer in his two gloved hands and slugs them down at the same time. "Men's prayer group," he answers.

"No shit?" Reggie says. "I seen a lot of that on the inside. Happens when you get old, ain't nothing else to live for."

The Riceville guy's sander is a big two-horse Craftsman Professional with inch-thick duct tape protecting the power cord. He's got teeth painted on the front of it like a tiger shark, a lead weight duct-taped to the midsection and what looks like a number twelve floor-sanding belt for traction. He's setting it up on the left side. The challenger's on the right, a new-looking blue Makita Power Pro with two lead pigs clamped around the handle and an oversize motor that looks like a custom job. Both of the sanders have the dust bags off so the dust can blow back like a jet trail, the exhaust adds thrust, and if you aim it right you can blind the other guy so he can't hold his power cord straight.

"You betting?" Reggie Dolliver asks.

"Just got here. Ain't seen what they can do."

The two racers plug into a power strip on the ceiling behind the starting line. Big Andy has a long-barreled western-style starting gun. He raises it once and the gamblers all edge over toward the finish to drop their money in one clam hod or the other. Reggie slides over and puts a twenty on the Makita and comes back to his seat. "Son of a bitch is fast. He smoked a Black & Decker Professional before you come in."

Wallace is behind the bar with his hand on the breaker panel. The two racers make sure their motor switches are on, then grab the oversized power cords and lean back to absorb the force of the start. The winner will be the first one over the far edge, drilling into the big sandpit at the end of the track.

Big Andy fires the blank, Wallace closes the switch and the belt sanders scream to life. They hold the wires for a second while the sanders gather traction and dig in, then they let go and the two machines screech down the bowling lane and bury their owners in a cloud of dust and smoke. But the Craftsman chews over to the right and knocks the Makita off the track so they have to run the race again. Half the guys scramble over to the clam hods to change their bets, but Reggie Dolliver stays put. "How's that cocksucker going to win if it don't run straight?"

Next race the Craftsman's owner hangs on to the power cord a second longer before letting go. His sander digs in, tracks down the groove and slams into the sandpit before the Makita can reach the finish line. The Craftsman's owner is a tall skinny guy with a cap saying ROSEN'S FLOORING, which is all the way up in Tarratine. Guys gather around him, checking his machine out, buying him drinks while the winners rake their profits out of the clam hod.

The next challenger is a Ryobi painted a godawful orange with a little Confederate flag on either side of the motor housing. Bets are taken, they hold the cord, they let go, and the Craftsman screams ahead down the groove, then the Rebel sander skews to the left and crawls up the Craftsman's power cord so the race ends in a blaze of sparks that blows a main fuse and puts out every light in the place. The weak little emergency lights blink on in the corner over the steer head, and there's Big Andy running over to the fuse box while Wallace is swamped with drink orders, stirring with his finger, trying to mix them up by feel.

Reggie Dolliver excuses himself and slinks his way among the crowd in the direction of the clam hods. Pretty soon he's back, folding a couple of twenties into his shirt pocket. "Take advantage of god-given opportunity, that's what I say."

"You learn that in the joint?"

"What do they say? 'Everything I needed to know, I learned in kindergarten.'"

"Jesus, Reggie, I thought you dropped out before kindergarten."

"I ain't talking about kindergarten. I'm saying I learned plenty up there, taxpayers' expense."

"How's the ship models?"

"Fuck them, that's for cons. I been taking computers down to the voc school in Stoneport. I got into home security. High tech."

"I heard. Any money in that kind of work?"

"Ain't nothing to brag about. But I got some ideas. Hey, I hear you got some trouble going out there too, don't know how that's going to come down on you . . ."

The lights snap back on. Instantly more belt sanders line up for their crack at the starting line. He grabs Wallace's arm going past with a tray of beers and orders a couple more Rocks and shots. He taps out a Marlboro and another for Reggie Dolliver. Reggie's not betting this time around. The sanders roar across the bowling alley and into the pit, everyone screaming, a dead heat. He says to Reggie, "Five cocksucking years."

"In the joint?"

"I ain't that lucky. License suspension."

"Hey. Think about it. You're still a free man."

"I ain't that free. I got payments. I owe the home equity even though I can't set foot in the fucking house. I owe the hospital. I can't even afford to fucking die."

"Tell you what," Reggie says. "I got a plan."

Now they've got three contestants on the track at once, the crowd's getting drunk, half of them holding a belt sander in the crook of their free arm. So many guys want to race it looks like they're going to start driving them right on the floor. Behind the bar, Big Andy's glancing at his aluminum baseball bat alongside the cash register.

Lucky laughs, chugs his shot. "I know where your fucking plans end up."

"No, this is hot. You're only in on it cause you and me's pretty near family." Lucky pulls his Rolling Rock a few more inches away from Reggie's, as far as he can get it without running into the guy's on the other side, big Indian biker from Riceville with a spiked bulldog collar on his wrist.

"I don't see as we're family," Lucky says.

"Maybe not. Down the road, though, who knows? Anyway, I'm wiring that new development, Split Acres, they got a gated entry so you can't even get in there, but you can see it from the water. Million-fucking-dollar estates. They got art up the butthole in them places, Louie the Nineteenth couches, buck-naked statues, old fucking masters, they got safes behind the pictures with stocks and cash, you name it. Got to be drugs too, rich bastards, every one of them's strung out on coke. I seen them. They can't even stand up half the time."

"So what's the point?"

"The point is this. I wire these fucking places for security, and I got the codes. Only you can't get anything out of there in a truck, they got this gate, they got a private cop. So all's I need is someone with a boat. And a little imagination, you know what I mean."

"What about your ankle bracelet? Ain't your parole officer going to be watching you on TV?"

"First thing we learned in security class, how to disable them things. I can set mine for anywhere I want. You'll get the hang of it. What do you think? You aboard? You ain't got nothing to lose."

"Just what I need," Lucky says. "Spend a couple of years getting cornholed up at Thomaston."

"You ain't going to get cornholed, Lucky. You're too old."

"I'm too fucking old for that shit too."

Reggie looks him over like he's a job applicant. "Just trying to help out," he says. "Think it over, no hurry. There's a window of opportunity, guys like us just got to pry it open a little, that's all. Cousin."

He gives him a family slap on the shoulder and they turn to the bar to focus on their shots and beers. Reggie's a moody bastard, he must be on some kind of pills. He gets so quiet and lost in thought, Lucky's ready to start talking to the Indian biker, then he feels the presence of two guys behind him, one on either side. Fucking Shag Island, he thinks. They're here. He puts the shot glass down and turns around slow and ready, but it's not. It's a tall lanky kid with his head shaved and his eyebrow pierced with a gold pin, big enough to look him right in the eye. Fucking Kyle, standing there in his bald skull wearing a leather jacket that looks like the Hells Angels gave it to the Salvation Army. Beside him is his fairy friend Darrell Swan, six inches shorter, little mouse-colored mustache, black sweatshirt with the sleeves cut off, brown veiny arms like he's been working out.

Lucky spits into the sea-green sawdust around his feet. The whole room smells like an electrical fire from the belt sander track. He looks at Kyle. "How'd you get here? You come in your little slant-eyed truck?"

"I ain't got it on the road. It's up to Heidi Astbury's on blocks."

"How come?"

"Ain't got no fucking insurance."

"I ain't got no insurance either. It don't stop *me*."

"Yeah, Heidi's cousin's a cop, he lives down the street, he stopped me and ran the insurance down and now he don't even let me out of the driveway. We come here looking for a ride."

"I ain't got room."

"Bullshit. We seen your truck out there. It's empty."

He's caught between Kyle and Reggie Dolliver and he picks Kyle. Couple more drinks and he'd be down on Split Point busting into someone's home.

"How far you going?"

"Couple miles. It ain't long."

He gets Wallace to sell him three bottles of Colt .45 under the table and waves Reggie good night. "I ain't rushing you," Reggie says. "Just think it over. And don't let it get nowhere."

In the RoundUp parking lot, the three of them thread their way to his truck through a hundred pickups. Kyle says, "Hey Dad, what's with the gloves?"

"Burnt my hands on the exhaust."

The three of them hoist themselves up into the GMC's high-lift cab and he starts her up. "Truck sounds like shit," Kyle says.

"Don't remind me. That son of a whore Virgil Carter put a hot Chevy transfer case in her, he got the year wrong and it don't even fucking fit. Where we going?"

He takes one of the Colt .45s out of the bag and goes to twist the top off with his work glove but it's not the twist kind. His hands hurt like hell from crushing the lead frames. He takes the top between his teeth and pops it off like they did in the old days, takes a swig, hands it across Darrell's chest to his son.

"Ain't you going to give Darrell none?"

"Here." He hands an unopened bottle to Darrell Swan.

"I ain't going to open it with my teeth. Fuck that."

Kyle comes up with a Buck knife and pops it off, then shouts instructions to his old man. "Next right. Head out the Sherman Road."

"What the fuck's out on the Sherman Road? Nothing but pulp-wood and coyotes after you pass the dump."

"We're going to Moto's place."

"Your Chinese sushi dealer? I ain't taking you out there."

"Come on, Dad. I ain't even living at home. What do you care where I go?"

"If we can't go to Mr. Moto's," Darrell Swan says, "would you mind swinging us over to Burnt Neck?"

"I ain't going to that shithole. Mojo's it is." He drops her into second gear and the hard-sprung GMC goes airborne with every bump. After the town dump, the Sherman Road turns to gravel and they raise a cloud of dust turned red by the taillights in the rearview mirror. "Yahoo!" Lucky shouts. "The Orient Express! I ain't been out here in twenty years. Used to jack deer on this land when we was kids, put the lights on them and shoot them right between the eyes. Your grandma didn't ask no questions, neither. We'd bring one in at night, we'd have venison pie next day for supper. Now they lock you up for that, can't even take a leak without breaking some fucking law."

They make a sharp turn and Kyle says, "Slow down, it's right around here." They haven't passed a house in miles, nothing on the roadside but scrub thicket and beer cans in the ditch, then they pass by a little unmarked opening in the shoulder, just a couple of up-right stones on either side, no sign, no mailbox, looks like a gravel pit road. "That was it," Darrell Swan says. "Them was the Zen stones."

Lucky says, "Ain't nothing but a woods road," but he backs her up and noses into the unmarked entrance. A sign nailed to a tree says

NO HUNTING NO FISHING NO TRESPASSING
GUARD DOG ON DUTY

The sign's got a silhouette of a German shepherd but someone has put its eye out with a .22.

Another quarter mile on the winding entrance road and they come to a big circular drive with a four-bay garage at the other end.

He knows right where he is, middle of fucking nowhere, they used to come out here in the back of Johnny Thurston's wood truck, feel up their girlfriends, jack off and smoke Indian tobacco. Now they're surrounded by orange floodlights and a big garage with ten-foot-high bays, all but one of them open: must be this Moto's personal fleet. One bay has a mean-looking black Humvee, backed in, showing a five-ton Warn winch and tow cable crisscrossed over the front bumper. He's seen the black Hummer a couple of times crawling through Orphan Point, windows tinted all around like it's Saddam Hussein inside.

The next bay's got a silver Mercedes-Benz 450 diesel Hitlermobile, and over beyond that's a turd-brown high-lift Nissan X-cab pickup. The fourth one has a big white Mitsubishi Fuso refrigerated truck that just barely fits inside, looks like anybody's clam truck. Must be what Moto uses for his sushi runs.

As soon as they pull up, a stocky little Chinese guy comes out and walks around the front of the truck. He's got a black sweatshirt on, sweatpants, and white running shoes. He sees the boys in the truck cab and busts into a big shit-eating Chinese grin. "Oh, these two. Carroll and Darrell."

"Kyle," Darrell says.

"Carroll and Kyle. Who is other gentleman?"

"My old man."

Dead serious, like a Commie guard, the Chinese guy shines one of those little black flashlights right into Lucky's eyes, then onto the Remington .30-06 in the back window, and back to Lucky again.

"You sure he is father?"

"What the fuck, Frank," Kyle says. "Mr. Moto said it was OK."

"OK, OK. Park here. Leave keys."

Lucky pockets the keys and hops down. He wants to check out the Humvee in the garage but as he gets closer he hears a low growl. That must be where they keep the one-eyed dog. "Nice friendly place," he says to Frank.

Beyond the driveway a big low house glows out of the darkness as if it's made from varnished teak. The path is lit by a double row of Chinese lanterns just like the ones they have at the My Lai restaurant, that's probably Moto's too. On the other side of the garage, stretching away from the circular drive, they've got a low chain-link fence surrounding an area washed by banks of orange lights like an illuminated playing field. "What the hell's that," he asks, "miniature golf?"

"Croquet," Darrell says. "Mr. Moto loves croquet."

Kyle and Darrell chat it up a bit with Frank, who gives them each a quick fake karate neck chop then walks over to the chain-link gate and lets them through. They call back to Lucky, "You coming in?"

Beyond the chain-link the bright green croquet lawn looks like AstroTurf under the orange lights. He's heard of croquet but he's never seen the game: a square of green lawn set with colored stakes and little wire hoops. Wilfred Beal is standing with a croquet club beyond one of the end stakes. Wilfred looks up from his croquet hammer and says, "Hey Lunt. Didn't know you played." He's teamed up with a woman in a tight red skirt and high heels, looks like a go-go girl from the tit club in Tarratine. The heels look like they're going to sink into the putting green, but they don't. Fake grass.

Then a short grinning heavyset Chinese guy in a white alligator golf shirt comes up and puts his arm around Kyle's shoulder. "This is your boy?" he says to Lucky. "He's good boy. He's working for me, no problem. I am John Moto."

"That your Humvee out there?"

"I used to have Range Rover. The Hummers, they kick Range Rover butt."

"Oh yeah? What's under the hood?"

"Eight-cylinder GM diesel. Three hundred horsepower. Come back in daytime, Mr. Runt. I take you drive around."

Moto has a long silent look at Lucky's gloves, then takes his elbow like a midget realtor, showing him the property. They walk away from Kyle and Darrell Swan and the croquet field, to a round white table next to a rock-bordered fishpond behind the garage. "You are fisherman," he says, "these are my fish." A spotlight on the back of the garage lights up the pool when they get near, must have a motion sensor. The pool's surface fills with big slow orange-and-white goldfish, eyes goggling out of their heads, gulping for air bubbles and swishing their fins around like they're going to drown.

"Them things breathe air or water?"

"They are imperial goldfish," Moto says.

"They good eating?"

Moto laughs the way people laugh when the subject is money. "That would be expensive even for sushi bar. They are three thousand apiece and they die like fries. Shipment every week."

"You get all this off of sea urchins?"

"Businessmen cannot be too specialized. Uni is hot today, other fish tomorrow. Uni season closes, demand gets very large."

"I hear you're dealing off-season. Ain't there a law against that?"

Moto laughs his little rich-Communist laugh again. "Highest law," he says, "is law of suppry and demand."

Frank the bodyguard shows up with a bottle of Johnnie Walker Black Label, an ice bucket and a couple of glasses. One thing you have to say for liquor, it tastes just the same whether you like who you're drinking with or not. He fills his glass till the liquid's bulging over the rim. Moto puts maybe a quarter ounce in his, clicks it against Lucky's. "What we drink to?"

"Supply and demand," Lucky says.

Without touching a drop Moto says, "Big demand now is jumbo lobster. In my country they are eager to impress. Greater lobster, greater the man is. It is like how do you say it? Pecker."

"Five and a half inch is the limit," Lucky informs him.

"So small for American man?"

"Not the pecker, the lobster. What we call the carapace. It's got to be under five and a half inches or we throw them back. That's a big fucking lobster, go four, four and a quarter pounds at premium price, that's twelve bucks at the dock. Past that, they're breeders. We got to conserve the stock for our kids."

Moto refills his glass but doesn't touch his own. "Your son, I observe, is not a lobsterman."

"He's got a chance," Lucky says. "He ain't out of high school yet."

"I am wondering maybe we do business," Moto says. "You know, your fine son speaks of you. I would buy five-pound lobster and up."

"Don't take them that big. Besides, there ain't a dealer in this state that would buy the catch."

"I have place to bring in," Moto says. "Nice quiet spot, no question ask. Five pound and better. I pay eight dollar a pound. Also roe."

"We don't take eggs. Wouldn't be no lobsters left if we did that."

"Roe is thirty dollar extra. Very important. I have customers. It is also roe stiffing the pecker, not here perhaps but in my country."

"If it gives you a hard-on there, it ought to do the same thing here," Lucky says. "We're all human beings."

"We believe we are different species, Mr. Runt. For example, you were once monkeys. We were not."

"That may be," Lucky says, "but I ain't doing it. Them big deep lobsters, you see, them's the breeding stock. They're like the oil wells, dry them up and we're all running on empty."

"Perhaps you are running empty already, Mr. Runt. Mr. Beal tells me your bad fortune. You wish to help out lobster fishing but they take fishing license away. I am a man of strictly business. As I see it you owe them nothing. Your fine son Darrell believes the same, as we have our saying, you receive shaft, you owe nothing back."

"I ain't geared up to take oversize lobsters. My trap heads ain't big enough, besides, they're wood, they'd get stove up out there. My engine's a piece of shit. Sternman I got's a woman, she ain't ever been offshore. I ain't equipped to even think about it."

"Money no object," Moto says. "I advance my fishermen all their gear. Come with me." They go through a back door of the garage building into a big storage space behind the turd-brown Nissan. Stacked up against one wall are eight of the biggest wire lobster traps he's ever seen, twice the size of normal ones with a head-end opening eight inches across. He fingers the escape vent in the parlor end, a two-pound lobster could swim out of that without brushing the sides. The voice is barely a whisper now, coming from inside the shadowy trap. *Lukie, them big ones is the future.* Moto's taking his elbow, turning him from the oversized wire traps to the black Humvee gleaming in the fluorescent garage light. "Work for me, you will have line of credit. Five, ten thousand, what you need to start up."

"Ain't legal to bring them fuckers within twelve miles of the shore."

"As I say, Mr. Runt, I have nice quiet cove."

"Can't be anywheres near here."

"Fifteen mile east, I have old wharf in Whistle Creek. Urchins come in all time year, why not robsters? Your fine son can show you where it is."

"I know where it is. My wife's uncle used to operate that wharf, years back, then it silted up. Can't get in there now."

"Moto Enterprises, we have dredge channel."

"Finest kind, Mr. Moto, you got it all figured out. You got the wrong fucking man, that's all."

"We see, Mr. Runt. I am good judge of fishermen. Also, sometime in robster trap perhaps package appears."

"I ain't running no drugs."

Moto puts both hands up, backs away like he doesn't touch the stuff either. "Not now of course. But who knows? Future is rong rong time. I call you Rucas?"

"Sure."

"Anytime, Rucas. Night and day."

Frank the bodyguard's back in the garage starting the reefer truck, must be time for the milk run. Moto gives him a friendly handshake, takes the Johnnie Walker and turns away, leaving his quarter ounce untouched. Lucky knocks it back.

Back at the croquet field there's no one left around. Frank the bodyguard is picking the varnished hammers up, wiping off the midnight dew before he stacks them in a white shingled garden shed. "Your boys take other ride," Frank says.

The tall garage doors are powering down as he climbs into the GMC cab and starts her up. Big Country 105 is playing Tanya Tucker.

> *She's got everything that a girl could want*
> *But she needs more, and she can't stop*

When he gets to the Blue Claw it's dark except for one small window where Fat Charlie is in there prepping tomorrow's menu. He's got Bon Jovi on, his eyes are closed, his face grinning and nodding like he's jerking off into the clam chowder, a specialty of the house. No Probe in sight, not even Doris's brand-new Buick. The town wharf is quiet. Out in the harbor somebody's got his running lights on. Too early for lobstering, it's probably Noah Parker going out beyond Shag Island on a pilot run. Fifteen miles offshore, Noah and Phil Parker will rendezvous with a tanker bound upriver for Tarratine, thousand bucks before the fucking sun comes up. Everyone's licking somebody's asshole, it's hard to find a man doing a clean day's work.

He slows down passing his own house, where the lights are out, all three garage doors closed up tight. Alfie could be right in there on the oil spot where he likes to sit and wait for the pickup to pull in. He tries to think of his wife sleeping inside, but he can't picture it without him in there too. He's out in the truck idling, staring up at his own bedroom till he believes he's in there, out in his truck and in the old brass bed with her at the same time, it's fucking crazy and his heart starts slamming in his chest. He reaches in the glove compartment for a handful of heart pills, then drives back past the unlighted windows of Lurvey's Convenience & Video and takes the right turn up Deadman's Hill. Halfway up is the Peek house, in Sarah's family since the Revolution, only now there's a Saab in the driveway with New Jersey plates. Peeks can't afford it anymore. He comes to the cemetery entrance, U-turns and parks facing downhill. The sprinkle of streetlights and yard lights outlines the sleeping town like a radar screen. The only life on the pitch-black harbor is the four-second red flasher on the Sodom Ledge bell and the ten-second white sweep of Split Point light. On one side of him is a Mazda pickup with a guy and his girl trying to work things out over the stick shift. On the other side, maybe a hundred feet away, his old man's lying there quiet in the ground and beside him is his grandfather, Merritt Lunt, all dressed up so you won't know his pecker got chewed off. There's a question on his mind but he can't ask it in a way they could answer because they're both of them stone cold fucking dead.

With the headlamps off, his night vision picks up a faint flash on the horizon where one kind of black shades into another, must be the Gannet Ledge bell, fifteen miles out. Canyons out there a hundred fathoms deep, big blind lobsters that have never tasted sunlight. They don't let him fish for his own country, might as well sell them to the Japanese.

He honks the horn and sends the couple beside him scrambling for their clothes, but the stones over Merritt and Walter Lunt don't move an inch. He blasts down the hill past the Peek house, and just to hear the sweet sound of his own engine keeps her in second gear till he's back on the Sherman Road and heading through the dark hackmatack woods towards Moto's place, past the Zen stones and the one-eyed dog to the four-bay garage with one door open and a couple of Asians leaning on the bumper of the black Humvee.

Moto's still up, the only figure on the lighted croquet field. "Why you take so long?" he asks.

"Had to empty out the truck, make room for the new traps."

He peels out of Moto's circular drive with a heavy load, sixteen oversize wire traps under a canvas tarp, you could stuff a human being inside one of those cocksuckers if he scrunched himself up. When he comes to the highway he turns eastward, speeds up past the dead RoundUp and doesn't stop till he's reached the Split Point Road and pulled his truck in front of the trailer where Ronette Hannaford lives. The windows are dark. A weird dog barks once across the street then goes silent like it's been choked. Jesus. He shuts the lights off, kills the engine, and slumps down to sleep behind the wheel.

10

THE ALARM RINGS in the middle of the night, he wakes out of a dream of eel nets and he doesn't know where the sound's coming from. He takes a whack on his side of the bed where the clock's supposed to be but it's not there. His palm cuts through the empty air and he almost falls off the low, tilted mattress. Way over on the other side the beeping blue-green digital numbers read 1:30. He reaches across the unknown body beside him and puts his whole hand around the clock and squeezes until the beeping strangles and dies. When he rolls back on his own side the room seems to move with him and he thinks for a moment he's aboard a boat, but it's only Ronette's trailer which is so fucking flimsy you can feel the floor bend when you breathe.

He's been asleep three hours. Night before they watched tag team wrestling on TNN. Pretty soon they were grappling on the trailer floor themselves, it was almost eleven before they moved to the bedroom and collapsed. Ronette likes to do it while wrestling's on, she's got one eye on the tube the whole time. Last night it was the Undertaker versus this new guy Goldberg the Rastling Rabbi, the Undertaker's sitting on the Rabbi's butt, twisting his leg back, Rabbi's screaming and yelling, Ronette's underneath him thrashing like a halibut, it drives her nuts. He doesn't give a damn, if that's what wets her appetite, what the hell.

Later she wanted another crack at it because she couldn't sleep, but his heart was still pounding from the first one and he didn't want to die in a strange house. He swallowed a handful of heart pills and went to sleep.

Now in the dark he reaches back under the covers groping for Sarah's familiar papery skin with the bones and ribs underneath, and finds instead a bedful of damp warm flesh coming awake, pulling him towards its mouth like a starfish, ready to do it again.

"Jesus H. Christ, Ronette. We got to get out there. It's twenty-five of two."

With the old Ford six in there, it takes three hours to reach the offshore fishing grounds.

Her face is blue from the clock light so it looks like she's under-water, then she pulls down the covers. She's got nothing on, her belly's getting bigger, her arms and shoulders are bulking like she's been shooting steroids along with Darrell and Kyle. Her nipples look like blue saltwater chocolate in the clock light, he wouldn't mind chewing on those for a few minutes, see what happens, but by sun-rise he wants to be twelve miles out to sea.

She sees him looking and pulls the covers up. "You're going to leave me, Lucky. I used to have a figure but now I'm a frigging whale."

They're on the back road passing the blacked-out welfare shacks of Burnt Cove, two barrels of Stoneport redfish in the truck bed smelling so ripe it's making the dogs howl in every house. For two weeks he's been dressing himself out of Uncle Vince's closet. He's wearing long underwear and two sweatshirts under his oilskins because they're fishing twenty miles offshore in a gray endless September fog bank cold as a witch's tit. Just thinking of it makes him reach into the glove compartment and wash down his morning pill with Old Mister Boston cherry brandy, a hit for himself, a hit for Ronette, and a hit for old Luther Webster when they pass his road, just the right taste at 3 A.M.

Snugged up against him with her knees drawn up on either side of the transfer case lever, Ronette Astbury lights him a Marlboro so she can steal a couple of deep forbidden drags. With her other hand she searches for a twenty-four-hour station. She finds Vince and Dolly way at the far end of the dial, lots of static but a great duet:

> *Goodbye, please don't you cry*
> *'Cause we both know I'm not what you need*

She turns it up. "Did you know Dolly Parton wrote them lyrics? Bet you didn't."

"I'd like to have a picture of Dolly Parton writing that song."

"What for? She don't write naked."

A big fall-colored bird whirrs low across the headlights into the roadside brush: partridge. Just over the Riceville line he turns on the Whistle Creek Road, then stops short for a doe and two late-summer fawns standing right in the road. The doe freezes in the headlights, the little ones scamper off. All by itself his hand reaches back for the .30-06 racked across the window behind his head.

"Lucky, for Christ sake. Hunting don't start till November."

"Always deer season after dark. That's what my old man used to say." The doe breaks out of her stare and follows her fawns into the alder brush before he can get the gun out. Her eyes are still in there watching as he drives past but she'd be gone before he could get out of the car. "If you was paying attention we would of had her. You could of shot right out of the window. She was waiting for it so hard it hurt."

"Lucky, you planning on teaching this kid to jack deer?"

"Don't see why not. Kyle learned."

"Yeah, Kyle learned. And look at him now."

"What do you mean?"

"I don't mean nothing, just don't want *my* kid turning out like that."

The Whistle Creek Road comes to an intersection with a stop

sign. He runs it, then the pavement turns to dirt. They're almost there. "Ain't nothing wrong with Kyle," he says.

"Nothing wrong if you ain't planning on grandchildren."

"What the fuck's that supposed to mean?"

"That Darrell Swan's the biggest fairy this side of Tarratine. Everyone knows that."

"You saying Kyle's queer?"

"You got to have your face rubbed in it?"

He puts the cigarette in his mouth and the cherry brandy between his legs and backhands her right across the mouth: *slap.* He comes off with the feel of her teeth on the back of his hand.

"Asshole," she says. "You stop this fucking truck and let me out." She's wiping her mouth with her thumb, looking at it for blood. "Nobody gets to do that, not Clyde, not my old man, and not you."

"I ain't letting you out. I can't move all this shit by myself."

They come to the wharf and he stops. "Fucking asshole," she says. "No wonder your wife moved out."

"I never laid a hand on Sarah. What the fuck you think I am?"

"I don't believe you. And supposing you didn't, so what does that say about *me*?"

She's still got her fist balled up over her mouth but he takes it and pulls the thumb out of the fingers and looks at it. "You ain't bleeding," he says.

She pulls away from him and opens the passenger door. "Let's get them traps loaded and get out on the water. You ain't fucking fit to be on land."

He stops under the single lightbulb on the corner of Moto's ice shed and tips her face up so he can see the mouth. She looks just like she did the first day he saw her serving coffee at Doris's, sad, wet-skinned, lips puffed up. Clyde must have slapped her around at home, her mouth always looked that way at the Blue Claw.

He tries for a kiss but she pushes his face away. "Least Clyde had some money," she says.

"Just leave Kyle alone."

"You never gave a shit about Kyle. Why start now?"

When he gets to Moto's wharf there's eight more oversize wire traps for him, hidden under a canvas tarp in case the law comes around. God knows who his source is, the things look like animal cages or prison cells stacked tier on tier in a con movie, nice and scrubbed. Old Luther's going to be a career wormer now his last customer's gone.

They steam through the dark a half hour or so out of Whistle Creek while Ronette knits a tiny green-and-orange sock under the worklight, all that's left of his old colors, then they enter the offshore fog bank and it's like a blind man going blinder, they can't see the bow from the wheelhouse. He switches on the used Apelco VHF he got off Harley Webster but they're too far out to pick anything up. He tries the broken radar again but all he gets is the blank black screen, raster line going around like a searchlight in outer space.

They scatter a gang of little gray sea-pigeons that whistle and vanish in the fog. They must be feeding on something, and where there's something, there might be something else. He reaches in the bait barrel and puts a couple of ripe redfish on a hand line with a gang hook and passes the line over to Ronette. She puts her knitting down but she doesn't pick up the hand line yet. "See this fog, Lucky? This must be what the kid's seeing. It must be just like this."

"What are you talking about? It ain't got eyes."

"That ain't true, Lucky. I heard this woman on TV, she said they can start learning to read before they're born."

"What the fuck? There ain't nothing to read in there."

"They ain't actually reading yet, it's called pre-reading."

"Pre-reading? That's the stage I'm at."

"Supposed to read to them even now." Then she doesn't say anything for a minute. "Or you can play them a book on tape. That works just as good."

"You're on the clock," he reminds her. "You ought to consider doing some work."

She takes the line and lets out a hundred feet and makes a couple of loops around the tow bitt in the stern. "We ain't going to get nothing," she says.

"Eight knots," he says. "Slow enough to trawl. Get a striper or two, might break up the macaroni and cheese."

"Don't complain. You was living off cat food back in that house."

He feels a shiver on the wheel and looks back. The hand line on the tow bitt's jumping around, then it pulls tight. "Come up here,

Ronette, and take the helm." He throttles down and cuts to starboard diagonally across his track to ease the strain on the light line, then hands the wheel over to his sternlady and puts on the canvas gloves. He brings the line forward, takes a couple of turns around the pot winch and hauls in a nice fat striper, maybe twelve or fifteen pounds, crazy god damn fish hit the bait at eight knots and doesn't know when to quit. It flails around the platform till he can crack it a couple of times with the billy and jerk the hook out and lay it down in the ice box beside the beer.

He spears another redfish onto the gang hook and throws the line back into the *Wooden Nickel*'s wake. "This next one's going to be for Moto. He wants a striper for the sushi bar, he's going to get one."

"He don't own us."

"He's going to. When we come in he's going to be waiting with ten thousand in his hand."

"Yen?"

"Dollars."

"Jesus, we ain't caught *that* much."

"It's an advance. We'll get rid of this piece of shit engine, stick in a V-8, get the radar fixed, give the hospital a couple thousand so they don't come after my fucking heart and take it back."

"Lucky."

"What?"

"I'm going to be needing something too."

All this time they're steaming south-southeast at eight knots through a fog so thick he can just see a hundred-foot circle around the boat, white mist sluicing in the windshield vent and condensing on his face so his mouth fills with the cold and bitter taste of salt. He shouts over the engine, "Hey Ronette, you think there's any planets with just water on them, no land?"

"What are you talking about? You can't have a planet with no land. What would you want with that anyhow, you'd never be able to get off the boat."

"Don't sound so bad."

Twenty-two miles out, the swells rise slow and black from the open Atlantic, the air's the color of a TV after the station goes off. She slips her oilpants on and he hands her the helm for the first haul. He gaffs the buoy and puts it around the old Pitts pot hoist, which can barely handle the heavy offshore gear. The motor pretty near stalls and the winch groans breaking the giant trap over the rail, but it's got a nice big one in there snapping the air with both claws. "Fucking thing's never seen light before," he says. "It's trying to bite the sky."

"It's got to be nine pounds," Ronette says. "I ain't grabbing on to that one."

He opens the trap and picks the sucker out and throws it thrashing and biting into her arms. "Catch." It snaps like an alligator and falls on the cockpit floor. Takes the two of them to subdue the huge bastard and cuff him with six thick green jumbo bands.

The next five traps have nothing, then they get a couple more godzillas in the next one, bigger than anything he's ever handled, the kind of lobster old Merritt Lunt used to haul off of Toothpick Shoal sixty years back, when the big ones were still inshore. One of them's a huge breeder female berried up with a quarter pound of eggs. All his life he's been conserving the lobster stock by throwing them back the minute he saw the eggs. *Sustainable,* that's what Kristen calls it, somehow she got the gift of words. Thirty fucking years on the water and nothing to show for it but a bad heart and a mortgaged boat, then he defends his homesite like anyone would and there goes his occupation, just like that.

He says, "Ronette, scrape the eggs off of that one, will you?"

"Do it yourself. No wonder them pro-lifers don't like abortions."

"It ain't a human being, for Christ sake. Can't you tell the fucking difference?" It was one of the Ten Commandments, *Lukie, you see them christly eggs, you throw her back,* but he makes himself do it because his old man's dead and right now that Isuzu-powered cunt's out there setting her traps on top of a shoal staked out by Merritt Lunt. With a hundred percent government support. He takes his hunting knife to the oversized female's underbelly and scrapes every last frigging purplish-green egg into the margarine tub. Five ounces at least, that's sixty, seventy more right there. They throw the big mother in the saltwater well and Ronette skewers a bag of redfish into the trap.

After they haul another dozen they wrap the last warp over the bitt and kill the engine and stop for a Rolling Rock. By now it's hot and the fog's scaled up so they can see a half mile at least. Not that there's much to see. No friendly lobster boats, no fields of traps, nothing but the long seal-colored ocean swells and the invisible territory of his new deepwater ledge, marked by his new buoys. Ronette sprayed them Day-Glo lemon trying to match her car, Bunny's Marine didn't stock chartreuse. She unfastens the straps of her oilskin bib and leans back for a Marlboro against the piles of coiled yellow hundred-fathom warp. He takes pity and gives her a sip of the Rock and a hit off his Marlboro. She smokes with one hand and with the other one rubs her belly like she's already rubbing the kid's head. "Got a little lobster trapped in there."

"Be the first god damn lobster that can read."

He feels the throb of twin GM diesels resonate in his own keel before he sees anything. Then a big white party boat comes out of the haze traveling north to south and swerves off to westward to avoid the *Wooden Nickel* and its field of Day-Glo traps. Dark shapes of passengers line the leeward rail, they're bundled against the cold, orange life jackets on the kids, binoculars and cameras around their necks. The captain veers back closer so his clients can capture the fishermen on film. He smiles and flips a large-diameter upright middle finger wearing a neoprene lobster glove. Take those snapshots home and blow them up, Merry Christmas! Love watching the natives going about their work.

He can read the stern now:

BALEEN STALKER
Norumbega

It's a fat double-hulled catamaran with a twisting motion in the swells, her white sides streaked with yellow trails all the way to the waterline from passengers heaving their breakfasts over the windward rail.

As soon as they pass the *Wooden Nickel* they speed up again, then slow down abruptly just inside the fog line and stop. This time it's Ronette getting the binoculars out.

"We ain't got time," he says. "Only thing they're doing is throwing up. Them whales must like it, that's all they bait them with."

"Take it easy, Luck, you ain't even done your beer. Besides, they got something over there."

The other boat's only a couple hundred yards south of the ledge, probably in sixty fathoms. He can't see anything at first, then a shape breaks the dark surface between the boats, heading their way, looks like a porpoise at first but the back keeps rising and it's a whale all right, what did those Indians get for whalemeat, dollar a pound? Figure it out, a man could live a year off one of those. The *Baleen Stalker* turns sharp to port and comes back to follow it, forcing the god damn whale to swim right through the field of traps and surface again close to the *Wooden Nickel*'s bow. Its breath sounds like an over-size porpoise and for a second his nose catches a septic-tank smell that cuts right through the bubbling stench of the redfish barrel.

"What a racket," he says. "They got to be carrying sixty people, they probably get fifty bucks a head, three thousand bucks a morning, then he goes back and gets another boatload of suckers after lunch and never takes his hand off the christly wheel."

"I'd pay fifty bucks," she says. "I love to see it when that big fin comes up."

"Sure it's big enough for you, Ronette?"

She puts the beer on the starboard rail and grabs both his suspenders, pushing her little belly up against the crotch of his barnacled orange apron till she almost shoves him backwards into the lobster well. "We go for the big ones," she says. "But we don't let them push us around."

His eye catches the color fishfinder with a huge blue mass moving along the six-fathom grid line like a submarine. "Son of a whore's right under us." They go over to the port side and watch the fin poke up in the light chop just beyond the shoal. Couple of strange-looking black seagulls wheel in towards it and fly low over the water. The whale-watcher can't follow it cause they don't want to snag up on all the buoys and toggles. "Ain't that cunning. Damn thing's using the traplines to keep that tourist boat away."

"They ain't that smart, Lucky. They're just animals. I heard their whole brain was the size of a walnut."

"Thought it was a Volkswagen."

"That's their heart, Lucky, their heart's the size of a Volkswagen, it's the truth, I heard it on TV."

He looks at her hard and thinks something but it won't come up in words. The whale surfaces again about half a mile away and the whale-watcher goes after it, but they have to arc way out around his trap zone and by then it's gone into the fog. He goes below and gets the .300 Savage out of the chain locker and puts it up on the rack where it belongs. She says, "Thought you wasn't supposed to carry a gun aboard."

"These here are federal waters. Only law out here is the Bill of fucking Rights, and that says you can have all the guns you want. Second Commandment."

"Jesus, anything moves out here, you have to take a shot at it."

"You move around plenty and I ain't shot at you."

"You better not, either, cause I been known to shoot back."

They haul another twelve traps and it's almost eleven. The sea breeze is already kicking up whitecaps so they have to stop. You can't frig around with a heavy trap in these seas, you'd get your rail swamped in a minute.

They've got nine big ones, pretty near five hundred bucks' worth, along with close to a pound of roe. Not bad. He turns the new stereo on but it's too far offshore to pick up High Country, so he puts in the new Tanya Tucker tape.

> *Every now and then*
> *You feel like jumping*
> *Off the deep end*

The Ford six's exhaust doesn't have the heat to get a flame off of, so he lights his Marlboro with a Bic and gives her the first puff. The fog's lifted some more so they can see the *Baleen Stalker* half a mile south, stopped dead in the water, they must have found more whales. "Know what I heard?" he says.

"What."

"Kristen was telling me this. This whole fucking ocean out here used to be dry land. Six, seven hundred feet higher. This ledge we're over would of been a hill."

"No shit? Was there any people back then?"

"Indians maybe. Indians, bear, dinosaurs, Christ knows what."

"Nothing but lobsters down there now."

He revs the engine up and puts her in gear and sets the loran heading back to Whistle Creek.

———

Mr. Moto takes Lucky into the little office over the bait shack and pours him a cup of green tea before they sit down to business. Moto's got a computer, a satellite phone, and a little black bank safe bolted to the floor. Out of the safe he gets a brown envelope and hands it over. "Ten thousand advance. I will take half boat price till you make up."

"My old man wouldn't of took this."

"You are not old man. You are alive. Old man is passed away. But you are not wanting so much? Five thousand maybe?" His little short-fingered hand reaches to draw it back.

"Hey. I need a decent engine, radar, new hauler. Them oversize traps are heavy. Got a mortgage payment too."

"But you not living home. Fine son tells me."

"Don't matter. I got the home equity for the boat."

"How it is going so far?" Moto says, pouring him another cup of seaweed tea. Then a big Chinese wink: "Not too ronely?"

"Plenty of fucking whale-watchers, we had fifty people staring at us the whole time."

"They were seeing whale?"

"Just a small bastard, thirty feet maybe. Size of my boat. You got any customers for whalemeat?"

The envelope has been sitting on the tea table all this time, but Moto pushes it in his direction. He's still wearing his orange bib oil-suit and he slips the envelope into the apron pocket. Out the window he can see the *Wooden Nickel* and his pregnant sternman swabbing the striper blood off the platform while Moto's dockboy, Curtis, shifts lobsters around in the cars under the float.

Moto says, "Why ask more trouble? Whale is U.S. crime."

"We're criminals already, look what the shit we're bringing in. Might's well go all the way. The Indians shoot them bastards with an elephant gun. I heard they got twenty thousand dollars off of one fucking whale."

Moto stands up and looks out the office window at Ronette scrubbing the deck down in her orange oilskins. "Evlything have price."

"Another thing, I thought you was going to bring that Humvee down so's we could try it out."

"Tomollow I bring Humvee. You fish tomollow?"

"Every three days," Lucky says, "long as it ain't blowing. We're on a roll with them godzilla lobsters, no sense quitting now."

He drops Ronette off in the driveway of the Split Cove trailer he now calls home. Ginger's right there pawing the screen door, she doesn't come anymore on these offshore trips. "Know something?" she says. "I ain't contesting Ginger. We been swapping that dog off every week since April. Next time I take her over to the wharf for her weekend with Clyde, I ain't going back to pick her up."

Sonny Phair, the next-door neighbor, is sitting on a four-wheeler with a sixteen-gauge shotgun across the fender rack, pulling his welfare checks out of a mailbox with five or six bullet holes in it. He gives a big grinning dipshit wave and drives the ATV in a wide circle around his hubcap-covered shack.

Ronette hops up on the running board and pushes her lips on the side window in a big moist kiss that leaves a little red cunt shape on the glass. *Smack.* He could see counting the ten grand again inside, couple of beers, get naked and fool around a bit. She loves doing it pregnant and he does too, big spongy udders, no more Magnums, there's a good side to everything. But instead he's got an appointment with his daughter Kristen at the Cockatiel Café in downtown Orphan Point. It's her last day before going off to school and she probably wants money.

"Can't get no blood out of a turnip," he speaks out loud.

Ronette says, "Who you talking to?" then without waiting for an answer she's inside the ripped screen trailer door.

He's just past the Blue Claw and turning onto Summer Street when a diesel pusher RV the size of a Greyhound bus pulls out in front of him and tries to turn left so it's going to crush him if he doesn't back up fast. He looks up in the RV's cab and the driver must be in his nineties, he doesn't care anymore, close your eyes and drive this fucker over everyone, what's the worst they can do to him, death penalty?

They say they're coming out with a sex pill, you can get it up when you're a hundred years old.

He glimpses this good-looking woman on the sidewalk in front of the health food store: black T-shirt, white shorts, green baseball cap with a ponytail sticking out the back. She steps out between a pale yellow Jeepster Commando and a BMW Z-3 and comes running to the open passenger window of the truck. "Daddy!"

"Hey sweetheart. See if one of them cars has the keys in it, and back her out so I can park."

She's up on the running board, looking in. She's got a tan, lipstick, a pair of port-and-starboard earrings with bits of colored glass. She says, "The Cockatiel has customer parking, out behind. That's why I picked it."

Inside, Kristen steers her old man to a back corner away from the AARP clusters in the window seats. The restaurant's all white inside with color photos over every table, lobster boats in the fog and pot buoys hanging on shingle walls, most of them taken at Clyde's wharf, old unpainted place stinking of gullshit and herring guts. "If them pictures smelled like they look," he says to Kristen, "this place would never sell another meal."

"Daddy, people come from all over the country to photograph Hannaford's wharf. It's a *motif*."

"I don't notice no pictures of old Albert taking a leak into the crab bucket."

"Everyone's not like you, you know. Some people see the beautiful side."

"Ain't no people in them pictures, just a bunch of shit-covered bait shacks."

The waitress approaches to take their order, picks up on the conversation and backs off. Then she sees who it is. "*Kris*ten."

"Wendy, this is my dad. Wendy's already at the U. We're going to be in the same dorm."

Wendy's wearing a little clip-on bow tie over a white shirt but the second button down from the neck has pulled open and he sits up straighter so he can improve the angle down inside. "I'm so glad you brought him," she says to Kristen. "We haven't had any real people here all day." She hands out the menus, then straightens up and closes off the view.

He leans back in his chair with his authentic oilskin pantlegs and trawler boots on either side of the little round table with the red rose sticking up out of a half-liter wine bottle. "Got any Rolling Rock?"

"We only have microbrews." Wendy laughs. "We have Wartman's Maple Ale, we have India Pale Chutney —"

"Just make it coffee and a cheeseburger."

"Cholesterolburger," Kristen says.

Her father says, "Extra cheese, french fries, large onion rings."

"We don't have a Frialator," Wendy says. "I'm afraid you'll have to make do with potato salad."

Kristen orders a latte and a tuna salad plate. She says, "Know what Mom says? She says you're in rebellion. And she's right. You're bigger than anyone in here and you're rebelling like a little kid. You're worse than Kyle. By the way, I heard you made up with him."

"Don't ask, don't tell, ain't that how they put it?"

"You know I'm off to school tomorrow. I have all these forms for my dorm, my student loan, it's hard to fill them out. They say, you know, 'If separated, father's address,' and I don't even know where you live."

"I'm staying in Split Cove."

"But Daddy, you *hate* Split Cove, you used to drive this round-about route for miles so you wouldn't have to drive through that town."

"Things change," he says, waits a minute then says, "I suppose you want some money for school. I ain't got any."

"Dad, I didn't ask you out to lunch for money. I wanted to see *you.* Money's no problem. I have a scholarship and a loan package and I saved a ton this summer. The Hummermans even gave me a bonus. I get to work in the cafeteria in exchange for meals. I can take out a loan for my room. The one thing is books. It's not like high school where they give them to you. You have to *buy* them. That's going to be four hundred dollars."

He can't believe it. *"Four hundred dollars?* That could get you a twenty-five-inch TV. Ain't that school supposed to be run by the state? Hardworking people shovel their tax money into that god damn place and you have to pay for your own books?"

"Daddy, you don't even *pay* taxes."

The waitress arrives with the coffees and the food. She's not much to look at now she's got her shirt buttoned up, no chin, lot of acne under the makeup mask. He turns his eyes back to the pretty girl across from him with her face smooth and suntanned under the green cap that says NORTH SAILS. "I've been talking to Kyle," she says.

"Talking Chinese or English?"

"English."

"What kind of shit's he filling your head with?"

"He's been staying with a cousin of your girlfriend, over in Burnt Cove. He says you guys are going to have a baby."

"Kyle should mind his own god damn business."

The chinless waitress is hanging around nearby, dusting the row of coffee urns, one ear out to hear what's going on. Kristen leans over the table till her cap visor's right over his potato salad and whispers, "It is our business, Dad. You have a family already. It's *us*." She started off with Sarah's serious look, but now she's starting to cry. He'd like to pat the back of her neck the way he did when she was ten, but his hands are too big to touch any part of her and all he can do is squint at the waitress till she comes over and tops off his dollhouse coffee cup. Kristen's pulling a pair of sunglasses out of her backpack, putting them over her eyes so they can't be seen.

He lays his huge lead-scarred claw over her hand beside her untouched tuna plate and asks her, "How you planning to get up to school tomorrow with your gear? Your boyfriend going to stuff it all in the Miata?"

"Nathan's gone back to Brandeis already. He's on the sailing team, so he had to leave early. We got kind of distant over the summer."

"Too bad," he says. "That was a decent little car. Your mother taking you up?"

"I guess. Her Lynx is kind of broken. Nobody knows what's wrong with it."

"Get some of them artists to look at it, over to the school. Sounds like you could use some wheels yourself."

"I could never afford it, my whole summer savings went into the first-semester bill."

She's got the sunglasses off now and she's stopped crying, but her eyes are still wet the way they used to be when she'd get hurt in the yard and come stand at the back door and look up and bite her lip with her front teeth.

"You know Virgil Carter?" he asks.

"That old guy with the used car lot? I know who he is. Don't you always say his cars are stolen?"

"Let's go to Virgil's," he says. "Maybe he's got something that'll get you up to school."

When they turn off the Eel Dam Road into Carter's Car Care, Virgil's in the garage with a blowtorch and a trouble light, burning the serial numbers off a '73 Corvette. He looks up and blinks a few times from the September sun. "Who you got here?" Virgil says, eyes bloodshot from acetylene fumes, looking puzzled as hell. Sounds like he's got Kristen mixed up with Ronette. "You planning to trade her in?"

"She needs a car for college. You got anything that runs?"

"This Corvette'd be nice for her. Got a 501."

Kristen pokes her North Sails cap into the little side window of the Corvette. "How is the gas mileage on these, Dad?"

"Round a gallon a mile," Virgil says. "Guess you're looking for something practical, little Mazda 323, maybe a Sube, a Civic, I got a couple of those, light wrecks, we can glue them up."

"She wants something American, Virge." Kristen's wandered off by now, she's looking at Virgil's front-line specials under the pennants he's got strung from a pine tree to his power pole.

"What do you want to spend, five, six thousand?"

"She's just going to college, for Christ sake. She ain't won the lottery. Let's see what you got out back of the trailer."

"Them are all shitheaps. You'd let your flesh and blood go back and forth to school in one of them things? You want her broke down on some lonely highway in the middle of the night?"

He's trying to see around back of the trailer but Virge is pushing him towards Kristen, who's looking at the row of convertibles under the SUMMER SPECIALS sign. "Her boyfriend drove one of them Miatas."

"Ain't got a Miata."

Over at the far end of Virge's specials he spies an old sixties Mustang ragtop, cherry red. "What's in that Mustang?" he asks.

"Little six, four-speed. That one's a classic, Lucas. It ain't in the Subaru range."

"Give her the keys, Virge, let her try it out."

He's got the Mustang's hood open while Kristen slides behind the wheel. "Want to know something?" she says. "All that time with Nathan and he never once let me drive his car."

"You going to let him drive this one?"

"In his dreams."

Virge comes back from the trailer with the dealer plates saying to Kristen, "Little six like that, no PCV, she'll get twenty miles a gallon easy. Don't race her now, honey, she ain't been run for a while." Soon as Virge puts the plates on she's off up the Eel Dam Road, top down, blond hair wagging in her wake like the tail of a golden lab.

"That's an Alabama car, Lucas, complete restoration, no fucking Bondo, never seen road salt. That's white leather upholstery and a brand-new top. You know them things is hard to find. I'd have to have nine-five for her."

"Christ, Virge, it ain't a museum piece. Needs valve work, you can hear the fucking clutch slipping from here."

Virgil takes out his can of Red Man and sucks a wad under his tongue and appears to think. Pretty soon he spits a red gob out on the tire of a Honda Civic. "Have to get eight for her anyway, at that I'm losing some."

"You ain't losing nothing. You stole the fucking thing."

"I got my overhead," Virge says.

He fingers Moto's envelope in the bib pocket right over his heart. "Cash sale," he says, "don't have to say nothing to nobody."

"That way I can do you a little better," Virgil says.

Lucky opens the envelope and counts off forty-five of Moto's hundred-dollar bills, folds them once, and shoves them down in his pants pocket. He leaves the remaining fifty-five hundred in the envelope and hands it over. By the time Kristen's back from her test drive, Virgil's coming out of the trailer with the paperwork and the ten-day plates. "Sign this here form, Lucas, it says you paid me six hundred bucks."

His only daughter throws her arms around his neck. "Daddy, I can't believe you're doing this. But how much *was* it?"

Virgil Carter finishes screwing the ten-day plate on the trunk and says, "Know what them billionaires say. You can't afford it if you got to ask."

Harley Webster's got an eight-cylinder Volvo Penta on the hoist when he pulls up to the Riceville boat shop. Harley breeds pit bulls in his spare time and his yard dog comes drooling up the minute Lucky steps down off the truck. He gives it a swift boot to the shoulder, the dog goes screeching behind an engine crate. They're pussies if you show them who's in charge.

Harley says, "Look who's back for another turbo. Heard you was done lobstering. Guess you won't be needing that boat for a while. Planning to sell her?"

"Fuck that. I'm doing offshore research now, foreign government contract. I'm going to need something better than that dipshit six."

"Got a 307 Olds in there, freshwater cooled, twice as strong as that little six. Finest fucking kind, hundred percent marinized, new starter, new alternator, ain't got a thousand hours on her. Guy out of Stoneport went diesel and traded on a 210 Cummins. Ain't going to last, neither. I got somebody coming down tonight."

"Tonight? Where is it?"

"Inside, on the small hoist."

The 307 has rust on the block surface and the saltwater cooling side, it's going to need a new manifold. He takes a pipe wrench off of Harley's shelf and cranks her over. Compression's decent. Takes a plug out and tastes the electrode with the end of his tongue. Little burned, not bad. Puts his middle finger down in the cylinder, runs it around the cylinder wall and licks the tip. Inside's decent but the outside's a mess. The pit bull's right there beside him ready to snap his hand off if he pockets a tool. He gives it a pat on the neck and goes out to deal.

Harley's swinging the hoist over the engineless Stoneport boat tied to the end of his wharf. His boy Peter's down in the cockpit with the bulkhead pulled, ready to guide the big Volvo into place. "Hang on, Lucas. We'll get this son of a whore in, then we'll talk."

The sun's starting to go down over Riceville harbor, it's catching the line of red and green channel markers and the hulls of a couple dozen of the fastest boats on the coast. Harley keeps the locals tuned up right. Out beyond the harbor is the open sea, with a smoky afternoon southwester cooking a mist off of the whitecaps, an eastern-rig trawler passing by, hull down, bound for Stoneport with a nice full load.

Harley has dropped the Volvo now and his son's down there shimming up the mounts. Now he can give Lucky his full attention. "Seen anything you like?"

"Looks like that Olds got a little wet."

"The fuck it did. Old fart never left the mooring."

"Whose was it?"

"You know him, Alan French. Senior."

"Alan's fucking boat sunk, everyone knows that. How long'd that piece of shit spend on the bottom?"

"Lucky, you find that 307 has touched salt water, I'll *give* you the fucking thing."

"Them growths on the flywheel cover, you sure they ain't barnacles?"

"No, them are just from hanging there in the fog."

"How much?"

"Twenty-five hundred installed, now you ain't got the use of Clyde's hoist."

"Harley, you owe me for that fucking turbo. Piece of shit blew up on me."

"Bull shit. You ordered that propane rig, I put it in."

"Two thousand."

Harley looks at his watch, squints his good eye down the road. He's blind in the other, the black part's gone white as a fish. "Guy's coming for it in twenty minutes. I promised him over the phone. Didn't know you was coming in. He gets here, he's got it." He pulls a cigar out of his tool apron and lights it like it's a fuse and when it's smoked down the other guy's going to show up and buy the 307.

"OK, for Christ sake."

"I got to be paid now, Lucky. That guy comes in, he's going to start screaming. I got to be able to tell that cocksucker the deal is done."

"I need something else too. Fourteen-inch Hydroslave hauler, good for offshore. You got one?"

"Finest kind."

"Throw in the Hydroslave," Lucky says, "we'll be even."

"What do you mean, throw it in? For Christ sake, Lunt, this ain't the Salvation Army, this is a fucking business. The Hydroslave's cherry. Out of the box. New, it's four thousand bucks. For you, because you are an asshole, it's three."

"Give you forty-five hundred for the package," Lucky offers. "Engine, hauler, hydraulics. You put them in."

"You come down and help me. Just so's you won't come back yelling your ass off like you usually do. We dig our own fucking graves in this world, nobody digs them for us."

He pulls the rest of Moto's money out of his pants pocket and hands it over. Harley sticks it in his tool apron without even looking at it. He throws a screwdriver off towards the block yard and the pit bull screams off to pick it up. "You come around next Monday good and early, we'll clean that V-8 up and stick her in that research vessel of yours, see how she runs."

He drives back up the Riceville Road filling the pickup cab with cigar smoke till he can barely see. The Indians knew what they were doing, zip the door of the tepee and light up. When he gets to the Carrying Place, where the road slopes down right next to the water, he stops the truck and looks out through the smoky windows onto the North Atlantic Ocean as if he's just bought it off of Harley Webster for forty-five hundred bucks.

Fucking Harley, how can he stay in business making deals like that?

11

HARLEY HUNG ON TO the *Wooden Nickel* a week longer
than he promised, so she's not ready till September eighteenth. He can't
sleep at all the night before. He dreams of Clyde Hannaford's Ramcharger parked in his garage between the Lynx and the ATV, wakes up,
swallows some heart pills with a half shot of 101, then goes back to the
same dream. He slips out of Ronette's bed and walks the wobbling
length of the trailer to the built-in couch on the far end and watches an
old NASCAR rerun till almost 2 A.M. Then he turns it off and walks
back down the hall to wake her because it's time to head out. His head
scrapes the dotted soundproofing of the trailer ceiling and his shoulders
brush the fake-birch veneer walls on either side. The floor rocks like a
deck. Soon as he wakes her, she stumbles into the bathroom and kneels
down without even closing the door and throws up into the head. She's
a real fisherman now, seasick on land, cast iron stomach out to sea.

"Quarter past two," he calls in. "Don't take all day in there."

Looks like a winter night outside, clear black sky above with the moon going down over Corey Prentiss's dog fence and a mist coming off the road that will mean fog after daybreak, then it will scale up after a couple hours in the sun. She's out of the bathroom now, getting her boots and oilskins on. "Going to have to borrow a pair of yours before long," she says. "Can't do the snap on these things."

He heaves the last six oversize traps onto the bed of the GMC and they're over in Riceville by ten past three, listening to Midnight Country all the way. Harley's not there yet, but the *Wooden Nickel*'s floating proud and high on the float under the dock light, with a note wedged onto his useless radar screen.

> 1 oldsm engine reblt $2500
> 1 shaft 2" bronze usd
> 1 strat pipe exast
> clean engine etc tunup
> new wood mount shims
> hoses instal
> 1 Hydroslav haulr usd hoses pump instal
> $3800 PARTS
> $700 LABOR
> $4500 PAID CASH

"So can't I add right," she says, "or ain't we supposed to have five thousand left?"

He casts the lines off the float and says, "You sound like the tax auditor. Some other expenses come up, didn't have nothing to do with you."

"I don't know, Mr. Mystery Man. I been out here every day with you side by side, bad days and good. I'm putting you up in my house rent-free. I got a right to know what become of the ten thousand, same as you."

"Why don't you ease off with your right to know and let me hear what this engine sounds like now we got the new shaft."

"I'll give *you* the new shaft," she says, "if you don't talk to me about the extra cash. I'm going to be needing some of that myself. I should say *we*. Me and this kid. *We* are going to need money. If it don't get invested in the boat it should go to us."

He throttles her up to 1500 to drown the noise. The Riceville channel beacons are silhouetted by a green predawn glow forming over the open sea. Beneath the glow, right where they're heading, the offshore fog bank rises like a wall of ice.

They're just spotlighting the Riceville entrance buoy when a fifty-foot stern trawler comes out of the dark right at them smelling of marijuana and illegal groundfish, and pulling a trawl of seagulls through the air. No lights. "They ain't giving way," he says to Ronette, who has gone silent. "And I ain't neither."

He flips the spotlight in their eyes and swings to starboard so the two hulls come within pissing distance but don't hit. Two silent Riceville bastards in the smoky wheelhouse, dark as Arabs, staring straight ahead while their stern wave breaks over his bow section. He gives them the finger and yells, *"Assholes!"* but the term is buried in their wake.

"They ain't going to see your finger in the dark," Ronette says. "You ought to install a light on the frigging thing."

"Thought you wasn't talking."

Finally they've got an exhaust hot enough to light a cigarette. He tamps out a Marlboro and gives her the first hit. She pours herself a cup of coffee from the thermos. He grunts and she pours him one too. They've cleared the channel and are headed out past the Virgins off to the eastward and the Bishop and the tall white birdshit-covered rock known as the Bishop's Dick. The greenish dawn is changing to dark orange over the mist and a cloud of gulls flies off the Bishop to follow them out, though they keep their distance cause he's still carrying the bloody wing. Ronette breaks through her anger and throws them a fistful of redfish guts.

He runs her up to 2200 on the tach. The 307 pulls like a loco-motive compared to that little flathead six, she won't win races but she'll carry them twenty-five miles out on the North Atlantic Ocean, and when the day is over she'll get them home. Even in the swells the new V-8 with the three-bladed H&H prop is taking them out at a steady fifteen knots on the loran.

Passing the Riceville flasher, the reborn *Wooden Nickel* throws enough spray to wake up the old blackback on the solar panel and send him gliding off into the fog. He locks the helm and puts on the new Tracy Byrd.

With calves like that you gotta be a cowgirl
They don't make calves like that in town.

She reaches for the tape control and shuts it off.

"Hey. I'm listening to that."

"You listen to me for a change. I want to know about the five thousand bucks. We're going to have bills coming up. I ain't insured, you know."

"You can get a midwife for a couple hundred and get it born right in the trailer. That's the way Danny Thurston did it. Five hundred total and the kid was fine."

"Lucky, we ain't going to have a midwife and we ain't going to have it in the mobile home. Dr. Hyman says I've got complications, I'm throwing up too much. You know how much that kind of stuff can run?"

"You kidding? Hospital's got a mortgage on my heart."

He turns the throttle up a notch, leaves the cloud of gulls behind in his wake. The new V-8's smoothing out now, getting acquainted with the shaft and wheel, cutless bearing's settling so she doesn't shake so much. "Smell them Japanese lobsters all the way from here."

"About the five thousand," she yells. "That would be what I'm going to need."

"I gave it to Kristen. I ain't like you. I got other mouths to feed."

"You gave your daughter five thousand bucks?"

"College," he shouts back. "It ain't free."

"You gave *our money* to *her?* Has she been out here with you day after fucking day, so far offshore the radio don't reach, baiting and setting these huge traps pregnant to pay off your advance? How *could* you?"

"That money came off of *my* boat. Kristen's *my* flesh and blood, raised in my own house."

"*Ex* house. Lucky, I don't know what that girl told *you,* but she's driving a brand-new convertible. Reggie Dolliver was hitching a ride, he ain't got a license, your precious darling picks him up in a Corvette and drives him to Norumbega with the top down. Now, somebody's got to be lying. Either she ain't telling the truth or you ain't. Did you give her our five thousand for a car?"

"Wasn't no Corvette, it was a Mustang. You couldn't look at a Corvette for six thousand bucks."

"See? You *did,* you bastard, you spent our kid's birth money on a *car.*"

He throws the Marlboro butt over the side and throttles her down cause the new shaft is starting to shake some in the seas. "Ain't none of your business," he says. "It's my fucking family."

She takes his free hand and holds it against the front of her oil-skins the way she used to in the old days, but lower down. The new bump in the middle is getting bigger than the other two. "*That's* your family," she says. "Right in there. Family is whose bed you're sleeping in. Family is who took you in when you got thrown out. Them others is history, same as your old fucking ancestors you're always yelling about. They're dead and gone. You get an impulse to buy something, buy it for us."

He tries turning the music up again and this time she lets him. She lights one up for herself off the exhaust and leans her back against his back, looking the opposite way.

> *Now I'm a guy and she's my girl and we live on the farm*
> *We spend the day, making hay, out behind the barn*

With the V-8 in there, cruising at fifteen knots, the sun's just a fogbound yellow ball on a horizon that's only a hundred yards away. He passes the last of the local Riceville traps with their old-fashioned glass toggles and moves into deep water so the fishfinder goes blank, eighty, ninety fathoms under the keel, farther than she'll reach. It's over an hour before the sounder comes up to fifty and starts flashing again, meaning they've picked up the north end of their new ground. All his life he's fished so close to the Orphan Point boats he could hear them take a leak over the side, now he's twenty miles from the nearest human being. Life is different out here, big fog-colored birds that probably don't lay eyes on dry land from birth to death. He's got a circle of maybe two hundred feet of visibility on the water, though straight up above there's a clear September sky with the day's first sunlight cracking through. He looks for the Day-Glo lemon buoy, should be shining through the surface fog right about here, loran's sounding off, the depth is right, he's just where he should be. But the buoy's not. Nothing but three or four seabirds adrift on a scrap of timber, purplish-gray water far as he can see. He whacks the loran with the heel of his hand and it blinks off for a second, then reads the same numbers when it comes back on. That first one was the only buoy he punched in. The rest of them he set on a course south-southwest down the ridge, about a hundred yards apart. He steams south for a couple minutes while the bottom shoals up to twenty-five fathoms. This is where he set four big ones close together, but there's nothing here either.

"Ain't been any storms," he says. "Don't know where them christly traps could be."

Ronette's got the binoculars and she's sweeping the fog line off to the southeast. "I think there's something way off there."

"They ain't nothing off there, cause I didn't set no traps down there. I laid the string off to westward along the shoal."

"No, Lucky, look."

He turns the wheel and steams over. At twenty-five fathoms there's a snarl of three Day-Glo lemon buoys twisted together with the handles in three different directions like a propeller.

"What the fuck."

She hands him the gaff but they're twisted so tight he can't untangle them.

"What are you going to do, Luck?"

"I'm going to haul all three of them bastards and see what's going on."

He waits for a down swell and hooks the snarl of pot warp over the rail cleat. The new Hydroslave hauler strains like a weightlifter, but it just heels the boat down till she sucks green water over the starboard rail, three traps are too heavy to haul at once. She hands him the long-handled rope knife and he feels the warps to see which is the tightest and cuts it free. "One more fucking ghost trap, four or five big bastards chewing themselves to death."

The cut line spirals off from the others and disappears. He throws a few more turns on the pot hauler and eases the other two close to the surface, the rail back down to the water with their weight. One trap, ripped halfway across the top, has scooped up a load of bottom mud and stones. The other funnel is ripped right through and another big rock's in there, the two of them must weigh five hundred pounds submerged.

No way he's going to untangle the two warps, traps are ruined anyway, so he takes the rope knife and cuts them free. The starboard rail jumps up from the relief.

The sun's scaling the fog up some and he can see the next buoy, back where it's supposed to be, so he steams up, slips it over the davy block and around the drum. Twenty fathoms of water and the Hydroslave sucks her off the bottom like a loose tooth. Ronette's peering down in the water watching it come up. "Nothing wrong with that one."

They haul it over and there's two jumbos inside, covered with deepwater barnacles and squirming with hunger, all claws intact. They'll run eight pounds apiece, at eight bucks a pound that's about a hundred thirty right there. They get the double bands on them and they're in the well.

"Look at that, Lucky, they're trying to crawl right up the side. I feel sorry for these big ones, they could be pretty near human."

"They was dumb enough to get caught, it's their own fault."

"You don't have no sympathy for nothing, do you?"

"Look at them lobsters close, Ronette. Look at that fucking water. It's twenty-five fathoms down there, freezing fucking cold, you ain't a hard-shelled bastard they're going to eat you alive."

They haul a dozen more traps and drop another eight godzillas into the live well, then Ronette drops her bib straps to peel her sweatshirt off and puts in a Trisha Yearwood classic.

> *Well, I've got a steady job that pays enough*
> *A pretty good car that don't break down much*

He pulls a Rolling Rock out of the ice box, bites the cap off, and gives it to her for the first sip with the foam drooling over the top and running all over her hand.

"Remind you of something?" he says.

She sticks her tongue out at him, then uses it to lick the foam off of the bottle neck. "Don't remind me of nothing. I ain't that kind."

She slips the orange oilskin bib down so she's just wearing a T-shirt with the neck ripped down to the Nike sign. She leans back on the cooler so her face points up at the morning sun. A good-looking woman looks good pregnant, everything she had before and more besides. Then he looks over in the well at his jumbo lobsters shuffling around near the pump outlet, some trying to crawl up in the saltwater pipe to escape, others trying to burrow under each other like rocks.

"Hundred pounds of them bastards, we're going to be pushing eight hundred bucks, just this one haul."

"Four hundred bucks for Moto, four hundred for your exes." She holds the Rolling Rock up so the green glass catches the sun and the inside looks like the sparkling depth of the sea.

"You should of stuck with Clyde, you'd be floating around the hot tub now."

"Clyde would of gave me the whole ten thousand and then some. Cheap bastard, no wonder your wife threw you out."

"How come you're out here then? Freezing your ass off, can't see a hundred feet, cold black water, and all the traps fucked up."

"There's one or two reasons, but I ain't going into them till after lunch." She's getting her sandwich out of the lunch pail. "Jesus, I'm starved all the time, I'll be a blimp before this is over. It don't come off, neither." She switches to "Don't It Make My Brown Eyes" on the *Country Legends* tape. She always puts that on when she's got something in mind. Works too, same way a dog hears the can opener. He fastens a trapline to the anchor bitt while she finishes her sandwich, then follows her down below. She's got one leg out of her orange Grundens before her feet hit the cabin floor.

These days, she likes to do it with her clothes half off, one leg in oilskins, the other sticking out warm and bare. The Nike shirt pulled up to her shoulders, bra unhooked, nice round pregnant tits swinging like jellyfish as the boat sloshes in the ocean swell.

Sometimes she's too much for him and it's over in a minute, but this time she's cool and slick as a sea cucumber, he feels he can rock in the crosswaves forever. Then she throws her eyes wide open and pushes him up off her with both hands on his shoulders. She pulls her head back so he's forced to look her in the eye and listen. "You can't do this with nobody anymore."

"Hell," he says, "you ain't that far gone. We don't have to stop *yet*."

"Nobody *else*. I mean it, Lucky. I'm going to be fat and ugly, but even so you got to promise you ain't going to do this with nobody else. Your womanizer days are over, you understand?"

She's crying while she says this. Big drops splash down on the blue nylon comforter she fetched out of Clyde's house when she went back to get her stuff.

His dick has already shriveled and popped out, it's curled up like a brine shrimp, so they might as well talk. "You afraid I'll be going back to Sarah? She calls the deputies if I drive past on the road."

"Don't make no difference if it's your wife or whoever. You cheated and lied on her when you was starting up with me, how am I supposed to know you ain't going to do that again? I ain't going to be your little honeypot at the Blue Claw. I'm going to be a fat old pig. How do I know you ain't doing it already?" She's pointing at his dick like it's in the witness box. "That thing don't tell me where it's been."

She dries her face off with the tail of her T-shirt but her tits are still staring at him like angry brown octopus eyes. "I ain't interested," he says. "I ain't got time."

She pulls the shirt down and pokes her free leg around trying to jam it back in the oilskin trousers. "You do, Mr. Lucas Lunt, and you know what's going to happen to you? Clyde gave me a handgun, you know. I'm going to hunt you down and shoot you where it hurts. And her too. I don't care if I have to bring the baby up in jail. Lots of girls do, no pricks giving you a hard time, and the medical care is free."

Then, just to sternward, there's an engine sound, not a lobster boat but a heavy Caterpillar eight-cylinder diesel turning a full-size three-blade prop, nice and slow. He puts his head up through the companionway. A big black dragger with its gear up is practically stopped just to sternward of them and the crew is staring like pirates over the port rail, every one of them with a shit-eating toothless grin.

"Jesus H. Christ," he yells, "if it ain't the god damn Trotts. You boys tired of fishing? You see anything you like?"

Anson Trott puts her in neutral and calls, "Picked you up on the radar, just checking if you was OK. Awful small little boat to be way out here. Didn't see nobody so I thought something had happened."

"We was below," Lucky shouts. The Trotts change from their shit-eating toothless grins to big belly laughs, drooling tobacco spit, stomping on each other's boots, flashing their black tongues. When Ronette pops her head out the companionway they close their mouths and start frigging around with their drag cable.

"OK, Lucky," Anson Trott yells back. "Guess you was. Ain't hauling, are you?"

"Hell no, I'm doing government research now."

"That's what we heard. Which government?" Har har. Anson throws his cigar stub into the space between the boats.

"Hang on a minute. You boys been towing that drag across my gear?"

"Ain't no scallops on that ledge. We're fishing ten miles south of here, just heading out and thought you was in trouble. Didn't know you had the lady aboard."

"I catch anyone dragging this ledge, I'm going to fucking shoot them."

In the shadow of his wheelhouse Big Anson Trott's got both his hands raised to the sky. "Believe you will," he shouts. "They say you're pretty handy with a gun."

Anson turns back to the helm and revs the diesel while his crew members elbow and goose each other all around and go back to work. The exhaust farts out a black storm cloud and they take off to the west-southwestward, swinging far over to avoid Lucky's field of traps. There's so much fish scum and birdshit dripping down the transom you can barely make out their name under the huge winch drum:

RACHEL T
Shag Island

"Them bastards," she says. "They can't let nothing drop. That's the thing about the god damn ocean, there's nothing to do out here but remember."

Last time he set another string half a mile southward on a sixteen-fathom rise, it's the shallowest shelf around. Steaming over there, he can feel the sea heave up beneath them where the deep swells get lifted by the ledge. The loran and fishfinder both say they're right on top of it, but the whole field of them has disappeared. "Bastards," he says. "Five traps gone to hell. Right here."

He's got the waypoint alarm set and the loran's beeping away.

"I remember," she says. "This is where we got the ten-pounder."

Another diesel sound, this one twins, then the squat white form of the cat-hulled whale-watching boat steams directly at them out of the lifting fog. The cat passes close enough to see her rail full of tourists throwing up, the crew running frantically from mouth to mouth with plastic bags. "Hey, look at them, they're all pregnant!" Ronette says.

The whale-watcher makes a sharp turn to port and the twin engines boil the water as she throttles up. "They must be on to something." Soon as he says it, they both spot a whale on the close, misty horizon, tipping its tail and jamming down into the water headfirst, just like the *Titanic.*

"I ought to drive one of them boats. Easy money, don't get your hands dirty."

"Cute little passengers," Ronette says.

"Cute little passengers puking all over you. Just my type."

"That's about all *I* do these days, ain't it?" She's fastening the oilskins now, pulling the bib over the Nike T-shirt, that's it for romance.

"Guess it's back to work," he says.

No answer.

The fog has scaled up to a hazy September sunlight and it's easy to spot the next yellow buoy bobbing like a fluorescent sea duck on the long green swell. This one's way off station too. It seems OK as he slows alongside and gaffs it, but he grinds her till the hydraulics smoke and she won't come up. "Something's onto her." He jams on the winch brake to lean over for a look. Same thing. There's three or four warps snarled up like a bucket of fish guts, strands coming out all over and a sunken buoy wrapped up in the whole mess. He grinds the hydraulics down till water spills out of the live well and sloshes over the rail. "She ain't going to come."

He looks up and sees the silhouette of the *Rachel T,* trolling along slow and easy as a drag queen. "Cocksuckers," he says.

The high-pitched double diesel of the whale-watching catamaran comes straight towards the *Wooden Nickel* on a collision course. Ronette says, "Look!" The cat's chasing a whale with its fin out of the water, herding the fucking thing at them till it tips up and waves its tail in the air not more than a couple hundred feet from their bow and dives straight down. There's something looped around its tail.

"You see the tail on that thing?"

"It had a rope around it, Lucky. You couldn't see that?"

"I seen something."

"If you can't see a god damn whale maybe it's time for glasses."

"I got glasses."

"You got *TV* glasses. You bought them at the Rite Aid. That frigging thing had a yellow rope on its tail. You know how one of them tail fins was cut into like a V-notched lobster? Well, the notch had the yellow line in it and around the thick part too."

"Anything attached to it?"

"I couldn't see."

Meanwhile, the whale-watcher boat crosses the *Rachel T*'s bow and disappears in the green smoky offshore mist. Lucky unhitches the tangled warp off his winch and heads south-southwest where the *Rachel T* is still slowly dragging along the fog line.

"We're going out and have a talk with them bastards."

"Who?"

"The Hot to Trotts, that's who. Them lines been fucked up by someone. Ain't no one else fishing this deep but them."

"No, Lucky. Don't you see? It's the god damn whale. It was your own yellow poly around the fin."

"Then get the gun out, Ronette. I'm going to shoot that son of a whore."

"You can't, Lucky. They're *protected.*"

"The fuck they are. We're twenty-five fucking miles offshore. It's every man for himself out here."

"Lucky, I think they're protected everywhere."

"They ain't protected from me."

They steam due west to the southwest tip of the ledge, where there's a string of undamaged traps that produce another eight big ones for the saltwater well. Plus the biggest starfish he's ever seen, clinging on to the outside as they brought it up. He holds the star up by the arms, pretty near as far as he can stretch. Ronette says, "I never seen one that huge."

"They feed on nuclear waste, that's what Wallace Eaton heard. You ain't going to want to be around when them bastards start coming inshore."

She rears right up on the washboard where Ginger used to sit. "Jesus, Lucky, don't let it get near the baby. Throw it *back.*"

They watch it pinwheel slowly down through the darkening sea layers till it seems to glow of its own light, then it disappears. They steam northward towards the waypoint for his last two strings, towards the center and high spots of the ledge, but there's no sign of them. No toggles, no sunken warps, nothing. Half the traps he set on the new grounds are wrecked or missing in the space of a week. The only clue's a loop of yellow pot warp that he couldn't even see.

Coming into the Old Cove via the Whistle Creek entrance, it's so shallow he feels the prop churning up the seabed, stern wave looks like raw sewage as it breaks on the harbor ledge. Right in the narrow dredged channel with the sounder reading under five feet, he sees an outboard roaring out towards him, then throttling down hard when they see who it is. Ronette, up on the bow as lookout watching the bottom, yells, "Hey Lucky, it's your own flesh and blood!"

Kyle and Darrell Swan have their shirts off and their open boat full of diving gear and a six-pack of Budweiser on the thwart, enough tattoos between them to start a freak show. They pull alongside and Darrell Swan hangs on to the *Wooden Nickel*'s rail with one arm.

Lucky says, "You been to Moto's?"

Kyle's got his hands on his hips, big dive knife on his belt, grinning skull tattooed across his shoulder. "Moto ain't there, Curtis is buying."

"Didn't know it was urchin season yet."

"Ain't no seasons in Whistle Creek. What I hear, there ain't no size limits neither." Kyle peers at the jumbo lobsters in the saltwater well. "Old Grandpa Walter, wouldn't he love to see that."

He throws Ronette's blue quilt over the well cover. "Walter Lunt's dead. Merritt Lunt's dead. Them days are gone forever. They ain't coming back. Man's got to feed his family, he does what he has to do."

"Can't see's you been feeding *us*."

"He don't mean you," Darrell Swan says. He's still hanging on to the starboard rail, scratching the snake tattoo on his forearm. Must be a new one, it looks raw.

"Oh yeah," Kyle says. "I hear there's another family on the way." He looks at Ronette, smiling in a slantwise goofy way that's the image of Walter Lunt. Directly to her, not even glancing at his old man, he says, "Guess I ought to say congratulations. You caught a big one."

She puts her hand on her belly like she just finished off a turkey dinner. "Don't say nothing you don't mean, Kyle."

Kyle stands up next to Darrell Swan on the edge of the *Metallica.* The two of them on one side pretty near bring the rail under. Ronette reaches over and pats their shaved skulls like a couple of tame seals. "Give me a smoke, would you? Your old man won't let me have any."

Kyle reaches down, pulls a pack of Camels out of his shirt and hands one each to her and to Darrell Swan. "Matter of fact," he says, "we're moving to Halifax."

"What the *fuck,*" Lucky spits. "Who said you could do that?"

Ronette moves over so he's facing the three of them together. "Jesus, Lucky, what do you think, he's *ten?*"

"Going to Halifax," Kyle repeats. "We made some money off Moto, now he's drying up and it's time to see the world."

"What's that supposed to mean, drying up?"

"Know that Humvee he had? Repo company came for it."

"No shit? Thought he had money up the ass."

Ronette asks, "What are you going to do in Halifax? They got urchins?"

"We ain't going to be fishing," Darrell Swan says. "We're going into international trade."

Kyle says, "Darrell's got an uncle in the pharmaceutical business." Darrell gives him a sharp swat on the shoulder, right on the skull tattoo. Kyle slaps him back. "He's my old man. He ain't going to say nothing. He works for Moto just like us."

"Catch you running drugs," Lucky says, "I don't care where the fuck you are, I'll come after you and kick your ass. That ain't what boats are for."

Kyle and Darrell both let go the rail and push off a bit, so the *Metallica* drifts ten or twelve feet off to starboard. Kyle says, "You can't do nothing anymore. You ain't got a house, you ain't got a license, you ain't even got fishing grounds. Only ass you'll kick will be your own."

Ronette comes over, leans closer to Lucky, offers a drag off of the Camel to calm him down. Over on the skiff, Darrell Swan's mocking her, he leans up against Kyle the same way, offers him the butt of his Camel, big shit-eating grin on his face. Ronette says, "Remember, Lucky, your heart. They're just kids." She stretches up and gives him a wet kiss on the cheek, trying to distract him. Out on the water Darrell Swan gives his son the same big kiss like a mirror image.

Ronette pushes him towards the wheel and tugs it to starboard, away from the outboard skiff. "Come on, Lucky, Curtis ain't going to wait all day."

"Just a minute, I ain't settled with that little bastard." He backs off from the skiff to get a running start, puts her in gear, revs the 307 and spins the helm to starboard so she points right at the midships of Kyle's dive boat.

Darrell Swan takes a look at the big white bow bearing down on him and lunges for the controls. The Merc outboard digs its prop to the channel bottom and douches the green Whistle Creek buoy in a plume of septic-colored spray. But Lucky's on their tail with the *Wooden Nickel,* yelling, "Halifax, bullshit. I'm going to sink them little cocksuckers on the spot."

The throttle's pinned, flames are gushing out of the 307's exhaust, and he's on track to climb over the *Metallica*'s stern and fucking sink them with Ronette screaming, *"Jesus, Lucky!"* and the rocks flashing on the color fishfinder like huge red spikes. All of a sudden Darrell turns the skiff sharp westward out of the dredged channel and planes through the shallows along the rocky shore. Lucky turns to follow but the one-fathom alarm's bleating like a smoke detector and the whole boat shivers when the keel grazes a boulder and glances off. He throws her in reverse to kill way, the stern wave climbs the transom and floods over the washboard onto the platform. He starts the pump and backs out of there with the sounder showing four-foot readings all the way back to the channel cut. "Sneaky little fucker."

"What'd you expect him to do, sit there and let you run them down? Your own kid, for Christ sake."

Beyond them, the *Metallica*'s still skimming across the Whistle Creek tideflats with those two tattooed son of a whores diving into the cooler like it's a family barbecue.

"Fucking degenerates, they don't give a shit. I don't know who I'm doing all this for."

"I do," she says. "So let's bring in them lobsters and get paid."

Moto's fish wharf looks a hundred years old, it's got planks falling through, the gangway's twisted, the pilings and crossties gilded with piss-colored algae and hanging with brown folded sheets of kelp. The bait shack and icehouse are frosted with gullshit like a wedding cake. The little office where Moto does the paperwork has a pane with a bullet hole in it and another pane boarded up, you'd never know he kept a computer in there and a safe with probably fifty thousand cash. Fucking Chinese, they're smarter than they look. He keeps the place looking bad so no one will notice. And the guy he has working for him as dockboy, Curtis Landry, is such an insane son of a bitch he could walk into the grand jury with Moto's outlaw transactions and nobody would believe a word. Curtis is a short guy but he's built like a mooring stone and he's an ex-con like Reggie Dolliver, only he did more time. He killed a guy once and served five or six years for it, and they still have him living in some kind of halfway house up in West Stoneport. Moto has to pick him up every morning and drive him to Whistle Creek. Maybe that's why Moto trusts him, cause the state's still got its hand around his neck.

Curtis doesn't move a muscle when the *Wooden Nickel* pulls alongside the float. He stands there with his thumb up his ass and lets Ronette jump off and handle the lines. He's watching her close enough, though, as she bends over and fastens the stern line. They probably don't get much up at the halfway house.

He says, "Hey Curtis, you want to hand over one of them crates? We got some counters in here."

Curtis spits some black chew into the lobster car under the float. "I ain't paid to move crates."

"Thought you was working here."

"Mr. Moto ain't here, I'm the buyer today."

"Well kiss my ass. You got promoted. Who would of believed it?"

"You want to wise off, mister, you can take them lobsters right on up to Massachusetts."

Ronette's struggling to drag a hundred-pound lobster crate across the float. He lugs out the second crate, between them there's fourteen godzillas that have to average eight pounds apiece. State ever learned about these, it would be ninety days for everyone, Moto on down. Ronette, she's an accessory, maybe she'd just get fined. The catch goes up on the scale and totals in at a hundred twenty-one pounds. Curtis dumps the giant lobsters into a float car with a lock and chain, case anyone snoops around. "Dock price is five-fifty. We'll go upstairs and figure it out."

Lucky flips his cigarette and it sizzles out in the rainbow of oil slick around the float. *"Five fucking fifty?* Moto's paying me eight. Get on the christly phone and call him up."

"Might be Mr. Moto's price. It ain't mine."

"That's bullshit. Half my traps got wrecked out there. I got to buy twenty more before I go out again."

"You going to take five-fifty or am I going to open the bottom of this here lobster car and let them go? We could use some breeders in this cove."

Horny little fucker, he's staring at Ronette's tits when he says that.

"You let them bastards go, you'll be down there breeding with them. You ever try it with a jumbo lobster?"

"Six bucks. Mr. Moto says that's it. Seven-twenty for the haul."

"Hey Curtis, you ever think of turning your boss in for the reward?"

"Mr. Moto treats me right. He treats all his help right, but me specially cause I been around and I know what the fuck is going on. Them other guys is just Japs, they don't know shit."

"I hear they all got black belts, Curtis. They can bust planks with their foreheads."

"They don't know shit," Curtis repeats.

They go up to Moto's office for the paperwork. Math is a real struggle for Curtis, you can see his eyes cross and his brain start to stall out like a plane about to go down. He's sitting in Moto's chair in front of the blank computer screen with his face right down against the paper and his fist around the pencil stabbing it at the invoice like a knife. "Ain't my fault," Curtis says. "Ain't Mr. Moto's neither. I heard it on Rush. The whole Asian money system's going under. They got a fucking depression over there. I seen pictures of bank presidents begging on the street. They ain't going to buy them lobsters off you because they can't afford no sushi anymore. This guy called in to Rush, he seen some of them Jap bankers eating rats."

"You're full of shit, Curtis. You been to Moto's place? They ain't eating no rats up there."

"God damn fishermen learned something about the economy, they wouldn't get fucked in the ass so much."

"You ought to know, Curtis."

At that, Curtis's eyes pop open. He stands up, spreads his arms out sideways, and starts coming forward across Moto's office like a rock crab. Lucky's reaching for a busted-off tuna gaff in the corner, he'll gaff the son of a bitch right through the neck, then all of a sudden they hear a German diesel snorting down the hill towards the bait shed. It's Moto in his Mercedes, leaving a cloud of dust behind on the dirt road and driving right out on the planks of the old pier though you can see the pilings sag under the weight. The diesel keeps flopping and farting even after it gets shut down. Up in the office, Curtis pulls back so his boss won't see him going for the clientele. Lucky puts the tuna gaff in its corner and says, "Jesus, Curtis, you'd think he'd drive a Lexus or something, seeing as where he's from."

Moto's got a black doberman with him in the backseat behind a cage wire like in the K-9 cars, looks like a big lobster trap with a dog in it. Then he's pulling himself along the dock rail towards his office and up the outside stairway railing like he can't climb so great. But he's grinning and happy when he walks in the office door.

Right away Curtis says, "Mr. Moto, tell this guy what the new price is on his lobsters. He don't listen to nothing."

"Six dollar."

"What the fuck?" Lucky bursts out. "Our deal was eight and you said it was going up to nine. Not down. Them things don't grow on trees out there. I'm going out thirty miles offshore, I'm fishing on a twenty-fathom ledge. They ain't like one-pound chicken lobsters crawling all over each other on the bottom. Them bastards is few and far between. I haul eight a day, I'm doing good. Six bucks a pound ain't going to cover gas and bait, never mind paying off your loan."

"Economy very poor this time. I am have to absorb ross myself. Five-fifty next time, I am afraid."

"There ain't going to be a next time at five-fifty. I can't afford to make the fucking trip."

Moto rolls Curtis Landry aside on the office chair and sticks his little brown hand into the desk drawer, pulls out a pocket calculator and pokes some numbers in. "You are owing me ten thousand dollar."

"Less the two we brought in."

"I am a poor man much like yourself. One poor man cannot cally another on his back."

"I need some cash before I can pay you off. I got a heart condition. I got pills to buy. I got a kid coming. Half my fucking traps got destroyed out there."

"You are in trouble with neighbor again, even thirty mile out?"

Curtis, the old con, his eyes light up at the sound of violence. "I hear you take care of yourself out there."

"Relax, Curtis. It ain't a fight. Fucking whale ripped through a trapline. Cocksucker had a piece of my warp right around his tail."

Moto pulls a fistful of folded bills out of his pocket and rolls off five brand-new hundreds on the office desk, the ones with the big heads that look like counterfeits, Curtis drools over the sight of them. Moto will be lucky if his dockboy doesn't kill him someday and stuff him in the lobster car.

"Remainder will be on company account."

"I'm going to need more of them big traps," he says. "Must of lost fifteen of them things."

"Best perhaps not set them in whaling zone."

"How the fuck am I supposed to know? It's the Atlantic Ocean out there, there ain't no yellow signs with whales on them. Them fuckers are probably going after the lobsters anyway, they'd eat a few dozen at once, no different from a fucking seal."

Just then Ronette shows up in the office. There's only one chair and Moto pushes Curtis out of it saying, "Up, up," and rolls it in front of her like a gentleman so she can have a seat. Moto is about the same height as Curtis but Curtis would outweigh three of him. Both of them standing tall come up to somewhere in the middle of Lucky's chest, like that guy Dolliver and the midgets.

Moto starts some water on a hot plate and gets out a box with four little black teacups, no handles. Pretty soon the water's steaming and he throws a green tea bag into each cup. Curtis's cup looks like a thimble in his thick fingers. Ronette holds her cup on the knee of her orange oilpants and says, "Mr. Moto, I hear your boat price is going down."

"I am truly sorry," Moto answers. "Eight dollar not possible."

"Well, you lent Lucky all that money saying the price would be eight, now how are we supposed to catch up at five-fifty a pound?"

"Six," Moto says.

With her sitting at the desk like that, everyone else standing, she looks more like the boss than Moto does. Ronette spent time as a dealer's wife, she knows what's going on. "Clyde Hannaford would never of let one of his fishermen get in debt like that."

Moto brightens up and says, "Oh yes, you are Mrs. Hannaford. Also seafood buyer."

"I *was* Mrs. Hannaford. I ain't no more."

"You now Mrs. Runt?"

"You kidding? Lucky ain't even got his lawyer yet."

"Excellent. I am not mallied either." Moto slides up closer to her with more hot water for the cup balanced on her knee. Sitting there in the office chair with the torn T-shirt sliding off under her apron and her hair frizzed up from the salt air, Ronette's looking just like a page off of the Snap-Lok Tool calendar in Harley's garage. The shirt's getting so tight on her, the head of her little sea horse peeks over the ripped neck. The orange oilskins bunch up so her belly doesn't show. Curtis is drooling into his tea, his ankle radio's lighting up the switchboard back in the halfway house.

On the desk there's a big color photo in a wooden frame, it's Moto and Wilfred Beal grinning on some Florida fish pier with a thousand-pound marlin hoisted up between them. Moto reaches under the photo and pulls a brown bottle out of the desk drawer and offers her a hit of it in the tea. It's got a red label with big yellow Chinese letters. "Sockey," he says. "You try."

"Sure."

Lucky sticks his cup out for a hit. Stuff's got an odor like acetone, but it does wipe out the dulse taste of the tea. Moto puts it away without offering it to Curtis, probably just as well. Short guys are mean drunks, every one of them.

Ronette says, "Six bucks a pound ain't enough for what we got to go through to get them things. Me and Lucas need more money. We're planning a family. We got to pay you off too, Mr. Moto. It don't feel good to have a debt around our neck."

Moto looks down at her neck like he can see the debt hanging between her tits and takes a sip of his green seaweed tea. "For you only, six-fifty a pound."

Ronette says, "We got to have more traps and line too. He tell you what happened to the gear? We think a whale wrecked it."

Curtis says, "What if the same thing happens again? You going to keep coming back for more loans? Mr. Moto ain't made of cash, you know."

Lucky drains the rest of his acetone seaweed tea and stretches his hand towards Moto for a refill. "Happens again, I'll kill the son of a whore."

Curtis jabs his elbow against Moto's and giggles like a girl. Rugged as he appears, he probably took it from behind a few times in the slammer. Don't care how big you are, somebody's always bigger. "Hee hee, I'd like to see that," Curtis says. "How you planning to kill a fucking whale? You planning to use a harpoon?"

"Shoot him. Whales got a heart, ain't they? They got blood. They got to come up for air. Three-hundred Savage, maybe a three fifty-seven magnum, same as we use for moose. Shoot the cocksucker in the right place, he's going to bleed to death just like anybody else." He looks at his favorite dockboy. "Ain't that right, Curtis?"

Curtis puts his cup down next to the hot plate and steps back away from Moto and starts spreading his claws again like he's about to come on even though the boss is there. Lucky's heart skips and speeds up, then settles in. He sets the tea down and spreads his feet apart, ready.

Ronette turns to Curtis, puts a hand on his arm to settle him down — "Curtis, he didn't mean nothing, he's just *like* that" — and the short fat fingers pick up the tea again.

Moto pays no attention. He's interested in the whale. "Just like red Indians," he says.

"That's right. The Indians go out in the Pacific Ocean and shoot the bastards out of a war canoe."

Ronette's having a tea refill with another splash of sockey, like she's been a fish broker all her life. She leans her head against Moto's elbow and laughs. "Listen up, Lucky. We bring one of them whales in, we got ourselves paid off. One fish."

"OK, I pay seven." Moto laughs back. "No need to kill whale."

Curtis grumbles, "Too god damn much."

"And I go five thousand more for gear," Moto volunteers. "You are ten thousand already, less two as you say. Thirteen thousand total. OK? No more. That is big debt for a small boat."

Curtis giggles again. "Supposing you was to take a shot at one of them son of a whores and you managed to kill him. How you planning to bring him in? You going to tow him into Whistle Creek? You can't drag a peeled eel through that slit."

Now Moto's got something up on the computer screen, he's checking his prices. "Whalemeat down too," he says. "Only ninety yen a pound. Seventy-five cent."

"That takes care of *that* dumb idea," Ronette says. "Now let's get the boat cleaned up and get the hell home."

"Wait a minute," Lucky says. "They run a half ton a foot, that's what I hear. That one's a short little bastard, maybe a boat length, say thirty-five feet, that's at least fifteen tons, come around twenty-four thousand bucks, same as my operation. Tow her in at night, all's you have to do is come in here with a big truck with a winch in the trailer box. We'll drag that sucker up the boat ramp, Curtis will chop her up, and it's off to Tokyo. No more fucked-up traps, and we're paid off. Hey Mr. Moto, can you get a ten-ton refrigerated truck down here?"

"You stick to robsters," Moto says. "Let Indian tribe catch whale."

The brown bottle empty, Moto gives them a ride back to where they left the truck in Riceville. He stuffs Curtis behind the wire in back along with the doberman and puts Ronette between him and Lucky on the pull-down center seat. His stereo's on Communist Public Radio playing the kind of music Kristen likes.

"Crassical," Moto says.

Ronette says, "Mind if we shut it off? It's kind of screechy on the ears."

"Anything you rike, Lonette."

She hits the seek button. In a minute she's got Real Country 103 and Vince Gill singing "When I Call Your Name."

> *I rushed home from work*
> *Like I always do*
> *I spent my whole day*
> *Just thinking of you*
> *When I walked through the front door*
> *My whole life was changed*
> *Cause nobody answered*
> *When I called your name*

"That's what we call classic around here," she says. "Mind if I smoke? I ain't supposed to but it's been a long hard day."

She pulls out a Marlboro and draws the ashtray out. A little spotlight comes on over the tray and the lighter. The ashtray still has the factory seal across it, never been used once. The minute she lights it there's the click of a Bic in the backseat, either it's the doberman or Curtis lighting up. Moto says, "Curtis," in a little whisper and you can hear him snuff out the butt he's just started, while up front Ronette is puffing like a smokehouse, pregnant or not, eyes closed, thinking about Vince Gill.

Back in his own truck driving home from Riceville, she's fishing around in the glove box for the Vince Gill tape. "Relax," he says. "You got it back home."

The instant they get in the trailer door and she peels her oilskins off, she's going through the pile of cassettes looking for Vince before the moment's lost. She runs around pulling the shades to keep the sunset out, then in the dark living room between the TV and the built-in, she circles her arms around his waist and tries to join them around his back but as always they don't quite reach. She closes her eyes, rests her nose beneath his armpit, and waltzes him in a slow circle over the wall-to-wall rug.

> *The note on the table*
> *That told me good-bye*
> *Said you've grown weary*
> *Of living a lie*

"Taking up where we left off," she says.

"Unless something comes up between us."

"Might of come up already," she says, pushing her hips in tight. "Sure you ain't hiding a lobster buoy in there?"

"Just the handle. The big part's underwater."

This time she rides on top of him like a kid on a Wal-Mart horse. He's hanging onto her waist so she won't throw herself off onto the trailer floor, at the same time he's watching a ceiling joint rock back and forth like the walls are about to come down, only Ronette beats them to it and grabs his chest hair with both hands, then screams and crashes down on him like old Clyde's arrived in his big Dodge Ram and shot her in the back through the trailer window.

They're lying there with a clamshell ashtray on the bed between them. One tit's pointing right up in the air, the other's drooped over a bit to the side and staring at him soft and quiet as a scallop. Her face is smeared up like she's been crying. That sometimes happens with Ronette, she'll come off like a stomp rocket, the next moment she'll start sniffling and her big kelp-colored eyes will fill with tears.

She takes her can of Miller High Life off the nightstand and balances it on her growing belly that's just starting to push up higher than her hips. "Just a little hill now," she says.

"That'll be a mountain before Christmas. You'll have toboggans going down the side of it."

"Maybe. Maybe not. I been to the doctor."

"Yeah?"

"I told you, Lucky. I got a complication. Dr. Hyman sent me to Dr. Sempert in Tarratine, he's such a geek, he says how much it's going to cost, I tell him I ain't married, I got no insurance. You know what he says when I tell him that?" She lifts the can off her belly and takes a slug, then pours a little on the end of her tit so the nipple stands up curious as an earthworm in the rain.

Lucky doesn't answer, just gets his own Miller's off of the trailer floor and takes a sip.

"He says, 'You might want to consider a termination.' That's the way he put it, *termination.* You'd think he was Arnold F. Schwarzenegger."

"Tad late for that," Lucky says.

"That's what I tell him. I'm past four months. 'Not too late,' he says. 'If I recommend it, they do it.'"

He stands right up on the trailer floor beside the bed. "No wonder they shoot them partial-birth bastards," he says. "Reggie Dolliver said he seen them on the Internet, whole page of abortion butchers, names and addresses, targets on their heads."

"No, wait, Lucky. I been thinking. Dr. Sempert ain't all bad. Maybe he's right. Look at us, we ain't got a pot to piss in. This ain't even our trailer. My uncle Vince, he used to keep this for when Aunt Rosie threw him out. They start fighting again, Vince is coming back in here, then what the hell are we going to do?"

"There's room. He gets the sofa down the other end."

"Come on, Lucky. Get serious. That's where the *baby's* going to sleep. And you got a heart condition. You got any life insurance? What if something happens to you? You don't even have a house no more."

"I got the *Wooden Nickel.*"

"Free and clear?"

"She ain't exactly."

"See what I mean? I got complications, we're going to have more bills. It ain't going to be like you, telling the doctors 'I got my heart, so fuck off.' We got to pay them or I can't take the baby in when it gets sick."

The Vince Gill tape has run out by now and it's real quiet. Outside the trailer he can hear the TV going over in Sonny Phair's little shack next door. Sonny's listening to the ball game, Sox and Toronto. Lucky tries to catch the score, then an evening wind rises and the aluminum trailer roof starts rattling and drowns it out.

"You ain't saying nothing," she says.

"I'm listening."

"You hear what I'm telling you? Dr. Sempert thinks maybe we ought to terminate. It's easy, they just take their little vacuum aspirator and it's like sucking a hair ball off a rug."

"We ain't doing it."

She turns her body towards him but keeps her head back so he can focus on her with his farsighted eyes. Even pregnant, with her clothes off she looks like jailbait, younger than Kristen. "It ain't your choice," she says. "It's mine."

"Then why are you telling me all this shit?"

"Just thought I'd see what you had to say. You wanted to, remember? You change your mind?"

"Wanted to what?"

"You know. Terminate."

He lights up a Marlboro, takes the last slug of Miller High Life, and sizzles the match out in the can. "Maybe I did. So what?"

"It ain't going to be easy for us two, Lucas Lunt. I'm giving you a way out if you want to take it. You can say good-bye and get in your truck and go back to your snow-white little house with your dead ancestors and your famous fucking wife. You won't have to feel the trailer shake no more."

He lies down again, turns his back to her and looks out the cracked bedroom window. By Corey Prentiss's yard light he can see his high-lifted GMC four-by-four parked next to Ronette's round little Probe, just like the two of them lying there in bed. Beyond that's the roofline of Sonny Phair's hubcap-shingled shack with the window open and Sonny all by himself drinking beer and yelling like a hand job at the TV. She's got her mouth against the back of his neck and she's saying, "I got an appointment tomorrow, Lucky. What am I going to tell him?"

"Tell him to stick his little vacuum cleaner up his ass. We been this far, we're going through with it."

She puts her arm over his shoulder and hangs on to him like she's clinging to a life preserver. She's not making a sound back there, she just buries her face in the hair of his back till it grows warm and wet, and pretty soon he's dreaming he's down in the Everglades with Wilfred Beal. Lucky's swimming around on his back and spouting a big stream of swamp water and watching Wilfred Beal up there on the flybridge of his tuna boat. Moto's dockboy Curtis Landry walks out on the pulpit and aims the harpoon gun at him, no escape, nothing but eelgrass and alligators all around. It feels like it's all over, he calls to Wilfred Beal but no sound comes out, and that son of a bitch Curtis is pulling the trigger of the harpoon gun, only what comes out of it is not a harpoon but a stream of piss, so warm and golden he lets it fall over his head and shoulders like summer rain.

12

THIRD OF OCTOBER, first big autumn storm's blowing itself out, wind out of the northeast for three days straight. It came right over the roof of Sonny Phair's hubcap-covered shack and shook Ronette's eight-by-forty like a paint mixer. Halfway through the blow a transformer went down, they've been in the dark for thirty-six hours in weather so thick you can't tell if it's night or day. Tarratine Hydro doesn't give a god damn about the shacks and trailers on the Back Cove Road, they'll be the last ones back on line. Ronette went off to work the lunch shift at the Blue Claw, so Lucky's left with ten pounds of frozen cod thawing out and a six-pack of Rolling Rock that's going to go rotten if it doesn't get consumed. The wind scrapes the last leaves off the two poplars by the driveway and rattles the trailer roof like a sheet of tin, which it is. That first morning he went over to Sonny Phair's and found him lying in his bed in front of a blank TV, voice so small you could barely hear him. "I get wicked depressed when the lights go out." He goosed Sonny out of bed and got some clothes on him and the two of them heaved five or six truck tires on top of the trailer to keep the roof on. Now the tires are clomping around like there's a horse up there, they should have roped them down. Ronette's got a battery-powered eight-track and Sonny lent them some oldies, so they spent the evening snugged up by the kerosene heater listening to Waylon Jennings in the dark. System goes down, that's when you know the survivors, they've got all they need.

He brings the gas lantern over to the kitchen counter and opens one of the Rocks. Thick-looking water drips out of the freezer compartment onto the floor and runs into another stream from a roof leak over the stove. Inside the freezer, the block of frozen cod's gone soft and started to smell a bit, but the chowder's always tastier anyway if it's a tad ripe, people ought to know that but they don't. He takes the whole ten pounds out and cubes it up with the cleaver and sets it to steam a few minutes on the gas. He hauls out a gallon of whole milk that's swelling the plastic bottle up and should also be used before it turns. Half a pound of salt pork, bottle of Rolling Rock, bag of onions, slice and dice, two sticks of butter. He's unwrapping the Land O'Lakes quarters when he hears a woman's voice in his ear so real it makes him turn around. *Too much cholesterol, Lucas.* He hoists his finger to the empty air and throws in a third butter quarter, waits for the voice to say something but it doesn't.

By now everything in the refrigerator's at room temperature. No use looking for a cold one, though the Rock is a better beer warm than a cold Bud. He opens a five-pound plastic bag of scallops that never got to the freezer compartment and a wisp of steam comes out. Bad sign. He was thinking of tossing a few in the chowder along with the codfish but they're some rotten, you can tell from the green spots. Maybe Corey Prentiss's rottweiler would go for them, never hurts to make a friend.

He turns the chowder down to simmer. He puts on his oilskin jacket and his trawler boots, grabs a flashlight and goes outside. Come to think of it, though, Corey might be in a trading mood. He drags his old Remington .30-06 out from under the built-in and wraps it in a green garbage bag to keep it dry.

The wind's still strong out of the northeast and there's rain slanting down through the ground fog onto the trailer and the GMC parked outside. The driveway and yard have a couple inches of bubbling rain on them and the road's awash on both sides, so he wonders how Ronette will ever get back from Doris's in her little low-slung Probe. The afternoon sky's darker than midnight. A high-lifted Dodge four-by-four sloshes down the road till its taillights are lost in the rain and wind. The guy waved but Lucky doesn't know him so he didn't wave back. A man's been in one spot for two hundred years, takes a while to cozy up with the new neighbors. He walks right up Corey Prentiss's driveway with the rottweiler barking and straining at its chain. He opens the scallop bag and lets a little rainwater run in to kill the stench, then tosses the whole load over the dog fence. They say dogs don't care for seafood but this one tears the bag open and wolfs down the whole five pounds, then starts howling again like he hasn't been fed for days. This time Corey throws the door open so you can see the light streaming out of his kitchen and stands there in the doorway in his undershirt, cigar in his mouth and rubbing his belly like he just got out of bed.

"Hey Corey, hope your dog likes scallops. I just fed him a five-pound bag."

"Well, ain't you considerate. Fritz got an allergy to them things, he'll be throwing up all night."

"That's tough, Corey. We had to get rid of them. They was getting ripe."

"Icebox don't work, huh? Come on in and have a drink. I got gas lights, gas stove, gas-powered refrigerator. I ain't dependent on nothing. We could have a fucking nuclear war, I wouldn't even know it. I got two years' worth of dog food in the basement."

"Finest kind, Corey. One year for the dog, one for you."

"That stuff ain't as bad as you might think. I try a little now and then. Man oughtn't to feed an animal what he won't eat himself."

He comes in out of the rain and takes the wet jacket off and plops down in Corey's den. Gas lamps sticking out of every wall, brass-colored Aladdin lantern with a green chimney hanging from the center of the room, behind Corey's drawn curtains it's bright as day. His hobby is taxidermy. He's got a whole fucking zoo in there, pheasants and deer heads, lacquered trout plaques on the wall, beaver chewing a tree in a glass case. A big moose head over the recliner faces the TV like it's watching the evening news. According to Sonny Phair, when Corey's wife died a couple years back he had her down in the basement half stuffed by the time the deputies showed up and took her away for a church burial.

Corey's also got a six-foot gun cabinet with every kind of rifle and shotgun known to man. First thing Lucky does, after he puts the deer rifle down and hangs up his wet oilskins, is accept a shot of whiskey with ice cubes and peer into the glass doors of that rack to see what's there.

"I been thinking of a large-bore rifle," he says. "Thought maybe you would swap for this Remington .30-06. I kept her good."

"What'd you, win the moose lottery? Thought you said you got a moose last year. Season's over anyway."

"Didn't even try this year. Where the fuck would I put a moose in that little place? Just want something a tad heavier around the house."

"I'm right with you on that one. Never know when a man might need to defend his home."

"You got a fifty-caliber?"

"I ain't. You're talking about a bazooka."

"That's what them Indians use on the whales. Out west."

"That's different. They're government subsidized out there. You and me, they don't even let us look at guns like that. Wait a couple years, you won't be able to buy a water pistol."

Lucky peers through the beveled glass of the gun cabinet. "Wouldn't mind seeing what you have."

"Take a look at this Ruger four-sixteen. That's what the elephant poachers use over in Zimbabwe. That's a three-hundred-grain softpoint, she'll expand to the size of an apple right in an elephant's heart, stop it cold. She'll pass through a two-inch plank and kill someone in body armor on the other side. I got a thousand rounds of them Rigby four-sixteens, down in the shelter. You never know."

The deal gets interrupted by a gust that shakes Corey's solid double-wide prefab till there's a crash on the roof like an antenna coming down. "Wind's backing," Lucky observes. "She'll clear off tonight."

"Maybe. You want to swap that little Remington for the Ruger?

It ain't exactly an even exchange, Lucky. How much you want to spend?"

"I'll throw in my four-wheeler, it's a Polaris 350 with a gun rack and deer winch. You just have to pick it up yourself over to my wife's garage in Orphan Point."

Corey thinks for a while, then says, "OK, I could use an ATV, won't be any roads left when the shit comes down. Your ex-wife better give me the god damn thing when I go after it. I don't want no domestic trouble."

He unwraps his side of the deal and rubs the moisture off the .30-06 with his shirttail. Corey takes the Ruger out of the gun rack and hands it over, stock first. The Ruger outweighs the Remington three to one. This is a bona fide African rhino rifle: commando sling, open sights, five- or six-shot clip and a nice checkered walnut stock that glows under the gas lamp like sunset on the flanks of a bull moose. Must have quite the kick too, the stock's got a recoil absorber thick as a crutch pad. Corey comes up with a box of Rigby ammunition from the steel drawer under the gun rack. "You ought to fire her a few times before you use her," he warns. "She'll rip your shoulder off if you ain't braced up."

"I'm going to try her out on that christly dog of yours on the way out."

"You go right ahead, Lucas. Save me the trouble. Say, you folks ready for the year two thousand over there? It ain't going to be pretty."

He turns around and slings the Ruger over his shoulder like he's back in boot camp at Fort Dix. "We are now."

On the way home the wind's stopped howling through Corey's satellite dish but the rain keeps coming down. The rottweiler's lying there strangely silent while the empty scallop bag floats around his yard.

Back in the trailer he gives the simmering chowder a stir and fills the clip on the Ruger, just to get a feel of the action. He's picturing himself out there in the clearing wind, shoulder braced against the pot hauler, sights lined up right on that son of a whore's eyeball. Take your time, wait till the sucker turns over, squeeze her nice and gentle. With a heart the size of a Volkswagen he ought to be able to hit the christly thing. Then a car splashes into the driveway and he slides the gun back under the built-in and throws a handful of pepper in the chowder pot.

Ronette comes blasting through the aluminum trailer door in her white waitress outfit, white skirt and shoes splattered with rain and mud. The door won't latch right and blows back open in the rain, so they both have to go out and wrestle it in. "Power ain't back yet?" she says.

"What's it look like?"

"I don't know, but it smells like cod heaven. Didn't know you was a cook."

"We still got the gas anyway."

They sit down to a couple of lukewarm Rolling Rocks and the hot chowder and another old Waylon Jennings, he listened to it with Sarah when they first went out, now she won't have it in the house.

"Turn it up, Ronette, so we don't hear the god damn wind."

I can't say I've always been proud of the things that I've done
But I can say I've never intentionally hurt anyone

"Lucky, it's fucking *raining* in here, can't you feel that?"

She's right, a wet breeze is blowing right through the trailer wall. Then there's a crash over the fridge as one of the roof tires vibrates to the edge and falls scraping down past the aluminum siding. After that even more rain comes into the living room. He finishes the last of his chowder and starts shining the flashlight around. A wall section has buckled between the kerosene heater and the gas stove and there's a two-foot-long crack opened up between the panels. Serious water is gathering on the floor and floating the carpet up. His first instinct is to look around for a bilge pump, then he gets up and throws his shoulder against the panel to try and straighten her out.

At first she seems to be bending back OK. "One more heave ought to set her in."

"Take it easy, Lucky. This place ain't the Rock of Gibraltar." Soon as she says that, his last heave splits the aluminum panel right off at the roofline and a whole wall section falls down onto the lawn. They're standing there right in the living room looking into the powerless night with the downpour pissing in from the direction of the two shadowy vehicles in the invisible driveway. "Jesus H. Christ, now you've done it."

"Weren't my fault. God damn wall's thinner than a beer can."

"It's a good trailer, you just found a weak spot, that's all."

"Bull shit. The whole fucking thing's weak. Watch this." He takes the next panel in both fists and pulls the edge back where it busted off from the other. It curls like a sardine top and the roof bends down till another tire slides off and splashes down on the flooded lawn.

"Holy shit, Lucky. *Enough.*"

He opens two more beers and they stand there watching the rain sluice past the big open square like it's a Sony projection TV. Every once in a while a lightning bolt flashes and it's like changing to another channel, you can see the chartreuse car and the red truck, Corey Prentiss's chain-link fence with the doghouse behind it, the naked poplar sapling in the front yard with the empty bird feeder flailing around in the wind, Ronette's fall-brown little garden with the blue crystal ball, just like a photograph. Then it goes black again and it's just the rain and the night and the two of them by the wet sizzling kerosene heater next to the open wall.

She cuddles up in her waitress outfit looking like the first time he laid eyes on her, she was a waitress in the RoundUp, brown-haired and cute as a pussy, flashing her half-carat engagement ring. He tosses his empty through the open wall into the dark and leans away from the missing panel in the direction of the bed. Then she says, "Lucas, maybe we ought to bring that wall back up before you get any ideas."

He gets his trawler boots back on and wades out in the swampy yard with the rain pouring down and tries to get his shoulder under the wall panel and jerk it back up in place. He can get down there and lift it up at an angle, but he can't keep it up high enough to push it forward to the roofline. Ronette's in there screaming about Noah and the fucking animals but she's not coming out to help. He's standing there holding the wall up slantways so all the water funnels right into the trailer, when a flashlight shows up like a lifeboat through the rain and fog. It's the next-door neighbor Sonny Phair, drunk as a mackerel, with a tarp draped completely over him like a boat ready for winter.

"Seen you needed some help."

"Sonny, get your head under here and prop up this son of a whore till I drive the truck up against it."

Now he's got Sonny under the wall panel, he can go over and start the pickup and slog it across the muddy yard in four-wheel granny low. With the headlights on high beam and the truck coming over at an angle, he can finally see. There's the trailer with a panel wide open and old Sonny Phair stone blind in his tarp, his legs spread wide, holding the panel steady as a sawhorse. There's the living room inside lit by the gas lantern, and Ronette standing in her waitress outfit at the table by the two bowls of chowder and the Rolling Rocks like she expects a tip. He creeps the pickup right up against the panel and slowly encourages her into an upright position, with Sonny Phair pushing alongside till the piece finally fits back in. Sort of.

He shuts the truck off with its grille up against the trailer panel and leaves her in that position for the night. He says to Sonny, "Long as that truck don't move she's going to stay put. How about some ripe cod chowder and a nice warm beer?"

Inside, they've still got a considerable drip down the wall where the panels don't join, but the wind's quieted down so it's not pushing the rain through quite so hard. Sonny pulls up a chair and stares like a stray dog in the direction of the chowder pot. He's a short, round, dark little guy with big thick hairy wrists and a long thick neck with veins and red streaks on it like a pecker. He eats a couple of bowls like he's never seen food before. "I been eating Nine Lives," he says. "I like the Ocean Platter best."

"Why don't you go up to the state agency in Norumbega, get yourself some food stamps?"

"Ain't got a license."

"Jesus," Ronette says. "You should of come over here."

"Don't want to get no obligations, if I can't pay it back."

Ronette gives him a third bowl of chowder and another Rolling Rock. Lucky gets out the new rifle from under the built-in and says, "Surprise. Look what I swapped off with Corey Prentiss."

"Looks like a cannon," Ronette says. "What do we want that thing around for, you and Corey planning to go to war?"

Sonny turns the gun around with the stock up, sticks it in his eye and looks down the barrel. Lucky says, "Ain't nothing to drink in there, Sonny." He takes it back and polishes Sonny's fingerprints off the blue steel with his shirttail.

Outside, the rain's coming down harder but the wind's slacked and gone north. "We may be out tending them traps tomorrow."

"Jesus, Lucky. It's a fucking hurricane."

"No, she's winding down. Be a swell offshore but no wind, next day it'll start blowing northwest and we'll be stuck another three days. Keeps slacking off like this, I'm catching the window in the morning."

"Crazy bastard," Sonny Phair says. He's eaten half the chowder now and he's going home.

"Thanks for holding the wall up, Sonny."

"Anytime. What friends are for."

He's in a dream with Sarah on one side of him and Alfie on the other, they're in a wire mesh jail cell full of cons and every one of them's using chopsticks to build a computer in a bottle. When the alarm rings he doesn't know who he's with or who he is. He reaches an arm out to slap the clock quiet, the trailer shakes all over from the impact so he knows he's not at home. He listens for signs of the storm but the wind's backed and died, just a little breeze on the north side ruffling a downed wire outside the window, he can hear it knocking against the kerosene tank. He can't see Corey Prentiss's twenty-four-hour yard light, that means the power's still down. Someone turns and gives him a kiss on the forehead, then slips out of bed on the other side. He still has to think *Who is this?* for a moment, then he figures it out. He hears her feeling her way through the dark corridor towards the bathroom, then a flashlight switches on and she shuts the door. He hears the whirlpool of the flush and the hiss of the tank filling, then the flush again.

He's got to haul today or they're going to lose everything in the traps. The traps could be hard to locate too, seas may have dragged them off station, and if they slipped off the ledge into deep water, they're going to be lost, they'll pull the buoys down with them forever.

Ronette flushes a third time and he rolls out of bed and feels for the flame gun to light a Marlboro and start the Coleman lamp. Going to be raw out there. Sarah would be up already with coffee and the weather report, handing him the one-piece union suit and the wool socks that are still back at Orphan Point. The best he can do is pull on one pair of pants over another one and the heavy Grundens oilskins over that. The trailer floor's buckling even more with the wall panel loose, the carpeting's still awash, the wind's blowing right through the trailer but it's just a fall breeze now, coming off the land.

He checks under the built-in to get the Ruger out and put it on the kitchen table, then knocks on the half-open bathroom door. "Anybody alive in there?"

"Jesus, Lucky, I ain't too sure."

"I got to go out today. You want, I'll go see if I can get Sonny Phair to go along. You can stay home and screw the wall back together."

"If you go out, I'm going with you. I'm your sternman, remember?"

"Well get moving, then, it's pretty near four o'clock." He boils water for a thermos of instant coffee and shovels in some sugar and Cremora, then some more. She likes it light.

"Let's bring some more of that Waylon Jennings. I got a cassette in the drawer."

He roots around among lipsticks, old wallets, address books, for the Waylon Jennings tape. "Soon as they get a kid in the oven," he says, "they go back to the old stuff."

They have to drive to Whistle Creek in Ronette's little Probe since the GMC's still up to its hubcaps on the swampy lawn holding up the trailer wall. He can't get his legs under the Probe's wheel, the seat won't go back far enough, so he lets her drive. She starts up, flicks the lights on, and puts the tape on to "Good-Hearted Woman." She's got a box of sugared crullers that she took home from Doris's. The high beams slash through the drizzle and light up the leafy road like a blind guy getting his sight back.

"Nice to have electricity," she says.

"Finest kind. Drive this little car right through the hole in the wall, leave the lights on, we could go right off the grid."

The high beams make their pathway of light between darkened houses, nobody else on the road, big branches and stray power lines strewn here and there across the way. Then the turnoff to Split Point and all of a sudden the darkness fills up with red, white, and blue strobe lights from half a dozen vehicles in both lanes.

"Must be a fire," Ronette says.

They slow down to see what's going on and a cop comes up and shines his light in the car, same fucking porkbelly deputy that kicked him out of his house. "You was driving a truck last time I saw you," the cop says, talking across to Lucky but shining his flashlight right on Ronette's tits. "Guy your size, I'm surprised you fit inside that little thing."

"Stopped to see if you needed any help," Lucky says.

"You can help if you can bring back the dead. If that ain't your specialty you better keep on moving."

Behind the cop there's the burned-out ruin of a trailer with the strobes blinking at a handful of charred uprights, a blackened refrigerator skeleton with the plastic panels melted, and an oil-drum wood stove with the tin chimney still straight up in the air, pointing to heaven. "Wouldn't of thought nothing could burn in all that rain."

As they speed up again he sees the ambulance strobes switch off in the rearview mirror. Ronette says, "I knew the old guy in that trailer. He was an Astbury on my mother's side."

"Father's, you mean."

"I got them on both sides and the middle." She snuggles over across the automatic shift lever to get close. "And now you're a blood relation. Someday you're going to be an old Astbury in a trailer just like Uncle Uke."

Back in the comfortable dark car again, Waylon sings,

> *A long time forgotten are dreams that just fell by the way*
> *The good life he promised, it ain't what she's living today*

"That Old Cove ain't the tightest spot in the world. Hope the fucking boat's still there."

"Didn't know you was the worrying kind."

"She was moored right off of the house in Orphan Point. First light after a blow, I'd look right out and see how she was."

"Welcome to reality, Mr. Unlucky Lunt. You ain't got shore property anymore. Life ain't a big old family farmhouse with a million-dollar view. It's a trailer in a mudhole, with a big crack in the wall made by some asshole in the middle of the night."

> *But she never complains of the bad times or the bad things he's done*
> *Just talks about the good times they've had and all the good times to come*

"You should of stuck with Clyde. Guy like that could of brought this kid up in style."

"Guy like that would of drowned the kid in the hot tub when he found out it weren't his."

"Ain't mine?"

"Ain't *his.*"

"Sure as fuck better be mine, I ain't doing all this for nothing."

Without the streetlight on the corner she misses the turnoff to the Whistle Creek landing and has to U-turn in the road and come back. Soon as they get down the steep driveway to Moto's pier, though, there's lights and action. Moto's got two parked vehicles shining their brights on his ice-house and his big white Mitsubishi Fuso reefer truck pulled right up close. No power here either. Curtis is up on the ramp loading seafood into the truck with Moto standing by one of the cars in a bright yellow rain jacket, urging him on. Not that he'd ever lend a hand to help. One thing you can say for the Chinese, they don't take to physical labor, unless maybe they're in prison with a gun pointing at their head.

When Moto sees the Probe he ducks away from the headlight like a shadow and doesn't come out till Curtis Landry peers down from off of the truck platform and says, "By Jesus, them Lunts is moving up in the world."

Then Moto slides out of the dark and shows his grinning face at the car door. Lucky powers down the window and leans back easy in the seat like the Probe's his, Ronette's just a chauffeur.

"Rucas, you come at right time, nine ton frozen squid lotting in here."

"Ain't got time to help out now. Curtis is a fast guy, he can do it. I ain't been out to them traps in more than a week. My boat OK?"

"Who can tell? No light on water yet. One little dory wrecked up on the float."

Lucky sticks his head out the window and sniffs around. "You're too late to get nothing for that squid. I can smell it from here. How about giving me a bucket of that for bait?"

Moto yells, "Curtis, take bucket of squid down on the float for Mr. Runt."

He carries the thermos and the Ruger in one hand and Ronette grabs the other to help her down the dark rampway to the pier. When

Curtis gets a glimpse of the gun in the truck headlights, he says, "Lunt, you planning to bag some more of them Shag Island women?"

"I'll bring one back for you, Curtis, if you think you can handle it."

"No thanks, they ain't my type. I like them alive."

"I bet you do."

They stand on the pierhead for a minute getting their bearings on the harbor in the first light. A couple of dories are beached on the granite ledge north of the pier. One of Moto's floats is ripped off the wharf but the one holding Lucky's punt is still hanging on, though the rope's stretched and the float sticks out in the current at an angle. He can hear the surge break over the entrance ledge out by the Old Cove daymarker. Even inside, the float's groaning up and down a foot or two as the long swells come in, but the chop's down and the wind's set to flatten the onshore seas. By the time they get out there it may be smooth enough to haul.

The dawn ratchets up another notch so they can make out the *Wooden Nickel* in the center of the cove. In the half-light the blue cabin looks black, she's like a big tough old blackback seagull riding the swell. Those guys are the predators of the ocean, they don't give a shit, you see them up there riding out a full-blown gale, they enjoy it, they're loners, they take what they need and move on. His boat's the only boat visible, she's got a bit of rain in her but she's riding proud at the end of her mooring chain. Down on the float, he flips the punt over and launches her in a trough, rows out to the stem end first and checks the pennant line. It's chafed almost halfway through up at the bow chock where the leathers wore off in the blow, he'll splice up a new one later. He grabs the davit to hoist himself up out of the punt the way he used to, then halfway up he gets a sharp pinch in the chest and has to let himself back down and take a breath. Then he works his ass up on the rail like an old lady getting aboard the church boat before he can turn around and step into the cockpit. Every time he starts to forget about the heart the fucking thing lets him know it's there.

The bilge has a few inches of water and the white life ring got ripped off the cabin top, that's all for damage. He scans the shore with the binoculars looking for the ring, but all there is is the two stove-in dories, a few tree limbs on the tideline, a handful of local traps and moorings dragged onto the beach. She's riding a bit low from the rainwater in the bilge but otherwise she checks out fine. The Olds V-8 catches for a moment on the second turn then stalls out. He opens the box and squirts some ether to the carb throat and hits the distributor cap with a spurt of WD-40 and she comes awake one plug at a time, never was an Olds that cared for water. He warms her up a bit, kicks in the bilge pump takeoff and lights a Marlboro while the three-day rainstorm spews over the transom into the little harbor of Whistle Creek.

It's bright enough to see surf breaking into foam on both sides as they steam out through the inlet ledges, passing the thermos between them. Ronette busts out laughing at the spot where the *Metallica* ran them through the shallows. They light a couple more Marlboros, Ronette Clinton tries not to inhale, they turn up the Waylon Jennings tape and stomp the Olds to a clean sixteen knots on the loran. The storm took his bloody gull wing off the antenna, so they're already dragging a bird cloud in their wake, every one of them wants to get his beak into Moto's bucket of rotten squid. They pick up the Old Cove daybeacon and in another mile the Whistle Creek flasher, then comes a white offshore fog bank like the cliffs of Labrador, too bad Moto's advance ran out before they got to the radar. The *Wooden Nickel* trudges uphill over the long swells, glides down and trudges up again, not a damn thing visible, just the green TD numbers on the loran clicking off their movement south and east.

The first trap's got one jumbo, maybe seven pounds, and a good-size cull but Moto won't touch it. If some Chinaman's going to pay three hundred bucks for one lobster he wants the whole thing sitting on his plate just like it was at the bottom of the sea, you can't blame him. What the hell, they'll keep it and boil it up at home, no sense throwing away good meat. Next two traps have a couple of jumbos each, so they're up to three hundred bucks in the first half hour and it's time for a beer. They sit up on the rail with Hank Junior singing "Rainy Night in Georgia" and watch the six big lobsters chase each other like a pack of squirrels around the seawater tank. He spots the gull wing in the scuppers and climbs up to duct-tape it back on the antenna. The cloud of birds draws back right away to a respectful distance.

The next set's up towards the shallow end of the deep-sea ledge. The fishfinder rises to thirty-five fathoms, then thirty, he can sense the swells shoaling under him, heaving the keel up, setting them down again in the trough. He steams up on the waypoint till the loran sounds off, but there's nothing there, just the circle of gray-green sea.

"We'll just head down to where that next buoy ought to be, see what the fuck's going on." The fishfinder says twenty-eight fathoms, then twenty-five and the fog thickens so he puts Ronette as lookout up on the bow. She's kneeling down with both hands on the anchor bitt as they head into the swell and the bow sweeps up and down.

All of a sudden Ronette raises her free arm and screams out, *"Rocks!"*

He can't believe it. There's no land out here for twenty miles. He throttles off and puts her in neutral so the boat turns broadside to the swells. It sways like a windshield wiper while he squints into the fog. Nothing but gray mist at first. Then, sure as shit, right off to starboard the water's boiling and breaking on a half-tide ledge.

"Jesus H. Christ. Supposed to be twenty fucking fathoms over there." He puts her in gear and heads the bow up, then idles over real slow for a better look, one eye on the fishfinder and the loran, both in agreement and bringing him right to the spot where they set their main trap cluster, should be five or six Day-Glo buoys nearby. The bottom graph shallows to twenty-three fathoms as they approach. A big swell lifts her by the stern and he sees a cloud of birds over the spot, but not much else. They get a little nearer and Ronette yells out, "Buoys! There they are!"

He sees one for an instant, then it's gone. On the next swell he looks down where the buoy was and the sea drops off swirling like an ocean whirlpool. Then the long gray barnacle-covered granite ledge rises right out of the water with two of his fucking buoys on it and his heart stops dead. The swell hoists him eight feet into the air and down again while he waits for the heartbeat to come. He can't breathe and he can't speak, but he does manage, without a heart, to throw the wheel to port so they don't go hard aground.

He bangs his fist once sharp against his chest and the cocksucker turns over and starts up again. He bangs his fist on the fishfinder to make that work too but it just flashes in weird computer letters: ERROR NO. 22. Then the screen goes black.

In a small high voice he says to Ronette, "Steer." It sounds like somebody else talking, not him. He should have taken a pill this morning, but with the lights out in the strange trailer bathroom he couldn't find them. Ronette's got the helm, she's brought her off to the southeast, so they can't see anything but gray air and blue-black water and a handful of following gulls. Now that his heart's pumping again he takes over and turns back on the loran plot, working her slow but steady in the quartering sea. When he bangs the fishfinder again he knocks it right out of its ceiling mount so it hangs swaying in the air by its data cord. He has to rip it off before it breaks the windshield, then he tosses it towards the hatchway but it bounces once on the hatch corner and it's over the port rail and gone. Last thing he read off it was *Made in Malaysia.*

"Jesus, Lucky, now you've done it."

"Plastic junk," he says. "Weren't worth fixing." He lets the seas drift him off to starboard as the waypoint closes in, but there's no buoys and he's right on top of an uncharted breaking shoal where he thought he had twenty fathoms all around. Fucking loran must be busted too. He whacks at it with the back of his lobster glove, yelling, "Piece of Chinese shit."

He keeps her bow just starboard of the swell and lets her slip southwest, where the water's got a deeper color. Then he hears surf breaking close to port.

Ronette's leaning on the port side of the wheelhouse so she can see. "That ain't no rock ledge, Lucky, it's *skin.* We're on top of a fucking whale."

Soon as she says that, they're up on a swell looking down at it, gray-black and barnacled, same length as the *Wooden Nickel* bow to stern. No wonder it looked like granite, it's got growth all over it, it's not moving and the waves are breaking across it like a shoal. On the far side of the whale's body it's lifting a long white arm fin like a guy drowning and waving for help, and the fin's got two or three coils of pot warp wrapped up in the armpit where it joins the body. The head's mostly underwater, with a bunch of small black-headed seagulls screaming around it like they're hungry for its eyes. Then it lets off a blast of vapor and steam that makes the seabirds screech and back off.

When the spout goes back underwater again the rear end of it comes up, and there's the loop of yellow pot warp around the black root of the tail. Now it's up close and he can see the rope clear as a wedding ring. He's got the engine in neutral now, idling back one or two wave crests from the whale so they lose sight of it in the troughs, then pick it up again. He's starting to figure out how the thing is caught. "That loop of yellow line ain't attached to nothing, it's them warps around his fin that's holding him down."

"He's a fucking *whale,*" Ronette says. "Why don't he just snap them cheap pieces of rope?"

"He's a weasely bastard, he's waiting to make his move. Look at the warts on him, he must have some kind of VD. Ain't no morality out here, cocksuckers do whatever they want."

"Yeah, that includes *us.* We better go back in, Lucky. You already had a stroke or something back there. You looked like you was dead."

"Happens all the time, I got nine fucking lives. I want to see what's on the other side of this bastard." He turns to starboard and cuts a wide slow circle to the northeast, goes out maybe a quarter mile past two more of his traps and toggles, then steams back on a loran course through the fog. The whale's lying quiet and sneaky as a spider in its yellow web, when they get near him he starts sloshing the right-hand fin around. That one's got four or five more loops around it, and a couple strands of pot warp going up forward towards the head. Ronette's got the binoculars on it. "No wonder the poor thing can't move. That piece of line goes right into the corner of his mouth."

"Bastard's got eight or nine warps on him. That's what happened to them other traps. He picked them up and dragged them along the bottom till they got wrecked. Cocksucker didn't get enough of my gear, he come back for more."

"Lucky, it ain't the whale's fault. He ain't no different from you. It's his territory out here, we set the traps on it. He must of swam into them at night. He's been here through that whole frigging storm trying to get rid of them lines and he's exhausted. We got to do something. We ain't going to just let him die."

"You just take the helm, sweetheart. I got to go below. Just jog her easy, don't sweat the wind, keep her southeast with her head up to the swell."

He goes down into the anchor box for the .416 Ruger and works the bolt once to bring the Rigby cartridge up. They're on a high swell again, and even through the cracked and grimy portside cuddy window he can see the spout of that bastard white and smoky against the black-edged fog.

When he goes up in the cockpit she takes one look at the rifle and says, "Lucas Lunt, what in Christ's name are you intending on?"

"Son of a whore took every trap off this fucking ledge."

"He didn't. We saw a couple off to the south of here."

"It don't matter. He gets away, he'll come on back through and finish them off."

"That ain't true, Lucas. We'll get on the radio and call the Coast Guard and they'll send somebody out here and cut him free. That's what they do. We'll never see him again."

"They'll cut him free and he'll be back again. That ain't what we bought that radio for. Besides, nobody lays a hand on my fucking whale. We got fifteen thousand dollars right here in front of us, half-dead. Gear he's ripped up, he owes us twice that much."

"What are you talking about, fifteen thousand dollars?"

"I mean my man Mr. Moto's going to shell out seventy-five cents a pound for that piece of meat. We shoot it and slice the gear free and drag the fucker into Whistle Creek and we are paid off. We don't owe that bastard a god damn yen."

She keeps a hand on the wheel and bites the joint of her thumb to keep from laughing. "Lucky, you are blind, deaf, and dumb. Moto was bullshitting you. He ain't going to buy no whale. What the hell's he going to do with it?"

"He's going to sell it in Asia. That's what they fucking eat. He'll get Curtis Landry to cut it up on the boat ramp with a chain saw and stuff it in the reefer trucks and ship it to the Chinese fish warehouse at Logan Airport just like a load of tuna. That baby's going to be sushi in the morning. You heard him the other day. Them Asians eat anything that swims."

"I heard him. He was bullshitting you. That little pervert Curtis was laughing up his sleeve."

"Curtis is a con. He never fished a day in his life, what the fuck does he know?"

She turns the wheel hard starboard and revs the engine and starts steaming southward towards the Day-Glo buoys. "Let's haul what we got left and get out of here, Lucky. This ain't going to be nothing for us but trouble."

He rests the Ruger in the crook of his arm like it's a bird gun. "Take her back, Ronette. You ain't the captain of this boat."

"You pointing that frigging thing at me?"

"I'm telling you take the boat back there so I can get a shot at that cocksucker or I'm going to do it myself. You think you're queen shit cause you got a kid coming. You know what? You ain't nothing but the sternman on this boat."

She lets go the helm and backs herself down into the cuddy, keeping her eye on him as he takes over. Resting the gun butt on the cockpit floor, he spins the *Wooden Nickel* around in a trough between two swells and once again steams back to the waypoint on a one-eighty reverse course through the lifting fog. He's got one hand on the bronze wheel spoke and the other on the Ruger's cold oiled steel. He ought to have his sternman at the helm, that way he could spend some time with his shot. Just like a woman, they fold when the shit comes down. He should have left her throwing up in the trailer and come out this morning with fucking Sonny Phair.

The fog's shutting down again by the time he's at the waypoint. He has to close in to a tenth of a mile, then four hundredths, then all of a sudden the thing's right under them wallowing in a wave trough off to port. The head is raised. It's got two of his Day-Glo lemon buoys around its neck. It's putting out a high wheezy spout like an old man blowing his nose. He hits the shift into neutral and puts the rifle up. He follows the top of it with the flip sight like a deer hunter looking for a neck or shoulder shot, only the cocksucker's got no neck or shoulders and all he wants to do is bury that softpoint .416 in its fucking heart. Not easy to take aim when the gun barrel and the target are both swaying in separate directions, the swell's bad enough, every time that bastard moves its tail that makes it worse. Then a long sea draws the boat away from the whale and holds it steady for a moment. His sight eye stops at the blowhole where the skin folds in, but it's a bad angle. You need to get right above that cocksucking spout and fire straight down inside. The hole has all kinds of warts and barnacles around it, it's armor plated, nothing's going to get through all that growth. The heart's too far under and he's not going to get a shot at that. He moves the sight down to the waterline beneath the spout and the barnacles and braces up against the pot hauler, waits for a long lifting swell, and takes a shot right at its fucking head.

The noise of the Rigby cartridge blinds him and the kick slams his shoulder around so he doesn't get to watch it hit.

He looks back and the whale's not moving or diving or taking much notice at all. Maybe it takes a long time for the news to reach the brain, their head is so fucking thick. Then he sees a piece of red meat the size of a bloody moose heart hanging off the wound. The gash is getting redder fast, and down at the whale's stern the tail's swinging from side to side like it's got its power back and it's going to thrash out of there even though it's caught by six or seven lines. Lucky puts the wheel hard to starboard and slips over a couple of seas westward to wait and see what it will do. He bolts a new cartridge into the chamber and the spent one rattles out and spins around steaming on the wet cockpit floor. The whale twists its chest towards him for a moment, right under the flipper where the heart must be. He braces up quickly for another shot. The whale rolls back so it comes in too high and spits off a slice of skin that skips away shining through the fog like a piece of quartz. Maybe the whale didn't feel that one, but the first one's got it bleeding hard up near the eye.

When he turns around, Ronette's got her head outside the companionway, not saying a thing, just looking up at him like she's a dog or something that can't talk, face all awash with tears like she's been wailing the whole time she was below.

He shouldn't have brought her. "If you don't say nothing," he says, "I can't say nothing back. Don't matter anyway." He spins the wheel to port and tracks back to the spot to check things out. There's three buoys floating on the surface holding up a snarl of lines and the whale probably down under that, but he can't see it and his fishfinder's gone. Now he spots a streak of red blood on the water, and over it there's five or six black seabirds he's never seen. Must be sea buzzards, waiting for the god damn thing to croak.

"We got to him," he says," but we got to get closer. We got to get right over the spout hole. Fucker comes up again and he's dead meat."

She waits awhile to answer. "I been beside you all this time, Lucky Lunt, but I ain't helping on this one."

"That's right, you ain't helping and I ain't going to forget it. I'm going on with it myself. That thick-skinned bastard, I got to get right on top of him this time. That's how them god damn Indians do it. They get right over them with an antitank gun and let them have it down the nose." He nudges the *Wooden Nickel* up and over a wave crest closing in towards the left flank of the whale. The only thing on the surface now is the root of the tail where the yellow line's wound around it, so he idles in forward and waits for the head of it to come up for another breath. "It's a god damn mammal same as you and me, can't hold its breath forever."

The whale rolls towards the boat and goes under, throwing its back up a couple of feet off the water, an easy spine shot on a deer but that thing's not even going to feel it. He lets it dive. On its way under, it shows the gear tangled beneath it. Ronette says, "Lucky, he's got three of your buoys wrapped under him. I seen them."

"If you ain't going to help, don't talk."

He throws her in neutral to cut the shaft vibrations for a better shot whenever the thing decides to come back up.

Then there's a rush of water on the port side, opposite the wheel, and the whale shoots up a couple of boat lengths away, rolls in the swell and throws off a spout of vapor that blows back over the port rail as a mist in the north wind. It smells like cat food. "Cocksucker went right under the keel." The eye's not quite out of the water, so it's hard to find the place for a head shot. He aims the Ruger just down and forward from the chunk he ripped out before. He lets a swell pick the stern up for a high shot angle and fires the third of five shots in the clip, the kick bangs his shoulder up against the hot exhaust. The blast and recoil blur his head a moment, then he can see the impact as the three-hundred-grain softpoint rips out another bloody chunk right at the waterline. It's not like any animal he's shot, these are fucking artillery shells but they're just scratching the surface, they're not getting him where he lives.

"Fucking Indians," he shouts. "What the fuck are they using on them things?" The whale lifts its tail six feet in the air and rolls hard towards the boat, then brings the tail down flat and a sharp fast wave breaks over the port side, he has to lay the gun down on the bulkhead so it won't get soaked. "Got to get closer and fire the next one right down the fucking blowhole."

Ronette reaches up through the cabin hatch and grabs the gun by the barrel, which is so hot he can hear it searing her skin as she pulls it down the companionway with her hands smoking, then comes back up again without it.

"Don't put it away yet," he says. "I ain't done."

"The fuck you ain't. We're getting out of here." She's looking at the red burn stripes on her hands.

"What the hell you talking about? Get that fucking gun back up here. Now."

"Don't order me around, you heartless bastard."

He steps off from the helm and shoves her in the face with the heel of his hand. An ooze of blood runs out of her mouth like squeezing a cherry tomato. She backs up till she's put the engine between them and kneels against the empty life jacket box. "Now stop fucking with me and bring the gun up." The gun's right beside her but she doesn't move. Off a couple of boat lengths to port the whale's boiling the water trying to escape against the drag of the gear. He goes over to the helm just to cock the rudder over to one side so they don't drift closer. As soon as he's by the pot hauler with his hand on the wheel Ronette pulls herself up through the companionway with blood on her face and the barrel of the rifle in her free hand. "About fucking time," he says, reaching for it while he leaves his other hand on the wheel, keeping the boat backed off from the rush of water around the whale.

She doesn't give it to him. She crosses to the port rail, across the beam of the boat from him. Then she raises the Ruger over her head with both hands and throws it as far as she can over the side. It spins a couple of revolutions in the air then hits the water. The wooden stock tries to hold it on the surface, then the steel barrel pulls it down.

Fucking cunt.

He crosses the boat in one stride to push her aside and stick his face over as if he could grab for it or at least see it on its way to the bottom, but there's nothing but afternoon chop and pink foam from the bloody whale. "Jesus H. Christ. That was a thousand-dollar gun. We ain't got nothing else aboard."

Now the whale's rolling sideways towards the port side of the hull. He looks right down the blowhole as it turns over. This would be the perfect fucking shot, it would go right straight down that windpipe to the heart. That bitch, she ruined it and now she's standing in the companionway lighting a cigarette while the fucking whale slides back underneath the boat. He spins the wheel to star-

board, puts the shift in forward and raises the throttle all at the same
time. Fuck her, he'll drive right up on the cocksucker and chop him
up with the propeller. The V-8 spurts to life, the boat jumps forward
a few feet, then she stops dead just like she's thrown a rod.

"Now what the fuck?" He jams the shift lever into neutral and
hits the starter. If she's got a thrown rod she won't turn over. But
the 307 powers right up and he puts her in forward and she stalls
out again. Could only be one thing. "Wheel's fouled. Cocksucker
wrapped a line around it." He shifts to reverse and revs her up, hoping to back the warp off the way it came. The whale's turning the
surface white over there like it's trying to drag all that gear southward towards deep water and every time the tail flips he feels a shiver
along the keel.

Ronette comes alive and yells, "Lucky, we're *attached* to it, we got
to cut them lines away." She goes for the long-handled rope knife in
the scuppers and when she comes up with it she points it at his
crotch like a harpoon. "That's right, I ought to slice it off and feed it
to that god damn thing. That's what they eat, pricks. They can't get
enough of them." She's got him backed right up against the pot
hauler, then the boat shakes and she turns and goes to look over the
side, so he can come up in back of her and pry the rope knife out of
her hand. The two of them bend over the port rail looking for a submerged warp pointing towards the whale, but if there is one it's too
deep to see.

"We fouled one of them lines on the whale," he says. "The shaft's
shaking every time it moves."

Thrashing around like that, the whale must have snagged every
piece of gear on this part of the ledge. And now it's trying to swim
forward on the surface, huge tired fucking animal with eight or ten
traplines around it along with an eight-ton lobster boat broadside to
the swell. He can't tell if it's moving any or just plowing the water in
one place. There's nothing to judge by, just the *Wooden Nickel* and a
thirty-five-foot whale with its two big side fins caught in pot warp,
more warp around the tail and one or two harnessed through the
back of its mouth like a fucking horse.

"We got to cut free," Ronette says. She looks like she's got a
mouth full of strawberries and the juice is dripping down her chin.
He'd like to kiss her, but his keen sense of timing tells him the

moment's not quite right. She grabs him around the waist of his bib oilskins so he won't fall overboard slicing at the warps. "Jesus," she says. "You got more barnacles than the fucking whale." He gropes over the port rail with the long-handled rope knife, in the direction of the twisting tail, trying to find the line and cut it free, only whenever he gets the blade on it the swell raises him back up. "It's down too deep," he calls up to her with his face almost in the water and his arm way in, then raised up in the air the length of the long-handled knife, then plunged up to the shoulder in the next swell as he gropes the knife through the black water feeling for the line. The only place where he can see pot warp is on the whale itself. With the stern to it, he can see a doubled length of taut green line reaching from the armpit of the right fin down in and right towards the boat. "We got to pull ourselves on top of that son of a whore and cut that warp where we can see it."

"How the hell we going to do *that?*"

There's one slack yellow line forward of the taut ones. He reaches down and hooks it with the long-handled gaff and slings a few turns around the Hydroslave. When he kicks in the hydraulics the yellow line tautens and draws the rail down and sideways till they're so close they can hear its lungs breathing in and out. The tail lying on the surface of the water makes a slow beat, stops, makes another beat, like it wants to stir the blood and water together. He reaches over the rail past the taut yellow warp to stab the son of a bitch with the rope knife, yelling, *"Die, cocksucker,"* but it blasts up a big spout of bloody steam and swings its tail towards them, then away. In that one motion it hauls the *Wooden Nickel* about a hundred feet to seaward. It may be tired but it's still dragging ten or twelve stone-weighted traps over the bottom, along with the crippled boat. It wants to get the fuck out of there and go home, same as anyone else.

All of a sudden it rolls so hard the rail goes under, but he can finally reach the two lines from the prop, a green one and a white one, stretched taut right under the surface in the direction of the whale. He waits for a wave trough and lunges his arm down with the long-handled rope knife and saws through the green one. It snaps free with the sound of a depth charge and throws the whale's weight onto the white one, then that one explodes and the whole strain's on the heavyweight yellow warp off the pot hauler, the rail scoops green water and the boat's going under sideways. He cuts the yellow line and it slashes into the water like a bullwhip as the *Wooden Nickel* comes upright, a foot of trapped seawater sluicing out the scuppers.

Fifty feet to starboard, with its lines off, the whale lifts its long white side fin up slow like it can't believe it's free. Suddenly the head drops diagonally under the boat, the tail lifts to the level of the wheelhouse roof, twists and slants down so close to the starboard rail that the hull shudders with a sharp scrape and crack, then the thing is gone.

Ronette says, "What the hell was *that?*"

"That was fifteen thousand fucking dollars." He turns and yells in the direction it dived in: *"Cocksucker, kiss my ass!"* Then to Ronette: "You hadn't of trashed the gun, we could be towing that son of a whore into Whistle Creek."

"Come on, Lucky, he would of been towing *us.* You wasn't going to win that one. But what was that *noise?* It sounded like we hit a ledge."

"Tail nicked us on the way down. It don't matter, we're out of here."

He throttles the engine up a bit in neutral and slams her in reverse to throw off the rest of the line. It spins a couple of revolutions, then shuts down. "What the fuck." He starts her again and puts the shift forward but it's not going into gear, must have line wound tight around the shaft. In calm water you might swim the knife under and cut the wheel free, but in the eight-foot swell you'd get your brains knocked out before you ever saw the line.

"Wheel ain't turning," he says.

"What's that mean?"

"Means we got to get ourselves a fucking tow."

She lights two cigarettes between her lips and hands him one with a string of blood on the filter end. "I shouldn't give you nothing," she says in a small voice. "Never again."

"You better start saving up for a four-sixteen fucking Ruger when we get in. They don't come cheap."

"Lucky, there's nobody out here. Even the whale-watchers ain't around. This radio don't reach back to Orphan Point. How you planning to get us towed?"

"Get on channel sixteen and call the fucking Coast Guard. They'll hear us, they got a hilltop antenna. That's what we pay our taxes for, ain't it?"

"We'll have to get rid of them lobsters in the live well."

"Coast Guard's all from Kansas, they wouldn't know a lobster if it was clamped onto their nuts. Only thing they care about is drugs."

She bends into the companionway to set the radio on channel 16, then turns back around before she even touches the dial. "Lucky, the floor's wet down there."

He looks down the hatch past the engine box into the cuddy. The piss bucket's floating over the cabin sole.

"Must of took some when the rail went under."

He cuts in the power takeoff for the bilge pump and revs her up to 1800 rpm. Down under the platform the pump sucks hose air for a few seconds, then takes hold and a steady stream of water pours over the starboard rail.

Ronette's already down in the cuddy and calls up, "Jesus, Lucky, the water ain't going down."

He cranks the engine to 2000. "She'll go down."

"It ain't, Lucky. It's *rising.*"

"Shit. Must of cracked a seam when the tail hit." He cranks the engine to 2400, high as the Olds wants to go. Meanwhile, Ronette's back on the radio poking the channel 16 key and handing him the mike. He squeezes the switch and says, "You on there, Coast Guard?"

He waits about thirty seconds, then yells in there loud enough so he'll reach them, radio or not. "Breaker, Coast Guard, you on this one?"

A girl's voice answers, she sounds about sixteen, Kansas accent, the idea of water seems brand-new to her. VESSEL CALLING COAST GUARD, THIS IS COAST GUARD NORUMBEGA GROUP.

He pokes the mike button. "You got anybody there that knows anything?"

VESSEL CALLING COAST GUARD, she repeats, THIS IS COAST GUARD NORUMBEGA GROUP.

Down in the cabin Ronette says, "It's wicked deep, Lucky, and it ain't going down."

"Come up and talk to this Coast Guard girl, I'm going to find that fucking hole."

He can't see any leaks down there but it's three inches deep over the cabin floor, the foam mattress is washing around among the loose floorboards like a water bed. The tunnel-of-love pillow has floated into the overturned yellow piss bucket, which bangs into the empty life jacket box every time they roll. It's good the engine's mounted high or she'd drown out. He opens the shaft cover behind the engine box where the bilge pump is cranking but it's too dark to see.

He calls up over the whine of the bilge pump: "Give me a flashlight, Ronette." He aims the beam back past the pump and the frozen shaft, and there's a garboard plank stove in with the sea spouting through the hull like a fire hose. Already the water's mostway up the shaft. Another six inches and the block will start going under, the bilge pump will shut down and then they're fucked. He reaches back into the empty life jacket locker, that's where she keeps the nylon quilt, turns back and drags it with him while he crawls under the cockpit floor. The power takeoff and bronze bilge pump are scraping his left side, the pump bearings are screaming like they're going to explode right in his ear. He gives the grease cup a half turn and she quiets down. He pulls himself over the shaft to the plank where the seawater's blasting in like an open hydrant. The hole is under a fuel tank so he can't get right up to it, but he shuts his eyes against the stream and pulls the wet heavy comforter past his face. He reaches forward to feel for the busted plank, then presses the fabric in a long line against the flood, trying to find the center of the opening. He's jammed in a crawl space a foot and a half high with a foot of water in it. Every time he breathes he's got to raise his mouth over the oily surface then put his face in again. His heart pounds like a pile driver, stops for a cigarette break, then starts up again. He feels for the long rectangular crack and rolls the quilt tight as he can make it, braces his feet against the bulkhead and jams her in there with all his strength. The nylon fabric grabs and catches in the opening and for a minute it seems like the sea is stopped, then he hears the water coming in at the aft end where the comforter's not tight enough in the slot. He backs up towards the cabin to get Ronette's sweatshirt and stuff it in the gap, then, just as he's feeling the fresh air with his feet, the quilt pops out from between the planks and shoots back against the bilge pump in the flood. He can't go back in there, the wet unfolded comforter fills the crawl space and the water's too fucking deep to breathe. Thank Christ that Olds is still high enough to keep turning the pump around.

He wipes the oil off his face and lies there for a moment with his ear right up against the engine box like old Dr. Burnside when he put his stethoscope down and laid his ear on your chest and had you breathe. Even with his boat filling up with water, for the time being he relaxes and listens to her hum just like she was on the test bench in the shop: camshaft balanced like a tightrope walker, power takeoff turning, valves like tap dancers, nice GM engine in the finest kind of tune, just a little gurgling now as the seawater reaches the shaft oil seal. Fucking Harley Webster, he did come through, she's running 2400 rpm in neutral with the bilge pump sucking like a blind French whore. But it's still coming in. He shifts his ear to the pump shaft spinning off the PTO, something's not right, a rubbery slamming sound like an impeller blade loose. The V-8's trying her hardest, you can hear it, but the busted impeller's putting her behind.

He pulls away from the engine box so he can hear Ronette working the Coast Guard. She yells into the mike, "This is a nine one one. We got a cabin full of water, when can you get here?"

PLEASE GIVE US THE LOCATION OF YOUR VESSEL.

"It's out here in the god damn fog."

Lucky yells up, "Read it off the loran."

"OK. Four four three one point two seven. Six seven four nine point zero three."

ROGER THOSE, MA'AM. CAN YOU GIVE US A DESCRIPTION OF YOUR VESSEL?

"It's half-sunk."

ROGER THAT, MA'AM. I NEED THE LENGTH AND COLOR. WHAT IS THE LENGTH OF YOUR VESSEL, AND THE HULL COLOR?

"Thirty-six-foot lobster boat. Wood. White hull, blue cabin, red bottom. Red, white, and blue, lady, the country wouldn't want to lose a boat like that."

ROGER THAT, MA'AM. MOW MANY PERSONS ABOARD?

"Two."

ROGER THAT, MA'AM. I WOULD LIKE TO HAVE ALL PERSONS ABOARD PUT ON THEIR PERSONAL FLOTATION DEVICES AT THIS TIME.

"I don't think we got any," Ronette says.

There's a long pause on the radio. Meanwhile, the water's reached the engine box, the mattress is drifting from side to side with the sea roll, and there's a long brown used Magnum rubber from the old days, head up and tail down, swimming after the mattress like an eel.

Then the voice comes back. *WE'RE GETTING A BOAT UNDER WAY TO THAT POSITION. PLEASE LOCATE AND PREPARE THE EMERGENCY FLOTATION DEVICES, SURVIVAL SUITS, OR INFLATABLE LIFE RAFT.*

"We ain't got none of those," she yells. "We had a life ring but it come off in the blow."

He's over his ankles in ice-cold seawater, standing between the engine and Ronette. His boots are full, it feels like they're screwed down to the cabin floor. Under the engine cover the block hisses when the water hits it. A cloud of steam bloats out around the exhaust pipe and the back cylinder misses. He grabs the throttle cable and pulls it harder but it's no good, crippled bilge pump's already maxed out. He lifts the cover off the engine box and gets a faceful of choking steam. The 307's running with its oil pan underwater but it's slowing down fast, and as it slows the pump slows. In a few minutes the water's over the carburetor float level and the carb puts out a wheezing little screech like a scared animal as it sucks water and one by one the cylinders die out. He's amazed how quick this happens, he's never watched a motor drown.

Up in the wheelhouse the Coast Guard lady sounds like she's painting her nails while she talks. *ROGER THAT, MA'AM. AT THIS POINT I WOULD REQUEST YOU TO LOOK AROUND YOUR VESSEL FOR ANYTHING THAT MIGHT SUPPORT A PERSON IN THE WATER.*

"When are you coming to get us?" Ronette screams.

AUXILIARY SEVEN SEVEN ZERO ONE IS GETTING UNDER WAY, MA'AM. ESTIMATED TIME TO YOUR LOCATION IS TWO HOURS FIFTEEN MINUTES.

"We're going to be dead by then. Can't you get a helicopter?"

OUR NEAREST HELICOPTER IS ON CAPE COD.

Then a thick yellow spark arcs back of the engine box and the radio hisses out. "Batteries gone," he says. "No more radio."

"Least we got the word out."

"We ain't going to be here in two hours."

"You heard her, we got to find something to hang on to."

"We can try floating the bait barrels."

"They ain't got tops to them, Lucky."

He's up in the wheelhouse with both boots off emptying them over the rail. Ronette's clinging to the steering wheel like it's a car and she can drive them home. The cuddy's full of water halfway over the engine box and the big coils of heavyweight pot warp are loose and sloshing around. Engine must be up to the cylinder heads, power gone, radio dead, loran screen black as night. The fishfinder found the seabed it had been calling to all its life. Oil-slicked water spreads over the cockpit floor, as the stern slants downward it's coming up through the scuppers that are supposed to drain it out. "Going to flood the live well, them lobsters'll swim right over the top."

Ronette shrieks, "Oh Jesus, the cigarettes!" She reaches down behind the gun rack where she keeps hers and looks into the box to see if they're wet. She takes two out and lights them both with a Bic lighter in the lee of the wheelhouse window. The boat's drifting free now, not attached to anything.

"Might as well have a smoke," he says, "ain't going to make no difference now."

His watch says two-fifteen. The Coast Guard lady said her last roger at one fifty-five. That leaves most of two hours and the boat's not going to float for half that time.

"Hope them assholes hurry up," she says.

No use telling someone what they don't need to know. "This was a glass boat," he says, "she'd be on the bottom by now. Engine's trying to pull her down, wood buoys her up, same as the fucking gun."

"And look what happened to that."

He reaches for the pint of Wild Turkey squeezed in with his stash of Marlboros behind the radar mount. The water on the platform's coming over his trawler boots as he pours Ronette's whiskey into a coffee cup and drinks his own right out of the pint. The low-set bronze steering wheel of the *Wooden Nickel* is touching the surface with its bottom spoke. The live well's flooded over and the first lobster has already found its way over the top, it's taking an underwater stroll across the cockpit floor.

"The lobsters," she says. "They're all coming out."

"They all got pardoned and they're going home. But it ain't going to do them any good, they'll starve with them fucking claws pegged."

"Can't we take their bands off, Lucky? They ain't going to survive like that."

"No chance. It's four feet deep back there."

They can't keep their footing on the flooded platform. They take the pint and the cigarettes and hoist themselves around the wheel-house to sit on the cabin trunk and watch the rest of the mammoth lobsters paddle over the side of their cage and down to the flooded cockpit floor. Few more minutes, they'll be floating right over the washboard and down to the bottom, handcuffed. The free ones will find them in the thirty-fathom darkness and have a meal.

It's getting to be a decent afternoon, nice and quiet without the engine or the seawater pump or the fishfinder's squirrelly chirps. The big swells of the morning are flattening out from the northerly breeze. A few points off the starboard bow he spots one of his Day-Glo buoys. "Cocksucker missed one," he says. Then the buoy disappears as the breeze lightens and the ocean fog bank creeps back over his offshore ledge.

Ronette takes another sip off the Wild Turkey and snaps up her orange oilskins. Her mouth is swollen up from the blow and numb with cold, so her words slur like she's drunk. "Lucky, what the hell time is it? They ever going to come?"

They both look down at his digital watch but it's filled with water and the numbers all read eight. "Must be an hour to go."

"How are they going to find us in this fog? Ain't nothing left of us to show on the radar screen."

She's right, but he won't say it. Way they're sinking, they're going to be invisible. "If you'd of kept away from the fucking gun, we'd be towing that bastard home by now. We'd be listening to Waymore, having a smoke."

"It was your fault, Lucky, we should of stayed away from the god damn thing, it's a curse. We'd be steaming into Whistle Creek with all them jumbos, get paid, pick up the car at Moto's, have a nice beer at home."

"Watch some wrestling."

"Ain't going to be no more wrestling, Lucky. Look, we hardly stick up over the water, even if they could find us they'd never see us."

"They ain't going to find us," he says. "Wind's pushed us way off that fix you gave them."

The fog's thickening up too, you can see only three or four boat lengths over the long colorless swells. They're sitting on the cabin trunk just a foot above the surface. Behind the wheelhouse, the long cockpit's already submerged. A stray swell heaves right over the foredeck and breaks across their legs. She grabs his arm with one hand, holds the Marlboros high above the spray. "Lucky, I'm freezing. Any way we can get that blue comforter below?"

"I tried to stuff the hole with it."

She shivers and draws closer. All she has on is the oilskin jacket over her purple sweater. "I ain't worried about myself, I seen enough. But I'm scared for the little guy. He ain't been anywhere. How're we supposed to say good-bye if we ain't even met him yet?" He takes a small swig of the Wild Turkey and passes it over. The bottle's light, it's getting near the end. Next time he'll bring a fifth instead of a pint. She looks at the label while she's rubbing her swollen lip. *"Causes birth defects.* Causes fucking defects in you too, Mr. Lucky Lunt." She takes the bottle and tosses it over the cabin side.

Lucky lunges for it even though it's open and it's already being invaded by undrinkable sea-water. He'd have to go overboard to get his hands on it, then it's gone. He raises his arm again, but this time she's ready, she twists out from under him and stands over the green icy water like she's going to jump. She stands in front of shotguns, she grabs hot rifle barrels with her bare hands, she probably fucking would. "Another thing," she says, still balanced there on the low edge of the slanting cabin top. "We ain't going to get through this, cause nobody's going to find us in this christly fog, but if we do, there ain't going to be no more hitting. Just one fucking touch and I'll leave you faster than I left Clyde Hannaford. Cause you ain't even got a hot tub. Besides that, you ever raise your hand against this kid, I'll kill you before I leave. I seen what you did to Kyle, and it ain't going to happen in my house. You understand?"

Suddenly the boat lurches even more to starboard, but she doesn't move. She's standing on the roof's edge, beyond the handrail, her feet wide apart, her legs angled back against the slant like she's in a wind tunnel. "Get the fuck back up here," he yells.

She doesn't move and she doesn't look back. "How are you going to make me come up there? You going to hit me?"

"I ain't going to hit you, for Christ sake. I ain't going in after you neither, so move off the fucking edge." He's standing behind her with his water-filled boots braced on the handrail, waiting. On the next swell, she turns and falls against his chest so he has to grab her and hold on. Her face is cold as seawater and she's shaking all over like a hooked fish. He walks her over to the other side of the cabin top to level the boat off, but now the prow's gone under and there's water over the cabin trunk. They can't sit on the handrail anymore, even the high one's immersed. Water breaking over their boots now with every swell, they have to stand on the cabin top and lean across the windshield to hold on to the wheelhouse roof. Beneath them through the wet glass he can see the spoked wheel's completely sub-merged and the companionway flooded to the dashboard, just the blank radar screen sticking above the surface. He can't see the com-pass, he has no fucking idea where they're pointing. Everything aft is deep below the surface, the davit's going under to starboard and the engine box cover is floating back up through the hatchway. The cabin's full of water, but there must be an air bubble trapped against the forward bulkhead keeping them afloat. Both bait barrels went over the rail when the stern dropped and they're drifting into the fog bank twenty yards astern. "Should of grabbed them bastards," he says.

As the wind rises again, they drift to leeward, still trailing the snapped green and yellow lines, and the whitecaps start breaking right across the trunk. The only space left's on top of the wheelhouse, hanging on to the radar mount. Ronette climbs first. She's trying to pull herself up the steep windshield by grabbing on the life ring mounts but she can't get a purchase on the slick blue paint or the wet glass. He puts a hand on her cold little oilskinned ass and pushes her up and over so she's sitting right up there hanging on to the radome with the bullet holes in it, but his heart is knocking like a one-lung diesel and he can't climb up himself. He rears a leg back and kicks the auto glass of the center windshield panel, right where the bullet went through, but he can't get his foot in there. He kicks again and again till he's wedged his boot tip in a round hole in the center of the windshield and can boost himself up and over on the cabin top, blowing and wheezing like a walrus. It's listing way over, they both have to hang on the Raytheon radome, only place you can grip the slippery fucker is by the bullet holes. Beneath them, down in the tilting wheelhouse, the box of cassette tapes floats free from its place behind the radar screen and the albums drift off over the starboard rail. Say good-bye to Vince's scrubbed face, Waylon's eight-string,

Tanya's white cowgirl outfit, big Garth in his ten-gallon hat, glint of Reba's dyed red hair.

Ronette leans over the low side of the wheelhouse top, trying to hang on to the radome and get her face over the side at the same time. "Hold on to me please, sweetheart, I got to throw up."

"Can't be the morning sickness. Must be three in the afternoon."

"Don't frig with me, Lucky. Just give me a hand so's I don't fall off." He's got one hand on the white metal frame of the radome mount and the other around her waist as she leans over and heaves it brown and liquid into the blue-black sea. It smells of whiskey and he almost goes sick himself. He's been on boats since he was born, he's lived on liquor for forty-eight hours without eating so there was nothing in his body but alcohol, he consumed a bottle of windshield-washer fluid on one cold lonesome drive, but he has never thrown up the contents of his stomach in his life. A couple of last night's cod chunks swim into his mouth in a sauce of whiskey but he swallows them back down like a hot lunch. When she turns around wiping her mouth she opens her eyes wide and smiles slantwise despite the blue cheese drool and the cut lip. "My God, Lucky, you're white as a corpse. Your heart still going? You look like you're already drowned." Now she's got tears leaking out through the sea spray. All that dried blood and vomit and caked white salt on her face, she's still a good-looking woman when she cries.

There's a big slurping sound as the cabin bubble busts up through the hatchway and the last of the wheelhouse air farts out through his boothole in the windshield. The cabin trunk's two feet underwater, whitecaps are breaking right over the wheelhouse roof where they're both half-seated on the radome now, hoping the fucker won't break off. The boat settles another half a foot as a swell breaks over the windward side. She howls as their boots fill with ice water but he barely feels it, his feet have gone so numb. "Should of stuck with old Clyde," he says. "You'd be dangling your toes in the hot tub."

"Wouldn't be pregnant, neither."

"Free, white, and twenty-one."

She lets go her hold on the bullet holes in the radome and grips on to the folds of his oilskins. Suddenly there's the aroma of barbe-cued steak on the wind, steak smothered in warm bubbly A.1. Sauce with a slight touch of gasoline from the rainbow slick forming around them out of the fuel vent pipes. He can't tell her what he knows, in a minute or two the whole fucking boat will go down, the two of them sucked to the bottom in their clothes and boots. Then she sits up straight. *"Lucky,"* she says. *"Listen."*

"Don't hear nothing. Only the wind and waves."

"Deaf old bastard. There's a *motor* out there."

"Ain't time for the Coast Guard yet. We'll be lying on that deep-sea ledge by the time them bastards get their pants on, going to be the lobsters' fucking revenge."

Then he can hear it over the wind noise and he instantly knows just what it is. It's a godawful old Caterpillar diesel turning a bent three-bladed wheel and drumming on the water through a metal hull. "Ain't the Coast Guard. It's a fisherman. Steel hull."

Then the sound is turning and going away.

She's standing up in a foot of water on the wheelhouse top, yelling blindly into the fog. *"Over here! Over here, for Christ sake!"*

A big sea breaking over the high side slaps him right across the back. He yells out, *"Over here, assholes,"* but it's not half as loud as Ronette and he ends up coughing and panting just like his old man when he died.

The breeze blows the fog open a bit on the port side to show a high black steel bow steaming right at them, it's got rust dripping off of every hull plate and a stench of rotten seafood so strong even the cloud of seagulls can't get close. The minute he lays eyes on it he hears the Caterpillar backing down and the bow swings sidewise so they don't run over what's left of the *Wooden Nickel*.

Soon as he sees the crew lined up on the bow rail he knows who it is, the whole fucking Trott gang in the stern dragger *Rachel T.*

Big black-bearded Captain Anson Trott's leaning over the rail with a cigar in his mouth the size of a bowling pin. One of the other Trotts has got the helm. They pull up close as they can in the swell and put her in neutral. Now the one with the arm missing joins Big Anson at the rail, along with another he's never seen before. That may be Carleton Trott, he's done some racing in a black thirty-footer with a six-cylinder John Deere. The other's the short squat thick-necked bald-headed little fucker that looks like a dwarf. There's no one steering, the whole crew's out at the port rail staring down.

Lucky shifts his grip on the radome and cups his ear so he can hear Anson Trott over the diesel. Big Anson yells, "If it ain't my friend Lint out of Orphan Point. Everything OK out here?"

"Finest kind," he yells back. "Riding a bit low, that's all. Too many lobsters in the hold."

"OK, big guy, just checking. We caught you talking on channel sixteen."

"False alarm," Lucky says. "Ain't nothing wrong here."

"How about getting your crew off of there, just in case? Then you can take your vessel on in yourself. We'll see the lady gets home safe and sound."

The bald-headed one is grinning and shaking his head, while Carleton Trott starts lowering a red boarding ladder over the port rail. They haven't got any small boats aboard, so Big Anson goes back into the wheelhouse and backs her down till the *Rachel T* comes straight to windward, then cuts her in neutral till the dragger drifts down on them and the ladder's about twenty feet away. They can't come closer, the *Wooden Nickel*'s right under the surface. That big steel hull bumps the lobster boat, she'll go straight to the bottom, no questions asked. Ronette's already trying to reach for the ladder, but there's a stretch of rainbow-colored water between the two from the escaped fuel. The one-armed Trott reaches his hook up and drags the orange rectangular foam life ring off of the *Rachel T*'s cabin top and dumps it over the rail to leeward so the wind sails it in the right direction, but the line on it clumps and fouls and the ring drops into the water ten feet away. Ronette's not saying anything, she's got a death grip on the radar mast but the cabin top under them is slanting down more, won't be a minute till she slides right in. Big Anson creeps the dragger forward across their bow and the bald-headed dwarf coils up the line and lifts the life ring again and flips it towards them with one hand like a four-foot Frisbee. This time it passes by close enough to grab. His feet slip right down the windshield and he's standing waist deep in frigid water on the high side of the trunk, but he's got his hands on the big orange lifesaver, which has a net bottom so you can't slip it over your head, you have to climb in.

Ronette's still up at the radome clinging on like a limpet and saying, "Jesus, I can't swim," but he pushes the ring against the slope of the windshield and coaxes her feet off the wheelhouse roof, so she lets go and slides down the stove-in glass with a cold splash that blinds him for a second with a douche of salt and gasoline, but she's safe, she's sitting on the ring like a swim float with her legs inside the nylon mesh. He's standing outside the life ring up to his chest in ice-cold seawater, feet braced on the handrails, steadying her with both arms. In the long swells the line first points way up at the big steel dragger, then way down. On their end the bald-headed dwarf's keeping it taut so they don't drift apart.

He turns away from Ronette for one last minute with the *Wooden Nickel.* His occupation's gone, along with his kids and the woman he married and the home he was born in, but he promised his old man he'd keep this boat till the end. He hangs on a moment to the only part still above water, then turns around to hop on the orange raft.

But the raft is gone.

The bald-headed Trott's hauling in on the fucking rope as Ronette sails off alone in the life raft towards the *Rachel T.* She looks back and yells something, it sounds like *asshole* but he can't be sure. Then she has to hang on with both hands and look forward as she nears the ship. All four fucking Trotts are up on the high rusty black steel rail laughing their dicks off while the dwarf Trott reels her in. Now she's alongside the dragger, they've got a tackle on the raft line, and the orange life ring rises straight up in the air with Ronette in the rope mesh like they're raising a halibut. Three Trotts reach out and pull her over the rail while Big Anson throws it in gear. The dragger lets out a black fart of diesel smoke and turns her stern away with the bent three-bladed wheel churning under the miles of cable coiled on the stern winch drum.

RACHEL T
Shag Island

He's giving them the finger with one hand and hanging on to the radome with the other, it's the last thing above water except the VHF antenna and the loran whip with the gull wing on it. He grabs the radome and pulls himself back on the wheelhouse roof, rips the wing off and throws it as hard as he can in their direction, but it just flutters into the water while the dragger's big stern reel dissolves into the fog.

Marlboros gone, Wild Turkey gone, day's haul over the side. For a moment, shimmering under the oily surface, the *Wooden Nickel* looks brand-new, he's standing there down in Moose Reach in 1970 with his old man and the Alley brothers, busting a bottle over the stem, then all of a sudden they're flying him back from Vietnam to bury a stranger that doesn't recall his name, and the *Wooden Nickel* is his. There's a thousand nights with so many girls he can't remember them, then he sees Sarah Peek walking with Clyde Hannaford and that's it, they're up on Deadman's Hill on the bench seat of his '68 Dodge plow truck, Willie Nelson on the eight-track with "Blue Eyes Crying in the Rain," the big black shift knob trying to get in on the act. She pushes the shift away and into neutral, they roll down into the cemetery among the stones. That was Kyle, then Kristen, and now this new one that won't have an old man, Ronette will raise it in the trailer with the GMC pickup holding up one side. She'll bring it back to Clyde, with his Irish setter and his undescended testicle, it won't be a fisherman but a fucking dealer. Well, that's where the money is, maybe Clyde Hannaford can save it from this christly life. The sea's a piss-poor companion, you can't trust it or anything in it, cold-blooded shadows, they don't give a fuck.

The hull shudders slantways underneath him with a burst of gasoline that flattens the water in a widening oilslick circle, the radar mast twists out of his hands and the boat turns so he's standing on the port *side* of the wheelhouse, nothing to hang on to, and it's going down. On the way over he grabs at the loran whip but it busts off in his hand. He yells once into the fog where they vanished, *"Cocksuckers,"* then he looks down. The sun's breaking out of the cloud bank now, so he can see beneath the surface. His legs look as short and thick in the water as the legs of that bald-headed dwarf. Beneath them the shadow of the *Wooden Nickel* catches the sunlight like a long red-and-white fish, a whale, son of a whore shaking with death and anger and bleeding from head to tail. Nice new V-8 engine too, he was coming to like that Olds.

The last bubble burps out of the companionway and the hull sinks another foot, it's not going to support him any longer. His skin is frozen and he can't feel a thing, fuck it, might as well suck water and drown like Merritt Lunt. They say he did it on purpose, his time was come, beats wheezing off in a fucking hospital.

Only thing is, he wouldn't have minded meeting that little kid.

Off in the densest part of the fog bank he hears the *Rachel T*'s engine, just a rumble at first but growing louder by the second. Jesus H. Christ, Anson's not satisfied with leaving him there like a bait bag, now they're coming to run him down. One by one he kicks the trawler boots off in case he has to duck under and swim. He can't feel any feet there, they're already frozen stiff. His hands are too cold to pull off the oilskins, there's two pairs of wet pants under them anyway, his legs weigh two hundred pounds apiece. Then his bare feet find the wooden lip of the wheelhouse top. He flexes them a few times to get the feeling back. He knows the boat so well his toes can feel the rain gutter on the wheelhouse corner, beneath that the bronze bulge of the portside running light, then the snap hook for the life ring that blew off in the storm. He loses contact for a second and floats free, then finds it again, six feet beneath the surface. The dragger slows down and steams close past him, so he can hear their worn-out tappets and the grind of the raw-water pump and, from the wheelhouse, the voice of Garth Brooks, clear as if he's up there steering the ship.

Operator won't you put me on through
I gotta send my love down to Baton Rouge

Their quarter wave hits him and his feet can't find the wheel-house anymore. Astern of the dragger the empty orange life ring drifts downwind right in front of his face and he grabs the safety line with both hands and lets his body float free. He turns around to catch a last glimpse of the red-white-and-blue shape sinking beneath him but he can't see it, just the plume of gasoline slick where it's still leaking out from the drowned carburetor and the fuel tank vent. Full unopened pack of Marlboros jammed behind the radar screen, they're twisting down through the cold green currents along with the wrinkly brown rubber, a cooler of Rolling Rock, the blue curtains pushpinned around the windows, and, hidden away under the compass mount, a high school graduation picture of Sarah Peek. He can imagine the Marlboros swelling up inside, all that wet tobacco, busting the box through at the seams, what a waste.

Minute she finds the bottom there's going to be big green lobsters poking around every fucking corner, just how they greeted Merritt Lunt when he went down.

He looks up and shakes his eyes to focus on the air again. Up on the *Rachel T* that must be the lobster boat racer, Carleton Trott, grinning like a monkey and starting to reel him in. Beside him is the one with the hook, Harvey, pointing and giggling like he's at a mud run. Big Anson beams down from the wheelhouse window, pleased as piss with his skippering to drag that piece of Styrofoam right past a drowning man.

They shut the wheel down so they can tow him up astern. Soon as they get him alongside the dragger reel, Carleton Trott's saying, "The little lady wanted to leave you for lobster bait, too bad Big Anse wouldn't let her."

"That's right," Harvey the Hook says. "Law of the sea says to go back for you, Anson's a law-abiding man. Har har."

The two of them stand there watching him pull himself up on the port side of the huge dragger reel and over the transom. The diamond-tread steel floor feels like sharpened ice on his bare feet. He's been in the water a long time and his body shakes all over from the cold. Big Anson's on one side of him now, Carleton's on the other. They're helping drag his knees over the steel transom that's so slippery from fish guts he's going to slide back in. Big Anse holds out a Mobil cup with something in it: black rum. He takes a pull and reaches the other hand out for a smoke. Carleton Trott gives him a Camel filter. "Bet you thought we wasn't coming back for you," Anson Trott says.

"Never crossed my mind."

"Just having a little fun, nothing better to do out here, ain't found a christly scallop all day."

Anson's got a remote mike on his belt that squawks, WOODEN NICKEL. UNITED STATES COAST GUARD VESSEL SEVEN SEVEN OH ONE.

Anson Trott pushes the mike switch and says, "This is the *Rachel T* out of Shag Island."

AFTERNOON, CAPTAIN. WE'RE TRYING TO REACH A VESSEL IN DISTRESS CALLED THE WOODEN NICKEL. HAVING A LITTLE TROUBLE WITH OUR GPS OUT HERE. YOU SEEN ANY SIGN OF THEM?

Big Anson pushes his mike button and says, "The *Wooden Nickel's* sank. They'd of waited for you, they'd both be dead. We got her crew aboard."

HOW MANY PERSONS, CAPTAIN?

"Two."

THEY SAFE AND SOUND?

"We're going to feed them and tuck them in."

THANK YOU, CAPTAIN. THIS IS COAST GUARD SEVEN SEVEN OH ONE, ON STATION FOR REPAIRS.

By this time he's looking around the dragger for signs of Ronette. The crew cabin aft of the wheelhouse has a steel door to starboard and two round portholes on each side, too salted up to see in.

"The lady was pretty near froze to death," Carleton says. "Zeke's took her up in the crew cabin to warm her up."

"That the bald-headed guy?"

Big Anson says, "Zeke ain't bald. His hair's just real short, that's all."

Carleton breaks into a shit-eating grin. "Zeke's old lady keeps it short. She don't use no clippers either. She just grabs onto Zeke's ears and rubs it off."

Harvey Trott doubles up laughing on that one, then waves the hook up and down over his crotch like he's jerking off with it. That thing must feel pretty chilly on your dick.

"Guess I'll head up to the crew cabin," Lucky says. "Wouldn't mind a warm-up myself."

"I was you," Harvey says, "I'd knock before busting in on them two. Maybe they ain't decent. How about staying aft awhile, give them some privacy." He gaffs another Styrofoam cup off of the stack and splashes it half full with the black rum. The foam makes a sharp screech sliding out of the stainless steel hook, it's one sound Lucky can't stand, he'd rather hear a drill going through his tooth.

He takes a hit of the rum to warm up and wash the screech out of his mouth.

Carleton says, "Guess we won't be seeing you down to Stoneport next year. Not on that sled anyway. Figure on trying to raise her?"

"Can't raise a boat out here," Harvey the Hook says.

Carleton Trott says, "Why not? They raised the fucking *Titanic,* she was two miles deep. They did that with a robot sub."

Harvey rubs his ear with the hook. "Hey Lint, think you can get ahold of one of them?"

"I ain't thinking about it right now." He gets up to go forward and find out what's going on with Ronette in the crew cabin, but his clothes are so cold and heavy he can't even stand up. Harvey and

Carleton Trott get on either side of him and hoist him to his feet. He's barefoot on the fish guts and scallop slime, every piece of clothing is soaked, his pockets are full of oily seawater and he can't move so fast. Suddenly his feet go out from under him and the two Trotts have to catch him on either side. Big Anson's got her on autopilot now and he steps down from the wheelhouse to the side deck just outside the steel crew cabin door. "Hypothermia," Anson says. "Carl, give him another drink."

"Let's get them fucking clothes off of him first."

"Take him in the crew cabin," Anson says. He goes for the steel door lever right beside them.

"No, Zeke's in there with the waitress. Take him up forward."

"What the fuck," Lucky says, "I guess I can fit in there too." He ducks past Big Anson and opens the door lever himself. Harvey puts the hook up to stop him but he shoves it aside.

Inside the crew cabin it's so dark he has to blink his eyes. He feels for a light switch alongside the steel door but he can't find one. Soon as his eyes adjust, there's bald-headed Zeke in a black T-shirt on a plastic chair with his feet in trawler boots up on the mess table. He's got a beer in one paw, with the other he's smoking a thick hand-rolled joint. Dirty light from the porthole catches the blue cloud around his head. He sticks the joint in his mouth for a minute so he can scratch his nuts, then takes a long suck and blasts it out in a sudden dense coughing puff like he's thrown a valve. When he recovers, he looks at Lucky in his wet oilskins, barefoot, and says, "Jesus, look what they pulled out of the trawl. Thought there wasn't nothing down there."

In the close heat of the crew cabin with the black rum in his throat and this asshole smoking like a grass fire, his heart settles and his shivering stops. He can't make out anyone but Zeke Trott in that shadowy space. "What the fuck'd you do with her?"

"Who, your sternlady? Guess she's gone sound asleep. I must of wore her out. Har har." He points a boot at the darkest corner, where there's a human body lying under a grease-colored blanket on a bunk. "We got them wet oilskins off of her and put her in one of Anse's union suits. It ain't exactly Victoria's Secret, har har."

He's about to go over and check her out when Harvey the Hook comes in through the steel door and bolts it shut with a side lever.

They must all have the crawling crabs, cause the minute Harvey sees Zeke over in the corner he starts scratching his own nuts with the hook. "Zeke, ain't that the waitress at the Blue Claw?"

"I thought I seen her somewhere," Zeke says. "Just didn't recognize her in them clothes. Her mouth ain't right neither."

"Looks like she got beat up. You get rough with the crew, skipper?"

Harvey takes another Styrofoam cup in the hook and pours it half full with his good hand. He holds it under Ronette's nose but she doesn't sit up, just turns away from the alcohol fumes in her sleep. "Wake up, honey, you ain't going to believe what we picked up in the drag."

Lucky says, "Leave her be, for Christ sake."

"What do you give a shit, you got a wife, ain't you?"

Zeke's still over in the corner with his big hairy hand on his crotch. He says, "Get out of the way, Harv, you're blocking the view."

"You want a view?" Harvey says. He puts the drink in his good hand and draws the blanket down with the hook almost to her waist. She's sleeping on her side facing the room and the union suit's half unbuttoned, so you can get a pretty good look. "That's a decent view, ain't it, Zeke?"

Lucky says, "What the fuck you up to?"

"Zeke thinks maybe she's hot."

Over in his corner Zeke says, "She's hot all right."

Lucky says, "She ain't hot. She's been in the fucking water. Cover her up." He feels the steel hull shake and twist a bit as the skipper revs her up and changes the heading to port, seaward, he knows from the way she strikes the oncoming swells. The big broken-down Caterpillar rattles like a chain in a washing machine, you can't hear a thing. He doesn't know where Anson Trott's taking her, they may be going back fishing for all he knows. Harvey's not pulling the blanket back either. He's standing right there with the union suit falling open and half of Ronette's tits showing right down to the tattoo. Harvey Trott dangles his hook in front of her like he's about to reveal a little more. Lucky says, "Put the fucking blanket back and let her sleep."

"Jesus H. Christ," Zeke says. "Don't he sound like the fucking skipper? Well, you ain't. Your boat's on the fucking bottom. You'd be fucking fish food if Big Anse didn't pick you up. Way we look at it, we kind of figure you owe us. Seeing as you would of fucking drowned."

"Nobody'd know the difference," Harvey Trott says, looking over at Zeke. He follows Harvey's glance and Zeke's not scratching his nuts anymore. He's got one of his short dwarf legs cocked up on the other and a single-barreled twelve-gauge shotgun across his knee. The gun's pointing over towards Lucky while his eyes are directly aimed at Ronette's tits. There's two of them and one's got a gun and the other one's got a hook ground sharper than a tuna gaff.

Without moving his head Lucky checks the room for weapons. There's a red fire ax on one wall and a short wire-handled ash poker hanging by the kerosene cookstove. It would be a nice feeling to bury that fire ax in the center of Zeke's wide blubbery back, but if he moved towards it he'd get shot.

He gets up slowly to go and pull the blanket back over her shoulders. Harvey lets him cross to the bunk, lets his hand almost touch the blanket, then the cold stainless steel of the hook is around his wrist. From over in his corner Zeke says, "Back off, Charlie. Don't go fucking around. You ain't nobody on this boat. We could fucking throw you back, nobody'd give a shit."

He pulls his arm out of the hook but Harvey gives a little twist while he's pulling it out and it comes off bloody. Harvey says, "We was just thinking of a little payment for that rescue work. Kind of like tit for tat."

Bald-headed Zeke roars, "That's good, Harv. Tit for tat. We got to get something for all that work and, mister, you ain't got nothing we want. Pull the blanket down some more, Harv. I want to see that union suit. Don't look half so good on Anson as it does on her."

He stares over at Zeke to see if he'd really pull the trigger. Zeke's got little black pig's eyes under the bald head, a gold ring in one ear, shit-brown Abe Lincoln beard with the mustache and lip areas shaved, neck like a swamp tire. His boots are still cocked up on the cabin table and the gun across his leg points straight at Lucky's chest.

He's worked himself closer to the fire ax on the wall over Ronette's bunk, but he'd be down before he got a hand on it. It would be a good idea to back away.

"Looks nice, don't she, Zeke?"

"I seen a lot more than that fore you busted in."

Anson's got the Cat diesel running hard right under the steel cabin floor, it's slapping like it's about to swallow an intake valve. You want to say anything in there, you have to speak up. But Ronette's sleeping right through it. She could be dead except every once in a while she shivers and tosses her head like she's in a bad dream saying *no.*

Harvey looks at him standing over her bunk and says, "Big Anse's got another union suit up in the head, why don't you go check it out. You're going to freeze your ass in them wet clothes."

His brother Zeke says, "Take your time, skipper. Maybe you'll find something to do while you're in there."

"Fuck you. I ain't leaving her alone."

Zeke says, "I told you, Harv, we never should have picked this asshole up. We could of took the waitress on a fishing trip."

"Still can," Harvey says. "He ain't going to do nothing."

"He's the one that shot Prissy Shaver."

"That's right. We could just drop him off to Shavers' wharf, let the dogs have him. He don't look so hot anyway."

His heart's skipping and pounding like the fucking diesel. He spreads his legs so he can stay upright on the vibrating steel floor.

"Finest kind," Zeke says. "Drop the cocksucker off to Shavers' wharf. *Then* take the waitress fishing. Harv, pull the fucking blanket down, let's see what she's got. The big guy can watch or not."

Lucky says, "Anson know about this?"

"Anson's family. He don't give a shit."

Harvey Trott hooks the blanket and draws it down to Ronette's waist. She makes a little sound in her sleep and tries to draw it back up but the hook stops it. She twists again, one of her tits slides out of Big Anse's white union suit and Zeke sucks in his breath like he's been shot, but he keeps the gun steady, right on Lucky's belly, and the twelve-gauge barrel follows his movement as he sways with the boat's roll. Harvey's still leaning over her, the hook's drawing the blanket down along the sharp high curve of Ronette's hip, then it stops short and pulls it back. All of a sudden Harvey sounds dead serious. "OK, Zeke. You seen enough."

"What the fuck, Harv? You gone chickenshit? You afraid of this asshole? We got the armament."

"I said that's enough."

Now Zeke swings the shotgun barrel on his brother and says, "Candyass faggot. You ain't even got a hard-on. Pull the blanket down."

Harvey draws the blanket edge down over her hips again and says, "Take a look, Zeke, you want to fuck around with that?"

The whole crotch area of Big Anse's union suit is red with blood.

Zeke sets the gun butt on the deckhouse floor and stands up so he can look, though he still keeps a couple fingers around the barrel. After a minute he says, "Rag come off, that's all. You ain't never seen minstrel blood before?"

"It ain't," Harvey says. "They don't bleed that bad." Harvey still has his stainless steel hook over the brown blanket edge. Ronette's body shivers with the chill, she reaches down in her sleep again to pull it up. Harvey jerks his hook back from her hand like a corpse is going after it. Now Zeke's staring hypnotized at the bloodstain, he's leaning towards his brother and Ronette for a closer look. He's forgotten all about the shotgun.

Lucky bends down over the bunk as if to see better, but he's got something else in mind. With both of them focused on the stain, he takes one big stride across the crew cabin and swoops his hand down on the gun. Once he gets his fist around the barrel it's easy to spin it out of that dwarf little bastard's grip. In an instant it's over, he's got the gun in both hands, his back to the steel wall. Bald-headed pervert, he must have raped her when she first came in, now he sees blood and he's freaked out.

The gun's a stainless steel single-barrel Mossberg, the kind you carry on boats so they won't rust. He can feel from the weight there's a shell in it. The safety is off and the hammer's cocked, fucking Zeke meant business. "So now you assholes back off from her," he says.

The bald-headed one's scared shitless and starts slowly working his way towards the black steel cabin door. The other, Harvey, he's an ex-con and smart. He stays right in front of Ronette's bunk. He's thinking, you got a shotgun, shoot me and you shoot her. He doesn't care, let him keep her company. It's Zeke that was in here alone with her.

Harvey Trott says, "Don't get excited, skipper. Fucking gun's got a flare in it anyway."

"That's right," Zeke says. "She ain't got shot in there, she's loaded with a parachute flare. I seen Big Anse put it in there myself."

Harvey doesn't move. He turns to his brother and says, "I told Anse we shouldn't of picked them up."

Zeke says, "Should of picked the girl up and stopped while we was ahead." While he's talking Lucky's looking right through the ratty Megadeath sweatshirt covered with fish scales, just like an X ray, and in there he's seeing a little round heart black as pig liver and jumping with pure fear. That bastard was in here alone with her for just enough time to rape her bloody. He's never shot off a flare before, but a shotgun's a shotgun, don't matter what's in it, even a flare will blind the cocksucker and set his clothes on fire, he won't fuck with women anymore. Ronette's bleeding to death, the boat's gone, license, house, wife, kids, what the fuck. He raises the gun point-blank and fires it right into the D of MEGADEATH so it will explode in his liver-colored heart. The blast echoes off the steel crew cabin walls like an atomic bomb. The flare comes off slantways out of the barrel and hits Zeke's arm and knocks him up against the wall. It's not like a bullet, he can see it as it cracks off Zeke and angles into the port rear corner across from the cabin door. The chute pops open and the red flare hisses and ignites. The cold dark crew cabin goes blinding red-orange like the inside of the sun. Zeke stands up star-ing at Lucky and rubbing his elbow like his arm's come off. Harvey puts his good hand around Zeke's waist, raises the steel door lever and leads him out on deck. Ronette's eyes are wide open, she's watch-ing the whole thing.

The flare keeps burning with a screaming hot light in the aft cor-ner but it's not hurting anything and the heat feels good. When he turns his eyes away from it, Ronette is sitting upright on the bed. She has the blanket drawn around her and she's trying to say some-thing but the noise of the flare and the diesel make it impossible to hear. Lucky yells at her, "That son of a whore lay a hand on you?"

She yells, "The hook?"

"No, the bald-headed one."

"Come over here and I'll tell you." He sits beside her as they watch the flare die, like a couple of campers by the glowing coals. "He wanted to watch me change clothes. He said we owed him. I said I'd wait till you came in, then I'd change, so he went in the head. I put the union suit on, crawled into the covers, and that's the last thing I remember."

"Fucking pervert could of done it while you slept."

"Done what?"

"You take a look at yourself down there?"

She pulls off the blanket and looks down. "Jesus H. Christ. I ain't supposed to be bleeding like that. I ain't bled since April the twenty-sixth. Oh Lucky, it's the baby."

"You sure it ain't that bald-headed fuck?"

She's got her face buried in her hands, opening the fingers so she can look down, then closing them again. "He didn't do nothing, Lucky, it's the baby."

"Got to get your ass to the emergency room." He opens the steel door and there's Big Anse with a long-barreled target revolver in his hand. Carleton Trott is close behind him with a shark club. They look at the dying flare, not much light to it but it's putting out black smoke now like a steak pit. Used to be bright as noon but now no one can see a thing. Carleton finds his way through the smoke and picks the gun off the side of Ronette's bunk where Lucky left it.

Big Anson's waving the pistol around and saying, "You crazy bastard, we fish you out of the fucking sea and you start shooting. What the fuck's wrong with you? You got a war going on?" He keeps the pistol on Lucky while he turns to Ronette. "And what's with you, sweetheart? You wearing the rag? Carl, get her some paper towels."

Lucky says, "Leave her alone, Carleton. She's pregnant."

She doesn't even cover herself while Big Anse takes a long stare at her, like she's in the hospital already and he's the M.D. looking her over, telling her there ain't going to be a child. Anse says, "She *was* pregnant, you mean. Bad enough taking her offshore in a shitheap like that. Woman in that condition, you got no right taking her out at all. I got six kids back on the island. My wife wants to travel, she takes the fucking plane."

Ronette's just looking at him, her eyes glowing from tears reflecting the last of the red flare. Big Anse puts the pistol in his belt and spits on the flare smoldering in the corner. It hisses and steams and then goes out. "Carleton," he says, "hose that fucking mess down and clean it up." He turns to Lucky. "You take care of your woman, like you should of done before. Lie her down and get her quiet. We got a busted arm up in the wheelhouse. We're supposed to be fishing and we're running a god damn hospital. I don't know why the fuck I stopped." He shoves the pistol in his waistband and slams the steel door shut. Carleton goes off for a mop and a bucket of water from the head. The old Cat diesel farts and whines when Anse puts the throttle to her and turns her hard to starboard. In a minute the engine's at its upper limit and the hull yaws and complains from the sharp turn. Wherever they were headed before, seaward or home to Shag Island, right now they're steaming towards the mainland fast.

He covers Ronette with the blanket and lays a hand on the hill of her hip while he watches Carleton Trott clean the flare up on the other side of the room. They haven't gone ten minutes when the diesel slows down, maybe she's running too hot. They're nowhere near land yet. Big Anse is shouting up on deck. The smoke is gradually clearing out of the crew cabin, long rays of red sunlight streak through the dirty fixed window on the port side. Just as he thought, Anson's been heading north. Now, though, they're dead in the water and he hears a second big diesel throbbing nearby, this one a Cummins six, good deal healthier than the Trotts' old Cat. He hears another shout, then another. He leaves Ronette and heads for the starboard door. Carleton stands in front of the door and says, "Anson said you wasn't supposed to leave the cabin."

"What the fuck's going on? Can't see nothing out of this christly window. It's covered with birdshit."

He steps back so Carleton Trott can open the door. Almost sunset and they're still on the high seas. The swell's nearly gone, a sharp land breeze carries the smell of fall. The other boat's on the other side where he can't see it. Carleton jumps out and goes aft to get around the crew cabin.

In a minute he's back. "Coast Guard's alongside. They're going to take her in. Both of you's going. See if you can walk her around the stern, get over on the leeward side, we'll put her over there with the hoist. Here's some boots, they're Anson's and he's going to want them back."

"Zeke going too?"

"Zeke don't want to leave the ship. He ain't hurt bad. He's coming on with us."

He gets Ronette up and wraps the blanket around her so it covers the union suit. He scoops her up to carry her but he can't balance in the sea swell so he has to put her down. He pulls her arm over his shoulder but she can't even hold it there, she's pretty much dead weight. She looks at him and smiles but she can't talk, she shuffles forward like he did when he was first walking after the heart job. Slow, looking down at her feet, one little step at a time. There's not much sea motion on the big dragger, otherwise she'd fall right over.

When they get around aft of the crew cabin there's a white-hulled Coast Guard auxiliary off to starboard, big black numbers 7701, the name *Robert J. Sweeney* on its hull. They've got two spring lines attached but the boats are still about ten feet apart, too much swell to bring them together so she can walk across. Big Anse is yelling into the handheld radio at the Coast Guard coxswain up on the bridge. Back on the *Rachel T*'s stern, Harvey Trott stands aft by the cable reel with his hook on the controls of the deck crane. They've got a four-point sling rigged with an empty haddock box to swing her over to the Coast Guard boat. In the wheelhouse he sees Zeke's low bald head over the helm, a bloody towel around his arm. Son of a bitch just got shot and he's running a ship. One by one the *Rachel T*'s deck lights come on in the gloom, then the lifeboat swivels its spotlight over so it's bright as noon. He hears the sound of Big Country 105 from the wheelhouse, fucking Zeke's listening to Reba McEntire. Ronette puts her head up for the first time and says, "It's Reba. 'Please Come to Boston.' That was on the album that went down."

Then Carleton helps her into the sling and she's up and over. Two or three coasties on the other side pick her up and walk her into the round aft cabin on the auxiliary, looks like a little white Quonset hut. Aft, at the hydraulics, Harvey the Hook swings the tackle back aboard the *Rachel T* and it's time for him to get in. Big Anson yells into the handheld, "You better take this asshole or we're throwing him over the side."

The radio voice comes back: DON'T KNOW IF THE SLING'LL HANDLE THAT MUCH WEIGHT, CAP'N.

"That's OK, he can swim over."

Carleton and Harvey Trott have the sling beside him and they're pushing him into it. The box stinks of marijuana and herring guts. Back aft Harvey jerks the hydraulics so he's going up and over the side like a space launch. Harvey stops the hoist right in the middle and dangles him over black water for a moment, then Big Anse yells, "Christ sake, Harv, ain't you frigged around enough?" The Coast Guard keeps their spotlight on him as he finishes his swing over the gap and drops on the afterdeck. Safe.

The auxiliary's smaller and lighter than the *Rachel T* and it's got a familiar lively motion, bit more like a lobster boat. He finds when he tries to get out of the sling that he can't lift his own weight. A couple of coasties in orange life jackets take him out and help him into the shelter cabin. One of them's a big sailor with no shirt under his life vest and a U.S. flag tattooed on his shoulder, another's a black guy with a Confederate accent and a gold tooth. The black guy takes him to the door of the Quonset hut and says, "Y'all are darn lucky to be alive."

Ronette is lying on one of the bunks with a small pale coastie standing watch over her like she's a drug haul. He's got a belt holster holding a stainless steel .45 and he's nervous, Anson must have told them there'd be trouble. She has a small olive-drab blanket barely covering her bloody union suit and the guy looks scareder than shit, but the blood's already dry and caking, not flowing out anymore. Outside there's a clatter as the *Rachel T*'s tackle swings back over the rail, the next moment the big Cummins opens up as the boat lifts and they take off over the long following swell like a jet ski.

She's wide awake now, half sitting up so she can sip a mug of Uncle Sam's coffee though the high-speed vibration is spilling it all over her GI blanket. The coastie, who's about fifteen, looks at Lucky and yells over the engine noise: "I'm supposed to assess the victim, sir, but I don't exactly know what to do. We didn't practice on any girls."

Ronette says, "Take it easy, sailor, it's OK. I looked down there myself and it ain't coming out no more." Then she looks over at Lucky and starts crying again. "You was right about today, Luck. You should of took Sonny Phair."

He sits beside her, and the Coast Guard kid's glad to let him take over. The kid backs all the way across the shelter cabin and sits down on a bench with his thumb rubbing the hammer of his handgun, he'd rather be back with a *Playboy* in his bunk. Over his head there's a locked gray metal cabinet where they must keep the rest of their arsenal, a pile of olive-drab blankets on top of it. The coastie says, "You can help yourself to one of those blankets, sir. You must be some cold after all that exposure."

"Don't need it," he says. But he pulls one down and unfolds it over Ronette's knees. If they sit close together on the bunk they can talk in a normal voice. "Way he's pushing this thing, they'll have us on shore in fifteen minutes. You just hang on, OK?"

"Lucky, it wasn't just blood coming out of me. I lost it. I know I did. I didn't feel nothing the whole time we was sinking but I got the cramps soon as I laid down. They was worse than a monthly. It's gone, honey, and I already loved that kid so much."

"You got to rest up," he says. "Another few minutes, they're going to transfer you again."

But all she can keep saying is, "I lost it. I know I did. I didn't deserve it for what I did to Clyde, and they took it away."

"You ain't losing nothing," he says. "You just got hurt when they pulled you over the side. Anyhow, anything happens, we'll make another, be pretty god damn easy, now we know how."

"Lucky, we ain't talking about a transmission. You can't just make another. Life ain't like that. That was a human being, he was starting to be my friend. You never lost nothing, so you don't know."

"I ain't lost nothing? Guess again."

He knows she knows what he's thinking about: the *Wooden Nickel* dropping upside down through its own fuel slick like a blood-red shadow.

"It ain't the same," she says, still looking down at the olive-drab GI blanket covering up the union suit.

The Coast Guard seaman's totally silent on the bunk, sitting right up at attention like he's going to be inspected at any time. Lucky yells over to him, "Hey, where are they bringing this thing in?"

"They didn't tell me, sir. The boat's out of Norumbega base."

"That's a long fucking way. Can't they bring her in closer by?"

"I wouldn't know, sir. I'm from Tulsa, Oklahoma. I did hear them talking about Burnt Neck."

"That's right," Lucky says. "They got a dock hoist there, they can lift her off if she needs it."

"What do you mean, *she?*" Ronette says. "They lifted you too."

"Well, I wasn't about to fucking swim."

She smiles for a minute, then her head goes down and she's crying again.

Lucky says to the coastie, "Know what the ETA is?"

"I don't, sir."

"How fast this thing go?"

"Twenty-four knots, sir, wide open."

"Think she's wide open now?"

"Yes sir, I think she is."

He feels the auxiliary making a wide turn to port, so they must have passed the Burnt Neck entrance buoy. Twenty-four knots, that's three times what the *Rachel T* would have done, they ought to be in by now.

Then the motor slows down and he hears boots on the starboard side of the Quonset hut. There's no portholes in the shelter cabin, but the minute the coastie opens the metal door they're hit by the flashing red and white strobe lights of the ambulance on the Burnt Neck pier. Behind the ambulance there's a crowd of local kids and drunks to check out the action, biggest thing that's happened to Burnt Neck since the genetic counselors came to town. The auxiliary bangs up sharp against the wharf pilings and the coasties jump off and tie her on. The high tide gives them a near horizontal gangplank, so they won't have to use the hoist. Soon as they've docked up, the paramedics come running with a stretcher, carry Ronette into the back of the white Ford medivan and shut the door. Lucky starts to follow but the cox says, "Got a few formalities, skipper, then you can go."

They're filling out paperwork as the ambulance backs off the dock, strobes flashing, all the wharf drunks and Burnt Neck Indian kids scattering out of the way. "You OK in those clothes, skipper?"

"Finest kind. I ain't got far to go."

The ambulance is gone, the crowd's headed for home to watch the playoffs, he's on the pier alone. The auxiliary swivels its decklight around and picks up nothing but drizzle in the smoky fog. Up on the night-lighted bridge he can make out the cox peering into the radar screen as he backs the *Robert J. Sweeney* away from the Burnt Neck pier. A teenage kid comes up to him, curious. The kid's holding a bottle in a brown paper bag. "Hey mister, what's that all about?"

"What'd it look like? It was the UPS, taking all the Coast Guard money to the bank."

"No shit? Looked like an ambulance to me."

"Hey," Lucky says. "You got a car?"

"I ain't got a license. I ain't sixteen. My brother's got a truck, though."

"Want to make a fast ten bucks?"

"Sure."

"Go get your brother's truck and come back down here and take me over to Whistle Creek."

"You buy some beer for me?"

"Sure."

"Cigarettes?"

"Anything you say."

In a minute the kid's back driving a beat-up Ford Ranger with no plates and the muffler dragging a plume of sparks along the ground. "Let's go to the store first," the kid says. "I ain't stupid."

"Nobody said you was. You're going to get picked up, though, this thing ain't registered."

"Ain't no cops around here, mister. Town can't afford them."

"You some kind of Indian?"

"Tarratine Nation," the kid says. "You see all this land?" He waves his hand towards a line of roadside trees, then a couple of trailers and a bottle-redemption shed, then more trees. "In the old time all this belonged to us."

The truck hits a pothole and a blast of hot yellow sparks fills the rearview mirror from the dragging exhaust. Lucky says, "Don't sweat it. You're going to own it again someday."

"You think so, mister?"

"Yup. You just hang on and be patient. We're going to get sick of the god damn maintenance and give it back."

The lights are still out when they reach Moto's wharf in the Old Cove. The Indian kid waves and bounces back up the road, he's got a carton of Winstons and a twelve-pack of Rolling Rock, he's happy. There's no taillights on either side of the Ranger, just a wake of sparks spewing off the busted muffler, then the kid's gone.

No sign of Moto or Curtis Landry or the reefer truck. The place looks abandoned, just like when it was a leftover from the sardine days. The smell of dead squid oozes like a tentacle under the reefer shed door. Ronette's Probe is the only vehicle in the lot, keys right in the ignition where she forgot them.

High beams are useless in the night and fog, he puts them on low to crawl up the hill from Moto's pier. Can't see anything anyway, just fog and more fog, the wind hasn't reached this place to clear it out. He's still so wet he feels underwater, like the *Wooden Nickel* down on her twenty-fathom ledge. She's had planks sprung before, refits, recaulks, blown engines, bent shafts, but she's always come out of it, just like Alfie the cat. Not this time, though. If he closes his eyes he sees her on the bottom, big nuclear starfish already crawling down below. Lobsters will find her, they'll breed like a cathouse once they settle in.

He feels for a tape in the glove compartment and it's Vince Gill singing "The Heart Won't Lie." He turns Ronette's stereo up loud enough so he can't think.

Before heading up to the Tarratine hospital he stops back at the trailer to get changed. The truck's just like he left it, sunk up to the hubcaps in the water and mud, front end propping up the side of the trailer. He pulls the Probe into the swampy driveway till he feels the front wheels going down, Mexican shitheap couldn't crawl out of a sandbox.

At least there's a light glowing in the trailer, TV's on too. Tarratine Hydro finally got the power back on. Corey's dog yowls away under the yard lamp on his side of the road, somebody ought to do the neighborhood a favor and shoot that fucking thing. On their side of the road there's a couple of lights glowing in the trailer windows, plus the dim, flickering streetlight outside of Sonny Phair's. And there's Sonny himself, cigarette in his mouth, black trawler boots over his union suit, taking a leak in the big puddle under the greenish lamp.

When Sonny sees the Probe pull in he buttons up and comes sloshing over in the boots, he's wading through water a foot deep as he crosses behind the truck. He's all excited. "Hey Lucky, you had your scanner on?"

"I ain't. I been listening to a Vince Gill tape."

"Some kind of boat went down, people was hurt, Coast Guard was calling back and forth. You see any of that?"

"I seen it. I seen the whole christly fucking thing."

"What, was you and Ronette out there helping?"

"Me and Ronette was out there sinking."

"No fucking shit. That whole thing was *you?*" Now Sonny's looking up at Lucky like he's a movie star passing through Split Cove on the way to his summer estate.

"You want my autograph?"

Sonny keeps saying, "I can't fucking believe it. Thought you was just another shitheel fisherman and now you're on the radio all day long. And that woman was Rhonda? Coast Guard radioed up to Tarratine for an ambulance. I heard the whole thing."

"You got a great scanner, Sonny."

"I got it on all the time, even if I'm watching TV. You never know. They was making that movie two summers ago, I heard Mel Gibson right on the radio."

Lucky's already peeling the oilskins off, throwing them in the back of the pickup while they talk. Under his wet wool pants his body itches like the skin's going to come off.

"I'm going in for some dry clothes, Sonny. Then I'm heading for the Tarratine hospital, see how she's doing. You want to go up with me?"

"Sure, anything. Want me to bring the scanner? It works off of a battery."

"You don't have to, Sonny. There ain't nothing left to scan."

Half-hour later they pull into emergency room parking. The whole way to Tarratine, Sonny's been puffing on this long wiry joint, slapping his knees like there's bugs on them, fishing around the radio for Lee Ann Womack songs. Lucky parks in the same place Sarah did when she picked him up after the heart job. Then it was snowing. Now the parking lot's strewn with yellow leaves from the first October blow.

Sonny stays in the car smoking his joint with the stereo on. "Don't go nowhere," Lucky shouts back. He turns around to get the keys but Sonny says, "Christ sake, I want to hear the radio. I ain't going to steal your car."

The young nurse at the emergency desk buttons her shirtfront when she sees him staring. "You a relative?"

"I better be. I slept alongside her last night."

"Guess that qualifies. You the husband?"

"No."

"We'll put you down as domestic partner. Dr. Radner will be right out. He has the rest of the paperwork."

He stands in the corner of the emergency room breathing the stench of death. The bubbling fish tank beside him has three or four guppies and minnows drifting belly-up on the surface and another half dozen on the way out. You'd think they could keep the fish going in a hospital. Across the room is a guy about to die of old age, looks like he can't wait. He's holding on the sides of his walker, just staring out the emergency room door towards the parking attendant's shelter like it's the tollbooth to heaven. His wife looks up from her *People* magazine and gives him a little nudge now and then to keep him alive.

A doctor comes through a door with a porthole, looks around for just a minute, then comes over to Lucky and takes his arm. "I'm Dr. Radner," he says. "I guess you've been through a lot too."

"I come in under my own power."

"Yes. The young lady wasn't so fortunate." The doctor flips a few pages on his clipboard, finds the right one. "Rhonda Hannaford," he says. "And you're the husband?"

"Domestic partner."

He checks a box. "I didn't get her insurance company. We didn't want to bother her with a lot of questions. We have her under mild sedation and she's resting."

"We ain't insured."

He grunts and checks another box. "We'll want to observe her overnight, Mr. Lund."

"Lunt."

"Oh, I'm so sorry. I can never read Portia's writing. Your domestic partner shows every sign of coming through this in good shape, despite a pretty serious brush with hypothermia. In many ways the pregnant female is the sturdiest organism on the planet. I'll be frank with you, we were afraid she'd lost the child at first. Now it looks like there's a sporting chance. You have other children, Mr. Lunt?"

"Two. They ain't Ronette's."

"No. She said this was her first. You are the father?"

"That's what she tells me."

"That's all we men are ever given to know. The EMTs said she wasn't very coherent about dates and times. We do have to figure out exactly how far along she is. Do you have the approximate date of conception?"

"Few weeks after the start of lobster season. Took us a short while to get around to it."

"And when would that be? We're a ways from the coast up here."

"Must of been early May."

"Barely five months, too early to induce. It wouldn't be viable on its own. We put a monitor on her. Hard to believe after what she's been through, but we have a faint fetal heartbeat. The female forms a cocoon of protection, sometimes to the point of sacrifice. We're going to do what we can."

"What's the odds?"

"Mother a hundred percent. Her temperature's up, her vital signs are fine. She'll bounce back tomorrow. The child, fifty-fifty. The next few hours are crucial. Wish we could guarantee survival but we can't. We're only human."

"Any chance of getting a look at her?"

"She's resting right now, no sense disturbing her. We'll be keeping a close eye on them, we should know in the morning. This your number?"

"Yes."

"We'll give you a call. I have to get back on station. You can go home now, you did a good job getting her in here. Give her a full night's sleep, get some rest yourself. We're here for you and we'll give it our best shot."

He's just about to go back and join Sonny Phair in the Probe. Then he spots the gift shop off the exit corridor, they've got a couple of Sarah's sea glass mobiles dangling in the shopwindow. One of them is a blue-and-white wing shape like the one he crushed that night in the studio, she must have rewelded it. It makes his hand ache to look at it, he still has black scars on his palms where they got sliced by the lead moldings. He ducks inside the shop and lifts the price tag to see what she's getting. Hundred and ninety bucks. And the tag says *Another craftproduct from Yvonne's Creations. Orphan Point.* He even has a splash of sympathy for Sarah, fifty fucking percent to a parasite like that. People like the Hannafords, they got everyone by the nuts, twist and turn all you want, it only hurts more.

Then he spots something over in the kids' corner of the shop. He steps over a couple of little Chinese girls playing with Barbie dolls in the aisle, way past their bedtime, then he has to move a white blanket that's mostly covering it, but under the blanket is the spitting image of an old-style Downeast lobster boat, four or five feet long, set up with rockers on the bottom to make it a cradle. The boat is unpainted, just plain pine strips on plywood frames with a cabin over and no place for an engine, but the kid wouldn't be needing an engine for a while. Whoever designed this model took the lines off right, they even cut the pilothouse side away to haul the traps over. Could paint her white and write *Wooden Nickel* on her stern, nobody'd know the difference except the size. He looks for a price tag. There's something dangling off the anchor bitt up on the bow. Three hundred and fifty bucks for that little thing, probably not twenty bucks' worth of wood in it, then they make you build it yourself, so you wind up paying them for your own labor.

The other side of the tag has the same label as Sarah's. Clyde's sister-in-law is everywhere: *Another fucking craftproduct from Yvonne's Creations.*

Meanwhile the saleslady's come up behind him. "Anything we can interest you in, sir? We close at eleven."

"Which end you supposed to put the baby in, the head go down in the cuddy, or the feet?"

"I believe the infant's head would stay outside. A mother worries if she can't see her baby's face."

"You really asking three hundred and fifty bucks for that thing?"

The saleslady bends down to check the tag. He gets a decent look down into the crack of her blouse but she's about sixty so it's a bit dried up in there. "That's right, sir. Three hundred and fifty. Then there would be the five and a half percent tax."

"What would you take for it?"

"I'm afraid we aren't allowed to bargain for our merchandise. The prices are all fixed by the management."

"OK. How's about if we just add it to the room charge? That would be under Hannaford. She's a brand-new patient, just come in."

"I'm afraid we don't allow gifts to be charged to patients' room accounts. It is a lovely idea but there's no way we could bill it. The hospital and concession are financially independent. We do accept credit cards, though. Visa, MasterCard, Discover, and American Express."

Over behind her the little Chinese girls have got all the clothes off two Barbie dolls and they're laying the dolls on top of each other, clucking and giggling like hens. Lucky remembers a small black leather case under Ronette's pile of cassettes out in the glove compartment of the Probe. "Don't sell them boat kits," he tells the saleslady. "And don't close up. I'm coming right back."

Out in the parking lot, Sonny Phair's slumped down in the passenger seat in a cross-eyed trance from smoking too much pot. He sees Lucky and says, "Your old lady coming with us or what?"

"She's staying overnight. Let me into the glove compartment." The leather case is filled with credit cards neatly arranged in little pockets, last thing left from her old life. Some of the cards are in her name, Rhonda Hannaford, some say Clyde Hannaford. He takes the whole thing back to the gift shop lady.

"Might have to try a couple of these, ma'am. Some of them got kind of maxed out." He finds a Rhonda Hannaford Visa with her own signature on the back.

"You're a designated user of this card, sir?"

"Designated driver, that's me."

He stands by the boat cradle while the Visa machine talks to Big Brother back in Tokyo. The unbuilt kits are stacked under the window against the wall. They're massive cartons with heavy copper staples, but he manages to pry an end open and check out the parts. No plywood slabs, either, you frame and plank the things just like a boat.

The saleslady comes by and says, "These kits are wonderful projects for the fathers while the mothers attend childbirth class." Then she goes back to her machine, see if his credit card worked. She wants to sell it, it'll be her big-ticket item for the week.

He's poking around in the box, checking out the frames. They're pretty solid U-shaped sections sawed out of clear pine. The planking's set up to be nailed and glued. For a moment he flashes on the garboard strake that let go when the whale slapped them, water starts flooding his brain channels, then he shuts off that part of his mind. Yvonne may be a bloodsucker but she's got a good thing going with this kit. The only real difference from a working vessel is the two big curved bases so you can rock it back and forth like the motion of the swells. That kid'll be getting his sea legs before he finds the tit.

The saleslady waddles back past the Chinese girls. The Barbies have put their clothes back on and they're having a cup of tea. "I'm afraid that Visa card didn't go through, sir. It sometimes happens even to the best of us. Did you say you wanted to try another?"

Old Clyde must have canceled her plastic soon as she left. He gives the lady a Discover with Clyde's name on it. "This ought to work, ma'am. Sorry about the other. We put all the swimming pool supplies on her and she must of went down."

"Is this your signature on the back, Clyde R. Hannaford?"

"No, ma'am. Clyde's my employer. He's got me authorized to sign the slip."

The lady goes off again to her Visa machine. He's already prying the staples up on the four cartons, checking around for the one with the clearest wood. They even throw in a little plastic bag of fasteners, everything you need. Which is a good thing, cause Ronette's trailer doesn't contain a single tool and his are down on the boat. He'll bum a screwdriver off of Sonny Phair, dig a hammer out of the truck. Sonny's a sign painter too. He'll fix him some chowder when they get back. Maybe after they get the hull built Sonny will bring his gear over and paint a name on the transom.

The saleslady comes back all smiles, patting her hair down, playing with the buttons of her blouse. Now his credit's been established, it's flirting time. He signs *Lucas M. Lunt* on the slip with big letters. Old Clyde will get a charge out of that. Three sixty-nine twenty-five including a twenty-buck tip for the governor. He puts the wallet in his back pocket and picks up the second carton from the bottom, the one with the best wood. He slings the boat kit over his shoulder and walks out. It's not a bad deal when you think about it. The box is pretty near the size of a small coffin, probably fifty pounds of nice presanded pine.

Sonny Phair's moving around in the passenger seat when he gets there. "Shut the god damn stereo off, Sonny, there ain't going to be enough juice to start the car."

"Jesus, Lucky. What are you carrying around? You got a dead body in there?"

"Boat."

"Boat? What kind of a boat?"

"Kid's boat. You build it."

"Crazy bastard. What do you want to build a toy boat for?"

"Sonny, you're going to have to move your ass so we can get this thing inside. Another thing. I ain't sure we got room to take you back."

"What the fuck?"

He opens the Probe's trunk and folds the rear seatback forward. He hauls Sonny Phair out of the passenger seat and stands him up, then folds the right front seat forward and down. The two of them slide the boat cradle kit into the trunk beside the kid seat and slant it over so it fits against the dashboard and they can just barely close the trunk.

"There. Them Mexicans ain't so dumb."

"Where am I supposed to fit?"

"Lay right on top of her, Sonny. Stretch out and get yourself some sleep."

When he gets back to the trailer the wall's sagged out again and the first thing he has to do is wade over and inch the pickup forward so the panel straightens back up to the roofline. He's thinking how he's going to brace it up on its own so he can get the truck out, but that will have to wait till the lawn flood goes down, no use trying to straighten that piece of shit up to his knees in muck. Besides, he's got a boat to build.

He unfolds Sonny from his berth on the carton and the two of them carry it inside. "Lights are on," Sonny says. "Phone work?"

He picks the phone up and it's dead. "Sonny, look in the book and get the number of that god damn phone company."

"How we going to call?"

"You're going over to your place and call them up."

"I ain't had a phone since August. They took it out. All I got's the scanner."

"Jesus H. Christ, Sonny, what the hell you good for? Go on over to Corey's house and use his phone. Take your twenty-two and shoot that fucking dog while you're at it."

When Sonny comes back he's got the gun but his head's down.

"Couldn't bring myself to do it," he says. "Besides, how you figure Corey was going to let me use the phone if I just killed his dog?"

"Jesus, Sonny. You were supposed to shoot the dog on the way *back.*"

"Lucky, I'm sorry. I ain't like you. I just don't have the guts."

"That's OK, Sonny, it's a democracy, a chickenshit's as good as anyone else. What'd the phone company say?"

"They said Clyde Hannaford was paying the bill for this number but he ain't paying it anymore. Cost you a hundred bucks to reconnect, another hundred deposit. No checks."

"Fuck. Well, you're going over to Corey's tomorrow noon, call the hospital, see how she's doing."

"Why don't *you* go over? She's your old lady."

"You know why? I'll tell you why. I don't feel like telling Corey about his fucking gun."

Sonny reaches into the pocket of his sweatshirt and says, "Check this out." It's a fifth of Jim Beam, cherry seal.

"No shit, where'd you come up with that?"

"Corey."

"He ain't so fucking bad. He want to come over and share it with us?"

"I don't think so, Luck, seeing how I got ahold of it."

"Jesus. Remind me to lock the doors around you."

"Don't worry, you ain't got nothing I want anyway. 'Cept maybe —"

"Forget it, Sonny. You wouldn't know what to do with a woman like Ronette. Now let's open this cocksucker up and try her out."

Next morning he wakes up and it's blowing some over the trailer roof but not too hard to go lobstering, he can smell the salt air coming through the trees. Then it returns to him, first like a dream, then like the real thing. He won't be going out anymore. He hits the snooze button on the alarm clock, hits it again in ten minutes, and wakes up nice and easy with the room already light. Half a quart's not much, he feels pretty good for an old man who just got coldcocked by a fucking whale. Last night the two of them watched the Winston Cup Talladega 500 till they fell asleep. Now it's 6:30 A.M. Sonny was up early and out of here, probably went home to jerk off.

He walks down the hallway of the trailer naked. Every step, the floor creaks and sags under his feet. He scratches his nuts and peers out the grimy window at the pickup jammed against the wall. He has a glass of clam juice and twists off the top of a can of sardines, but they remind him too much of Alfie so he opens the screen door and throws the sardines outside on the flooded lawn. The water is down a bit, you can see most of the tires on the GMC, the cinder blocks under the trailer are coming into view.

The boat gets built first, though, then he'll look at that fucking aluminum wall.

He searches around for his Ricky Craven Pro Team mug and mixes a quick cup of instant Nescafé to get his pills down with. The trailer looks better inside than when they left. The wall-to-wall carpet's still pretty wet but at least nothing's floating around the floor. Last time they were home, Ronette had her morning sickness and she left the head in pretty bad shape. He takes the toilet brush to it with some Comet and it comes out nice. A trailer's about like a boat, they're shitheaps if you let them go downhill. He'll get some good self-tapping screws later and screw that fucking panel back onto the wall studs and seal it with duct tape, that will make a decent fix and he can drive his truck out. If you're going to have a little kid crawling around, you can't have a blizzard coming through the walls.

Up at the north end of the trailer on the bedroom floor he finds a space big enough to empty the boat kit carton on. Then he's got to walk out and look for a hammer in the pickup, with Corey's pride and joy yelping at the end of its chain the minute he goes out the door. No sign of Sonny Phair, though the hubcaps are rattling and his shack seems to be shaking up and down. He must be in there thinking about Ronette.

The coffee's done so he gets a Rolling Rock from the fridge and sits on the damp carpeted trailer floor and gets to work. The sawed pine smells like a boatyard in spring when they're planing the hull planks down. The kit has an instruction book about twenty pages long but the damn thing might as well be in Japanese, his glasses are twenty fathoms down there with the *Wooden Nickel*. Anyhow, it can't be too fucking hard to build a five-foot boat. Doesn't have to float anyway, just rock back and forth to put the kid to sleep.

He takes the ten U-shaped frame sections and lines them up bow to stern in the right order. The third and eighth frame members have an extra flange on them for the rockers. He starts with those two, flips them upside down so he can pound on them, and nails the keel strip to them, then the first of the hull strips, the garboard strake that butts against the keel. He bends the thin flexible strip up towards the bow and tacks it into the stem piece, repeating that process for the garboard strip on the other side. The next strake was the one the whale got, and for a moment he's back there with a blue quilt trying to bandage his gashed hull, but this one could be plugged with a handkerchief, no problem, and he tacks it on. The next pair of strakes follows, then the next, just like the Alley brothers, and before the morning's over he has a hull.

The pictures in the manual show the rockers going on next, before the hull gets flipped over upright to attach the cabin. The rockers have a couple of long Phillips-headed screws fastening them back into the frame members directly above them, he'll need to go to Sonny's for a screwdriver. He's been sitting on the wet rug for three hours straight and it hurts like hell to unfold his legs and get up, but he does it, and makes another stop at the fridge on the way out. Outside, it's a clear late morning with a stiff northwester finally coming in. Even the lawn puddles have whitecaps on them. Across the street Corey's going out to the doghouse with a bowl of Alpo, the dog's standing up on its neck chain like a human being. Over at Sonny's a cockeyed face shows at the window. He's up, he's got a beer going, good way to spend a windy Monday. He borrows the Phillips head from Sonny and wades back past a pickup that's become part of the house.

Screwdriver in hand, he faces the kit plans again. If they're going to use the lobster boat model as a cradle, it's got to have rockers. If they're going to bury it in the ground behind the trailer, it won't be needing them. Doctor said fifty-fifty but it's a new day, might as well hope as not. He starts screwing the rockers on.

By noon he's got the deck fastened and the cabin framed up and she's starting to look shipshape. All that's missing is the propeller and the engine box, but if you put in a motor there wouldn't be any room left for the kid.

He's just tacking down the wheelhouse roof when he hears someone at the door, sounds like a dog scratching at first. It can't be

Corey's, that thing's across the road howling like a timber wolf. Maybe it's Ginger, smelling her way back from Clyde's with a tale to tell.

Turns out it's Sonny Phair with his white Sherwin-Williams cap on and his arms full of brushes and paint. Sonny grabs a beer out of the fridge, then takes a long whistle when he sees the boat cradle up underneath the trailer window alongside the unmade bed. "Can't launch her without a paint job," Sonny says. "I brought my acrylics over, them things dry in half an hour."

They spread newspapers over the blankets and lift her up on the bed so they can each paint a side. In an hour she's got a white hull and a blue cabin top and a red bottom, Sonny even threw a little sand in the deck paint for the nonskid, you can't tell her from the original.

They have a couple more beers and watch the Silverado 150 while the paint dries. Sonny says, "I'm going to paint the name on her stern now."

"You can't. You've had six of them beers and it ain't going to look right."

"I've painted five hundred fucking boat names and every one of them I had a six-pack before I started out. I know what I'm doing. You just got to arch up the letters a bit so the name don't have a smile."

He pencils in the slight upward bend across the transom, then pencils the letters. He takes a bottle of black model-airplane paint and fills in each letter so it's nice and crisp against the white.

WOODEN NICKEL

"Looks like the real thing, Lucky. Only thing she needs is a home port. You want me to paint Orphan Point or Split Cove?"

"You don't need to paint nowhere, Sonny. Just the name. We'll put the port in later."

"Don't touch her for a few minutes," Sonny says. "We don't want to fuck up a perfect job." Sonny cleans his gear up from around the bed, then turns to the boat. "You know, Lucky, we could go into business. Build some more of them suckers over the winter and sell them up to that craft shop in Orphan Point."

"Yvonne's."

"Ever see the junk they sell in there? Work of art like this, add a few details, it could go for a thousand bucks. Think about it."

"I will."

Sonny lugs his paints and brushes back to his shack. Lucky watches him from the window coming up to his old place covered with tar paper and old license plates and hubcaps, big scanner antenna on the roof, whole fucking structure would collapse if the junk didn't hold it up. Sonny tries to get the door open with his foot but he trips and the paint and brushes drop all over his feet. He's shitface drunk. But he didn't make a single mistake painting the stern.

He waits for Sonny to come back but he doesn't show up. For some reason his heart is kicking in his chest like he swallowed a live rabbit. He gets a beer to wash down a handful of heart pills.

After a half hour, he picks the boat cradle up with a few sheets of newspaper still stuck to the rockers, lugs it the length of the trailer into the living room so he can look it over while he watches the Louisville Speedway qualifier on channel 38. It's a damn good thing the TV doesn't come in on the phone cable, he'd have a blank screen along with the dead phone. That's why you got to bust up the monopolies, bastards will leave you blind and deaf at the same time.

The trailer widens out at the living room end so it's got a bit of space for the dinette set and the TV. He moves the table and the three chairs so he can place the boat cradle in the center of the room with the bow pointing towards the television and the transom towards the door. It looks half-decent, considering it was built in a day and painted by a couple of drunks. If he keeps it, he's got some ideas for decoration. He'll stick a radar mast on the wheelhouse and build a little pot hoist the kid can pick things up with. You're never too young to learn.

He puts on a George Strait album, *Blue Clear Sky,* and opens a Rolling Rock. He's looking at the boat with one eye and the race with the other when he hears a car splash into the driveway and stop short. Big American V-8, maybe they're just using the yard to turn around. He's right. Pretty soon the car backs out and he hears it head back up the road.

Then someone's walking up the metal steps outside. He starts to go for the door but it opens on its own before he can get there. It's

Ronette. She's just standing in the trailer doorway holding it open, wearing a long gray coat he's never laid eyes on, and behind her the sky's clearing and the sun glints off the metallic chartreuse Probe. First thing she sees is the boat cradle with the name *Wooden Nickel* and the two rockers underneath the hull. She kneels down beside it in the gray coat and runs her hand over Sonny's acrylic paint job, her eyes wide open like it's the real thing, hauled off the bottom by the robot sub. Then she stands up and puts her arms around his neck like they're slow dancing and buries her face in the old sweatshirt he's had on since he got back from Burnt Neck. Her body pulses a little, maybe from crying or laughing, he can't tell which. He has a question for her, but George Strait's singing "I Can Still Make Cheyenne," and there's no hurry, so he lets her rest there awhile before he asks.